THE IMPOSTER

ANNA WHARTON

THE IMPOSTER

MANTLE

First published 2021 by Mantle
an imprint of Pan Macmillan
The Smithson, 6 Briset Street, London EC1M 5NR
EU representative: Macmillan Publishers Ireland Limited,
Mallard Lodge, Lansdowne Village, Dublin 4
Associated companies throughout the world
www.panmacmillan.com

ISBN 978-1-5290-3739-5

1 3 5 7 9 8 6 4 2

A CIP catalogue record for this book is available from the British Library.

Typeset by Palimpsest Book Production Ltd, Falkirk, Stirlingshire
Printed and bound by CPI Group (UK) Ltd, Croydon, CR0 4YY

Visit www.panmacmillan.com to read more about all our books
and to buy them. You will also find features, author interviews and
news of any author events, and you can sign up for e-newsletters
so that you're always first to hear about our new releases.

For Gracie

ONE

She treads carefully through the carnage. Plates and pans litter the kitchen floor, and rice has been scattered from upturned bags across the pretend parquet. On the counter, pointing towards the microwave, lies a banana – half peeled and turning brown. She presses the door of the little oven and it springs open, revealing a bowl welded by porridge to the small, transparent plate inside. She pulls the sculpture out and it separates in her hands as she does, crashing to the floor. Cold lumps of porridge splatter up Chloe's trouser legs.

'Is that you, Stella?'

A voice from the living room.

She checks the clock on the wall. 5.09 p.m. She should still be at her desk. She sighs.

'It's me, Nan. Stay there, I'll be through in a minute.'

Chloe bends down and picks up the bowl. Making a cup of her hand, she scoops the porridge back into it.

'Stella, is that you?'

'Wait there, Nan—'

'Stella?'

Stella has been dead for years. Nan rarely remembers. Chloe plays along with her, knowing the world she's in now is as real to her as this one is to Chloe. A world where her imagination has won and her daughter is still living.

Nan appears in the gap between the two rooms. Chloe

looks up to see her standing there. She tries hard to picture this place when it still had doors and hinges. It feels impossible now. So much has changed. There have been different carpets over the decades, ones she only knows now from photographs. The years have drawn new curtains at the windows, new units in the kitchen, new furniture carried in and out through the hall. But Nan has always been a constant. She is Chloe's constant. She is everything.

'You're not Stella. Who are you? And what have you done to my kitchen?'

'You left your porridge in the microwave again, Nan,' Chloe says. 'And why are all the cupboard doors open and the cans on the worktop?'

Chloe sits back on her heels. She pushes her hair behind her ears, only remembering the gloopy mixture on her hands when she feels it stick to her cheek. 'Oh, for God's s—'

Nan has that look she knows. Chloe's good at reading faces – she's had a lot of practice. Nan's face now looks like a lost little girl. She knows that one too well.

'Who are you? Why have you messed up my kitchen? Where's Stella?'

Chloe looks down at the lino floor and sighs at the mess.

'Stella?' Nan calls over her shoulder, and then to Chloe, 'Get out of my kitchen.'

Her face is full of panic. Chloe stands up and walks towards her.

'Nan,' she says. Then louder: 'Nan.'

Nan covers her ears and starts to cry. 'Stop shouting at me. Where's Stella? I want Stella.'

Chloe glances at the kitchen clock. 5.13 p.m. She pictures her empty seat at her desk. The same desk her boss thinks she's sitting at right now. The same one with mounting paperwork. Nan's face crumples and Chloe looks around the only home she knows. She sighs, pulling Nan into her chest. Porridge clings to her shoulder, but Chloe holds her until Nan's body relaxes into her own.

'Stella hasn't been here for months,' she sobs. 'When is she going to visit?'

'Soon, Nan,' Chloe says and places a kiss on the top of her head because, at times like these, that's what she knows she's meant to do.

Twenty minutes later Chloe closes the door behind her, feeling the safety of the key clicking inside the lock. The hallway has disappeared behind a thick curtain that guards the door when she's not there. Not against intruders, but against Nan wandering out.

Nan is tucked up in bed now, a ham sandwich on her bedside table, tea in her flask. Chloe has reattached the note above the cooker reminding Nan not to turn it on, hidden the lead to the kettle and promised her she'll be home again soon.

She makes her way back to the office in the dusk, through back streets, up and down kerbs – six minutes' walk by shortcuts others are too afraid to take. Luckily she's always felt more at home in the dark than the light.

Orange street lamps illuminate different patches of path. A group of teenage boys jeers from the swings. One throws an empty can at her as she passes.

She walks through the underpass, takes the stairs two

at a time, pushes through the double doors. The daytime buzz of the office has made way for a hum now; computer screens are black and lifeless; coats lifted have left the backs of chairs naked. A note from her boss, written in angry spidery handwriting, waits on her desk:

That's the third time this week you've done one of your disappearing acts.

She screws it up and pushes it deep into the rubbish bin. Beside her a tower of filing wobbles a polite reminder. There is still porridge on her shoes. She doesn't know where to start. She never does.

After a few moments, her screen falls back to sleep. She checks the time – nearly six. They're being replaced by machines; this newspaper archive is moving into the new millennium and finally switching to digital. Chloe can't afford to miss any more time off work, she's already in competition with a motherboard for the only job she's ever known.

The day's newspaper lies open on her desk just as she left it: two gaps in the top right-hand corner, her scalpel filling the place where the stories once sat. She grips the small knife and turns the page.

As the hours pass, the sky darkens outside. A beep from the end of the office signals the arrival of the cleaner. He bundles in, knocking his Henry hoover against filing cabinets that protest with a metallic yelp. The rustling starts, the emptying of bins, and ceiling lights dozing behind frosty panels flicker into life to keep him company. At the other end of the office, Chloe begins to file away the stories she's gathered, the thick pile of envelopes thinning out in her hand until there are none left.

It's late, black licks at the windows, and the tinny sound from the cleaner's headphones edges closer. Chloe returns to her desk and switches off her computer. Today's newspaper is a skeleton now, picked of flesh. She pushes it deep into the recycling bin.

TWO

On the walk home she thinks of Nan. She's tired and all she wants is sleep. She hopes she won't find her clawing, cat-like, at the door.

When Nan misses Stella, it stirs the ache inside Chloe. It reminds her every time that she is the last one left to love. She pulls a photo from the breast pocket of her coat. It's her favourite, a black and white one of Nan and Stella. Nan must be around thirty, Stella is only six; she has white-blonde curls and she's missing two front teeth. They're on a beach in Cornwall, the shadow of St Michael's Mount looming behind their shoulders. This picture anchors Chloe on the days when she feels lost. She likes to imagine Granddad watching them through the viewfinder, nose pushed up to the camera's black leathery body, teasing them to say 'cheese' the way he always did. Not that she remembers.

There's something about that photograph that she loves: ghosts of the past looking out at the future, a sunny day on a sandy beach, the way Nan's hand grips Stella's shoulder. She runs her finger across them, the picture-perfect family frozen in time. She smiles as she slips the photograph carefully back into her pocket.

She fishes her phone from her bag. Three missed calls. She recognizes the number – social services. She dials her voicemail then decides against it and quickly hangs up, ignoring the messages.

She likes walking in the dark, as if threat wraps her in a safety blanket rather than strips her bare. Children are meant to be afraid of the dark; she never had much choice other than to find comfort in it.

She knows these streets, the houses that fail to pull their curtains at night, with their own families tucked up safe inside – on bad days it has felt to Chloe as if they are goading those like her, the ones on the other side of the glass. On good days she stares in, and it isn't difficult to find something she envies. Tonight, though, she doesn't need to linger; she's tired and she wants to get home.

She turns the corner, and moments later her key is in the door. The house is still inside, just the shuffle of her footsteps moving on the Axminster carpet in the hall. Too tired to eat, she takes the stairs, pulling herself up on the rail installed for Nan.

She opens the door to her own room slowly, wincing as the carpet shifts underneath it. She can't bear that voice calling out in the night for Stella, to ask again who Chloe is and why she is there. She needs one night of no questions, no explanations already made a hundred times before and instantly forgotten.

The next morning, Chloe finds Nan standing in the middle of the kitchen. Every cupboard door is open again, the contents cover the worktops – cans of rice pudding, dozens of them. She looks up and sees her.

'Oh Chloe, dear, I'm glad you're here, I can't seem to find the teapot.'

It's then she smells it, an odour of waxy burning plastic.

She rushes into the kitchen in time to see the electric kettle begin to melt on the gas stove.

'Nan!'

She opens the window, coughing, while Nan starts emptying more cupboards.

'Nan, stop!' she says. 'We've got teabags. Sit down, I'll make you a cuppa.'

'Teabags?' Nan says, shrugging. She wanders off into the living room.

Chloe cleans up the kitchen and boils a pan of water on the stove. She goes outside and dumps the burnt kettle in the bin on top of the last one.

She takes the cup of tea in to Nan in the living room and sits down beside her, fingers wrapped around her own warm mug.

'Lovely,' Nan says. 'You look smart, where are you off to?'

'Work, Nan.'

'Remind me,' she says, taking a sip, 'where do you work?'

'At the local newspaper.'

'Oh, a reporter! That's it.'

Chloe considers explaining the archive again, telling her of the cuttings system that the reporters rely on, of how she dissects the local newspaper each and every day, filing lives away into drawers. But instead she says, 'Yeah, that's right, Nan.'

'Stella would have loved that.'

Chloe takes a sip of her own tea. Nan has buried Stella again while she slept. She's better today. Chloe thinks of the missed calls from social services. She and Nan are managing just fine. They don't need anyone else.

She cooks Nan's porridge and gets her washed and dressed, handing her a toothbrush on which she's squeezed a small slither of white and blue striped paste.

'You did the same for me when I was little,' she says.

'Did I?' Nan replies, frothy toothpaste dropping down her chin and into the sink. She spits and rinses and Chloe gently pats her face dry.

Downstairs she sits her down in front of the TV, fills her flask with tea and hands her the remote control.

The clock on the wall makes her think of the note Alec left on her desk. But this morning, everything is going to plan, she'll even make it to work on time. She dots a kiss on Nan's forehead.

'Where are you going?' Nan asks.

'To work, Nan, I told you. I'm going to be late.'

'But you can't, not today. Not when someone's stolen my greenhouse.'

By some miracle, she manages to arrive at work on time. She'd walked Nan out into the garden, and it was only as they stood among the plastic terracotta pots and the earthy smell of dried compost that she was finally persuaded that her glasshouse was still there.

At the office, the same as every morning, Chloe follows the path that has been worn into the pale blue carpet tiles all the way down to the archive. Alec is waiting there, arms crossed over his bony chest. He makes a point of checking his watch.

'Alec, I—'

'Save it, you can explain to Malc. I've asked Sandra for an appointment for us to see him.'

'But—'

'Like I said, save it.'

She slumps her bag down on her desk, the buckles making an angry riposte.

'I hope you got all that filing done last night?' Alec says.

'Yes, of course.'

'Well, that's one good thing,' he says, limping over to his desk and returning with a pile taller than the one that had taken her until ten the night before. 'You can do mine now too.'

She spends the morning buried deep in the archive, keeping out of Alec's way and working through his pile of files. It's easy to hide there, among the filing cabinets that stand buttressed together, three in a row, back to back as if checking which is the tallest among them. There are four rows like that, each of them labelled A to Z with tales of the city. Everything is there, from the waggiest tail competition winners at village fetes to the secrets those names on the front would rather keep hidden: drink driving bans, domestic assaults. Chloe has read and filed it all. Most citizens of this city have no idea they've left a Helvetica trail of crumbs creating a picture of their lives, starting with their birth announcements and running all the way through to their own death notices. The archivist is the guardian of all that's happened over the years, the first stop for reporters on deadline to write a story. No one knows this city and all its stories better than Chloe.

She surveys the archive, across the tops of the grey filing cabinets, up to the tomes containing back copies of every newspaper they've ever printed. It's all going to be gone soon. Replaced with two computers. Just two. But what's an archive without that human touch?

At lunchtime, Chloe stands in line for a coffee. On her phone she finds another missed call from social services. It makes her stomach turn over inside her coat and she quickly pushes her phone deep inside her bag. In front of her in the queue, a woman laughs loudly into her own phone. The woman has long blonde hair and, when she turns around, a perfect smile with teeth straight out of a toothpaste advert. She smells of a musky, confident perfume that Chloe would never think to wear.

The barista calls out her name – Amanda – and the woman steps forward for her coffee, still laughing loudly into her phone. Amanda doesn't worry about answering her phone. Amanda has only good news from her phone. This makes Chloe think of social services again.

The cafe is busy, packed with bodies, and Chloe could say with all honesty that she didn't see Amanda turn around so quickly, that she hadn't realized she'd stepped straight into her path as she did. She could say she only realized what had happened when she saw the stain spreading across Amanda's perfect camel coat.

'Look what you did!' Amanda says.

She's not laughing anymore. Staff fuss around her, mopping at her coat with paper napkins instantly dyed tan.

Chloe steps past the chaos; she's forgotten all about social services. Instead, with a smile, she orders her latte.

'What's the name?' the barista asks, standing poised with a cup and a black marker pen.

Chloe watches the woman leave, now swearing into her phone. 'Amanda,' she says.

The barista scribbles it onto the side of the cup without question.

Alec leaves early to take his wife for one of her hospital appointments. Chloe has never asked him what's wrong with her. It grates that he can take so much time off.

Once he's gone, she starts sifting through the pile of cuttings that need to be scanned to the new system. She opens the flatbed scanner on her desk. Bright white light shines through the fine newsprint; she places the lid down again, clicks the icon on the screen, and watches as the image appears seconds later.

DOCTORS DIDN'T BELIEVE I HAD CANCER

Chloe enlarges the story, zooms in once, twice, and then starts reading.

> FOR thirteen years, Karen Stanmore was fobbed off by doctors who believed she was making up stomach pains.

Chloe reaches for her own stomach.

> The thirty-five-year-old city woman even convinced herself that her pains and tiredness were psychosomatic, but after being admitted to hospital with suspected appendicitis, surgeons found a cancerous tumour that had been growing inside her for more than a decade.

Chloe reads on as the office thins out around her. At the back of her mind nags a vague memory of a collection, talk of leaving drinks. Perfume spritzed at desks travels the length of the newsroom towards her, tangling together in the air around the archive. She hears a cork popped, plastic cups passed around. One appears at the edge of her desk filled with something pale and fizzy she hadn't asked for. She doesn't look up, too engrossed in the story about Karen Stanmore and her stomach cancer.

It's almost 6.15 p.m. by the time she's finished googling the rare cancer the doctors finally found. She ticks off all of the symptoms until she's satisfied there's nothing black growing inside her. The office is quiet when she next glances up, but there are still another five or six files to get through. The phone rings on her desk. Without thinking, she snatches the receiver from the cradle.

'Archive.'

'Chloe?'

Her stomach sinks into her seat.

'It's Claire Sanders, social services. I've been leaving messages on your mobile.'

'Oh yes, Claire, sorry, I—'

'We need to speak urgently about your grandmother's care, the sale of the house . . .'

She starts talking without invitation, about 'assessment reports', 'needs meeting criteria', 'care homes', 'financial eligibility'.

Chloe goes back to the article about Karen Stanmore's tumour.

THREE

Nan shuffles through the cemetery, clutching the daffodils inside gloved hands. The bright yellow of their happy heads stands out against the grey of this Sunday morning.

'Have I been here before?'

'Yes, Nan,' Chloe says.

She doesn't argue.

Chloe walks slowly behind her, keeping hold of her at the elbow; the disease that started somewhere in her brain has worked its way into the tips of her toes, making it easier for her to fall these days.

'Are you sure I've been here before?'

'Yes, Nan.'

'And who do we know here?'

'Mum, Nan.'

'My mum?'

'No, mine, Nan.'

'Oh, sorry to hear that, dear. Was she nice?'

Chloe guides her left up a winding path. She obeys without question, past lines and lines of neutral mottled headstones, each engraved with names and dates to sum up the soul lying beneath. Chloe has never found grave-yards creepy, not like some kids. She remembers late-night dares that she was certain would reward her with friend-ships she wouldn't otherwise be entitled to. She'd hear them laugh, their hurried footsteps fleeing as she wandered inside the darkness. Too humiliated to leave, she'd sit down among the stones to read them, fantasising about the people who kept her company that night, and all the ones that followed. Chloe preferred these ghosts to the living – they weren't anywhere near so cruel. You knew where you were with dead people.

At the top of the path Chloe and Nan turn right and walk across the wet grass until they stand in front of a shiny black headstone: *Stella Hudson. Who fell asleep . . .*

The pair of them are silent for a moment.

'Stella Hudson,' Nan says with a sigh.

Chloe puts an arm around Nan and pulls her closer. She knows what to do, she has watched people in cemeteries for as long as she can remember.

'Was she one of my old neighbours?' Nan asks.

Chloe thinks for a second of explaining, while Nan stands looking puzzled at the grave. Instead, she tells her yes, and crouches down closer to the earth, closer to Stella.

'Oh look, someone's left some flowers here,' Nan says.

Cellophane wraps the pink carnations they brought last weekend in an untidy hug, the petals curling, browning at the edges. Chloe pulls them from the vase at the foot of the stone; their slimy stems follow.

'I know,' Nan says, her eyes brightening with a new idea, 'we can put these daffodils in there.'

Chloe takes them from her and peers into the vase, picking out a few dead leaves, and one long, thin slug. She fishes the creature out, examining its shiny back in the palm of her hand, before discarding it onto the grave next door.

'Oh, there's no water left,' Chloe says, picking up the vase.

Nan tuts slowly.

Chloe stands up and looks round. 'Listen, stay here, I'm going to find a tap.'

She walks away without thinking, then quickly retraces her steps back to Nan. She zips up Nan's parka, securing it under her chin, and pulls the hood up over her white hair.

'Stay here, OK?' Chloe tells her. 'I won't be a minute.'

Nan nods.

Chloe hurries back the way they came, turns right, and takes another gravel path winding past more headstones. A wooden sign marks the Garden of Remembrance; she follows it, and sees on the other side of the garden a squat log-panelled hut. Inside there is a tap.

She fills the vase quickly, then makes her way out towards the path back to Nan. Only as she does, she spots a memorial stone. She stops and stares, then bends down for a closer look. She pulls her coat sleeve up over her hand and wipes it across the small black marble stone. It is a memorial for a little girl.

'Not a nice job, is it?' a voice behind her interrupts.

She turns to see a man in his seventies, wearing a flat cap and wiping at his rheumy blue eyes with a white handkerchief. He points at the plaque. 'But we've got to remember them somehow, ent we? The only way we know how.'

Chloe nods. She looks up towards the path where she had left Nan.

'Irene usually does this for our Katy – our granddaughter, like – but winter's got her bad this year, terrible chest infection, so I said I'd come up here today, just check on the babby. We don't get up as often as we'd like

– perhaps why we haven't met before. It makes you feel bad, dun'it, when you can't come as often? Still, you never forget, you always carry them in here.' He pats his chest, and coughs a little as he does. He glances at her vase then. 'Be careful you don't put too much water in there, otherwise the birds come and get a drink and, well, it makes the plaque messy, like, them doing their business and all, if you know what I mean.'

Chloe tips a little water away onto the grass. She is about to hurry back to Nan when he starts talking again.

'Relative, is she? Daughter?'

Chloe doesn't reply.

He bends forward, squinting a little, and takes a closer look at the stone. 'Oh, 1979, must make you . . . a sister?'

'Oh, I . . .' She looks down at the daffodils in her hand and realizes how he came to this conclusion.

'Ah, well, she'll be glad to have you looking out for her, that's what big sisters are for, ent they?' He smiles and wipes at his eyes once more with the handkerchief. 'You want to get some plants in here, you could spread out a bit—'

'Oh, I'm not—'

'Oh, don't worry about having green fingers.' He lifts his hands in protest as Chloe shuffles from foot to foot. 'There ent much you need to know. First of all, take a look at the soil.' He picks up some and rubs it between his fingertips; his fingers are a reddish purple, the years having hardened them against the cold. 'The type of plants that will grow and thrive all depend on the soil at your feet. You want to think, is it gritty, sandy, or does it form a solid mass – like clay?'

Chloe shuffles on the gravel path.

'You could have a lovely perfumed rose bush here,' the old man continues, 'or annuals, lots of bright colours. You could plant them every summer and then . . . whoop, up they'd come in spring. Cheer the place up a bit. And don't matter about nature, worms keep the soil aerated, birds eat the greenfly, only thing you don't really want are ants' nests – millions of them you'll have, all those tiny creatures hard at work underneath, yet never a good look crawling all over the soil. My Irene can't stand the things – can't say I blame her. Anyway, talking of Irene, she'll be wondering where I got to. I'd better stop chatting and get off.'

Chloe watches him cross the garden to pick up a trowel he'd left by Katy's grave. He pats the top of the stone as tenderly as if it were his lost granddaughter's own warm head, then follows the gravel path out towards the exit, lifting his arm as if he knows she's watching.

Chloe turns back to the stone then. She takes one daffodil and trims the stem with her fingernails, leaving it inside the vase, then hurries back up the gravel path towards Nan.

She turns left at the top, retracing her steps, just as she had taken them a few moments before. Only something is different. Her eyes scan the cemetery, quickly, then frantically. She spins on the spot, looks behind her, in case she had taken a wrong turn. But she knows this place. She wouldn't make a mistake. But then, if she hadn't, something is missing. That's the moment when the dread begins to swell inside, starting in the soles of her feet and spreading right up to the top of her head, collecting with it her blood, the sound of which bangs inside her eardrums.

'Nan!' she calls out to the empty cemetery. She is nowhere to be seen.

Chloe spins this way and that. She squints, staggering between the headstones, sure that she'll see it, that flash of navy – Nan's parka – but there is just grass and stillness, the odd petal that has blown in from the latest floral tribute.

'Nan!'

She runs back the way she came; perhaps Nan has gone looking for her. But the path is empty. Her heart thudding now, she runs back, all the way to Stella's grave, as if by some miracle Nan is small enough to be hiding behind it. Of course not. But that's when she notices it, a copse at the back of the cemetery, an opening just large enough for Nan to squeeze through, yet the trees are knitted together too tightly to get a look in from here. She runs over to it, hesitating at the entrance. Surely Nan wouldn't have gone inside. But now she's had that thought she can't leave it unattended. She takes a first step in, dry leaves crunching underfoot; a twig from underneath her own step causes Chloe to start.

'Nan, please,' she cries.

Silence answers her.

She goes further into the undergrowth. There is no path in here and so she kicks at bushes, hearing the sound of berries and leaves dropping within each footprint she leaves behind. The deeper she goes, the denser it becomes. A mossy, damp, earthy smell fills her nose.

'Nan?'

She looks back. She can't see the cemetery now. What if Nan has reappeared? What if she's looking in the wrong place? She can't think when she panics. Instead she goes deeper, dipping and ducking under branches; she snaps several in two to pass, scanning the undergrowth for a swatch of Nan's white hair. Perhaps she's slipped. Perhaps she'll find her hurt. The thought flashes more panic through her veins. She walks, she calls. Sometimes, where tendrils have stitched themselves together, she almost has to crawl to make a path through, bending and folding herself under low-slung branches, pushing on through the bramble.

'Nan?' she calls, and stops. Was that her voice? She scrambles to turn around, to listen, and a thorny bush nips her skin, tearing the flesh in a neat, straight line. She's tangled now, in brambly twine, nature's own barbed wire. She fights to free herself, pushes back through the bush until she sees the light and she hopes – no, she prays – that Nan will be waiting where she left her.

She emerges to the stillness of the cemetery, bleached grey headstones and the odd tumbled-earth grave. But no Nan. She sinks to the ground. She's gone.

FOUR

The hard plastic chairs at the police station are pinching the back of Chloe's thighs. Finally, an officer opens the door into reception and calls her name.

'I hear you'd like to report a missing person?'

'Yes . . . yes,' she says.

He leads her down a long corridor to a small room. They sit each side of the table, upon which there is a recording device – not that he switches it on. But Chloe's eyes quickly dart around the room and she slides her hands underneath her legs.

'I hear your grandmother went missing at the city cemetery?' the officer says, flicking through a small black notepad.

'Yes, that's right. I was just getting some water and . . . well, when I went back . . . I mean, I searched, everywhere, I even went into this little wood at the back of the—'

'And you say she has dementia?'

'Alzheimer's, yes. She was diagnosed two years ago.' Chloe taps the top of the desk quickly. 'I mean, I don't know how she just disappeared like that. She can't even walk that well . . . I only turned my back for a second.'

'And you're her primary carer?'

'Yes.'

'Does she have a social worker's contact details that we could take?'

Chloe hesitates. She knows what this will mean. She sits forward in her seat.

'Look, can't you just get out there and find Nan?'

The officer sighs and takes his notepad in one hand. 'Chloe, officers have already been given a description of your grandmother and they'll be keeping a good eye out for her. I'm sure they'll find her safe and sound soon enough. In the meantime, you and I just need to complete the relevant paperwork here at the station. Now, if you don't mind, her social worker's details . . .'

Chloe wakes with a start, shaking off the rest of a dream she's had a thousand times before. Anxiety is somehow always waiting for her in the night; it's constantly there, just under her skin. She opens her eyes quickly as she remembers Nan. She quickly leans over and finds her mobile on the floor beside her bed, but the screen is blank. It is still only 5 a.m. She lies back down on her pillow, but when she closes her eyes the same faces are there. She feels helpless. She gets out of bed, gathers her clothes up from the floor and dresses quickly. But at the bottom of the stairs she looks out the window, onto a dawn that has yet to fully rise, and wonders what she is supposed to do. Nan is still out there. There has been no news overnight. Or at least she has heard nothing. Should she stay here and wait for her? It feels as if she should be doing something else, something more practical. But what? The police insisted they would do everything they could.

She pulls the thick curtain back from the door, wondering why she'd even bothered to draw it across last night when Nan was still out there. She opens the front door and feels the cold rush in. She shivers at the thought of Nan wandering the streets.

By the time she leaves, the sun is dyeing the night sky orange. She pulls the front door shut behind her and looks up at Nan's little semi, darkness behind each window. The adjacent houses still sleep, families that haven't long moved into the area tucked safely behind each of them. The neighbours' front door is right next to her own; their path is decorated with glazed terracotta pots and in one a rainbow windmill smiles out at the morning. It belongs to the little girl who sleeps in the room above the front door. She's five or six, and she always stops to say hello. Chloe couldn't describe what she looked like – her eyes are always trained on the little girl's hands, one always locked tight inside her mother's.

A small wind blows and the plastic sails spin happily. Chloe tightens the belt on her coat and heads up the path towards the road.

In the lift up to the office Chloe studies her reflection in the mirror. The cold morning still clings to her cheeks and there's little she can come up with to comfort herself that Nan is safe and warm somewhere. She plucks a stray leaf still tangled in strands of her dark hair; she must have collected it in the copse yesterday. She goes back over the scene, asking again how Nan could have just disappeared. It doesn't feel right to come to work on a day like today. But what else is she going to do? Perhaps the right thing is to stay busy. She imagines that's the advice they'd give in films. The lift announces the third floor, and she steps out towards the newsroom, leaving more foliage from under her footstep.

It's still early and the beep of her security pass announces her arrival. The editor, Malc, stands by the news desk, hands in his pocket, swivelling on his heels between the news editor and the assistant editor as they decide on that day's splash. He doesn't look up as she makes her way towards the archive. No one ever does.

Chloe reaches her desk and checks her phone again for missed calls, just like she had when she got into the lift three minutes earlier. There's nothing, no news. She places it on her desk beside her keyboard.

She's not due in to work for another hour and a half, but she knows she needs to keep busy to distract herself from checking her mobile phone. She's always preferred the archive without people. Her eyes fall to a plastic orange crate beside Alec's desk – a job they've both been avoiding. The crate contains some of the oldest files that need scanning ready for the new electronic system. She turns the scanner on and watches as the bright white light beams back from beneath the flatbed.

She works on automatic; she knows how things operate here. Each file is a small brown gusset envelope, just slightly bigger than a postcard. Most have a few dozen cuttings folded neatly inside, the girth of the envelope a giveaway to the stories that have dominated the head-lines over the decades. Some have even multiplied, giving birth to one or even two more envelopes. In those cases the files will be marked *cont.* and numbered. But the first one she picks up, although thick, has only one line on the front: *KYLE; ANGELA.* It's written as all the

others are: neat capitals in black marker, double under-
lined in the top right-hand corner. Just the way Alec
likes it. She has always appreciated the archive for that,
the safety within the order of everything. How she needs
that today.

Chloe turns the file over in her hands, noticing how
some of the seams have started to give way. She pulls
its insides out as carefully as a surgeon, the envelope
collapsing without them. Dozens of cuttings scatter
across the light grey melamine of her desk, fanning out
like a neutral paint chart, instantly revealing the length
of time this particular story has dominated the headlines. The older cuttings are various shades of pale
yellow and ivory – daffodil white, perhaps; the newer
ones are magnolia.

Chloe picks a cutting at random. It's an old one, she
can tell from the folds that have been impressed over and
over by the hammy thumbs of reporters. She takes extra
care not to tear the fine newsprint as she peels it open,
stirring it again with oxygen. The cutting resists as she
stretches it awake, but a second later it is laid bare in
front of her.

POLICE GIVE UP SEARCH FOR MISSING ANGIE

She immediately thinks of Nan and glances at her
phone. Nothing. She checks the volume, makes doubly
sure the ringtone is on. Still nothing.

She takes the cutting and places it under the scanner.
The white light flickers beneath the cover, and as she
waits questions accumulate. Who is Angie? Why is she

missing? And most importantly for Chloe right now, why did the police give up their search for this person?

When the clipping appears on her screen a few seconds later, she zooms in quickly – once, twice – and starts to read:

> YESTERDAY, police revealed the search for missing Angela Rose Kyle has finally been scaled back. The four-year-old disappeared on 27 October last year, after a trip to a city park with her father Patrick Kyle.

She checks the date on the cutting – 3 May 1980. More than two decades ago. She quickly thumbs through the pile for a more recent cutting, then another; each one still talks of missing Angie and is accompanied by a school photograph of the little girl, her dark hair in two bunches, a milk-tooth smile. Chloe stares at the first cutting she picked up in her hand – this girl has been missing for twenty-five years. She continues reading:

> Devastated Mr Kyle told police how he left his daughter on the swings at the deserted park for less than a minute while he went to lock his car. When he returned she was gone.
>
> Dozens of officers combed the surrounding area, while police divers dredged the nearby river for the youngster. But despite a nationwide appeal for information about the missing girl, all leads have proved fruitless. Now, six months on from her disappearance, police have been forced to scale back their search.

Chloe pauses, her gaze shifting to his wife, Maureen. Her pain is less visible than his, worn on the inside so her face has become nothing but a shell. Chloe glances between them, from the man to his wife. His arm around her shoulders in the photograph, his knuckles white, his grip on her tight. Chloe picks up another cutting at random from her desk, this time his hand wrapped around hers. She picks up another, another, another. It's the same in every picture. Their togetherness carrying the pair of them. Chloe only feels the pinch of envy for a second – how could she feel it for any longer when she reads on?

> Detective Inspector Tom Newton, of Peterborough Constabulary, told this newspaper, 'Over the last few months we have carried out searches of Ferry Meadows and the surrounding areas. Police divers have dredged the Nene and locals have been out in force alongside officers covering many acres of grass and woodland, but sadly there have been no sightings of Angela since the day she went missing. Like the family, we will never give up hope that Angela will be reunited with her parents, but with no new leads we've been forced to scale back our operations. We would like to take this opportunity to thank the public for their help in the search and remind them that an incident number will remain active in the hope of new information.'

Chloe opens up the next cutting, then the next, earlier ones before the police scaled back. Staggered across her desk, the headlines fit together like pieces of a jigsaw.

GIRL, FOUR, MISSING FROM LOCAL PARK

FEARS GROW FOR MISSING ANGIE

MOTHER'S PLEA: 'GIVE BACK OUR ANGIE'

FOUND: CLOTH CAT – BUT WHERE IS ANGIE?

She goes back to the original cutting.

> DI Newton refused to be drawn into speculation about what might have happened to Angela, although he admitted that police cannot rule out the possibility that she may have been abducted.
> 'We are not closing the case, and we still hope that Angela will be returned to her parents. I'd like to reiterate that without the discovery of a body we can only assume that Angela is alive and well. I would once again urge the public to come forward with any information that may help police – however insignificant it may appear to them.'

Chloe knows the cranks who would have got in touch back then, the same people who phone the newsroom with promises of stories if only the news editor dispatches a reporter to their home. Some people are prepared to do anything for attention. Some people just want the company.

> Patrick and Maureen Kyle, of 48 Chestnut Avenue, are said to be 'inconsolable' at the thought of the

police hunt being called off. A statement from Mr Kyle released through police said, 'Angela is our life, our love, our everything. An open wound will be here in our hearts until the day she is returned to us. We will wait for the rest of our lives for the day we are reunited.'

Anyone with any information should contact DI Newton at the city's police station.

Chloe reads the cutting over and over, checking Angie's age against the date, and doing the maths in her head. Angie was the same age as Chloe was in 1979, and so if she is alive, she'd be twenty-nine too. She closes her eyes and tries to picture her now. What really were the chances of her still being out there? Her mind flickers then to the worst outcome: a young girl dead in a shallow grave, never properly resting in peace. She shudders when she thinks of Nan. Is Chloe the only person right now who can imagine the pain this couple feel to this day? Instantly she feels so desperately, so sadly connected to them. Just twenty-four hours in the Kyles' shoes has taught her something of what they've been through.

She checks her phone again. Nothing. She drops the cutting onto her desk. She can't be here, not now, when everything is a reminder to her that Nan is missing. She could have picked up any file, and yet she'd chosen that one. She checks the time – it's nearly eight. She's too worried about Nan to do anything here, and anyway, it feels empty, pointless while Nan is still out there somewhere. She pushes back from her desk on her swivel chair; there is still time to get to the police station and back before 9 a.m. She leaves the office the same way she came in. Only this time she feels the editor's gaze follow her out.

FIVE

Chloe pushes open the thick heavy doors to the police station. She scans the benches that line the walls in case Nan is waiting there in reception. She can almost picture her: a puzzled face, shivering from the cold, but there, all the same. Instead a skinny man sits in a battered leather jacket and dirty jeans, and a woman in her fifties opposite clutches her handbag as though it contains precious forensic evidence.

Chloe walks up to the reception desk and presses the bell. An overweight woman slumps slowly towards the window.

'Yes?'

'I'm enquiring about my nan, she's missing. I just want to know if there's been any news?'

'Name?'

'My name?'

'Your grandmother's.'

'Oh, Grace Hudson.'

'Has an officer been in touch with you to say there've been any developments?'

'Well, no, but—'

'Then I think it's fair to assume there haven't been any sightings. Have we got your contact details in case any of our officers need to get in touch?'

'Well, yes, but—'

'Then we'll be in touch if there's any further news.'

The woman goes to walk away but Chloe taps quickly on the safety glass.

'Please, I . . . Can I just speak to the officer I spoke with yesterday? It's important.'

'Do you have new information?'

'No, I just need to know they're doing everything they can.'

The woman rolls her eyes a little and taps something into her keyboard, then she picks up her phone to make a call.

'He's coming down.'

'Thank you.'

She slopes off back to her crossword.

Chloe sits down on the benches, next to the woman clutching her handbag. The woman shuffles an inch away.

Chloe waits for twenty minutes before PC Dunn puts his head around the door.

'Chloe? Do you want to come through?'

She follows him – too slowly it seems. He walks quickly, weaving this way and that through the corridors, through double doors – another set – and she struggles to keep up. He's tall, well over six feet, and his straight black trousers don't quite meet his ankles. He chooses a different interview room today and they sit down. He takes out the same tiny notepad from his top pocket and the same tiny pen.

'I hear you have some further information for us?'

'Well, no, I . . . I just wondered if there's been any news?'

He sighs, shaking his head and putting the lid back on

his pen. 'Not as yet, I'm afraid, but you can rest assured we're doing all we can.'

Chloe can't help but think of the woman and her crossword behind the desk.

'We did manage to speak to the social worker, what was her name . . . ?' He flicks back a few pages in his notepad as Chloe's hands squeeze one another in her lap.

'Claire Sanders.'

'Claire Sanders, yes, that's right. She said that she's been trying to get Mrs Hudson into a care home for some time but there's been some resistance . . . from yourself, would that be?'

'Well, yes, but it's only because, well, we can manage, you see? Nan doesn't need to be in a care home, she's got me, and . . . and I've got her and—'

'Yes . . . although with the greatest respect, Mrs Hudson is currently missing – we've got officers searching for her now. You're not really managing, are you? Perhaps if she had been in a care home, this wouldn't—'

Chloe's phone rings in her pocket, finishing the sentence for him. She scrabbles through her coat to reach it. Even PC Dunn sits forward in his chair.

A name flashes up: Hollie. Her best friend. Chloe shows the policeman.

'It's just my . . . er . . . hang on, hello?'

'Oh my God, Chloe, I just picked up your text. Are you OK? Have they found her?'

She quickly tells Hollie she's at the police station, there's been no news. The two arrange to meet at a local coffee shop. She puts the phone down and PC Dunn closes his notepad.

'Chloe,' he says, 'I know you're worried, but I can assure you we're doing everything we can. Seventy-nine per cent of missing people are found within twenty-four hours.'

She thinks of the girl in the cuttings. 'And the rest?'

'Let's be positive, eh?'

He leads her out of the station. There's nothing she can do but follow.

In the coffee shop, Hollie wraps her in a big winter-coat hug.

'Oh hun, I can't believe this is happening.'

'Me neither,' Chloe says as she pulls out a chair and sits down. She looks over the menu, but she's not hungry. Instead they order coffees to help them thaw while Chloe quickly fills her in. Hollie reaches her hand across the table towards Chloe, and she stares at it lying limp on top of her own. Chloe feels the gratitude swell inside her for Hollie's unswerving loyalty.

'Listen, it's not your fault, you know that, don't you?' Hollie says.

Chloe shrugs.

'They'll find her, just you wait and see. I bet loads of people go missing like this and, well . . . I'm sure it's all going to be fine.'

Chloe stirs her coffee.

'I know, it's just . . . she's all I've got.'

Hollie pushes her long blonde hair back behind her shoulders and stirs more sugar into her coffee. Chloe sees how she glances up at her every now and then as she turns the teaspoon round and round inside her mug. Chloe shuffles in her seat.

'Your nails are nice,' Chloe says.

Hollie stops stirring to admire them. She has these gels done, long nails that curl slightly at the top. They're always painted like miniature portraits, with little flowers or glittery tips. Hollie calls it her guilty pleasure, though Chloe isn't sure what she has to feel guilty about and has never asked. She wouldn't have them done herself, though she has walked past the kind of nail salons that Hollie visits. Chloe has never so much as put nail polish on her own fingers. She knows they must look odd sitting here in this cafe together. From the outside they are a mismatch, Chloe knows this. She's always felt like the fat, ugly friend next to Hollie. But Chloe can honestly say she's never resented her for it, perhaps because Hollie is the most loyal person she knows. Most people aren't to be trusted; they always break promises in the end. But not Hollie. Chloe can't remember a single time she's ever let her down. And it wasn't Hollie's fault their lives turned out so differently. It could easily have been Chloe sitting across the table now, her nails perfectly manicured, her hair freshly blow-dried. She often thinks about this when she walks past happy dogs and their owners in the street, how easily someone might have stopped at the next kennel along. At the end of the day, it all comes down to fate. Which is why Chloe tends to take it into her own hands these days.

'Hello? Earth to Chloe?' Hollie laughs.

'Oh, sorry, I was miles away.'

Hollie drops her hands back on top of her friend's.

'You're bound to be,' she says. 'It would be a shock for anyone. Is there no one else you could—'

Chloe looks up quickly, and Hollie stops herself.

'No, of course there isn't,' Hollie says.

Now it's Chloe's turn to look down into her drink.

The good thing about Hollie is she knows not to probe; perhaps that is why their friendship has endured. Hollie understands there's a time to speak in clichés, that there's safety to be found there for both of them. Chloe has seen it in other friendships she has observed, this dance two women can become accustomed to, a way of keeping their shared history preserved in politeness. Not that she can call to mind any other female friendships she's enjoyed.

Hollie takes a breath. 'Do the police have any leads?'

Chloe shakes her head, and as she does a tiny twig drops onto the table. Hollie collects it and holds it up like a question mark between them.

'I searched a copse near the cemetery when I found she was missing, it must be from then.'

Hollie looks concerned.

'But I feel helpless, just waiting for news,' Chloe says. 'I keep thinking, what if I missed something? Maybe I should go back for another—'

'Chloe, you must leave it to the police, they know what they're doing.'

Chloe nods.

'But if there's anything I can do, even if you just need company. You know you could always come over to us, Phil wouldn't mind you staying for a few—'

'I'm fine,' Chloe says quickly.

Hollie looks away, scolded.

Chloe's voice softens then. She never means to hurt her friend. 'Honestly, you're right, they'll find her.'

'They will,' Hollie says. 'And you'll let me know if there's anything I can do to help?'

Chloe nods, relieved her best friend has heard, as always, what was left unspoken.

'Of course,' she says.

Then Hollie dips her eyes, and with a whisper she says, 'But when this is all over, we should . . .' Her voice trails off.

It's times like these when something ugly stirs inside Chloe. She knows it's all right for Hollie, she had a family to call her own, she didn't have the same chopping and changing that Chloe had. And now she has Phil, a new build on an estate and – Chloe notices – a new ring on her finger.

'Is that a . . . ?' she says, grateful for a reason to change the subject.

Hollie twiddles the gold band of tiny navy stones around her ring finger.

'Oh, no, not an . . . no, it's an eternity ring. Phil gave it to me for our eighteen-month anniversary.'

'I didn't know people celebrated an eighteen-month anniversary,' Chloe says.

Hollie shrugs. 'We do.'

Phil works on an insurance helpdesk, like a lot of people in this city. He has the same small-town haircut, wears the same small-town uniform. Chloe used to see a lot more of Hollie before she met Phil; now she makes excuses so she doesn't have to go round to their house for spaghetti carbonara and stand in their kitchen admiring their matching kettle, toaster and bread bin. Something about it makes Chloe feel claustrophobic.

Chloe starts playing with the tiny sachets of sugar and sweetener on the table. She empties them from their tub, separating them into white and brown sugar and sweetener and stacking them in piles.

'I'm so worried about Nan out there, all alone.'

Hollie picks up her spoon and stirs her coffee.

'I'm all she's got in the world.'

Hollie shuffles in her chair and looks around the cafe. She sticks out her hand across the table. 'These are actually sapphires, and these' – she points to two barely there white dots – 'these are diamonds.'

'Nan has a ring just like it.'

'Phil got it from that new place in town, by the market. He chose it.'

She blushes when she says that. Hollie and Phil share the same birthday. Chloe has always thought that makes them more like brother and sister. Hollie is besotted by him. Chloe finds him the dullest person she's ever met. She's often wondered how Hollie can find their life together enough, their weekend visits to garden centres or Saturdays spent looking for matching tea, coffee and sugar caddies. But then it depends on what you came from. They say you can go either way.

'Hey, do you remember a story of a kid going missing when we were growing up? Angela Kyle?'

Hollie thinks for a moment, then shakes her head. 'No, not that I . . . no,' she says, dismantling Chloe's sugar archive to take more for her coffee. 'Oh, hang on, the little girl at the swings? I have a vague memory of people talking about it when we were kids. Hasn't it been in the papers too?'

'Yes, Angela – well, the papers called her Angie.'

'Yeah, sort of. I remember her parents doing interviews about it, pleading for information and stuff. God, haven't thought about that in years. She'd be about our age now, wouldn't she?'

'Yeah, she would.'

'What made you ask?'

'Oh, nothing, just a story I'm working on. I was just surprised I'd never heard about her disappearance before, you know, being the same age. She was never found, you know. There can't have been many girls our age who went missing when we were growing up. It must have made people nervous for years afterwards, that's probably why you remember it.'

'Yeah, well I know what you're thinking, and remember, it's in the papers because it's rare that people aren't found,' Hollie says, and she taps Chloe's hand as she says it as if trying to reassure her.

'But it does happen. The police officer told me seventy-nine per cent of missing people are found within twenty-four hours, but what about the other twenty-one per cent? What happens to them? To people like Angela Kyle?'

Hollie sighs. 'Oh Chloe, don't go overthinking, you know what you're like.'

Chloe shifts in her seat.

'Nothing like that is going to happen to Nan, OK? The police are going to find her any minute and bring her home and you'll be back to slinging cans of rice pudding in the bin in no time.'

Chloe smiles a little.

'Thanks,' she says.

'Any time,' Hollie smiles back.

'Anyway, how are you? I've been talking about myself so much I—'

'Don't be silly, I couldn't believe it when you texted. Phil's just got a big promotion at work – huge pay rise – he's taking us on holiday. Fuerteventura, can't wait!'

'Oh, lovely.' Chloe feels hot; she glances around the cafe for an open window.

'And the new place is looking good – we've painted the spare room. It's tiny but it looks much better, you know, fresh lick of paint. You should come over, we're having friends around on Satur—'

'Oh, it's OK.' Chloe starts slipping her arms into her coat and winding her scarf around her neck. 'At the moment I'd rather just . . . you know, what with Nan missing . . .'

'Of course, of course.' Hollie looks away as she does up her coat.

Chloe stands up from her chair. 'I'd better get back to work, but I might go to the cemetery at lunchtime, you know, just in case . . .'

'Oh Chloe, it's far too cold for that, and anyway, she's got more sense than to be hanging around there. If she's anywhere, it'll be back at home, won't it? You'll probably go home after work and find her sitting there with a cup of tea.'

At the mention of tea, Chloe remembers the melted kettle she threw away. And then the fact she's already ten minutes late for work.

Hollie stands up to hug her goodbye. 'Promise you'll let me know when they find her?'

SIX

After work, Chloe leaves the office and heads for the shopping centre. She walks against the tide of shoppers, scanning the crowd as she does for a navy parka, white hair and a wobbly gait she would instantly recognize. A group of teenage schoolgirls, skirts rolled up above their knees, pass her going in the opposite direction. Chloe stares at the tight circle they make. One bumps Chloe with her bag. They walk on chattering.

Chloe finds the department store and heads towards the electricals. Inside, she browses different models of kettles, walking alongside rows and rows of them. She watches the people around her, the couples taking time to choose; some pick up one kettle to test how it feels in their hand, how it feels to pour. Chloe copies them, testing kettles well out of her price range, before choosing one exactly the same as Nan's last.

Nan's house is a museum of her life. It makes Chloe feel safe that Nan's world moves more slowly than the outside one, the things and people take longer to change. Chloe can relax in there. Outside the doors, the world is less reliable. The people are too.

When she was a child, she had a favourite teacher in year three. Her name was Miss Moore. Chloe had a book then, about a little girl who loved her teacher too, and when she read it she always thought of herself and Miss Moore. She once saw Miss Moore trimming a hedge outside her house. She often wished she could go into that house, that she could look behind her red front door. The teacher in the book left the school, and Chloe felt sure that Miss Moore would never do that to her. Then one morning she arrived at school and there was no Miss Moore in front of the blackboard. There was Mr Chadwick. The next time she walked past Miss Moore's house she reached over the fence and pulled all the heads off her pink roses. It had made her feel better but only for a while. She feels safe with Nan, and she knows Nan feels safe with her, and that's more than you can ask from a lot of people. In the electrical department, she feels wet tears on her cheeks. When will Nan be home?

She looks up and sees someone watching her. She dries her eyes. Hollie is right: the first thing Nan will want when she comes home is a cup of tea. And she will come home. She has to.

Chloe takes the kettle to the till. She waits in line to pay, gripping the box. A man and his daughter stand not far from her. The girl is about four, her hair in a plait, a navy pinafore peering from under her cerise woollen coat. She thinks of the missing girl in the news cuttings. Chloe watches her as she plays, balancing her shiny T-bar shoes on her dad's giant ones and giggling as he walks her round in circles in his great big footsteps.

'Excuse me? Madam?'

Chloe spins round. She hadn't noticed the cashier calling her forward.

'Sorry,' she says, smiling back at the little girl and her dad and placing the kettle on the counter.

'They're lovely at that age, aren't they?' the cashier says.

At that moment, the father looks across to the tills and the cashier waves at the little girl. The man smiles back.

'Oh, yes,' Chloe says, fishing inside her purse.

The cashier rings up the kettle on the till.

'Right, that'll be twenty-five pounds, please,' she says.

Chloe pays as the man and the little girl start to head for the exit.

The cashier presses her receipt into her hand.

'Hold on to these moments,' she says. 'They grow up so fast.'

And it's only then that Chloe realizes what the cashier is seeing. She pauses before she takes the receipt and follows the man and his daughter out of the shop, imagining the cashier's eyes on them, their perfect threesome. How easy it is to belong in another's eyes. It's only when she's out of sight of the till that she turns back on herself, taking the escalator up to the first floor, watching the man and the little girl skipping at his side until they disappear from view.

Chloe is soon outside again, the cold biting against her cheeks. She pushes her chin into her scarf, and her footsteps quicken towards home. She walks past the glow of shop windows until they become those of cosy front rooms. She can't bear to look inside tonight at neat family scenes. All she can think about is getting home. She pictures turning into Nan's street, seeing the house lit up from the inside, as if it has all been a bad dream. Cars filled with families pass her as she follows the path out of the city centre; small kids stare out at her from steamy back windows that they draw on while mum and dad ride up front. She stops for one at a junction, and when it turns right, she's about to step out into the road when a faint orange glow from a street light illuminates the sign: Chestnut Avenue. This is the street mentioned in the cuttings, the one where the missing girl had lived – where her parents continue living, still waiting for her to come home.

Chloe peers down the road as she crosses. The wide avenue curves after the first few homes, thwarting her curiosity. As she walks away she tries desperately to remember which number house they lived at. Was it 48? She can't be sure. She'd only know from the very oldest cuttings when life was different and people didn't need to worry about weirdos turning up on their doorstep.

She carries on walking towards Nan's house. She had no idea the Kyles lived so close by. She pictures their living room, just like the others she had walked past, yet in her mind's eye theirs is colder, an emptiness that just won't shift. She knows something of the pain of being stuck like that, although she's only had twenty-four hours without Nan, not the twenty-five-year hell they have endured.

Chloe opens the front door, hoping to find Nan behind it, standing confused in the kitchen, rummaging through cupboards. She's even willing to be called Stella if only she is here. But the house is still and cold.

She plugs in the new kettle and watches as it boils, steam rushing into the tiny kitchen. She makes a cup of tea and takes it into the living room. Inside, her eyes wander across the mahogany-stained sideboard and all the paraphernalia Nan has kept on it for years: the cut-glass fruit bowl filled with nothing but dust; the gold carriage clock Granddad got when he retired that ticked for years longer than his own heart. She pauses in front of a framed photograph of him and Stella. She puts down her tea and picks up the frame with both hands. Stella is a little girl, sitting on his lap; she's wearing knee-high socks and a tartan skirt, her hair cut in a cute little bob that her curls refuse to obey. They are unmistakably father and daughter. How can it be possible to envy intimacy trapped inside a black and white photograph?

She leaves the picture face down, and as she does, catches her own reflection in the leaded glass. Without Nan for context she looks like a stranger in this house.

She kneels down and opens the bottom of the sideboard where she knows the family photo albums are kept. She pulls them out until they lie scattered across the busy patterned carpet. They smell musty, of decades trapped inside. Cross-legged, she sits down among them. She pulls out the giant red one first and hears a soft crackle from the waxy sheets as she turns the pages one by one. There's Nan and Granddad on their wedding day, Granddad looking so handsome, so fresh from the war he's still wearing his uniform. Nan, a woman much younger than Chloe is now, her hair cut into a similar bob to Stella's. She roams through the pages of their lives together, fast-forwarding through their various homes, past baby photos, catching angles of houses and cars she's sure she recognizes – photographs and memories blurring into one. It doesn't take much to plant a story inside your head, then water it and watch it grow.

She flicks through and watches as Nan ages. There are photos of her in cone-cupped bikinis sunbathing on the rocks in Ibiza, and others of her as a young mum, a baby on one hip as she poses proudly beside their new VW Beetle.

She flicks through the albums quickly, like a flip book, watching the lines deepen on Nan's face as first her daughter and then her husband disappear from her side. The photographs stop abruptly then, a few pages short of the end. Instead a large blank fills the space.

Chloe closes the album, and sits with it in her lap in the dim light of the living room. A whole life contained in these albums. But what use are they to Nan now when the memories, the captions for each of those photographs, have already bid her brain farewell?

Chloe puts everything away. She heats up a can of rice pudding for supper, then sits in Nan's chair, looking out of the living room window. She watches the street, hoping to see a familiar figure appear under the orange glow of the street lamps. Instead it's just a fox that scuttles by.

Chloe watches TV for a while, skipping channels when she can't focus on any one programme. She looks outside again. It has now been twenty-eight hours since Nan went missing. Chloe knows her chances of being found are falling with each hour that passes. In a newspaper story a reporter would describe her as clinging to hope. She thinks of the Kyles, how they first feasted on it, until even hope became famine. She settles down in Nan's chair. The standard lamp in the window a beacon to return Nan home. Its long fringe shade casting shadows across Chloe's face.

SEVEN

Chloe has an uncomfortable night on the sofa, twisting and turning in half-dreams the way she often does. She wakes throughout the night to check her phone, the living room close enough to hear if there were a knock at the front door. At some point she must drift off into a deep sleep because her ringing phone jolts her awake.

'Yes?'

'Chloe?'

'Yes.'

'PC Bains here from Acton police station.'

She tries to stem her fear of what they might say. 'Acton?'

'Yes, in west London. The reason I'm calling is because I have a Mrs Grace Hudson here at the station and . . .'

Chloe sits up quickly, on the edge of the sofa cushion.

'. . . she's a little disorientated and dehydrated, but otherwise well.'

'Oh, thank God.'

She presses the phone to her chest because it feels like the right thing to do. She composes herself and takes instructions from the police officer, promising her she's already on her way.

Nan is OK. Disorientated, but OK.

She's home. Or not quite. She's in Acton. Chloe sieves back through the photo albums in her mind. Nan and Granddad's first home was in west London; they'd both

47

been born there and had only moved up here when Grandad got a job at the brick factory. Nan had gone home.

Chloe takes the fast train to London even though it's more expensive – she refuses to be slowed by twice as many stops. It is still early morning and the train is filled with commuters, and the scent of pressed shirts, fresh aftershave and plastic cups of hot tea. She calls her own office and leaves a garbled message for Alec. She knows it will be greeted with more eye-rolling, but right now – this minute – she needs to get Nan back.

She texts Hollie too: Nan ok, in Acton. Not sure why. On train to get her. So relieved. xx

Chloe sits upright in her seat, willing the scenery to flash past faster at the windows. Even two inches closer to the edge of her seat will mean she pulls in to London quicker. When the trolley comes around she buys a KitKat and a Diet Coke. It fizzes as she pours it into a beige plastic cup.

The train heads out to the edges of Fenland. There is still frost on the ground and birds stand on the woolly backs of sheep to keep their feet warm. Everyone is useful to someone.

Takeaways and betting shops lead Chloe to Acton police station from the tube, and like a trail of breadcrumbs these garish signs will lead her back the way she came. When she reaches the counter she's panting, as if she had been holding her breath all the way from Peterborough.

'My nan . . . Grace Hudson . . . she's h— I mean, she's been found. She's here.'

The officer behind the counter gestures for her to slow down.

'OK, let's start at the beginni—'

'It was PC Bains who called me, she . . . she said Nan was here, that she was fine. Dehydrated. Please, I just need to see her.'

'OK, OK . . .' the officer says, more sympathetic than impatient. He taps something into his computer. 'Can you tell me your grandmother's name?'

'Grace. Grace Hudson.'

Chloe scans his face for recognition while he studies his computer screen. She learnt a long time ago to read faces for the bits people don't tell you.

'Would you like to take a seat and I'll let PC Bains know you're here.'

'Is she here? Nan, I mean.'

'If you could just take a seat,' he says. He indicates towards the bench behind her, blue and shiny, matching the Met Police logo.

Chloe waits in reception – just like on the train – on the very edge of her seat. She scans each person in uniform who walks by in case she can identify PC Bains. She distracts herself by picking the dry skin around her nails until red bleeds into her cuticles.

She hears a voice down the corridor. Nan's voice. She looks up. PC Bains is walking along the corridor towards her, her arm hooked around Nan's elbow, talking to her as if they're old friends. Chloe stands up and rushes towards them like she knows for sure they'd do in films.

'Nan,' she says.

Nan looks at her like they saw each other just five minutes before.

'Chloe, whatever's happened, dear? You look like you've seen a ghost.'

PC Bains pats her arm. She has a Brummie accent when she speaks. 'She's been worried about you, Grace. You went wandering, didn't you? You've caused your poor granddaughter all sorts of worry.'

'I don't have a granddaughter.'

PC Bains gives Chloe a sympathetic look.

'Yes, you do, Grace. She's here to take you home. You've been missing for two days.'

Nan looks at her. 'Have I?'

Chloe puts an arm around Nan. 'Why did you come to Acton, Nan?'

'I was lost,' she says. 'I wanted to come home.'

'But you don't live here, Nan.'

'Well, that's what they keep saying. But my house is there. I tried telling them it was my house.'

Chloe glances at PC Bains for some kind of explanation.

'It turns out it's where she lived when she was a little girl,' she says. 'She stowed away on a train from Peterborough apparently, managed to slip through the barriers, even onto the tube, didn't you, Grace? The owners of the house found her inside their shed this morning. You gave them quite the fright, Grace.'

'Twenty-three Rothschild Road,' Nan says, 'but who were those people? Where are Mother and Father?'

'Don't worry about that now, Nan,' Chloe says. 'The most important thing is that you're home. Or nearly anyway, we need to get the train back—' She looks up and around inside the station, as if to get her bearings.

'Oh, it's OK, I think that's all sorted,' PC Bains interrupts, and as she does a figure appears walking down the corridor behind her, clutching paperwork. 'I believe you and Claire have met before?'

Claire Sanders, Nan's social worker. Her blunt bob swings around her cheeks. The jubilation Chloe felt at seeing Nan is instantly replaced with a dread that surely shows on her face. The mask slips. She feels it.

'Oh, Claire's been ever so nice, Chloe,' Nan says. 'She says she'll give us a lift home to . . .' She turns to PC Bains. 'Where are we going again?'

'Peterborough,' Chloe and Claire answer in unison. The social worker has her car keys in her hand, her handbag tucked under her arm.

'Shall we?' Claire asks. Nan and Chloe follow her out of the station.

EIGHT

From the outside, the new place for Nan looks more like a hotel than a care home. There is a shiny sign reading *Park House Care Home*, sprinkled at the corners with illustrations of spring flowers.

Chloe takes Nan's arm to lead her inside.

'Do we know someone who lives here?' Nan asks.

'Come on, Nan,' Chloe replies, 'let's go inside and have a look around.'

Claire Sanders walks behind them, so close she's practically inside their footsteps. Chloe tries to pretend she's not there at all, but it's not easy when she's interrupting constantly, pointing out different facilities before they've even stepped inside. Chloe concentrates instead on ignoring the ugliness that collects inside her veins.

The women are introduced to the matron, Miriam, and they follow her along a burgundy carpet peppered with yellow diamonds, around a giant glass window that looks out onto a small courtyard filled with tropical plants.

'Park House opened around twenty-five years ago, and we're currently home to thirty-one guests . . .' Miriam explains as they walk.

'It's pretty here, isn't it?' Nan says.

Chloe doesn't need to turn around to know Claire is smiling behind her.

'We're just starting a major renovation, extending the site to incorporate some of the land either side of us. We will be adding six new bedrooms, and an adapted kitchen to support residents to be independent for as long as they can – for some, just being able to keep making their own cup of tea can make a real difference.'

Claire smiles and nods. 'The facilities here are what makes Park House one of the top ten specialist dementia care homes in the region,' she interjects.

Chloe ignores her.

They're back where they started. Chloe glances at the matron, confused.

'We understand that people with dementia like walking,' she says, 'so this circular corridor with the garden in the middle means they can walk for hours safely and enjoy the view while they do.'

Clever, Chloe thinks. Not that she says it. She's been determined not to like this care home since Claire had told her she'd found the 'perfect place' for Nan when they got her back home.

'She doesn't need a perfect place,' Chloe had snapped at her. 'She's got one, right here with me.'

Not that it had made any difference.

'Grace needs twenty-four-hour care, Chloe,' Claire had said, 'and you have a job, it's impossible for you to be there for her all the time, as much as I know you'd like to be.'

She wanted to say that's what Nan had always done for her, that it had always been the two of them. But what was the point? It would only sound saccharine and sentimental to a social worker. Instead, she'd swallowed it down and so here they were.

The matron shows them a couple of bedrooms. They

remind Chloe of ones in motels – not that she's ever stayed in one, but she's seen them on television or in movies. These rooms have nice touches: bedside tables and vases, black and white pictures of the city in years gone by. Claire points out to Nan that the resident in this particular room has covered one of her walls in photographs of her grandchildren. Chloe tries to move her on by taking her elbow and leading her out the room.

'Hasn't she got it nice, Chloe?' Nan says.

Chloe nods, quickly, and Claire smiles at her as Miriam leads the way. Claire lingers in the room and catches Chloe's hand as Nan follows Miriam.

'I think she likes it, do you?' she asks.

'Let's not be too hasty,' Chloe replies.

By the time they catch up with Nan she's in the communal room chatting to two residents who ask her to join them in a game of cards.

'Will you come back for me a bit later, dear?' she asks. 'I just want to have a chat to these nice old folk.'

Claire looks from Chloe to the matron. 'I think that's settled it,' she says.

Chloe wants Claire to hurt, as much as she is hurting now. Her hands twist inside the deep pockets of her coat, her fingernails cutting crescents into her palms.

Nan sits happily with her new friends as Chloe walks over to a huge window that overlooks the grounds. There's a small wooded copse beside the care home. An area of it has already started to be felled – presumably this is where Park House will be extending, Chloe thinks. Beyond that, she can just make out a lake. It's a bright day, despite the cold, and the sun twinkles in golden silvers on top of the water. As she turns around, a nurse is bringing a cup of tea to an old man in an armchair beside her.

'Excuse me, where's that?' she asks her.

'Ferry Meadows,' the nurse answers. 'Lovely view, isn't it? On a clear day you can even see the steam train running along the back of the park.'

While Nan plays cards Claire and Chloe unpack her things, hanging her clothes in the small wardrobe and putting photographs on her new bedside table.

When they've finished, they call Nan in to have a look. She wanders into her room with one of her new friends and picks up a photograph of Granddad taken just a few months before he died.

'My Hughie,' she says, holding up the picture frame. 'You'll meet him, of course, when he's back from the war. Doesn't he look handsome?'

Her blue eyes turn paler when she talks about him, as if they become a window back to her youth. What good does it do to pull her back into a world where they're separated by death? Right now he's as real to her as Chloe is standing in her doorway. Nan looks up and sees her.

'Oh, hello, young lady,' she says. 'Are you here to take the drinks orders? I like a drop of Drambuie in the afternoon when I'm on holiday.'

Claire tries to comfort Chloe with clichés on the drive home. Chloe answers her by gazing out of the passenger window.

'She's in the best place, Chloe,' Claire tells her.

Chloe wonders why she has to make it sound like Nan is dead already.

She starts pressing buttons on the door – she needs to get some air in the car. Claire sees and puts her window down by pressing a button on her steering wheel. Her hatred of Claire is only increased by this gesture, and the fact that Claire doesn't seem to notice only irritates her more. But what does she expect? How would Claire like it if she had taken the one precious thing she has in the whole world? She'd seen it once, on her keyring, a boy – or girl – with ginger hair, around eight or nine. On the back of the keyring it read *Best Mum Ever*. Chloe doubted it. It didn't seem fair that her kid was at home, waiting for Mummy to come and play house when she had spent her day destroying another. Not that Claire would understand her loneliness, her loss. For some reason it's the photograph of Angela Kyle's parents that pops into her head, and she feels that connection again, as if they are the only two people in the world who might understand how she feels.

Claire drops Chloe outside Nan's house. She turns to wave until Claire has driven away. But she doesn't go inside, not yet.

Instead she waits until she sees the car go round the bend and then she puts her keys back in her coat pocket and walks in the opposite direction.

Chestnut Avenue is a long, broad road curved at each end, disguising both where you came from and where you're headed. Neat brown-brick semi-detached houses stand two-by-two and small front gardens peer out from behind short walls topped with privet hedges. Beside each house is a driveway, some still with the original garages; others have expanded and swollen, giving birth to extensions and extra bedrooms over the years. Between the pavement and the road there are grassy verges and planted occasionally within them, guarding each pair of houses, are the great trees that give this street its name. Throughout the decades, these trees will have seen it all. It is in many ways an unremarkable street, but to Chloe, its symmetry has a certain perfection to it.

Chloe walks towards the curve in the road, crossing a junction, onto the next part of the street. All the time she walks, she tries to picture it twenty-five years ago. She passes a Catholic church on a junction and peers inside the thick wooden door. In her mind's eye she sees the younger versions of Maureen and Patrick, the ones in the black and white photographs that filled the newspapers that autumn back in 1979, and she imagines them just a few years before, filing into this very church each Sunday, a tiny Angie in their arms and a congregation made up of neighbours who cooed over the new baby while her parents took communion.

She counts the numbers down from the hundreds and finally she's standing in front of number 48 – the address she'd checked in the earliest cuttings.

She looks up at what is still quite obviously a child's bedroom – Angie's bedroom? No, surely not after all these years? There isn't much to see: a thin strip of what looks like pink curtains peers out from behind double glazing, and the outline of a light shade hanging from the middle of the room. She looks harder, tries tiptoes, but the reflection of the trees in the window blurs the lines, and she can only just make out the shape of the paper light shade in the shadows cast behind the glass. A car rushes by and when she looks back, the outline is gone.

There's no movement behind the front door of number 48. There is no car on the drive either. Chloe steps forward, drawn to the house as if it were a magnet and she was metal. The Kyles know what it's like to lose something, a family member, or have them snatched away. She doesn't know why she came here to find comfort; instead she thinks of Angela Kyle and feels a pinch of guilt. At least she knows where Nan is now, even if it isn't with her.

She looks up at the child's bedroom again. A cloud has crossed the sky, obscuring the view through the glass with its reflection. Now she can't even make out the light shade. She turns on her heels and heads home to Nan's.

NINE

Chloe hasn't been in the office for two days, so she arrives early, hoping to creep in and camouflage herself among the filing cabinets.

Alec is already there when she arrives, his nicotine-stained fingers working through a pile of brown envelopes. Her first thought is that one of them might be the Angela Kyle file, but no, it's there waiting on her desk, just as she left it on Monday.

She mutters good morning. Alec coughs in response, then he picks up a pile of envelopes and heads deep into the archive. His clothes leave a stale breeze. His silence unnerves her. Should she follow him into the dense forest of filing? She closes her eyes and tries to think what would be happening if her life were a TV show, but nothing comes to her.

She turns on her computer, wishing she could muffle the fanfare it makes as it loads. As the office starts to fill, she casts glances over both shoulders in turn, the weight of the Angela Kyle file feeling reassuring in her hands. She peers inside, the spine of every single cutting so neatly folded; her fingernails pluck at them as if they're tiny guitar strings.

She empties the file and spreads the cuttings out on her desk, every so often aware of Alec passing by and glancing in her direction. Smaller cuttings offer tantalising tasters, words leap up from the melamine: *missing girl, heartbroken parents, search, desperate, hope fades.* But she knows the real story – the whole story – is folded away within the larger cuttings. She hasn't been able to stop thinking of the Kyles, especially not last night when she had returned home alone, when she'd felt the silence in the walls of that empty house. Is that how it has felt to these parents since the day Angela went missing? She feels she must be the only person who has some idea of what they are going through, and that likewise, they would understand her, and in many ways that made her feel less lonely, just the thought that someone would understand.

She picks one of the articles at random, opens out the double-page spread on her desk.

LOCALS JOIN SEARCH FOR MISSING GIRL

She starts to read, but Alec limps past again so she quickly presses the article underneath the scanner. Her heart races as the pixels begin to appear on her computer screen.

There is a picture of Angie in this one, a grainy black and white reception class photo, a milk-tooth grin, hair in two bunches.

Missing: Angie, four, the caption reads.

The main picture is of locals searching through long grass alongside police, watched over by her parents, and underneath: *Heartbroken: Parents Patrick and Maureen Kyle*. She lingers on this picture of them, their fingers knitted tightly together in gripped hands, the two of them united in their grief for their precious missing child.

A reporter enters the archive and, thinking it's Alec, she quickly labels and closes the file. Then she picks another:

THE IMPOSTER

MOTHER: 'HOW CAN MY GIRL JUST DISAPPEAR?'

This time a colour piece from a feature writer who hasn't worked at the paper for ten years. She had gone back to the family for a revisit:

> MAUREEN Kyle sits opposite me on the sofa in their cosy sitting room. There is not a thing out of place and yet, it's very clear that something is missing from this tableau. She appears poised, collected, but as her eyes rest on a photograph of her missing daughter, little Angela – or Angie, as her mum and dad call her – that calm exterior cracks, and the tears flow. 'One minute she was here, playing in this living room, and the next she was gone. It doesn't seem right. How could my daughter just disappear like that? How can any child disappear without trace? Somebody somewhere must know something.' Her husband, Patrick, inches closer to her on the sofa and reaches for her hand . . .

Footsteps around her, Alec's uneven gait. The scanner greedily eats up detail she herself longs to consume. The office is getting busy, Chloe knows she needs to look busy too. She picks another cutting from the pile.

ANGIE LATEST: POLICE DIVERS DREDGE RIVER

The next one:

BOGUS SIGHTING WASTES POLICE TIME

61

Another:

LOCALS RALLY FOR ANGIE VIGIL

The next couple of hours pass as the news rolls in from the wire. Reporters empty their shorthand pads at the news desk, and the editor's office door opens and shuts as the day's splash is decided upon. Among the chaos of the newsroom, Chloe works diligently through the Angela Kyle file. She knows it wouldn't ordinarily take this long, that she doesn't need to read all the cuttings. There are some she manages to resist, especially when she feels Alec's eyes on her. But when he's lost among the metal filing cabinets, when she hears the clang of the drawers as he removes and replaces files, she takes those few precious seconds to find out more.

ANGIE'S FATHER IN SHOCK ARREST

Her stomach turns under her desk. This one she has to read.

> POLICE swooped last night on the home of missing city girl Angela Kyle, arresting her father in a shocking turn of events. Patrick Kyle was taken to the city's Bridge Street police station and questioned for two hours after an anonymous tip-off from the public. But the bungling act by police proved to be the result of nothing more than a prank call, and Mr Kyle was released without charge. The city's police chief has since apologized unreservedly to the Kyle family.

> Speaking exclusively to this newspaper, Patrick
> Kyle said, 'Yes, it was upsetting, but it also reassured
> us that the police are taking our daughter's disap-
> pearance very seriously. We welcome every lead
> being followed up, we support the police in inves-
> tigating every suspicion, it's the only way that we
> will get our Angie back.'

There's another picture – the same again. The pair of
them united. Impenetrable. Their loyalty to their daughter
constant, steadfast, intoxicating.

By mid-morning the sandwich man arrives and Chloe
tears herself away from her desk to buy a tuna baguette
from the trolley. She keeps her eye on the file all along for
fear that Alec might take it. He still hasn't spoken to her, but
she comforts herself with the thought that she's insignificant
enough for yesterday's absence not even to be noted.

Eleven thirty rolls around, the newspaper is put to bed,
and the editor's office door opens. Alec approaches her
desk.

'Er, Chloe . . .' he says, coughing a little into his hand,
'Malc would like a word in his office, if you'd like to . . .'

His sentence trails off, but he gestures for her to follow
him.

She gathers up her notepad and pen, as if trying to
convince the both of them that Malc might need archive
material for a big story. Alec glances at the stationery in
her hand but says nothing.

Inside the office Alec closes the door. Malc is behind
his desk, elbows spread wide behind his head. He doesn't
ask either of them to sit.

'Chloe,' he begins, 'this isn't the first time you've been in this office, is it?'

She shakes her head.

'Sorry?'

He has pockmarks on his cheeks.

'No.'

'No,' he repeats, 'and I think the last time you were in here, we talked about the same things: time-keeping, unauthorized absences from the office, general tardiness in your performance . . .' He checks each felony off on fat fingers. 'Am I right?'

She nods.

'Sorry?'

'Yes.'

He knits those same fingers together and leans forward on his desk. 'So my question to you is, what are we to do about this?'

There is silence in the room. Chloe looks at Alec, who straightens up as Malc starts to speak again.

'Alec tells me you were absent during office hours three times last week, then this week—'

'I . . . I know it looks bad—' she starts and instantly regrets interrupting him because when he speaks again, his voice is so loud it startles the sound of her own blood from her ears.

'—and today's Wednesday, and you've only just decided to "pop back in"?'

He leans back abruptly on his office chair, bobbing back and forth a little. There is enough silence then for her to decide to fill it. She's good at talking herself out of situations, she knows what people want to hear.

'It's just my nan,' she says.

Both men roll their eyes a little.

'She's got dementia and I've been trying to care for her . . . she gets confused, you see . . . and she went missing . . . and the police, well, they found her in London . . . and I had to go and get her . . . now she's in a home and—'

Alec interrupts this time. 'Chloe, we've been as patient as we can be. How many times have we heard—'

'Yes, I know, Alec, and I'm grateful, I really am, but now she's in a home and I won't have to—'

'Until the next time,' Alec mutters.

Chloe wraps one arm around her middle and bites her fingernail.

'It's a written warning this time, Chloe,' Malc says, and then as if to underline the point, 'Your last warning.'

She swallows the rest of her sentence, and nods quickly before he changes his mind. Just another warning. She can deal with that.

Alec thanks Malc and they leave the office, shuffling awkwardly in their haste to get back to the safety of the archive.

She speeds through the rest of the Angela Kyle file – she can't afford to have Alec commenting on her work again today – but she doesn't put it back in the archive. Instead, when Alec isn't looking, she slips it into the top drawer of her desk. She'll wait until he leaves to put it in her bag. Chloe is taking Angela Kyle home.

At Park House that evening, one of the care assistants shows Chloe where Nan is sitting in the recreation room. Chloe doesn't recognize her at first; she looks smaller here somehow, like she's shrunken, and takes up less room than she had in her living room with its fake mahogany dado rail. Like the wood moulding stitching together two parts of the wall, Nan held herself and Chloe together too. She was the lynchpin of their family life. Here she appears as anonymous, as tiny, as any other resident. Seeing Nan like that, across the room, unsettles her for a moment.

Chloe takes a few steps towards her, but Nan doesn't turn around. She watches her silently, this small woman with her delicate frame, her fragile shoulders barely filling her mauve cardigan.

'Nan?' she says, more quietly than she might usually. For some reason, this alien environment is making a mockery of them. And as if she feels it too, Nan doesn't turn around.

Chloe stops then. Which world is she inhabiting in this moment? Is it one where she's brought Stella back from the dead, or is Granddad off fighting in the war? She never knows what she will face. It used to be day to day, then hour to hour, now it is more likely minute to minute. Faced with such shifting sands, is it any wonder they both let her disease win from time to time? There is another way of dealing with this illness after all: the days when it unwittingly swells their family from two to four could be seen as a gift. A chance for them both to pretend. As if this thief of time that creeps into her brain is letting them both live a fantasy.

As Chloe gets closer she sees that Nan is smiling.

'Nan?'

She doesn't respond.

Her hair has been shampooed and set, a brooch she hasn't seen except in photographs is pinned to her jumper.

Her smile is slicked in coral lipstick too. She's never seen Nan wearing lipstick before.

'Nan?'

She turns around.

'Who are you?' she says.

'It's me, Chloe?'

'I don't know anyone called Chloe.'

'I'm Stella's daughter,' she says, 'your granddaughter.'

Nan laughs then, really laughs. Her coral lipstick makes a giant 'O' on her face. 'Stella's only a baby herself, she doesn't have any children.' She turns back to looking out of the window then, still chuckling to herself. 'I'm just waiting for her to come home from school.'

Chloe leaves her there – in, when, the late fifties? – while she stands beside her in 2004. Instead she sits down in an armchair and waits in case the years catch up with her. They both look out of the window that overlooks the gardens. Just a few feet away, on the other side of the glass, a thrush pulls a worm from the lawn and above it, a blue tit clings to a bird feeder. The two women sit in silence for a while and that feels like enough to Chloe, enough just to be next to her. To imagine their hearts beating in time.

There is no way of telling how much time passes like that before Nan turns to her.

'Chloe, dear,' she says, 'how long have you been sitting there?'

'Not long,' she replies.

'Have you had a cup of tea yet? I'd love a cup of tea.'

Chloe glances at the full cup beside her, cold now, of course, tan already staining the porcelain.

'Shall we go and have one in my room? I'd love to show you all my pictures.'

Chloe is happy to have her back. She helps her out of the armchair and they shuffle slowly together to her room. Chloe forgets how much she slows down when she's around Nan and suddenly feels sad that even these last few days have stripped some memories from her. Goodness knows what they've stolen from Nan.

Inside her room, Nan sits down on the bed. She picks up the photograph of Grandad taken just before he died. He's sitting on the beach at Sheringham eating chips with a wooden fork.

'Do you remember that day?' Chloe asks her.

She nods. 'Is that Hughie?'

'Yes, that's right. We all went to the seaside together, do you remember?'

'Were you there too?' Nan asks.

'Yes.'

'What did you say your name was again?'

'Chloe.'

'Chloe. I don't know a Chloe.'

'Nan, you . . .' She sighs. 'Don't worry, let me go and get that cup of tea.'

'Lovely,' Nan says as she leaves. 'I just fancy a cuppa.'

Chloe leaves the room for the kitchen a few doors down. She doesn't have the energy today to go over the same story she has told a dozen times or more before: the day they went to Sheringham, the seagulls that swooped down and pinched chips right out of their hands. She'd been careful every time to patiently colour in as much detail as she could think of. It's frustrating always having to start at day zero. She boils the kettle and pours water over two teabags. Some days she wishes Stella was still there, to back her up, to persuade Nan too. But it would be different then, it wouldn't be just the two of them. Nan would have to share the love, and although there are days when Chloe misses a mother's touch, at least she has Nan all to herself.

She heads back a few moments later with two cups of hot tea.

'There you go, Nan.'

She smiles at her – that flicker of recognition; Chloe captures and pockets it. That'll have to do today. She takes a sip.

'I'm waiting for my daughter Stella to come home from school,' Nan says. 'It's nice to have a cuppa – a bit of a breather – before they're home, isn't it?' She laughs.

Chloe nods, drinking from her cup. She tastes the resentment in her mouth. Stella never erased from Nan's mind, and yet Chloe instantly forgotten while she makes a cup of tea.

'How old is your daughter?' she asks.

'Six,' Nan says, 'little terror. Good job I've only got the one.'

Chloe nods again. She's not tempted to explain any more, she's happy to leave Nan back in 1956. Because if Stella is six, then Chloe doesn't even exist.

TEN

7 November 1979
PETERBOROUGH ADVERTISER

MOTHER'S PLEA: 'GIVE BACK OUR ANGIE'

THE mother of missing city girl Angela Rose Kyle has made an emotional plea for her daughter to be returned and told for the first time of the last few hours she spent with her.

Four-year-old Angela – or Angie, as her parents call her – disappeared from a play park in Ferry Meadows a week ago.

Her devastated mother, Maureen Kyle, made the appeal through this newspaper for her safe return: 'I'm begging, if there's anyone out there who has our little girl, please, please give her back. We just want her home where she belongs.'

Mrs Kyle, supported by her husband, Patrick, spoke to this newspaper from the family home at 48 Chestnut Avenue.

'It's the details you worry about as a mother. If someone has taken her, I wonder if they are doing the little things, the tiny things you do on automatic as a mum: brushing her teeth at night; tucking her in with a blanket; rubbing her tummy when she's not feeling very well; stroking her head if she has a nightmare and can't get to sleep. Angie has nightmares sometimes about wolves in her bedroom – do they know that? Does whoever have her know that she wakes in the night some-times seeing wolves in her dreams? Will they know what to do when she cries, and what if she cries for me? Did she call for me when they took her?'

Chloe looks up from the floor of Nan's front room. She's been reading for the last hour, cross-legged on Nan's Axminster, the cuttings spread out around her. Many are still folded; some are opened, scattered headlines making a path between the sofa and the carpet-covered pouffe. She reads on:

'That last morning was so mundane, just like any other day, and yet it's still so vivid and I don't want to forget a single moment of it. Angie had a bath with her favourite Mr Men bubbles. I washed her hair and made it stick up on her head with the foam, just like I always do. I can still hear her gig-gling. I wish more than ever I could still smell those bubbles on her skin . . .'

Chloe pauses to look at the photograph of Maureen. She must be about thirty years old, but the prettiness of her has been swallowed by grief. In the photograph she clutches a screwed-up tissue in one hand, Patrick's fingers wrapped around her other one, his head leaning on her shoulders, although it's unclear who is propping up who.

She pulls the cutting closer to her nose, to get a better look at these two. At these perfect parents. Finally, she discards that cutting for the next.

ANGIE'S DAD: 'I'LL NEVER FORGIVE MYSELF'

ONE hundred days after the disappearance of four-year-old city girl Angela Kyle, her father has given a heartbreaking interview to this newspaper.

Reliving the nightmare of that day on 27 October 1979, Patrick Kyle recalled the last moments at the play park with his little girl before she went missing: 'I still remember her face every time I pushed her on the swings. "Higher, Daddy!" she said – she was fearless that girl. She was sweet, funny, bright, happy, caring. She laughed and laughed as I pushed her higher.'

Mr Kyle had taken his daughter for a play at the park in Ferry Meadows. The pair had only been there around ten minutes when he realized he'd left his blue Ford Escort unlocked. He turned his back to walk the fifty yards to the car park to lock it and when he returned, Angie had vanished.

'As her father, of course I blame myself. I was meant to be her protector. I held her in my arms when she was just a few minutes old, I rubbed her tiny nose against mine, I promised her then that I would look after her, that she had nothing to fear, that I would always be there and . . . I wasn't, was I? I'll never, ever forgive myself for turning away for those few seconds.'

But that was all it took. Chloe knows how it feels – after all, isn't that how she'd lost Nan?

Except her story had a happy ending. This cutting is from February 1980, and it is now 2004 and there is still no news. How does anyone go on like that? Left suspended between hope and grief. Life and death. Yet knowing every day that a call could come or she could walk through the front door.

She unfolds another cutting, careful not to pull too hard on the newsprint as she feels its resistance. Chloe shakes her head, doubting reporters ever treat the cuttings with the same respect. But she is in the business of preservation. Lives, stories, they're one and the same.

She rearranges herself on the floor, lying now on her front as she opens up another half a dozen cuttings and lays them out, one on top of another, a run-through of all the ups and downs of the case. One cutting includes a reception class photograph; Chloe scans it for Angie. She finds her, as easily now as if she'd attended the very same class. They were the same age, Chloe reasons, she might well have.

SCHOOL FRIENDS' VIGIL FOR ANGIE

CHILDREN at the school attended by missing city girl Angela Kyle have held a private assembly to pray together for her safe return.

Students and parents at Dogsthorpe Primary School filled a packed hall on Friday and remembered Angie with songs, pictures and performances. Maureen and Patrick Kyle were also present for what the headteacher described as a 'celebration' of Angie's life.

Headteacher Vanessa Cooper said, 'Angela is one of our reception class pupils and is a very popular little girl with lots of friends who miss her dearly. Many of the students' parents and teachers have been aiding in the search for Angie and we realized the children wanted to do their bit too. The children were very clear they wanted to hold a "celebration" of her life.'

In the days leading up to the assembly, the children made colourful posters and chose some of Angela's favourite songs to sing, including 'I Can Sing a Rainbow'.

One of her friends, Rachel Barker, five, told this newspaper: 'Angie is my best friend and I miss playing hopscotch with her.'

She picks up another cutting, pulling her pale blue notebook alongside it and writing down Rachel's name. She's not sure why, but it feels like something that would be useful to remember.

PARENTS PRAY FOR ANGIE'S RETURN

THE parents of missing city girl Angela Kyle made a late-night visit to their local church to pray for their daughter's safe return.

Maureen and Patrick Kyle are said to be 'devastated' at the disappearance of their daughter five days ago from a play park in Ferry Meadows.

Desperate for any information, they turned to their local congregation, who arranged a special mass to pray for news of little Angie.

Father Martin Cunningham, priest at St Gregory's Church, conducted the service. He told this newspaper, 'I've known Maureen and Patrick and their families for more than a decade. In fact, I married them just six years ago. I also baptized little Angie. They are both devoted to their daughter and, as you can imagine, this last week has been agony for them. But their faith is strong and that's what is giving them the strength to face every day at the moment – that and the hope each new day brings that Angie will be found.'

More than a hundred worshippers packed the church last night to pray for the family.

'The power of prayer can be an incredible thing,' Father Cunningham added. 'And right now it's fair to say that we are praying for a miracle.'

She writes down *Father Martin Cunningham*. Underlining it. Twice. On and on she goes through the cuttings, searching for more details, names, dates, places that might be worth revisiting. One cutting mentions a sighting in Highbury, north London. She writes it down, then scribbles it out when it's later revealed as a hoax. Then writes it again, this time with a question mark on the end.

She searches for more tiny details about Angie, finding the name of her cloth cat and writing *Puss* in her book. In one article, Patrick Kyle mentions she was wearing shiny new red shoes the day she went missing. That goes into her notebook too. Each little detail she writes, feeding this ridiculous fantasy at the back of her head that maybe she could find some missing detail that the police overlooked.

Chloe looks up at the street lamps peering in from between the heavy curtains. Were the detectives this vigilant? She doubts it. To them, Angela would have been just a job. But it already feels much more than that to Chloe. After everything she's been through, she – more than anyone – understands. She just wishes she could help.

Chloe reads on until the inky words swim in front of her eyes and her back aches from lying on the carpet. She flicks back through her notebook; five filled pages, not bad. For now.

She folds all the cuttings away carefully, putting them back inside the brown envelope and tucking it into Nan's sideboard alongside the photo albums overnight. She makes a vow to reopen the case in the morning.

Chloe and Nan have been visiting the cemetery every weekend for as long as she can remember, but dementia has changed everything. With a disease like that, old routines must give way to new ones. Except, Chloe doesn't like change. She scratches at her arm as she squeezes the last of the toothpaste from the tube, an itch inside she can't reach. Toothpaste is another thing to add to the shopping list, and, she decides, another reason she can't go to the cemetery this morning.

She takes the Angela Kyle file with her when she leaves

home, company for the bus journey to the supermarket. When she arrives she wanders aimlessly between parents pushing screaming toddlers in trolleys or scolding older children taking a ride on the end of them. Those are the types of families she can stomach; the ones who walk together in neat little sets, pushing the trolley in sync, make her aware of even the skin that covers her. She wriggles uncomfortably within it. Every time.

In the cereal aisle, a little girl in stripy dungarees is trying to persuade her mum to buy a brightly coloured packet of princess cereal. Chloe stands, her basket suspended on her arm, as she watches them. She thinks of Maureen Kyle. What she would give to have a similar argument with her daughter given her time again? Surely she'd let her have her way. As the little girl pleads with her mother, Chloe is tempted to remind the woman that life is short – what does a box of cereal matter? But the woman has now answered her phone, tucking it between her neck and her ear, and she's turned her back on her daughter. Chloe shakes her head and thinks of the split second Patrick turned around. The girl starts to wander as her mother runs through her shopping list with the person on the end of the line. Chloe follows her. The little girl picks up more colourful boxes of cereal. She calls to her mother to show her, but her mother barely notices. Chloe steps forward, just an inch or so. She looks around her. If only someone had intervened when they saw Angela on her own, might the Kyles' story have ended differently? The little girl wanders further from her mother, towards packets of multi-coloured corn loops. Chloe traces her footsteps, looking back at the mother every few seconds. Under her arm she feels the weight of the Kyle file in her bag. For all this mother knows, somebody could be watching this little girl now. They could be stalking her, ready to pounce when they're sure her mother is distracted enough not to notice.

'Mamma,' the little girl calls. She picks up a box of cereal, turning it upside down and shaking it, delighting at the sound.

Chloe quickly takes a step back from the girl as her mother turns around in time to see the mess she makes as it pours out of the box. The woman sighs into her phone, exasperated, and hangs up. Then strides over to her daughter and chastises her. Chloe takes some Weetabix from the shelf and moves on with her basket. Another parent who doesn't realize how lucky she is.

Chloe continues shopping, aware of the lone figure she cuts among all the others with their loaded trolleys. In the cosmetics aisle she is still thinking of the little girl. Distracted, she throws a tube of denture paste into her basket. It's only when she finally reaches the checkout that she remembers she doesn't need to buy it anymore.

'I picked this up by mistake,' she explains.

The cashier nods without speaking.

Chloe is about to tell her about Nan, to explain, but then she notices her name badge: Sharon Kyle.

'Kyle,' Chloe says. 'That's an unusual surname.'

The woman looks up. 'Is it?'

Chloe can't help herself.

'Are you related to a Maureen and Patrick Kyle?'

The woman puts a bunch of bananas on the scales and looks up to the ceiling. 'Nope, no relation.'

'Oh, OK, I just thought . . .'

Chloe carries on packing her shopping in plastic orange bags.

She tries again: 'They had a daughter, Angela?'

The woman shakes her head.

Chloe pays and leaves, convincing herself that they must be related somehow. She asks herself again what might have happened if this were a detective show? She stops still on the pavement, even thinks of going back. Surely a detective wouldn't have let a lead like that go? If she'd been a relative, Chloe could have told her that she was revisiting the case for new clues; the woman might even have offered to help, perhaps given her an interview.

As she walks to the bus stop, she has a fantasy of her name appearing alongside a newspaper article. She goes over the headlines in her mind, before settling on a triumphant *Angela Kyle reunited with parents*. She's smiling as she gets on the bus. She arranges her shopping at her feet, and wonders whether the police interviews of the time extended to wider family and friends. Aren't most missing children taken by someone they know? She's sure she's heard that before. She takes out her notepad from her bag and makes a note to look up that statistic. She swaps her notepad and pen for a cutting from the Angie file. She opens it out on her lap.

WE'RE STILL WAITING FOR ANGIE

Below it two faces, weathered by a decade of grief, Patrick and Maureen sit holding a framed photograph of Angie between them.

TEN years after the disappearance of their four-year-old daughter from a city park, Patrick and Maureen Kyle have revealed they will never give up hope that she will be returned to them.

The devastated parents, of Chestnut Avenue, Dogsthorpe, told this newspaper they still believe Angela will be found.

'Although the case was closed many years ago, the police never found Angela's body,' Mr Kyle said. 'And without a body to bury there is every chance that Angela will walk back into our lives one day. As long as we live, we'll never stop hoping that will happen. We'll always be waiting for her.'

Chloe pulls the cutting up closer to her nose, searching the eyes of Maureen and Patrick – for what, she isn't sure. It's obvious from this photograph that time has taken its toll on the two of them. Patrick's once-black hair is now peppered with white around his ears; he's grown a beard too which is filled in with grey. Two deep frown lines now fill the space between Maureen's eyebrows, her hair not long and loose like it was when she was a young mother. It's now cut more practically, less carefree. It must have broken her heart to trim off the locks that Angie herself had once touched.

'Never trusted him,' a voice behind her says.

Chloe feels someone leaning over her left shoulder.

She turns around. A middle-aged woman leans back in her seat once again.

'How do you mean?' Chloe asks.

'Always thought he was hiding something.'

'Like what?' Chloe folds the cuttings, as if that small gesture will protect Maureen and Patrick's ears.

'Well, how many dads do you know who take their girls out to the park on the weekend?'

She sniffs, and Chloe thinks, though resists the urge to say, she doesn't know any dads.

'That was it, wasn't it?' the woman continues. 'He left her, didn't he? Well, I always thought he looked a bit shifty. Leaving a little girl in the park like that, even for a second, he deserved everything he got if you ask me.'

The woman pulls her handbag up under her large bosom. Sniffs again.

'Well,' Chloe starts, 'it was only for a second . . .'

She has no idea why she's defending Patrick. Perhaps after this time spent within the story, she feels some kind of loyalty to Maureen and Patrick, like they're friends. Yes, like she knows them. She sits up a bit taller then. After all, hadn't it only taken a second for Nan to go missing?

'Don't matter how long, you don't leave your kids,' the woman says. 'Not even for a moment. How she stuck with him all these years I don't know. If my husband had come home without any of ours, I'd have strung him up myself.'

Chloe turns back to the cutting and reopens it. She tries to see Patrick as this stranger does. But to her, Patrick looks shattered, the same as his wife beside him. Hadn't he also welcomed the police enquiry, even when they arrested him? A guilty man wouldn't do that. Her fingertips feel clammy where she's clutching the cutting. How could anyone think they got what they deserved?

No one deserves to lose a child. Especially not these two, not when they had clearly cherished her so much.

'That little girl was about the same age as my Jessica at the time,' the woman starts again, only this time Chloe doesn't turn around. 'We were all saying the same thing in the school playground: it had to be him involved, police just couldn't pin anything to him. And they do these appeals every year – what do they say?' She leans forward to read the headline, then mimics them, '"We're still waiting for Angie." Well, she ent coming home. She's gone, ent she? Gone the minute he took his eyes off her. Wouldn't be surprised if he didn't know where an' all, you mark my words.'

Chloe has heard enough. She pushes the cutting back into her bag and looks up for her stop. It's not the next one, but she decides to get off anyway. She gathers up her shopping, and as she does, two oranges roll out and down the central aisle of the bus. The woman tuts. Chloe feels the anger burning inside, her temples throbbing. How could someone say that about Maureen and Patrick? No two parents are more devoted than they are. If only she had been lucky enough to have been their daughter. Chloe would have killed for parents like that.

As the doors close she hears the woman say to the passenger sitting next to her, 'Well, I was only saying.'

ELEVEN

There's chaos in the newsroom when Chloe walks in on Monday morning. On days like these Chloe has learnt that it's best to shuffle straight towards the archive, losing herself among the filing cabinets until tempers calm.

'What's happened?' she whispers to Alec as they stand opposite each other in the archive, separated by metal, her filing B, him L.

'No front page this morning,' he says, slamming the L drawer shut. Chloe feels the reverberation of it inside the B drawer.

Nothing causes more panic here than a Monday morning without a splash. Malc is a micro manager, very often calling reporters into the office to brief them on stories himself. The one day of the week that he's forced to spend with his family is a constant source of anxiety to him. He must spend all Sunday hoping for a story to break, Chloe has often thought. Alec said he should have stayed as a news editor; some people just can't let go.

Malc's office door slams open and shut throughout the morning until almost midday when the paper finally goes to press. It's cost them money and he snaps at Sandra, his PA. She types faster outside his office. Alec and Chloe instinctively make their footsteps lighter inside the archive. But five minutes later, Sandra pops her head in among the piles of filing.

'Malc wants to see you in his office,' she says, and then, looking directly at Chloe, 'Both of you.'

Chloe and Alec glance at each other, then shuffle back to their desks to collect notepads and pens. Perhaps Malc has a special project he needs them to work on, a nostalgia spread of city photographs for the centrefold, that sort of thing.

Only when they step into his office, Sandra closes the door behind them. Chloe and Alec watch it shut, then turn to Malc. He's leaning back on his executive chair, feet up on the desk. Nobody speaks at first, until Alec coughs.

'You wanted to see us?'

'Yes,' he says. His voice has a hard edge. 'There's a file missing from the archive – Angela Kyle. I want to know where it is.'

Chloe swallows hard. Angela Kyle. She grips her notepad and waits for Alec to speak.

He taps his chin with his pen and mutters, 'Angela Kyle,' to the ceiling.

'You might have seen we were in dire straits this morning?' Malc says.

They both nod.

'Well, that's because our splash fell through. That was meant to be it, an update from the parents about this missing kid.' Chloe tightens her grip on her pen. 'But the Sunday reporter – he's new – he couldn't find the file in the archive and so he cancelled the bloody interview.'

Malc leans forward on the chair, resting his hands on the desk and lowering his voice. 'So I'd like to know where the fuck it is.'

He stares at them, and in the space it takes for his eyes

to flicker from Alec to Chloe, the heat burns inside her cheeks.

'Chloe?' Alec says. 'Didn't I see you scanning that file in on Friday?'

She pauses for a second, glancing between their faces, trying to weigh up the best way out of this. She's usually good at this, but the words she needs aren't coming today, instead – just like Nan's – they're stuck inside some road-block in her brain. She stumbles, not knowing what to say. And she knows what's coming, the panic, and then anything could happen. She wants to keep silent, but both men are looking at her.

'It's just the file . . . well, it broke, and I took it home to fix—'

But she doesn't make it to the end of her sentence. Malc stands up behind his desk, taking a deep breath in, and beside her she feels Alec shaking his head slowly.

'You,' Malc says, jabbing at the air between them, 'you're the reason I have some *shitty* story about council bins on my front page this morning.'

'I . . .'

'Weren't you just in here last week? Didn't I just give you a written warning, in fact?' He rustles through the paperwork on his desk, finally holding up a piece of paper. 'Yes, here it is. The ink isn't even dry and yet you're in here again.'

She nods, unsure if that's the best response.

'So no more warnings, that's it. Taking files off company property, that's an instantly sackable offence, isn't it, Alec?'

Alec suddenly looks startled. 'Well, I—'

'Alec, see her out of this building this second.' He pauses to jab the air towards her again. 'And make sure you get that file first.'

Malc steps out from behind his desk then, and Chloe jumps back as he storms out the office, the cool air he leaves behind him changing everything.

She and Alec stand there, side by side. It's a moment before he speaks.

'Chloe,' he says sadly, 'you know so much better than this.'

Alec had been kinder than she'd imagined, promising her he'd speak to Malc again and make an appeal on her behalf. But the word 'sacked' is zigzagging around inside her head as she pushes out of the glass doors of the building. She stands on the pavement alone now, watching traffic rush past, people filled with purpose, a box in her arms, a hard lump inside her throat.

She looks up at the third floor of the building, barely able to take in what has just happened. Was she really up there just a few moments ago? And ten minutes before that, wasn't she in her beloved archive, filing away envelopes like she's done every day since she left school? She stands for longer, the white noise of the traffic rushing by hardly registering. It's only the feel of her phone vibrating from inside the box, inside her handbag, that snaps her back into full consciousness. Could it be Alec? Has Malc admitted he acted too hastily?

She answers it quickly. 'Hello?'

'Chloe, hi, Claire Sanders here. How are you? It's not a bad time, is it?'

She glances inside the box. She'd told Alec there was nothing she needed. But by the time he'd found a box, emptied it, tested its endurance, she felt she needed to find things to put in it. She looks down at the pathetic contents that sum up thirteen years at the newspaper: a few pens, an old diary she hadn't even filled in, a calendar from two years ago, small change she'd found in her drawer and a tampon. As she gathered up her things she was already calculating how long she could afford to live without a job. With no social life, she'd accumulated decent savings, and at least she had a roof over her head.

'I'm fine. No, not a bad time at all.' Chloe tries to keep the emotion from her voice.

She balances the phone and the box as she listens, the phone slipping from under her ear every now and then, the traffic whizzing past, but she picks up the gist of the conversation.

'. . . so to fund your grandmother's care, we're going to have to sell the house . . . Chloe? Chloe, are you still there?'

TWELVE

Chloe doesn't go back to Park House the next day. Or the next. Instead she phones them to see how Nan is and a cheery nurse tells her she'd enjoyed bingo that morning. Nan hates bingo, not that she tells him that. In Park House Nan is different; she's reinvented into someone who wears coral lipstick and dabs at her bingo card.

'Would you like us to see if she's around to speak to you?' the nurse, Sam, asks.

Chloe is aware of the pause that stretches between them down the phone line. Is there any point? Will Nan even know who she is today?

'No, it's OK, just let her know I called.'

'Of course.'

She thanks him, trying to imitate his cheeriness as she hangs up, then returns to the quiet of her empty bedroom.

She checks the time; she's arranged to meet Hollie this afternoon. But she has time to drop in on one other person before she's due to meet Hollie.

There are a few people in the cemetery when she arrives, mostly those kitted out with gardening gloves and secateurs – a routine to fill the empty days retirement leaves.

She enters via the gate on the far side today and walks beside a freshly dug grave, earth churned up, waiting patiently for a new guest to lie in its soil bed. From this entrance she turns right towards Stella's grave and from the path she can just make out her headstone and the daffodils she'd left here two weeks ago, their dull heads bent solemnly now. She walks over and crouches down towards Stella, feeling the coolness of the earth rush to greet her.

'Hello, Mum,' she says to the air, and then looks around, but of course there's no one there to hear. This isn't a TV drama, she reminds herself, no one is watching.

She touches the stone and feels its cold penetrate her palm, then she leans back into the ground and reads the headstones either side of Stella's: son, father, brother, sister, mother, daughter. Labels. Who really are we if we don't belong to someone else? She feels guilty then. She puts it down to the daffodils, their browning petals making this grave feel unloved, enough space made for guilt to slip in. She pulls them from the short vase and hears her knee crack as she gets up off the grass. She regrets now not bringing more flowers to replace these.

She takes the path down towards the watering shed and inside dumps the daffodils in the compost bin. But as she turns to leave, she sees it, the same black granite stone she'd come across the other day, and the same matching single daffodil standing up in the vase. That one needs replacing too. Only as she goes to take it, she has a closer look at the stone, and this time she notices the name – it can't be. She blinks, making sure her eyes aren't playing tricks on her. But it's there, for all to see: Angela Kyle. She can barely believe it.

Slowly, she crouches down, removing the old daffodil and laying it down on the gravel path beside her. She takes her thumb and rubs it across every bronzed letter scored into the stone, still incredulous at her discovery.

Angela Rose Kyle, aged four,
taken from us 27 October 1979.

Always loved, never forgotten.

We pray for the day when we will meet again.
Mummy and Daddy

She pulls her hand away from the stone and examines it, as if somehow it had provided a direct link between her and the Kyles. As if somehow this shared touch was all the confirmation she needed that fate was at that moment encouraging them towards one another. And somewhere deep inside, the emptiness she had been feeling since she had packed that pathetic box in her office lifts ever so slightly.

She steps back from the stone and checks her watch. She'd better leave now otherwise she will be late for Hollie. But as she walks further away, she is aware that she's actually nudging closer – although to what, she doesn't know.

'So you just stumbled across the grave?' Hollie says, stirring her coffee and frowning into her cup. 'Just like that?'

'Well, it is a cemetery, Hollie. I just feel so sorry for the parents.'

Hollie nods, but Chloe knows this look. She'd expected it. Chloe doesn't understand why Hollie doesn't feel more sorry for them. She had hoped she might ask more questions. But she can tell she doesn't want to talk about it, and now inside Chloe feels that familiar sting of shame for even mentioning it.

'And that's all you've been up to?' Hollie says.

Chloe tries not to sound too disappointed at the change of subject. 'Oh . . . well, this and that.'

'Like?'

'Well, like I said . . .'

Hollie nods and puts down her teaspoon. Chloe hopes she'll ask her more about them now.

'Isn't there something you can do? Appeal or something? Have you contacted HR? I mean, they can't just fire you.'

'I know, but it's different – on a newspaper, I mean. Different rules apply; it's like kitchens.'

'What about kitchens?'

'Well, chefs and stuff, nothing's done by the book. You do something wrong once and you're out. It's the same in newsrooms.'

'But there are procedures, Chloe, you need to speak to HR. You can't just get sacked for taking time off, you're meant to get warnings. And Nan was missing, for God's sake, the police were involved, and it's not like you didn't let them know. How can they be so uncaring?'

'I know but—'

'It's against the law. Do you want me to have a word?'

'No.' Her eyes quickly meet Hollie's.

Her friend looks affronted.

'I mean, no, no thanks,' Chloe adds.

There's a pot of brown sugar on the table between them, a silver spoon sticking out of it. On the end of the handle is a picture of a yellow beach and blue sea, *Jersey* written underneath. Chloe picks up the sugar on the spoon, letting the granules drop back into the pot, grains of sweet sand. She's back on a Cornish beach, conjuring up a memory of sand pouring through her tiny fingers, building sandcastles with Granddad, Nan and Stella, just like in that photograph, shoulders turning pink in the sun, knees in warm sand, donkeys walking up and down the beach beside them. Is it any wonder people want to escape their lives every summer? Pretend to be someone else, if only for two weeks?

She looks up at Hollie. 'Can we talk about something else?' Chloe says. She wonders whether Maureen and Patrick ever took a holiday with Angie. She can't remember reading anything in the cuttings. If Hollie wasn't sitting here, she would take out her notepad and pen and write down a reminder to have a look.

'Of course, but I hope you've signed up with some job agencies. Even if you just got some temp work while they sort all this out, it'd be better than hanging around in ceme—'

'Can you imagine it, though? Losing a child?' Chloe interrupts.

'Sorry?'

'I mean, just never knowing what had happened to her. It was OK for me, in a way, because even though Nan didn't come home, I know where she is, I know she's safe, that she's alive, but the Kyles . . . they just have to live in this limbo, this not knowing.'

Chloe picks more sugar up with the spoon, watching the granules fall slowly off the edge.

Hollie dips her hazel eyes into Chloe's eyeline and reaches for her hand. She lowers her voice when she speaks.

'It's awful, Chloe, it really is, but don't go taking on

the worries of the world right now, you've got other things to think about. Seriously. Like getting a new job.'

Chloe nods in a way she hopes will reassure her friend. 'I guess.'

'So you'll sign up with some job agencies? Today?'

She nods again. Hollie starts putting on her coat and scarf.

'Listen, I'm sorry I haven't got more time, but Phil's taking me out tonight. It's the anniversary of our first kiss.'

'Do people celebrate that?'

Hollie shrugs. 'We do.'

'I just can't help thinking how empty their lives must have been all these years. I mean, imagine—'

Chloe looks up towards her friend, but Hollie's picking the skin around her thumb. When she looks up again, it's like she never even heard Chloe.

'Did I tell you we're going to Lanzarote by the way?'

Chloe looks up. 'Wasn't it Fuerteventura?'

'Oh yes, it was, but you get more for your money in Lanzarote. We're staying in a five-star *spa* hotel.'

'Oh,' Chloe says. But she's looking at the teaspoon. She has never been to a spa hotel, and she would bet the Kyles haven't either – it's not really their style.

'Chloe,' Hollie says, putting her hand on her friend's arm.

She looks up.

'Give up this silly fantasy. Please. Find yourself a job, that's what you need right now, a healthy distraction.'

Chloe puts the spoon down and starts pulling her coat on. She loves Hollie but sometimes she wishes she would mind her own business because all it does when she doesn't is stir up all those old feelings.

'Do you want a lift? I'm only parked down the road,' Hollie asks.

'It's OK, I'll walk. It's not like I'm in a hurry anywhere.'

'OK, good idea, you'll pass a couple of recruitment agencies on the way home. Pop in.' She checks her watch. 'It's not even five yet.' She rolls her coat sleeve back down, then leaves a kiss on the top of Chloe's head. 'Call me soon, yeah? And promise me you'll speak to HR.'

After she closes the door behind her, the waitress carries over a tray rattling with empty cups and takes theirs from the table.

'Can I get another one of these?' Chloe asks, pointing at her empty cup and beginning to remove her coat. She picks up the spoon again, studying the little beach on the end of it. She wonders if Maureen and Patrick ever took Angie to Jersey.

THIRTEEN

Everyone at Park House has lost something. For some it's an item of jewellery. One lady, three doors down from Nan, has been searching for months for a pearl necklace she last wore in 1947. Chloe watches her sometimes, rifling through magazines, boxes of backgammon with torn corners, or down the backs of sofas, gathering nothing but crumbs under her fingernails. The other residents are used to her; they sweep their feet out of the way, or pick up their cups of tea and knitting without even breaking conversation. She mutters to herself while she's searching, telling tales of the times she wore it to no one in particular, taking herself all the way back to pre-war dance halls and their parquet floors, and never catching sight of the beads. It's an unwritten rule in the care home that everyone exists in their own time frame. Some residents sit alongside each other separated by decades, each as real to them as the year their neighbour finds themselves occupying in the seat next door.

Another thing people lose is time – that's very common. Yesterday, Chloe was making a cup of tea for Nan when a man started talking about politics; he was furious about something, gesticulating wildly, so much so that one of the nurses asked him to keep his voice down.

'Well, of course it's all the Prime Minister's fault, it's all down to Edward Heath,' he protested, in case he could persuade the nurse that the ex-PM himself was the reason residents were struggling to hear *Countdown*.

Nobody corrected him.

Time is mostly misplaced, which often makes the communal area one big waiting room: for news; for a visit; for a loved one to return from a war that ended more than half a century ago. And that is the most painful thing that people lose – family. This morning Chloe heard one lady ask at least a dozen times where her husband was, the nursing staff gently reminding her he had died five months before. Every explanation wet her cheeks with fresh tears.

'Terrible for these old folk,' Nan says suddenly, looking round from their game of rummy. She leans in closer. 'Some of them are a bit . . .' Her finger draws circles at the side of her ear until she's sure Chloe understands.

Chloe nods – she is the cleaner today.

'It's marvellous they let you have a little break now and then,' Nan smiles. She's wearing a cerise pink blouse that Chloe doesn't recognize.

'That's a nice colour on you,' Chloe tells her.

'It's not mine, it's Edna's. She lent it to me because I haven't got any of my own clothes here. I must have left them in my old house.'

This happened the other day, when Nan couldn't see the fitted cupboard doors in her room. She'd been wearing the same clothes for three days before anyone thought to show her the clothes hanging neatly inside her wardrobe. In the end one of the care assistants took a photograph of them and stuck it on the outside.

'Do you not have a photo stuck on your wardrobe door anymore, Nan?'

'Hmm?'

'Do you—' she sighs. 'Nothing.'

Chloe also knows that we all have reasons for ignoring the truth sometimes, when a story we tell ourselves or others sounds better. The Kyles must have done it over the years, told themselves a story to make the truth more palatable. She wonders where they might have started.

Chloe hasn't been back to the cemetery for four days. She's done what Hollie said. But she hasn't been to the recruitment agencies either. Instead, she's been here, hiding in this timeless no-man's land.

'It's your move, dear,' Nan says. 'Dear?'

'Oh, sorry,' Chloe says.

Nan doesn't look up from her cards. She has a look of concentration on her face, the same, Chloe decides, as she had when she studied her word-search book while Chloe sat cross-legged at her feet as a child, gazing up at her cartoons until her neck ached and she switched to lying on her front. Stella must have been out working then; she had a job in a local pub so Chloe stayed with Nan and Granddad on those nights. She'd sometimes hear her come in late at night, whispers from the hall floating up the stairs. 'Has she been OK?' she'd ask, and then, 'I don't know what I'd do without you, Mum.' Then a few moments later, a perfumed kiss in the dark.

Or that's how Chloe likes to remember it.

She puts down a card and looks up at Nan again.

'I've been working on a story at the office recently,' she says, forgetting for a second she's meant to be the cleaner.

'Remind me, what is it you do, Chloe, dear?'

Chloe is relieved to realize Nan has forgotten too.

'The newspaper,' she says.

'Oh yes, a reporter.'

'Yes, and I . . . I've been working on a new story.'

'What's that about then, dear?'

'It's quite sad really, a little girl who went missing.'

'Oh, how dreadful.'

'Yes, she was only four.'

'Where did they lose her?'

'At a park. Not far from here actually.'

She looks up. 'London?'

'No, Nan, we're in Peterborough.'

'Yes, that's it. Are you going to help them find her?'

Nan looks up from her hand of cards and Chloe feels that seed of an idea that she's been tending unfurl a little further. Nan's blue eyes are bright. She thinks of Maureen and Patrick Kyle, and wonders whether a disease like dementia would grant them the gift of living in a world where Angie is still alive.

'Do you think I should?' Chloe asks.

Nan breaks into a great big smile. 'Oh yes,' she says, reaching out and taking her hand in hers, cards fluttering down to the floor. 'Those poor parents.'

'OK then,' she says, 'I'll find her.'

Nan smiles.

'It'll mean I'll be busy at the office, I won't be able to visit so often.'

Nan looks up. 'What could be more important than finding a lost child?' she says.

Nan studies her then, for that second longer until

Chloe looks away. Then, suddenly Nan looks down at the floor.

'Oh, I've dropped all my cards,' she says, rolling her eyes. 'How are we going to finish our game now?'

'It's OK, Nan,' she says, 'you'd won already.'

Her cheeks pinken, complementing her blouse.

'Had I?' she says, clasping her hands together. 'How wonderful.'

Chloe puts the cards away in the packet as Nan chats to one of her new friends. She walks across the room to place them back in a drawer when the view from the window catches her eye. She wanders over and stands in front of the huge window; another resident is sitting in a recliner beside it, her wrinkly hands on the lace doilies that cover the arms of the chair.

'I took my Sarah there the other day,' the old woman says, seemingly to the glass.

'Sorry?' Chloe says.

'Ferry Meadows,' she says. 'My little girl. She did have a lovely time on the swings.'

Chloe smiles at her. Someone else trapped inside a memory.

'Oh, right, lovely.' She starts towards Nan but then she has an idea. She glances back out the window; it's a nice day, the sun dipping in and out of the clouds, casting shadows across the lake. It's windy, crisp, spring starting its annual and inevitable tussle with winter.

When she reaches Nan she puts a hand on her shoulder. 'I tell you what, Nan, I'm just going for a quick walk. I'll leave you with your friend and see you back here in half an hour.'

'OK, dear,' she replies.

As Chloe walks away, she hears Nan say to her new friend, 'What a nice young lady.'

A short path leads from the back of the care home directly into the park itself. There's a quiet bit of road to cross where drivers are warned with a bright triangular sign of elderly people crossing, but there's no traffic today and so within a few minutes Chloe is standing in front of the lake she could see from the window of the recreational room. It's a park she's been to many times before, and in that instant a thousand sunny days come back to her: picnics with egg and salad cream sandwiches; school trips canoeing on the lake; a spring walk searching for ducklings. Always making a special guest appearance in other people's families. But never during any of those times had she known what else this place represented. On cue, as if she were part of a film set, a gust of wind picks up, and there's a sudden chill sent across the air. It feels wrong now, she thinks, that life went on for everyone else, while they swam and sunbathed and tore up bread for ducks, and yet in this very same place it stopped still for the Kyles.

She walks slowly around the lake, slowing her footsteps to a more respectful pace. On a small island in the middle of the water, Canada Geese collect lichen and moss to line the nests they're building ready for spring. She comes to a little wooden bridge that leads to the back of the park; in the summer, white plumes from steam engines form clouds that sit above the treetops here. She follows the path to the left, out towards a place she knows she'll recognize from pictures. Here the grasses grow tall, the terrain is wilder, the flat landscape somehow more rugged, surrounded by tall trees that sway more savagely than they do around the lake. It's more remote here, cut off from the joggers and their puff-panting, and even the dog walkers weaving this way and that with their extendable leads.

Chloe spins around on the spot, scanning the tops of the trees for where she came from and just making out the apex of the roof of Park House in the distance and the scaffolding that towers over it for the new extension. She thinks then of what that matron had said on their first visit and realizes that Park House wouldn't have been part of the landscape back then, it wouldn't even have been built; perhaps it was still foundations and rubble, yet to be hauled up from the ground. But who could have guessed it was just a stone's throw away from where Angie disappeared.

She carries on walking until she spots it: an area where woodchip covers the ground. She recognizes it by the car park it backs on to – the play park where Angie disappeared.

The playground is still, the swings hang limply on their chains. The newly installed slides here didn't know this place in 1979; they weren't witness to what occurred here that day twenty-five years before. Chloe opens the short yellow gate; she goes inside, feeling the woodchip beneath her leather soles, the soft shutting of the gate behind her, the creak of its hinges. She sits down on a swing and pushes at the ground with her feet. After a few pushes, she takes to the air, her figure cutting through the quiet eeriness of the day. She closes her eyes, envying

Nan's ability to time travel. She thinks of her playing backgammon with her new friends, enjoying a conversation that can run on loop unhindered.

And then it happens again, a flash of something, like the wrong photo slide loaded into a projector. A split-second memory of this same place, but not now – then. Chloe opens her eyes quickly, her feet skidding abruptly on the ground, woodchip scuffing at her soles. The swing comes to a wobbly halt. She looks around. At once everything is the same again. She blinks, but it's gone, like the echo left over from a dream. The car park is empty, but she knows another car once filled a place in there – Patrick's blue Ford Escort. She pictures him, popping back to lock it while Angie played on swings like these. Just like when she lost Nan, he had turned his back for a split second. And then what? Maureen was right, how can a child just disappear? What exactly had happened to Angela Kyle?

FOURTEEN

It's almost midnight when Chloe arrives at the office. As she approaches the glass doors in the darkness, a sudden thought hits her – what if they've changed the keycode since she left? She lingers outside a moment, biting her nails, trying to avoid an obvious search for the CCTV cameras, instead turning her head and momentarily allowing her eyes to flicker up to check the angle of them. Behind her, the odd car drives by on the black road. One slows and she quickly turns her face back to the door, keeping it down to avoid recognition. Her fingers hover on top of the keypad as if, for a second, unsure whether to go through with this plan. But there's no going back now. She punches in the code, wincing as each number she presses sounds its own tune, and then she hits the lit key symbol. A second later and she is inside.

She takes the stairs two at time, keeping her head down to avoid the security cameras nestled in the top corners of each floor.

On the third floor, at the double doors to the newsroom, she takes her keycard out of her coat pocket. She stares at it in her hand. Slowly, she draws it up to the sensor. She's amazed to see the light turn green. There's a beep and the door handle releases into her hand. She crosses the threshold.

The newsroom is in darkness except for the odd desk

lamp left on, a tiny flash here and there from a sleeping printer.

She walks down the blue carpet path, forgetting as she does that each light disguised in the suspended ceiling above her will blink into life, lighting her way. Either side of her, the windows instantly turn to mirrors. She watches herself in them as she walks – an intruder. She looks away and moves quickly, purposefully. She doesn't intend to stay long.

Her melamine desk has now become a dumping ground for boxes; even her swivel chair has three lever-arch files stacked on it. She stands, paying a moment's respect to the graveyard of her working life. Suddenly, from the other end of the room, she hears a click, a rumble. She jumps, ducking down before realising it's the coffee machine. But it reminds her, she needs to work quickly.

Chloe heads into the archive, quickly finding the drawer marked KR–LA. She pulls it open, the scratch of metal tearing through the silence. She finds the Kyles.

Kyle; Amanda
Kyle; Norman
Kyle; Sharon
Kyle; Patricia
Kyle; Angela.

Bingo. She pulls it out, it's more creased than she remembered, but when she peers in, she can see all the cuttings are there, packed away in a tight weave.

The nearest photocopier is outside the editor's office. She presses the standby button and wills the machine to life. It clunks and clicks, waking dozy from slumber.

'Come on,' she whispers to herself as she taps the top of the machine. 'Come on.'

She counts the seconds until the green light on the 'ready' button flashes and when it does, Chloe empties the cuttings onto Sandra's in-tray. Then she starts unfolding them one by one, smoothing out the creases, putting one under the scanner at a time, watching, satisfied, as copy after copy appears in the tray beneath.

'Come on,' she says again to no one but herself.

She curses when she has to pause to refill the A4 paper tray.

She goes on and on like this, the pile in the tray getting thicker, stopping only to feed the machine more paper. One eye on the door at the top of the office which is once again plunged into darkness.

As the pile grows so does her excitement. She takes one copy from the stack at random; the photographs aren't perfect, some emotion in the faces of Maureen and Patrick has been replaced with inkjet splodges, but the rest is there: the words, the detail. That's exactly what she needs.

In the silence of the office, the machine spits out copies into the tray, a rhythmic mechanical beat.

And then something else. A bleep at the other end of the office. The release of the door. A cough. The click as half a dozen ceiling lights flicker on above the reporters' desks. Chloe ducks behind a tall spider plant perched on Sandra's desk and watches as a late-shift reporter heads towards her desk. Chloe freezes. Wincing now at the copier, glancing between the machine and the file. She has just a few cuttings left. She makes a quick calculation.

Could she manage without them? No, she needs every cutting, every detail. Any missing part of this jigsaw might be the most vital.

Chloe sticks her head out from behind the plant. The reporter is typing away at her computer, oblivious to her hiding outside the editor's office. The light above Chloe has gone off now, but she knows the second she moves it will flicker back into life, alerting the reporter. And then what? Could she be arrested? Charged with breaking and entering? Is it even stealing if she's only copying?

A huge wad of cuttings waits in the copier tray, at least half a packet of A4. She pictures someone finding them in the morning. Surely that would pose more questions? No, she's not leaving without them, or the rest of them. She has to finish.

She takes a deep breath, though her heart is pounding. She steps out from behind the plant with the last few cuttings in her hand, willing a pretence of confidence into her stature. She doesn't look back towards the reporter's desk, not at first. She just carries on, telling herself she's working overtime, making it look like that too. She even dares to hum a little to make it feel more realistic – if only to convince herself.

Finally, it's done, the machine spits out the last sheet of A4 and Chloe scoops them up quickly, pushing them into her handbag. She winces at the creases that appear in the paper – it's hard to erase that archivist in her – but she has to hurry.

She returns the file to the archive, takes one last look at her old desk, and then, with as much confidence as she can muster, walks down the long carpet of the office. Her hand grips the strap of her bag on her shoulder; underneath it, she feels her heart is hammering inside. As she gets closer she sees the reporter is wearing earphones as she types. Perhaps she'll even be able to slip right by? She's level with the newsdesk now; just a few more feet to go until she reaches the doors. She looks straight ahead, fixes her eye on her target.

But then:

'Hey.' She hears a call. She ignores it, increases her pace a little. Then again: 'Hey.'

Chloe freezes, her elbow pressing her bag tight under her arm.

She turns in time to see the reporter removing the earphones from her head. She's a young girl, the one who arrived to replace the guy who left, whatever his name was. She's got short blonde hair and the smell of cigarettes and a cheap burger sits in the air between them.

'Bloody council meetings,' the reporter says, coughing. 'Why is it they always leave the one thing that you're there to report on until the end?'

Chloe isn't sure if this is a question she's meant to answer. She shrugs. She looks at the door. She wants to go.

The reporter looks her up and down. 'You're working late,' she says.

Again, Chloe isn't sure whether this is a question. But at least this reporter still thinks she works here.

'Yeah, we're preparing for the new electronic filing system so . . .' Chloe tilts her head towards the archive and shrugs and the reporter turns back to her computer screen. She knows other people don't find the archive as fascinating as she does. She feels a sadness then in her chest. Chloe starts to walk away. Just two more feet and she's out the door.

'Wait,' the reporter says.

Chloe freezes again. The reporter gets up from her desk and walks over. Chloe is sure she catches her glance at her bag.

'You don't have any change, do you?' the reporter asks.

'Sorry?'

'I could kill for a coffee, but I've only got notes.'

'Oh . . . oh yeah, sure.'

She quickly – too quickly? – takes her bag from her shoulder, conscious not to open it in front of the reporter. She goes over to the picture desk to fish out her purse. The reporter looks pleased when she hands her a shiny one-pound coin.

'Oh, thanks so much, I owe you one. I'll give you it back tomorr—'

'Forget it,' Chloe says quickly. The last thing she needs is this reporter asking for her at the archive. 'Honestly, don't even think of paying me back.'

'OK, I'll buy you a drink next time there's a leaving do. In fact, isn't Sam on Subs off this week?'

Chloe shuffles her weight between her feet. 'I . . . er . . . I don't—'

'Yeh, drinks at the Tut, I think. I'll buy you a drink, I couldn't get through tonight without caffeine.'

Chloe pauses for a moment, long after the reporter has returned to her computer. No one in the office has ever offered to buy her a drink at a leaving do. No one has even asked her if she's going to one. She looks at this girl with her bright pink nails and her black leather handbag, a celebrity magazine peering from the top of it. Might they have become friends if she hadn't been fired? She'd never had a friend at work.

The reporter has turned back to her screen.

'See you tomorrow then,' the reporter calls without turning round.

Chloe hauls her bag back onto her shoulder, the weight of it replacing a sudden emptiness. She heads towards the door, the brightness of the hallway beyond like a beacon to safety. She's out the doors, down the stairs, out into the street.

It's only then that she allows her breath to return to normal.

She's done it. She's got the file.

Her hands are still shaking when she gets back to Nan's house. She rummages through Nan's bureau for some Blu-Tack then runs upstairs to her room. She shakes the photocopies onto her bed, and they land on the eider-down with a satisfying thud. Then she gets to work.

She starts by removing a couple of pictures from the wall, then the pins that had held them there. They leave faint smoky outlines of themselves, but she'll soon cover them. She flicks through for the earliest cutting from the pile, dragging a stool from Nan's dressing table so she can reach up to the top left-hand corner of the room. She works from left to right, up and down on the chair until her thighs burn, but she won't stop. She tacks each copy up with four tiny bits of pale-blue putty, and once she's done the top two rows it's easier, faster, not having to mount the stool. She works without stopping, a need to see what she's had in her mind all day.

An hour and a half later she stands back and there it is, the whole story of the Kyles covering three walls of her bedroom – just a few leftover cuttings creep around the next corner. It irritates her that they don't all fit, but she would never have left them. No, here she has everything.

She shrugs her shoulders a few times, massages the knots that have appeared in them. She's tired and it's nearly 3 a.m. She gets into bed, lying on her right side, an arm stretched under her pillow, so she can study this new newsprint wallpaper. She squints ever so slightly and the words blur to grey and, just for a second, it's as if the photographs of Maureen and Patrick have been chosen from her own family album. Just like that, she has her very own archive. And under its gaze, she sleeps.

FIFTEEN

The phone ringing on the floor by her bed wakes her up. Chloe answers it still half asleep.

'Oh, sorry, I didn't wake you, did I?' Hollie says.

'It's OK,' Chloe answers with a yawn. She rubs her eyes and watches the room come into focus. She smiles to herself. Hollie is chatting away on the other end of the line, but Chloe lies back on her pillow, satisfied with the wallpaper that greets her. Now she wakes and sleeps inside the story of the Kyles.

'So, how come you're so tired? . . . Chloe?'

'Oh, I . . . Sorry, I was miles away. I had a late night.'

'Oh?' Hollie says. 'Doing what? Did you go out?'

Chloe glances about the room guiltily.

'Reading?' she says, wishing she hadn't made it sound like a question.

'Oh, I love getting lost in a good book like that. Phil bought me a new one the other day. Now, what's it called . . . ?'

Chloe's eyes wander back to the wall. Her gaze honing in on one cutting. She reads the headline from her own pillow:

Did police waste time to find Angie?

She feels proud of herself, and, if truth be told, she would like to tell Hollie. But she knows too well what she would say. The same as she always does.

'. . . so I was just ringing to say that I've got you an interview.'

'What?' Chloe sits up in her bed.

'Yes, at Phil's firm. I was telling him what had happened and apparently his place are looking for an admin assistant at the moment. It's just filing and stuff . . . well, I don't mean *just filing*. But you know what I'm saying, it would be perfect for you.'

Chloe thinks of the envelopes in the archive and everything and everyone they contain. That isn't *just* filing. And this, a job, this isn't what she has planned. Her hand already feels clammy round the phone.

'Filing what?' Chloe asks. Not that she cares.

'I don't know, insurance records, what does it matter?'

It matters, Chloe thinks.

'Anyway, give Phil a buzz, he's waiting for you to call. I think he said they could see you Friday. I'm so excited for you. Imagine, Phil could be your boss.'

Chloe winces inside as Hollie does a little excited squeal. She hangs up, promising Hollie she'll call Phil. She turns back to the cuttings. No, starting a new job is not how she has pictured this playing out.

She throws the phone to the floor and instantly forgets the call. She leans back on her pillow and admires the Kyles, trying to decide how she will spend the day, which part of their story she will study, because she's already got a new job now, or at least a project.

She pushes back her duvet, and pads across the room. She stands in front of one long wall covered in cuttings and closes her eyes. She sticks out her finger, swirls it in the air and dots it down at random. It lands on a story about police dogs searching Ferry Meadows. She's already been there. She closes her eyes and tries again. This time it lands on the story about the school children celebrating Angie's life.

That is how Chloe will start.

She arrives at the school just after 2.30 p.m.

'Sorry, I'm late,' she says to the receptionist. 'I have a meeting with the deputy head at two thirty?'

'Not to worry, her previous meeting has overrun anyway.'

'That's OK then,' Chloe says.

The receptionist asks her to take a seat. She removes her coat and folds it over on her lap. Then crosses her legs, and refolds her coat. She hasn't been inside a school since she attended one herself. She feels conscious of her own skin on her bones. She tries to distract herself by looking at the children's artwork. On the walls are giant red letters, each spelling out one of the school values. Chloe reads them: *Empathy, Respect, Courage, Honesty*. Her eyes flicker across that last one.

Beside the words are photographs of children in their uniforms. The little girls in the pictures wear blue gingham dresses – a summer uniform Angie never got to wear. Then, along the way, tucked away slightly, not far from the receptionist's office, is another photograph. Chloe's breath catches inside her throat. She stands up and steps a foot closer. It's the same school portrait of Angie that was printed in almost all of the newspapers, and underneath, in copperplate handwriting, no name, just four simple words: *Always in our hearts*.

She knew she had been right to come here.

An office door opens and a woman says her name as she walks towards her with a hand outstretched.

'Naomi Taylor, deputy head, so sorry to have kept you waiting.'

'Oh, that's OK,' Chloe says, tearing her eyes away from the photograph. 'I was late myself.'

The woman wears dangly earrings and for some reason, Chloe flicks her own hair away from her shoulders.

'Anyway, let's get on with the tour,' she says, handing Chloe a school brochure. 'How old did you say your little one is?'

'Er, four,' Chloe replies quickly.

'Right, and remind me, do you have a boy or a—'

'Girl,' Chloe answers.

'OK, so as she would be entering reception, shall we start there?'

Miss Taylor walks slowly, lingering on schoolwork on the walls, talking Chloe through the history of the school and setting out its values. Chloe longs to run her hands along the walls as they walk. She imagines Angie doing the same. If these walls could talk, she thinks. Then supposes they wouldn't be able to give up any clues. Miss Taylor pauses outside a classroom.

'After you . . .' Miss Taylor says, opening the classroom door.

The room is filled with noise where at least thirty children are scattered among tables and chairs, with a few lying on the carpet on their bellies, reading books, their legs bent and crossed in the air above them.

'Looks like we've turned up at golden time,' the

deputy says, introducing Chloe to Mrs Bryant, the teacher, and her assistant. Miss Taylor talks Chloe through things like 'Key Stage One' and other terms she's unfamiliar with. She makes an effort to nod and appear interested, all the time her eyes roaming the room, taking in everything from the tiny chairs to the whiteboard. Although surely it would have been a blackboard in Angela's day? It was when she was at school.

'And has this always been the reception classroom?' Chloe asks.

'Yes, ever since the school opened in 1974,' she replies.

Chloe nods and looks around. In the corner there is an old white butler sink that has clearly never been replaced. There's a little plastic footstool in front of it, and Chloe pictures Angie climbing up onto something similar to wash her hands back when she was here. There's a doorway on the other side of the room through which sunshine spills light across the floor. She pictures Maureen and Patrick standing there each afternoon to collect their daughter, the sun dipping in the sky, an amber glow warming the tops of their heads as they waited. She smiles as she imagines Angie looking up at them from the carpet with their halos of afternoon sunshine – these two perfect parents. But then she corrects herself: no, no, it would have only been Maureen, Patrick would have been at work. Strangely, she can't remember seeing anything about what he did in the cuttings. She makes a mental note to check. Chloe wants to imprint everything about this room in her mind, right down to the poster paint smell. It all builds up a picture. A picture that she has stepped into, that she is now a part of, and that surely brings her closer to the Kyles?

'Shall we continue?' Miss Taylor says, guiding her elbow.

Although Chloe has already seen everything she needs.

That night, back in her bedroom at Nan's house, she writes down what she can remember about the school in her little notebook. On her phone there is a message from Hollie: Phil said he didn't hear from you today. Make sure you call him. Xx

She taps out a message saying she had come down with a migraine. It is true at least that she goes to bed early. Then she deletes the message.

In bed, she lies underneath her duvet, wrapped up in the story of the Kyles, and when she sleeps she'll dream of turning their heartbreak to hope.

The church is empty and Chloe stands in the middle aisle, looking up at the huge vaulted ceiling and the dark beams that criss-cross overhead. She pictures Angie as a baby in her parents' arms. Is this what she might have seen?

Chloe felt sure that the priest who was mentioned in the cuttings, Father Martin Cunningham, might have something to add to her investigation. Only when she'd arrived, the noticeboard read that the priest's name was Father Matthew Purcell. And inside the church, as she scanned the lists of priests' names scored in gold on the ornate board on the wall, it turned out Father Purcell had only been at St Gregory's for the last two years. She could see from a photo of him that he was young – a child himself when Angie had disappeared. There was no point in interviewing him.

Still, she walks through the church, her hand trailing on the backs of empty pews. She lights a candle for Angie and drops a pound coin into the tin. It rattles inside as it lands, breaking the silence. Chloe stares at the flame, knowing Maureen and Patrick well enough to understand how much this small gesture would please them.

It has definitely been easier to throw herself into this task since she photocopied the file. She's waited, the last couple of days, for her phone to ring, for Alec to demand her security pass back. She has been terrified that she was spotted on CCTV, or that the reporter has been down to the archive to give her back her money. But as the days have gone by, she's started to relax inside her own skin again. She even had a dream two nights ago that she solved the crime and brought Angie home and was given back her job at the paper as a reward. She'd not only solved the mystery but saved the archive, and the Kyles, how they had loved her for it.

She sinks down on a pew, picturing for a second a packed church, Maureen and Patrick doing the same, elbow to elbow with friends and neighbours. Then she sighs. It always comes back to Maureen and Patrick, every lead, every hunch, every new clue she finds among the photocopies tacked to her bedroom wall. She knows the real answers to what happened to Angie must lie with the Kyles. But how can she possibly get to speak to them?

She's never completely trusted silence, but here in this church, she feels peaceful – she feels heard. There's an effigy of Mary at the altar. Chloe walks towards it, she reaches out to touch the cool marble smoothness of it. Mary stares back at her, as if she knows, as if she sympathizes with the enormous task Chloe has in front of her. Are these the same eyes that Maureen and Patrick had stared into when they prayed for their daughter's safe return? If only she knew. If only Chloe could have been the reporter who sat down and interviewed them. And that's when it happens, a split-second moment that feels something close to divine intervention. Of course she needs to speak to the Kyles – there really is no other way. And it wouldn't be *such* a stretch of the truth to interview them for their annual colour piece. But it would be a way into their house, a way to eke out the details detectives couldn't, to discover the evidence others had missed. And by the time anyone realizes Chloe wasn't strictly who she said she was, then Angie would be back and no one would mind. In fact, Chloe would be a heroine. Her dream of saving the archive would come true. She looks up to Mary, her gaze at once forgiving. The fact that this idea had come to her here – here, of all places – is surely a sign that it's the right thing to do. That if God could forgive a little white lie, anybody could.

SIXTEEN

She wakes to find the sun streaming through her curtains, which already feels like a good omen. She spends longer choosing what to wear; it feels important to get it right. She settles on black trousers and a red silk blouse with a slit neck. She stands in front of the mirror as she tucks the top into her waistband. She pulls it out. Tries it again. It's missing something.

In Nan's room she rummages through her wardrobe, pushing aside hangers home to fur and felt and lamé that will never be worn again. She pauses at a drop-waist black and gold dress from the eighties. She saw this dress in a photograph inside the album she looked at on the night Nan was missing. Granddad's arm resting on one of those padded shoulders. She pauses for a second, her hand running over the material, and then, when she sees what's next to it, she pushes it aside. She pulls from the hanger a plain black blazer. She tries it on in the mirror. Her long dark hair falls over the padded shoulders; something doesn't look right. She takes it off, pulls out the padding, and slips back into it. The arms are a little long, and it's a bit wide for her frame. And – she sniffs it – it smells of mothballs. But then she remembers seeing a bulldog clip in Nan's bureau and she runs downstairs to get it, cinching it in at the back. Now her reflection is perfect. She dots some of Nan's Lily of the Valley perfume behind each ear and on her wrists. She tries on one long plastic beaded necklace and then another, leaving the jewellery scattered across Nan's dressing table. No, this will do. She twirls one more time in front of the mirror and sees the bulldog clip again. She just needs to remember not to take her coat off once she gets inside the Kyles'. She'll remember, of course she will.

It's only a ten-minute walk from Nan's house to Chestnut Avenue, but Chloe takes the long way round so she can stop at the newsagent's on the way. Beside the till there's a stationary section, a slim red ring-bound reporter's notebook. She buys it and a biro, remembering to test it on the paper first. She hands over the money to pay and leaves the shop transformed.

As she comes out of the newsagent's, a couple of teenage boys move their bikes from the pavement outside the doorway. She catches her reflection in the window as she walks away: notebook and pen in one hand, blazer, smart trousers. She even feels like a reporter. She pictures herself then, thirty minutes from now, perhaps Maureen making her a cup of tea while she sits on the sofa opposite Patrick, taking notes in her pad. She'll glance around the room, jotting down detail to colour in the story; nothing will go undiscovered, no stone unturned. The cashier in the shop hadn't even questioned her buying a shorthand pad. She stops still on the pavement – she doesn't know shorthand. Can she fake it? After all, she's seen what reporters scrawl in their notepads. Would the Kyles know the difference? But she doesn't like the thought of deceiving them. She checks her watch, there isn't time to buy a dictaphone. Yet the thought of abandoning her plan now when she is already so close, so prepared, is impossible.

'Too late now,' she whispers under her breath.

She carries on walking. Nerves collecting inside each step. For the first time ever she has sympathy for reporters sent out on door knocks. Is this how they feel? She's never thought about their job outside of the office, just complained if they didn't return files back to the archive. She puts her nerves aside. She's doing this for Angie, for the Kyles, so they might finally get some peace, some answers. After all, someone needs to keep hope for the missing. She remembers her own visits to the police station. They were hardly dynamic in their approach; twenty-five years ago they were probably even worse. She's got to remember to stay focused.

She arrives at the house and watches for a while from the other side of the road. She pictures Maureen and Patrick pottering behind the walls, busy in their permanent state of pretence and waiting. She imagines Angie's absence as something they pull on each morning as routinely as their clothes.

Unlike some of the other houses in this street, this one hasn't sprouted an extension from its side. The old wooden gate hasn't been swapped for a wrought-iron one either. The only update appears to be the double glazing and the new front door, brown uPVC to match the colour of the brick. Chloe looks up at the bedroom window she'd glanced into two weeks before, but for some reason she can't see the same light shade, and the curtains seem different too. She squints harder, makes a sun visor with her hand to see more clearly. She checks the number – 48. It's definitely the right place and yet somehow it feels different. She puts that down to nerves too.

She heads towards the short gate. As she pushes it open she notices tiny flecks of blue paint flake off on her palm. She slips her hands into her coat pocket, enjoying the thought of them collecting inside. She's surprised that Patrick hasn't sanded this down and repainted it, but perhaps the Kyles prefer to keep everything as it was then – a blue that Angie would recognize if she came home. She pictures Angie as a tiny girl, racing ahead of her mum, pushing at the same paintwork that is now scattered over her hand. For a second, excitement replaces the nerves. Respectfully, she closes the gate back onto the latch.

At the door, her hand hovers over the knocker. A white rose is etched into the stained glass above it – perhaps this is some tribute to Angie? She remembers the type of detail included in the colour pieces she's read on her wall and gets out her notepad and pen – this will all be useful. Then, before there's time for the doubt to creep in, she knocks and stands back from the front step. This is it. She clutches her reporter's notebook to her chest as she hears footsteps beyond the door frame. She clears her throat. Shuffles from foot to foot. This is it. A figure appears behind the mottled glass, the blurry outline of a hand reaching for the door handle. This is it.

There's the crunch of draught excluders as the door opens. Chloe takes a breath, shapes her face into a smile.

'Can I help you?'

A woman stands there, but it's not Maureen. Chloe feels her face fall. This woman is young, even younger than her. Her hair is pulled back into a tight ponytail, she wears dangly gold hoop earrings and grey jogging bottoms with fluffy pink slippers poking out the end.

'Maureen?' she says. She doesn't know why because this woman looks nothing like her.

The woman stands, one hand keeping the door pulled closed behind her, to stop the cold running amok down her hallway.

'Maureen?' the woman replies. 'Is that what you said? She don't live 'ere no more. It's our place now.'

With that, the woman is nudged to one side as two small children wriggle into the space beside her legs. One of them, a girl with mousy hair, about six, looks from Chloe to her mother.

'Who's she?' she asks her mother.

As she does, two more faces appear: toddlers, a boy and a girl, not twins but close in age; they have grubby food-stained mouths and are both wearing romper suits that are unbuttoned at the bottom, the fabric swinging between their chubby scuffed knees.

'No one,' their mum replies. 'She's after the old lady who used to live here. Now get in, it's freezing out 'ere.'

The door is pushed shut, another crunch from the draught excluders and then, outside, everything is still. Chloe stands there for a moment. On the other side of the glass she hears the woman's agitation at her kids; one starts to cry. No Maureen. No Patrick. No Angie. They've gone.

Chloe grips the reporter's notebook as if it might steady her. She takes a step away from the door and then back again. It can't be right. She goes to knock again, then decides against it. She steps back, checks the number – definitely 48. She heads back down the path slowly, through the flaking blue gate. She's in such a hurry to leave, she forgets to close it after her. She takes another look back at the house and sees the woman watching her from the window. It can't be right, something must be wrong. Patrick and Maureen wouldn't have moved. They couldn't have.

She walks home slowly, her shoes dragging on the pavement. She tries desperately to think of explanations. She passes a bin and dumps the notepad and pen into it. What if it had been Angie knocking on that door? What then? She can feel the ugliness rearing inside. And something else: anger, hurt. Hot black stones that burn inside her belly. After all these years of saying they'd wait for Angie how could they have just upped and left?

By the time she gets back to Nan's she's stumbling to get her key in the lock. When she does the hallway is blurred with angry tears. She slams it behind her, catching a bit of Nan's curtain in it. She pulls it out, too hard, the top of it coming free from the rings, and it hangs there, limp, useless.

'How could they just leave?' she cries to an empty hallway. And then again louder, 'How could they just *leave?*'

She runs up to her room, half expecting to open her door and the cuttings to be gone too, as if she had imagined the hurt and pain in Maureen and Patrick's eyes. But the cuttings are there, waiting for her, mocking even. She scans them quickly, her finger tracing the lines, one after another, after another, until she finds what she's looking for:

'Angela is our life, our love, our everything. An open wound will be here in our hearts until the day she is returned to us. We will wait for the rest of our lives for the day we are reunited.'

Liars.

Her hand grips the top of the paper, she pulls and the whole page comes loose from the Blu-Tack. It hangs there, limply. She thinks of the curtain downstairs. She thinks of Nan in the home. She thinks of Claire Sanders taking Nan away. Now taking her house too. She thinks of Malc sacking her from the archive. She thinks of Maureen and Patrick – why had she ever trusted them? She pulls harder, the cuttings rip. She pulls the next and the next. It feels better. She uses both hands then, ripping at the cuttings with her fingers, feeling stronger with every tear. She goes faster and faster. She sees Maureen and Patrick's faces tear in two, words split on the wall, on the floor. Fake words, lies. She stamps on them.

What's the use in keeping them anyway?

She pulls again and tears and rips and all those fake words gather in a pile on the floor. She pulls again and again, snatches and slashes until the wall is bare and the woodchip shows through. Until just a few dots of pale blue putty or their greasy marks remain on the paper, and those smoky shadowy outlines of the pictures that once hung there. In places even the lining paper is torn. Not that Chloe cares. At her feet are the scattered remains of the cuttings, the stories, the headlines, the pictures, the quotes. All lies.

Then, among the rubble, the panic comes. She searches

quickly from one article to another, to another, desperately trying to find one of the earliest. She picks it up with two hands, scans through the lines for the address. What if it was her fault? What if she had got the house number wrong? But there it is, unchangeable. 48. The same house she went to. Nothing had changed in black and white, yet in real life, everything had.

She sinks down among the paper on the floor, kicking one cutting off her shoe, and feels her throat constrict with hot tears.

Maureen and Patrick were meant to be different from all the rest. What a fool she's been. They are exactly the same.

SEVENTEEN

It's the afternoon before Chloe finally pulls herself up from the floor of her own shattered archive. She only does because she'd promised to visit Nan. Not that Nan will remember. But the staff will. She walks out of her bedroom with cuttings stuck to the soles of her shoes. One trails out of the house after her. She peels it off her shoe and allows the wind carry it off up the street.

It's just after 3.30 p.m. when she boards the bus. She changes twice and watches children in various school uniforms walking home, skipping alongside Mum or Dad. She plays a game from her seat by the window, trying to spot the parents who would move away from their kids should they disappear. She doesn't find a single one.

Chloe arrives at Park House just after the residents have had afternoon tea.

'There's a few muffins left in a dish in the communal room if you're peckish,' one of the care assistants tells her.

She shakes her head. She has lost her appetite.

'Your grandma has been really looking forward to seeing you.'

They both know she's lying.

Chloe walks past the communal room on her way to find Nan. From the circular walkway she sees the backs of half a dozen white heads waiting patiently for their own visitors. She feels something akin to one jigsaw piece fitting into another inside her. At least here she is needed and she feels a tiny flame reignite. She longs to be needed by somebody, and for a while she had forgotten that that person is Nan.

Nan is lying on her bed when Chloe arrives at her room.

'Oh nurse, thank goodness you're here.'

'It's me, Nan,' she says, approaching the bed. 'It's Chloe.'

Her brow crinkles. 'I don't know a Chloe.'

Not today. She can't take it. Not today of all days.

Chloe reaches for her hand. 'You do, Nan.'

'No.' She shakes her head. 'I don't know a Chloe. Nurse!'

Chloe sighs, she lets go of her hand, she steps back. What should she do? Go all the way back home? She makes for the door, and then when she gets there, she closes it. Not today. Not today of all days. She turns around.

'Nan,' she says. 'Please, you do know me.'

She pleads with her. She can do this. She can make her remember. She's so determined she doesn't see the way the old woman flinches, how she huddles herself up to the wall.

'Nurse!' Nan cries.

'No,' Chloe snaps, going back to make sure the door is shut tight. 'We don't need a nurse, you know who I am. Don't say you don't.'

She walks back to the bed where Nan is cowering. She switches quickly to a calm voice and tries again: 'You do know me, Nan, I'm Chloe.'

'I don't!'

'Nan.'

'Stop, I don't. Nurse!'

'Nan!'

'Nurse!'

Nan reaches for a red button next to her bedside table. She presses it furiously, over and over, as Chloe tries to stop her. The two women grapple, Nan trying to hit the button, Chloe fighting against her. She grabs her wrist, too hard. Nan cries out.

'We don't need a nurse,' Chloe says through her teeth. 'We don't need anybody.'

The next thing she knows, the door flies open. The matron appears in the doorway, her eyes wide.

'What on earth is going on?' the matron asks.

Chloe looks from the matron to Nan, seeing for the first time the scene as she does. Nan is trembling against the wall, her arms covering her face. Chloe's hand flies up to her mouth, as Miriam crosses the room and Nan clings to her like a frightened child.

'I . . . I'm sorry,' Chloe says, backing towards the door, watching as the matron sits down beside Nan and puts an arm around her. She sees her notice Nan's wrist, now pinky purple, the colour already setting in her skin.

Nan is crying now, telling the matron over and over, 'I don't know anyone called Chloe.'

The matron speaks gently to her. 'OK, Grace,' she says. 'It's OK. This is your granddaughter, she's come to see you.'

Nan is crying. Chloe knows it is her who has made her cry. Another care assistant, Gemma, rushes into the room.

'I heard the alarm,' Gemma says, breathless, assessing the scene.

Chloe looks between the three women. What has she done?

'I didn't . . . I just . . . I just wanted to see her,' Chloe says.

The matron gives a nod to the care assistant who replaces her next to Nan, then Miriam leads Chloe out of the room gently.

'Come with me, Chloe,' Miriam says. 'Why don't you have a cup of tea in my office while Gemma takes care of your grandmother?'

Chloe nods. She looks back at Nan but she's crying, her knuckles white where she's gripping the nurse's hand. Chloe knows then she's lost her. Today to Gemma, tomorrow to whoever else she happens to trust more than her. It's over.

She follows the matron out of the room, a cavity in her chest where her heart should be. The disease has won. It's over.

EIGHTEEN

'Oh God, Chloe, are you OK?'

Chloe peers around the door frame, daylight streaming through the three-inch gap. She squints.

'Yeah, I'm fine. How did you—'

'I've been calling and calling.'

'My phone's been off. I lost my charger.'

'What's wrong?'

Chloe reaches for her stomach.

'Oh, you know, twenty-four-hour bug, something like that. I'd invite you in but . . . germs.' She shrugs. 'Should have a red cross painted on my door!'

Hollie laughs a little, more to be polite, but Chloe can see she's worried. 'You sure you're all right? You don't seem yourself.'

'I'm fine, honest. Just haven't had any fresh air in twenty-four hours, it's making me feel a bit . . . woozy.'

'It might make you feel better?'

Hollie tries to peer around the door. Chloe lifts her arm towards the top of the frame, the sleeve of her dressing gown hiding much of the hallway, but she still sees it, Hollie's eyes roaming the gaps: the busy, patterned carpet, the hall table, Nan's shoes by the front door.

'Do you need anything from the shops?' Hollie turns to point as if to remind Chloe where they are. 'I could go grab you some supplies. Honestly, it's no bother.'

Chloe sighs. Hollie isn't going to leave.

'Give me two minutes to pull some clothes on and I'll come out with you. You're right, I need the fresh air.'

Hollie goes to lift one foot inside, but Chloe pushes the door just a little. 'Two mins,' she says, closing the door shut.

When Chloe reappears, Hollie is sitting on the low wall at the front of Nan's garden. She's looking up at the house. 'Nice little places these. Me and Phil looked at one round the corner from here.'

'Did you?' They start walking. 'Hey, how did you know which one was Nan's?'

'I came over that time just after you moved in, don't you remember? But Nan was ill, so we went to the coffee shop instead. Shall we see if it's open today? You could have some dried toast or something?'

Chloe looks like she might be sick and Hollie looks concerned.

'What do you think it is? Something you ate?'

Chloe shrugs. 'Best not to get too close, though.'

They walk in silence for a while, Hollie glancing this way and that up and down the road.

'It's a nice road, I remember thinking that last time. Quiet.'

'Nan's lived here since they were built.'

Hollie looks surprised to hear this.

'Surely she must know everyone round here? Or rather they must know her – know her family, I mean.'

'Here we are,' Chloe says as they arrive at the coffee shop. Actually, it is more of a greasy spoon and if Chloe really had been ill, the chip fat odour alone would have been enough to turn her stomach.

Suleyman brings over two laminated menus, putting them down on the table, and Chloe studies the black hairs on the back of his hands.

'How's your nan, feeling better?' he asks.

'Yeah, thanks, Suleyman.'

He walks away and Chloe whispers to Hollie, 'I can't be bothered to explain.' She nods. 'How are you anyway?'

'Oh, I'm fine. No news. More worried about you really, I couldn't get hold of you . . .'

'Yeah, like I said, I lost my charger, I'll have to buy another one.'

Hollie looks back at her for a second. She can see Hollie's unsure what to say next. She knows this look. But she knows Hollie well enough to know she'll keep her confidence. That she knows there is no alternative.

'Oh, that's annoying,' Hollie says, 'they're expensive as well. Especially when you haven't got a job . . .'

Chloe quickly looks down at the menu.

'I'm going to have the sausage, egg and chips,' she says.

'Do you think that's wise?'

'Why?'

'Your bug.'

'Oh yeah, you're right.' She turns her attention to the blander sides as Suleyman returns. 'Just some toast for me,' she says, handing back the menu.

'Without butter?' Hollie prompts. 'It's probably best.'

'Oh, yeah . . . without butter.'

Hollie orders a coffee and poached eggs on toast.

'How's the job search going?' she asks when Suleyman's gone.

'Not bad, yeah,' Chloe says. 'I might have an interview lined up through one of those recruitment agencies.'

'Oh yeah? Which one did you go for in the end?'

'Oh . . . I . . . I can't remember, I spoke to so many . . .'

'Phil says he never heard from you about that job.'

'Yeah, I just didn't . . . it didn't seem my kind of thing.'

'It was filing, Chloe,' Hollie says.

Chloe starts fiddling with the pot of ketchup; it's one of those giant tomato ones, the ones with the dark green lid that are always clogged with congealed tomato sauce. Chloe has always thought they were impractical.

She sees Hollie biting the corner of her lip, glancing between Chloe and the menu. She's looking down, her finger tracing the list of food as she speaks.

'And what about Nan? How is she doing?' Hollie asks.

'Oh yeah, good. I've been visiting her.'

'Chloe, I . . .'

'Well, I wasn't going to just dump her in that care home and—'

'No, of course not, that's not what I'm saying. I just think, well, maybe it all happened for a reason. Maybe it's for the best.'

'Anyway, what was it you were calling about? Just a catch-up?' Chloe says, trying to take the heat out of the conversation, to veer Hollie into different territory.

'Sorry?'

'You said you'd been calling me?'

Hollie reaches down to the handbag at her feet. She rifles around inside before pulling out a newspaper cutting. It's folded a couple of times, but Chloe can tell from the typeset it's her newspaper, or at least it was. She knows what's coming: the job pages, Hollie's highlighter pen.

'I was flicking through the jobs section, you know, having a look for you really – Phil's old job is being advertised, but anyway – and I saw this.'

Hollie unfolds the paper and lays out a spread on the table in front of her, ironing out the creases with her fist. The archivist in Chloe winces. She doesn't recognize it at first, but then Hollie flips the page so it's the right way up.

'It's that couple, the one who lost their daughter, and I just thought it was such a coincidence because you only mentioned her the other day to me, do you remember? You said you were working on the story and I guessed this was it, this update and . . .'

As Chloe stares at the newspaper the rest of the cafe with its chequered red and white tablecloths retreats into the background.

'It was her, wasn't it?' Hollie asks, tilting her head to read the name upside down. 'Angela Kyle?'

Chloe's eyes dart across the spread, from headlines, to pull quotes, to the pixels of Maureen and Patrick Kyle until they finally collect in some recognizable fashion in her brain. She hadn't known them at first, age and grief having taken their toll on their faces, weather and worry having beaten new lines into them, their hair greyer – and lesser in Patrick's case. But these are the present-day colour versions of Maureen and Patrick. She reaches out just as Suleyman appears at the table with the food.

'Here we go, ladies, one poached eggs on toast, and one plain toast no butter.'

He puts the small plate down right on top of the headline. Chloe picks it up quickly and, as she does, she takes it in for the first time:

WE'LL NEVER GIVE UP ON OUR ANGIE

Chloe gasps then – a kind of half-gasp, half-laugh. An exhalation of disbelief. Hollie looks up.

'It is them, isn't it?' Hollie says.

'Yes,' Chloe replies. 'Yes, it's them.'

'It says here they've moved,' Hollie says between mouthfuls, 'that's what the piece is about. At first I picked it up thinking they'd found her or something, but it's just a piece saying how they've moved to . . . oh, hang on.' She leans forward then, over her eggs, rubbing one finger down the newsprint, blurring the ink as she reads upside down. Chloe winces as Hollie dabs her black-stained finger down, smudging the words. 'There, there it is. Low Drove. That's out in the Fens, isn't it?'

Low Drove. Chloe has never heard of it.

Hollie chews on her toast, mentioning two more villages Chloe hasn't heard of. 'Yeah, it's between them somewhere. Tiny place, I think me and Phil drove through it once when we were going to a garden centre. One road, blink and you miss it – that kind of place.'

Chloe is half listening, half reading. Scanning and reading and mouthing the words to herself until she's not listening to Hollie anymore at all because this, this is all the proof she needed.

Chloe takes a bite of the toast but she can't eat now, and not because of some fake stomach bug. It's as if every hope she'd lost these last few days has been returned to her, as if wrapped up in this news cutting is a gift. But with the elation comes a horrid sickening feeling. She pictures all those torn and shattered cuttings, a feeling now that it was she who had let down Maureen and Patrick. It was she who had lost faith in *them*. The toast rolls around and around in her mouth. Finally she swallows.

She picks the paper up and reads the headline again.

WE'LL NEVER GIVE UP ON OUR ANGIE

'Come on, eat that toast, it'll do you good. Actually,' Hollie says, 'you're looking better already, bit more colour in your cheeks. It must be the fresh air.'

Chloe looks back at her friend, tearing her attention away from the newspaper cutting for a split second.

'Can I . . . can I keep this?'

'Yeah, course.' Hollie fills her fork with another mouthful. 'Keep it, Phil will only screw it up and use it for kindling in our wood burner. Did I tell you we had a wood burner installed? You should feel the heat it kicks out, we didn't even have the heating on the other night and . . .'

But Chloe is busy reading:

A HEARTBROKEN couple have finally moved from their city home twenty-five years after their daughter went missing, but the pair insist they have not given up hope of her return.

Four-year-old Angela Kyle disappeared from Ferry Meadows after her father Patrick took her to play at a park there in October 1979. Mr Kyle and his wife, Maureen, have appealed for information on their missing daughter, but despite an extensive police inquiry there have been no new leads. For the last twenty-five years they have stayed in the same house, even keeping her bedroom as a shrine to little Angie, should she return. But last week they swapped their Dogsthorpe home for a Fen village.

'It doesn't mean we have given up hope of Angie being found,' said Maureen Kyle from their new home in Low Drove. 'I'm still as sure today as I was twenty-five years ago that Angie will come home one day, but it's been hard staying in the same place, surrounded by all those memories, every fresh lead and every fresh disappointment. We needed a new start.'

Chloe looks up at Hollie. She can't tell her what she's thinking, that it feels to her as if Maureen is reaching out of the newspaper to reassure every doubt she's had over the last few days. When she pictures those cuttings pulled from the wall and kicked under her bed, her temples throb and the cafe feels small and stuffy. She leans back and takes deep breaths, her forehead tingling with sweat.

Hollie looks up at her, her knife and fork wavering mid-air.

'Oh, you're not right, Chloe,' she says. 'Look, you've

gone all pale again, and you haven't touched your toast.' She wipes the last of her own toast around her plate quickly. 'Come on, let's get you home.'

Chloe says goodbye to Hollie on the doorstep. She had to shuffle from one foot to the other, as if she needed the loo, until Hollie got the message.

As soon as she closes the door she runs up to her bedroom. There, on her hands and knees, she pulls out all the photocopies she'd pushed under her bed, releasing them from the tight angry balls she'd screwed them into.

She curses herself as she goes, curses herself for doubting Maureen and Patrick. Two parents who had proved time and again, year after year, how devoted they were to their little girl. She should have known them better. She knows, deep down, the past is always there, just under her skin. Life filtered through a lens of distrust is the best way of avoiding disappointment. But Maureen and Patrick are the first people who have ever proved her wrong. And surely that's got to mean something.

NINETEEN

Out in the Fens the roads are long and straight. There's often a camber each side which slopes into a grassy bank and then further still into a dyke, one side or the other, occasionally both. Through the windscreen of the bus, it looks as if the road is a giant grey play mat rolled out for a child to run toy cars up and down. The lumps and bumps in the road make Chloe's stomach pitch up and down. Or perhaps that's just nerves.

It's been a while since the bus left Peterborough, crossing over one anonymous roundabout after another until the buildings faded away into flat countryside. From the A47 Chloe had spotted the lonely little Eel Catcher's Cottage abandoned in the middle of a field, its thatched roof still withstanding the elements. On school trips to the coast, kids had made up stories about a wicked old woman who lived there and ate children for her supper.

The sky is bigger here. The grey clouds hang low, appearing, in the distance, to touch the tops of the trees that provide a windbreak for the crops – the only thing that breaks the Fenland for miles. The bus slows and stops to let people off as it passes through one village after another – Parsons Drove, Murrow – each little more than a string of bungalows with long neat gardens, interrupted only by the occasional empty petrol forecourt.

Chloe shuffles to the edge of her seat as a cluster of houses appears. She wonders each time if this village sign will read Low Drove, yet time and again she is disappointed – or perhaps a little relieved.

When she moves she feels the news cutting Hollie gave her crinkle inside her coat pocket. She's brought it with her to make sure she's got the right place. There it is again, that churning inside. Is today really the day she's going to see Maureen and Patrick? Because that's all she wants to do, just look. She'd already decided that before she left home. That's why she didn't take the same care when dressing. All she's going to do is find the house, see where they live and perhaps – if she's lucky – catch a shadow at the window, or a glimpse of them pottering in their garden.

Time passes looking out the windows. The sky has darkened and black clouds hang heavy, threatening to burst. Her hand reaches for the cutting in her pocket and holds it there, tightly. In her other pocket is her mobile phone; she'd made sure to call Park House from the bus station before she left the city to check on Nan. It didn't feel right to call from the road. One of the carers told her she was doing a still-life art class this morning. Chloe had never known Nan to paint.

The driver applies the brakes, and she looks up just in time to see the next village sign flash past on the left. Low Drove. She stands up and a couple of the other passengers lift their faces. The bus comes to a halt and the doors open.

'Are you sure this is the place you want?' the driver says, looking up the empty road.

'Low Drove?' she asks.

He nods, looking her up and down. She thinks of Angie.

'Yes, then.'

'Right you are.'

She steps off onto a grassy verge. It's only when the bus pulls away that she sees just how isolated this place is. The road is without markings. On the other side a weeping willow slumps across the tarmac. The back of the road sign is a hundred metres behind her and, in the opposite direction, the back of the bus receding into the distance, its indicator flickering as it turns right out of the village. She stands still and the wind whips around her. She pulls her coat tighter but it doesn't make much difference. Further up the road she sees a few houses, and – she squints – a red Wall's ice cream sign swinging in the distance. The only sign of life. She walks towards it, the edge of the road crumbling into earth. Why would Maureen and Patrick want to live here? Why would anyone? It offers nothing more than isolation. Is that what they want? To disappear? But then why do the interview in the newspaper, telling everyone that they've moved here? In case Angie comes home, she supposes.

The photograph on the cutting shows them standing outside a yellow-brick detached Victorian house with a short privet hedge, but Chloe doesn't see many houses at all, let alone this one. As the red sign gets closer she hears it creaking and, in that same moment, a string of four seventies bungalows comes into view. They are the same grey brick she's seen in other villages, long gardens that run up to the road, windows with net curtains, a sensible car in the drive. She walks past and catches her reflection in the window. Inside, she sees tall armchairs topped with lace doilies. She knows that style. This is a place for the old.

She reaches the red sign – it's a newsagent's. She goes to push open the door, but it's firmly shut. She checks the opening times. Wednesday afternoon: Closed. Who does that anymore? She pulls the cutting from her pocket, careful to hang on to it in the breeze. She studies the photograph of the Kyles, looking for some clue, a tree or a landmark, and then searches the road again. She walks on a bit further, but there's nothing here. Along a bit, opposite the newsagent's, is one tall red-bricked house with a nursery alongside it. Through the polythene she spots muted yellows, pinks and reds – roses probably. Otherwise, this place is grey. She walks back to the newsagent's and stands outside, looking up and down the road. They've got to be here. Why would they have done an interview letting everyone know where they'd moved to if they weren't really living here? She puts her head up to the newsagent's window, just in case anyone is there in the back. The cold of the glass pushes against her nose. She cups her hands either side of her eyes to get a better view. Her breath fogs up the glass. She steps back, wipes it away, and then she sees it. A postcard in the window:

Lodger wanted.
Room for rent in Elm House, Low Drove. Would suit single professional. Preferably female.

There's a phone number, but it's the name that makes her gasp out loud.

Contact Mrs Patrick Kyle.

Maureen. She scans the road again. Elm House. So that's where they are. It's as if that postcard had been waiting for her. But where is Elm House? She walks again, the length of the village, all the way to the sign reading Low Drove, and then all the way back to the sign she'd seen from the bus on the way in. But there is no Elm House.

She goes back to the bus stop and looks across at the weeping willow, at its branches scraping the ground. That's when she spots it: the lane the tree is hiding. She crosses, makes her way through the fronds of willow and a lane opens up in front of her. It's narrow, not much wider than one car, the verges scarred with tyre tracks. And there, in the distance, on the left-hand side, a pale yellow-brick house, a short privet hedge, a blue car in the drive – Elm House.

Just a look, she reminds herself.

She walks until she's opposite the house. She waits on the other side of the road, staring at the orange keystone above the white double-glazed front door, spreading outwards to the net curtains at the two bottom windows, slightly askew, a sign perhaps of the leftover chaos from moving. She pictures them surrounded by boxes, trying to find a perfect place for everything.

A sheet hangs at a window upstairs. They haven't had time to find curtains to fit yet, and there, at the other bedroom window, a light shade she's sure she recognizes. She narrows her eyes, but wind hurries the clouds along; suddenly the changing reflection of the sky in the window obscures her view. Was it a trick of the light, or a beacon welcoming her home?

TWENTY

'Can I help you?'

Chloe jumps and turns towards the gruff voice that has broken the quiet. On the driveway stands a man. He's about fifty-five, his hair greying, curly and wispy; broken veins stain his nose and cheeks crimson. His jumper strains against a stomach out of proportion to his otherwise slim frame. Chloe knows this man. This man is Patrick Kyle.

'You lost?' he says.

He watches her while she finds the words, his brow furrowing, his arms reaching across his chest.

'I . . .' She doesn't know what to say, thoughts race through her head until she remembers. '. . . the postcard.'

He looks confused.

'In the, er . . . in the newsagent's window?' Chloe says.

'Oh that,' he says, looking Chloe up and down. 'Well, you'd better come in and meet my wife, this is her brilliant idea.'

He doesn't wait for her before he turns, heading past the blue car, down the driveway towards the back of the house. Chloe stands still on the opposite side of the road. Does he want her to follow, or is he going to bring his wife – Maureen – out here? Her hands are clammy in her pockets. He turns around.

'Well, come on then,' he says, gesturing with his arm. 'Unless you can see the room from the road.'

Chloe crosses the road without looking – not that she's seen a single car since the bus dropped her off. Patrick waits for her at a small gate which leads into a large back garden. It's laid to lawn except for stepping stones which line the route to a washing line.

'Maureen!' he calls. He turns around to see she's stopped still. 'Well, come on, girl, do you want this room?'

'Oh . . . I,' she starts, but before she can explain the back door flies open; a woman appears, an empty plastic washing basket under her arm. Her hair is almost all grey now, just streaked in places with the black that Chloe knows from the earlier cuttings, as if someone has come along with a fat paintbrush and missed bits. Maureen is still pretty, despite the marionette lines running down the sides of her mouth that give her a rather sad leonine face. But had Chloe ever seen her looking any other way? This is her, without a shred of doubt – this is Maureen.

'We shall have to be getting this in Patrick, it looks like it'll be pouring any min— oh, who's this?'

It's only then she sees her. Chloe is standing a few feet back from Patrick, in front of their car. Maureen reaches to fix her hair.

Patrick waves a little towards her with his right hand. 'She's come about that bloody advert you've got up in the newsagent's.'

'Oh Pat, will you stop moaning about that, especially when we've got a girl standing on our driveway who . . .' Her voice trails off. 'Oh, never mind.' She dumps the washing basket in Patrick's arms then and straightens her clothes. 'Here, Pat, make yourself useful while I chat to . . .'

'Chloe,' she says, but the wind steals her voice. 'Chloe,' she tries again, louder. Blood is pumping at her temples. It's really them.

'Right, OK. Well, ignore him, Chloe. He thinks we're fine here rattling around in this big house, but I told him there's nothing wrong with lining our pockets with a bit of extra cash. Why don't you come in and I'll show you the room?'

Chloe nods, hardly able to believe that it's been this easy, that after everything she's read, everything she knows, she's been invited into the Kyles' home. Just like that.

'Mind the step, love, it's a bit high that one, has taken me some getting used to.'

Inside the kitchen is a black and white chequered lino. Chloe wants to tiptoe, to look and feel without disturbing this place with a single footstep. It feels like a film set, everything on show a prop: the set of knives on the wall, the dead cactus in the window, even the cobwebs that keep it company.

A terrific bang from outside makes her jump – a clap of thunder. The skies open immediately.

'There, I knew it was going to come down any minute . . . hurry, Pat!' she shouts out the doorway as she fills the kettle at the sink.

He shouts back something indecipherable.

'You'll have a cup of tea, won't you?' Maureen says. 'Well, you can't go out in this downpour now. Sit down, sit down.'

Chloe's head is spinning. How had it been this easy? She pulls out a white wooden chair from under a small pine table. It scrapes on the floor. She sits down on it and looks around the room. The draining board is stacked with plates from lunch, two mugs, a large saucepan with a potato masher still standing up straight in it. On the fridge a magnetic diary is filled with nothing more than doctor's appointments. In the kitchen window above the sink are four wooden letters which spell out hope. She's reminded again of her purpose, not to allow anything to cloud why she is here. They don't know it, of course – not yet – but she's here to help them, to investigate Angie's disappearance, maybe even to *solve* Angie's disappearance. Maureen sees Chloe looking around.

'Oh, don't mind us, will you?' she says, lifting a pile of papers from the table. 'I was just clearing up when you arrived.'

'It's OK,' Chloe says, casting her eyes further around the room. 'Don't feel you have to—'

'Well, I guess you take us as you find us, especially if you're thinking of living here.' Maureen shrugs.

Just then Patrick comes through the back door with the washing. She rifles through a few shirts on top of the pile. 'Oh Patrick, it's soaked.'

'Not much I can do when the heavens open like that,' he says. He glances at Chloe again. He seems surprised to find her sitting at his kitchen table. It's she who looks away.

'Take it upstairs and put it in the box room, I'll get the airer out later.' She tuts as he leaves, then turns to Chloe. 'Milk? Sugar?'

'Yes, two, please.'

She turns her back to open a cupboard opposite.

Chloe scans the contents. Everything looks ordinary enough except, just before she shuts it, she's sure she sees a child's cup, some cartoon character etched onto the side. Patrick returns. He pulls out the chair next to her, then has a change of heart, sitting himself down on the one opposite. Maureen puts the tea in front of her.

'Did you make me one of tho—'

'You didn't say you wa—'

She sighs, opening the cupboard again to get another mug. Chloe glances for the same cup but Maureen closes it so quickly she doesn't see a thing. Patrick picks up the newspaper and flicks straight to the horse racing. Chloe scans the room but there's nothing to see, it's just an ordinary kitchen. What had made her think she could come in here and find a clue to Angie's disappearance? But the truth is, she didn't expect to be in here at all. Maureen brings her own tea to the table and pulls out the chair between Chloe and Patrick.

'We haven't been here long ourselves,' Maureen says, taking a sip. 'Ouch, too hot.'

'No?' Chloe asks. 'What brought you out here?'

She sees the way Patrick looks at her quickly from under his eyebrows.

'Fancied a change, didn't we, Pat?'

He changes position in his chair as if that will do as substitute for answering her.

'We got sick of the city in the end, tired, you know. We wanted some peace. It's nice and quiet out here, see?'

'Yes.'

'But what about you? Young thing like yourself, what brings you to Low Drove?'

Chloe swallows her tea and feels it scald the back of her throat. She coughs.

'I . . . er . . .' She hasn't thought about this. She coughs a little more. 'I suppose I'm after peace, too. It's just I lived with my Nan until recently and, well . . .' Chloe pauses, she swallows. 'She died, quite suddenly, and . . .'

'. . . you just needed a change,' Maureen says.

Chloe stops and looks up at her. A connection made across the table.

'Yes,' Chloe says, the heat of the lie still lingering inside her throat. Unsure whether it was really necessary to bury Nan to live with the Kyles. Perhaps it was just easier.

'Yeah, well, we know what that's like, don't we, Pat?'

He grunts a little, moving the racing pages of his newspaper an inch or so.

'Oh?' Chloe asks, but Maureen doesn't elaborate.

'It's isolated out here,' Patrick says without looking up. 'For a young girl on her own, like. You sure you wouldn't rather be in the city, somewhere that's got a bit more going for it?'

Is he trying to be helpful or put her off? She looks at Maureen.

'Oh Pat, I'm sure that Chloe is old enough to know what she—'

'Yeah, well, I'm just sayin—'

Maureen reaches out and puts her hand on the back of his. He stops talking.

'How old are you, Chloe?'

'Twenty-nine,' she replies.

Maureen swallows her tea, not blinking. She seems

unsure how to answer Chloe. Instead, she gets up from the table.

'Well, I'd best be showing you the room then.'

Patrick doesn't follow them upstairs but Chloe feels him watch them leave the kitchen. Maureen leads her through to a hallway with parquet flooring. She glances into two rooms. The back room seems to be the main living room, and the door to the front room is pulled to, open enough only for her to spy peeling wallpaper and dusty floorboards, boxes stacked inside. When she turns back, Maureen has stopped on the first step of the stairs.

'Like I said, we haven't been here long so we're still getting the place together.'

'Yes, of course,' Chloe replies.

Chloe follows her up a grubby runner and, at the top, on the left, there's a window, the sill covered with dead flies. Why haven't they cleaned them up? It seems an easy thing to do.

'Will be nice when you get it how you want it,' she says, filling the silence, anything to make this situation feel natural. Still pinching herself inwardly that she is here, walking up and down the insides of the Kyles' own home.

'Yes, it's got a lot of potential,' Maureen says.

There are five rooms leading off the landing, each with closed doors. Maureen points to them in turn.

'This is the bathroom.' She opens the door and Chloe dutifully pokes her head inside. There's a modern suite, navy and white tiles on the wall. She nods.

'It's got a good shower,' Maureen says, as if to persuade her. 'That's our room there at the front, next to us is a box room. That's the spare room, and this here is the room we're renting out.'

On the wall just outside the room, a brass crucifix clings to the anaglypta. Chloe quickly looks away.

'Here we go,' Maureen says, stepping inside. 'It's a bit stuffy.' She swats at tiny motes of dust as she crosses the room to open a narrow window at the top of a larger one overlooking the back garden. Chloe stands in front of it, staring out at miles of unbroken flat Fenland, now soaked in rain.

'Nice view,' she says, searching the landscape for a glimpse of another house on the horizon and finding nothing but fields.

'We think so,' Maureen says. 'When we moved, we wanted somewhere quiet.'

Chloe turns back and smiles, trying to work out how she should be behaving, what she would say if she didn't know what she already knows. In the end, she settles for 'Where did you move from?' It comes out naturally, she hopes.

'Peterborough,' Maureen says, without elaborating.

'Right,' she says, feeling the sting of duplicity. She thinks of the notepad she dumped in the bin, how she wishes she still had it. She couldn't write here, in front of Maureen, of course not. But the minute she left, before she even got back to the top of the lane, she would be writing notes for her own archive.

Maureen wanders around the room. Chloe follows her. There is a single iron bedstead in the left-hand corner, made up with a white valance sheet that reaches down to the floor and a blue and green floral duvet. Opposite there's a wardrobe so tall it looks like it might topple over onto the mahogany-stained floorboards. And in the right-hand corner of the room, a closed door that appears to lead to an adjoining room. It is locked with a shiny silver padlock. Maureen opens the wardrobe and the hinges creak loudly.

'Must get some of that WD40 on that,' Maureen says to herself.

Chloe pokes her head inside, inhaling the musty smell of mothballs. She knows this smell from Nan's house; it feels like some familiarity to hold on to.

'It's a bit sparse but that's how people seem to like things these days – minimal, I think they call it.' Maureen says. 'But if you wanted anything else, a rug or something, I'm sure we could find you one.'

Chloe strolls around the room, hoping Maureen won't hear her heart thudding inside her coat if she's over by the window. She fingers the duvet for something to do, to buy herself seconds. What does she say? She hadn't expected any of this.

'Yes, it's very nice,' Chloe says. 'Obviously I've got a few places to see . . .'

'Yes, of course,' Maureen says. 'Perhaps it's too quiet out here, for a young girl like you.'

Chloe looks out of the window, at the miles of fields beyond, a bland lifeless landscape. She tries hard to pic-ture the single person who would want this room. Surely it's too isolated here for anyone, including Maureen and Patrick?

'The only thing would be getting into town each day. I work there, you see,' Chloe says.

Maureen nods. 'I think there's a bus that runs regularly, Pat might know.'

'Yes, there is. I came on the bus today.'

She buys a few more moments in the room discussing bus timetables, ticking off on her fingers fictional times when she'd be leaving and coming home, basing it on her old office routine, of course. All the time she's studying every detail of Maureen, the way she wrings her hands, then straightens out the pinny she's wearing. How every so often she tucks a loose tendril of hair behind her ear, even if it's not there. How long has she wanted to be here? No detail is lost on Chloe.

'You might be better closer to your work?' Maureen suggests. 'Not that I want to put you off.'

Chloe feels the jump of panic inside, the thought of letting Maureen talk her out of the room she doesn't even want.

'Hmm, maybe. Has there been much interest?'

'You're the first,' Maureen says. 'The advert has been up two weeks already.'

Chloe's mind settles again. She tries to say all the right things then; she discusses the price and appears to do a quick calculation in her head, nodding to make it seem doable. She even tests the mattress on the bed; it's firmer than the one she has at Nan's. She's surprised when she makes the comparison, as if she's playing with the idea of actually taking the room.

'Well, it's very nice. Can I let you know?'

'Of course,' Maureen says. 'As you can see it's available immediately, just give me a call once you've seen the other places.'

Chloe's cheeks flush with heat, knowing there are no other rooms to view. She quickly turns to leave the bedroom before Maureen notices.

The two women step out onto the landing and Maureen closes the door behind them. As Chloe follows her down the stairs she looks back at the room next to the one they're renting out. Maureen hadn't opened that one and it's locked with a shiny padlock, identical to the one she saw on the door inside the room. She resists the urge to ask Maureen what's in there, but curiosity rattles inside.

Back in the hallway, sun streams through the glass panel at the top of the front door, lighting up the parquet flooring.

'The clouds must have cleared,' Maureen says. 'There might even be a rainbow.'

Chloe glances out the glass. Yes, Maureen might well be right.

On the way back to the kitchen, Maureen stops to show Chloe into the living room at the back of the house. Patrick is sitting on a squashy grey leather recliner that looks out of patio doors, watching the horse racing on the TV. They have a big teak sideboard, not too dissimilar to Nan's, and settled within it – the reason Chloe is here – that framed photograph of Angie. She fails to suppress a gasp, but luckily Maureen doesn't hear her above the sound of the TV. She's busy pointing out something in the garden to Patrick, a bird she's seen, perhaps. She tells him to turn the TV down. Chloe can't take her eyes off the photograph, or maybe it's the other way round – as if Angie is the one watching her.

Chloe shuffles uncomfortably under her gaze. Not that Maureen notices. She carries on talking, oblivious. When she glances back Chloe makes sure she nods and smiles, her eyes constantly flickering back to Angie up there on the sideboard in her navy pinafore and her bunches. Would it be too much of a giveaway to ask about her? Will she get another chance to be this close to the Kyles again?

'She's pretty,' Chloe says. Unable to resist.

Maureen smiles up at the picture, her voices softens. 'Yes, our Angie.'

Chloe waits for something more, not daring to ask. But that's it. Nothing more. The words hang there in the air between them. She decides not to press it. Instead she scans the rest of the room: a crossword book on the pouffe, a gold carriage clock on the sideboard, a plate painted with a wintery scene on the wall. Maureen and Patrick must only be in their fifties, yet this room, this house, feels so old-fashioned. It's like they're stuck in a time warp. As if not having a child grow up in their home has aged them prematurely.

'Chloe likes the room, Pat,' Maureen says. 'But she's got a few other places to see.'

'Right,' he says, not looking up from the telly.

Maureen turns to Chloe.

'Don't mind him, he's not used to a lot of change.'

The two women go back into the kitchen. The garden is bathed with sunlight now. Maureen looks at her washing and tuts. 'S'pose I could chance putting it out again.'

'Would you like a hand?' Chloe says. 'I really wouldn't mind.'

Maureen stares at her a moment. Was that too much?

'Thanks, Chloe, but you must have so much you've got to get on with.'

'Honestly,' she says, 'it's no bother. In fact, I'd like to.'

Chloe climbs into bed around ten. The journey back from Low Drove was quicker than she had anticipated. It's always the same on the way back from somewhere – the city seemed to arrive too quickly. She missed the openness of the countryside then, the stillness of the landscape, the big sky. Perhaps that's what had attracted the Kyles to the Fens. What had felt isolated and exposing when she'd arrived now seemed in hindsight the ideal place for a new start.

She'd called the care home to check on Nan when she got home. When they told her she was sleeping, she felt relieved. She'd made herself a salad with pilchards for dinner. Nan used to eat them on toast for breakfast; she couldn't stomach the smell in the morning, but you get used to the different habits of people when you live with them. She wondered what irritating habits Maureen and Patrick might have? She hadn't noticed anything while she was there, in their home.

She pushes herself deeper down under her duvet, turning this way and that, the mattress feeling too soft now compared to the one she'd briefly sat on at Elm House. She screws her face up, turns over on her pillow, again, and again, imagining how much more comfortable she'd be in the Kyles' spare room.

She closes her eyes and tries to picture herself there, and she can, she can see herself sleeping in that room, eating breakfast with the Kyles each morning round that small pine table, calling goodnight to them as she got ready for bed. She opens her eyes, reminding herself it's nothing more than a silly fantasy. Isn't it?

She can't sleep, though. Not with all this going through her mind. Instead she sits up and turns on the light. She takes her pale blue notebook and finds a pen beside her bed, and sits there, deep into the night, writing down everything she can remember from Elm House – even down to the little wooden hope sign in the kitchen window.

TWENTY-ONE

'Packing to go where?'

Chloe cradles the phone in the crook of her neck, trying to zip up an overstuffed weekend bag with one hand, then two. The phone slips. She scoops it up from the peach eiderdown.

'Hollie? You still there?' she says, slumping down on the bed.

'Yes, I was just asking you where you're going? I mean, what you're packing for.'

'Well, I didn't mean packing . . . more just having a sort-out . . . I was thinking of going away for a few days, well, weeks . . . well, I haven't really decided. I . . .'

She scratches the back of her neck, cursing the unzipped bag, the clothes spilling out of it, wondering why she'd even mentioned it to Hollie. If she hadn't, she wouldn't be having to answer any of these questions. The bag stares at her from the end of the bed.

'Really?' Silence. 'Go away where?'

'I don't know . . . maybe the coast, just . . . I don't know . . . a change of scenery.'

She shakes her head to the air. It's the best she can come up with.

There's a pause on the other end of the line.

'You don't have to keep doing this, Chloe. You could come and stay with me and Phil . . .'

Chloe rolls her eyes.

'Chloe? Are you still there?'

'Yes, I'm still here.'

'I mean, well, if you're feeling a bit lonely. I've told you before, we've got our box room and—'

'I'm fine,' she says, perhaps too cheerily. She curses her own mistake. She tries again. 'I'm fine.'

'We've just done up the box room, I got this lovely duvet cover and matching lampshade from . . .'

Chloe thinks then of the blue and green duvet in the Kyles' spare room. She can imagine Maureen picking it out, making the bed, ironing out the creases with her hand and standing back to admire her work.

'. . . and you don't want that happening again, do you?' Hollie is still talking.

'Sorry, what?' Chloe says.

'I was just saying, about the last time and all that trouble wi—'

'Hollie, I've just got another call waiting, can I call you back?'

'Yes, yes, of course, I'll sp—'

Chloe hangs up and flops back on the bed. Her phone slips out of her hand onto the floor. She started packing this morning as an experiment – just playing with the idea of moving to Low Drove. She wasn't really going to go, of course she wasn't. She just wanted to see what it felt like, being Maureen and Patrick's lodger. The whole thing is ridiculous. She stands up and starts taking the clothes out the bag, just like she has done several times that morning. She can't move to Low Drove. She pauses. Can she? Chloe returns the clothes to the bag. But moving there, that's not the same as simply investigating. No, it's much more intrusive, deceitful even. She takes the clothes out again. But how can it be? It's not like she's there to do harm to the Kyles. Quite the opposite. She wants to help them.

Anyway, however hard she tries she can't escape how it felt to be there, in the Kyles' home, how natural it had seemed. By the second cup of tea she had with Maureen, after they'd put all the washing out on the line, she'd felt so at home. Even Patrick didn't appear to notice her there, as he walked in and out of the kitchen between races. And the thing is, she could actually see herself there, living with them, waking up in that bedroom every morning, sitting on those little white wooden chairs each night for dinner. It felt right. And suddenly this room – with its giant built-in white wardrobes – feels small somehow, like she's outgrown it, like it's time to move on. She thinks of the calls from Claire Sanders, the threat of selling Nan's house to pay for her care. Perhaps this has all happened for a reason? Perhaps it is time to move on?

A dull buzzing comes from the carpet. Her phone. She leans over the side of the bed, sighing. She expects to see Hollie's name, but instead it's Park House. She grabs the phone.

'Hello?'

'Hi, Chloe, it's Miriam Cropper here from Park House.'

'Hi, Miriam, is everything OK?' she stands up from the bed.

'Well, I'm afraid your grandmother had a bit of a fall this morning.'

'Oh my God.' Chloe starts pacing the room.

'She's OK – nothing broken – but it's given her a bit of a shock, as you'd imagine. We thought we'd better let you know.'

'Yes, of course. I'll come straight away.'

Chloe puts the phone down. In an instant all thoughts of Maureen and Patrick and the house at Low Drove evaporate. Even the bag on the bed looks ridiculous. How could she have thought about leaving Nan? It had taken one phone call to remind her just how vulnerable she is, just how much Chloe is needed here. She abandons her packing and leaves for Park House.

Nan is in bed when she gets there. She has an angry purple bruise that extends the length of her right forearm, a tiny cut on her cheekbone and various scratches on the backs of her hands.

'Nan?'

She opens her eyes slowly and looks up at Chloe. But even that is an effort and she closes them again and sighs. She looks tiny, tucked up in pale green sheets. As fragile as a little bird. Chloe moves silently across the room, pulling the leather chair closer to her. She's never anticipated a time when Nan would seem so frail. She knows in that moment she's exactly where she should be. Nan lifts her hand to her and Chloe takes it, giving it a gentle squeeze, carefully avoiding the fine cuts.

'Is that you, Chloe, dear?'

'Yes, it's me, Nan, I'm here with you.'

'Oh good.'

They sit in silence for a while. Chloe watches the gentle rise and fall of her chest, her bones suddenly so thin, so delicate, reminding her of how easily a fall could break one. As a child, wouldn't Nan have been the one to pick her up after a fall? She's reminded in an instant how quickly roles are reversed.

Someone has put a few white flowers from the garden in a short blue vase beside her bed.

'These are pretty,' she says.

Nan turns her head slowly. 'Yes, snowdrops, my favourite.'

They sit there, the two of them, holding hands. Nan closes her eyes, but she's not sleeping. After a while, she opens them again.

'What time is it?' she whispers.

'Just after four.'

'In the morning?'

'No, Nan. Afternoon.'

'You didn't have to leave work to come here, did you?'

'Nan, it's OK. Don't go worrying about something like that. My boss wanted me to make sure you're OK.'

'Did he? That's nice. It's all my fault, I shouldn't have gone down to the garden, but it was raining and I thought I'd left my washing out and—'

'Shh, Nan,' she whispers. 'Just rest, it doesn't matter.'

'But I've made ever such a lot of trouble for everyone.'

'Don't be silly, you haven't made any trouble at all. We just want you to get better.' Chloe gives her hand a tiny squeeze. The bones inside feel as if they might break within her grasp. The bruise up close is a rainbow of colours. How could something like this have happened here? Didn't they tell Chloe that she would be safe? They'd promised her Park House would take better care of her than she had. But there hadn't been any broken bones – no falls – on her watch. She curses Claire Sanders, she curses the nurses here. She feels bad now – sitting here, holding Nan's hand – when she thinks of standing in Maureen and Patrick's house. She feels deceitful, wrong. As if she's betrayed Nan. She doesn't deserve this. Nan needs her here, that much is obvious.

'I'm here, Nan,' Chloe whispers. 'I'm not going any-where.'

Nan turns her head the other way and dozes on her pillow. Chloe creeps out when she knows Nan is finally asleep, closing the door behind her. Outside in the corridor, she heads towards the matron's office. She's in there sorting through paperwork. Chloe makes an attempt to knock on the door.

'Do you have a minute, Miriam?'

The woman behind the desk looks up, her face instantly set with a professional expression.

'Of course, Chloe, come in.'

She gestures for her to take a seat.

'How's your grandmother doing this afternoon? I haven't had chance to catch up with Marina yet.'

She wonders how other relatives would deal with this, if they were making a complaint. How would they handle it? She wishes she had a script to follow. People in films make things look easy but they have someone directing them, Chloe just has to make things up as she goes along.

'She's very weak,' Chloe says. 'She's mostly sleeping. Whatever happened? She seems confused, she's saying something about going out into the garden?'

Miriam sighs. 'Well, like many of our residents here,

Grace likes to wander . . .' She pauses before she continues, her eyes flickering over Chloe in a way that makes
her feel she should be the one feeling uncomfortable.
'There's an area at the back of the garden, mostly hidden
by shrubbery and, for whatever reason, she was down
there and she somehow found a hole in the fence leading
onto the building site.' She pauses, linking her fingers. 'We
don't believe in keeping our residents prisoners.'

'But she's meant to be safe here. She's meant to be well
cared for. This never happened when I—'

Miriam puts her hands up. 'Chloe, I know this has
been a shock for you too, but I can assure you that your
grandmother is well cared for here. If there's one thing
thirty-two years in this job has taught me, it's that you
might think some of our residents come in here with these
brain diseases, but they very much still have a mind of
their own.'

'I know,' Chloe says.

'If your grandmother wants to go for a wander down
the garden, there's not much we can do to stop her.'

Miriam laughs a little, and Chloe joins her because it
feels right, letting the air back into the office, reminding
themselves that Nan is a person before a patient. Chloe
is back then inside Maureen and Patrick's house; that
light, excited feeling she'd felt when she was there returns
to her.

'I know, it's just . . .'

Miriam looks across the desk at her.

'Well, it's just I have this opportunity – with work. It
might take me away for a while and, I won't be able to
relax if—'

'Chloe, this was a one-off, it won't happen again. I can assure you of that. Of course you must take this opportunity, and you're only on the end of the phone, aren't you?'

'I guess,' she says, letting Miriam convince her.

The matron leans across the desk.

'You *must* take this opportunity, you can't put your life on hold. We'll take care of your grandmother. That's our job.'

Chloe nods, torn between the image of Nan in her bed and the house in Low Drove.

'I'd better get back to her,' she says.

Miriam nods. 'Of course.'

But something has changed when she gets up and leaves her office. Despite the shock of Nan's fall, it feels like something invisible has shifted. As if there was a reason this all happened – to grant her permission to go to Low Drove.

When Chloe gets back to Nan's room she's still sleeping. Chloe settles down in the chair beside her, sipping her tea as she watches her. She enjoys listening to the steady whistle of her breathing. She thinks of the evenings they'd sat in her living room, watching *Corrie* together, when it always felt enough just to be beside her. It's difficult to pinpoint now when she had begun to need something more. It always is.

Nan sleeps on and off for a couple of hours. When she sighs or her eyes flicker open for a second, Chloe reaches for her hand and she goes back to sleep. By six o'clock the scent of dinner creeps under the door. There's a knock and a care assistant – Sam – appears, offering them both a plate of mince and potato with some watery cabbage. Chloe takes two plates and puts them on the side. Nan stirs and Chloe helps her sit up so she can eat. She straightens her nightie, tying the ribbons across her bony collarbones so she doesn't feel a draught.

'Here you are, Nan,' she says, offering her a small forkful of mince and mash.

She takes tiny mouthfuls.

'Good, well done.'

Nan smiles every now and then, each portion Chloe persuades her to eat adding more colour to her cheeks.

'I remember you doing this for me,' Chloe says.

'Do you?' Nan takes another mouthful, swallows it. 'When was that then?'

'When I was a little girl.'

Nan watches Chloe over the next fork she puts into her mouth. She eats silently for a few moments.

'Did you know Stella?' she says, her blue eyes watery.

Chloe lifts another fork to Nan's mouth, but she takes her time to swallow, as if the memory of Stella sticks in her throat.

'Yes,' Chloe says finally, 'I knew Stella.'

Nan's eyes sparkle, but no longer with tears. She's away somewhere else then, taking forkfuls of mashed potato, but not here, not in this room.

'Here, try a little cabbage,' Chloe says.

Nan eats it, smiling to herself.

'She was a lovely little girl, wasn't she?' Nan says after a while.

Chloe nods.

'A shock of blonde curls, do you remember?'

Chloe thinks of the photograph that she keeps in her pocket, her favourite picture of the two of them.

'I do,' she says.

Silently, Nan reaches gently for a tendril of Chloe's black hair and winds it around her fingers into a question mark, then stares at her granddaughter.

'Here, Nan, finish this last bit.'

After a moment, Nan opens her mouth obediently. She'll do anything for a few minutes back with Stella. How many people wouldn't give anything for that time again? Chloe could do something, she could add colour to Nan's memory.

'Stella adored you, followed you everywhere,' Chloe tells her. She waits for her eyes to light up.

Nan laughs. Chloe feels calm return to her. She wipes a little gravy from Nan's chin with a tissue.

'She did, didn't she? I used to call her my little shadow, do you remember that?'

'I do,' Chloe says, smiling.

She goes to give Nan more, but she shakes her head.

'You've done really well, almost all of that.' She shows her the near-empty plate. 'You must be getting better.'

Chloe goes to stand up and Nan grabs her arm, softly, but urgently.

'You've been ever so good to me, Chloe, not just today, but . . . before I came here, I mean.'

'Don't be silly, Nan.'

'I mean it. I don't know what I'd do without you.'

'Well, it's just us now, isn't it?'

'Yes,' Nan says. 'I suppose it is . . .'

Chloe doesn't know why this feels like goodbye. She thinks of that weekend bag on her bed. She remembers the words of the matron, reminding her that she's got to take this opportunity, that she can't put her life on hold. But Nan *is* her life. She turns away from her. She knows what she needs to do.

'Chloe?'

'Yes, Nan.'

'Did you ever find that little girl?'

She stops for a second, those incisive moments that cut through the fog still catching her by surprise.

'I'm not sure.'

'I've been thinking of those poor parents and, well, I know what it's like to lose a child. You will help them, won't you?' She reaches for Chloe's hand, and she stares at her, for a second, straight in the eye.

'I'll do everything I can, Nan.'

'Good,' she says, as Chloe removes one of the pillows propped behind her and helps her settle back down under the covers. 'Good.'

She's asleep again a few moments later, exhausted from the exertion of eating, but stronger somehow. Chloe lets her sleep, dropping a kiss on her forehead as she leaves.

'Bye, Nan,' she whispers. 'I promise I'll come and tell you when I've brought Angie home.'

As she leaves Park House, she's already dialling Maureen's number.

TWENTY-TWO

The kitchen table is set for three. Chloe hesitates before pulling out a chair. Instead she hovers, waiting for Patrick to take his place. He chooses the seat nearest the doorway into the hall. Maureen transfers a steaming casserole dish from the oven to the worktop.

'Sit yourself down, Chloe,' Maureen says, indicating which chair to pull out.

She does as Maureen suggests, wincing as it scrapes on the lino floor, wanting to make herself smaller, less noticeable. As a child, Chloe was convinced that if she made herself quiet enough, people wouldn't notice her still there, hanging around after tea, or after the credits on a film had rolled round.

It's her first night at the Kyles' Low Drove home and they've invited her to eat with them. The kitchen windows are steamed up, although they disguise nothing but blackness beyond. The room is filled with the thick meaty smell of beef and carrots, which makes her think of Nan, and it's only intensified when Maureen pulls the lid off and starts serving up on blue and white willow plates. Patrick sniffs at the plate she serves him.

'Smells good, Mo,' he says.

'Thought I'd do something special for Chloe's first night,' she says, smiling to herself as she ladles carrots and dumplings onto each plate.

She sets them down in turn at the table. Chloe feels the heat from her plate rise to meet her cheeks. She waits for Maureen to sit down before she picks up her knife and fork, but Patrick wastes no time and digs in.

'Don't wait for me, Chloe, you start eating,' Maureen says. 'I'm just going to butter some bread for Pat.'

He sticks up his thumb without looking up.

Chloe picks up their cutlery. It feels alien in her hands, heavier, not like Nan's old bone-handled set which had fit so well.

'Sorry, Chloe, can I just get to the . . .' Maureen asks.

Her chair is in the way of the fridge. 'Sorry,' she says, shuffling forward and bumping into the small table.

Patrick's forkful of food spills down his cardigan.

'Oh, sorry,' Chloe says, standing up to get him a tea towel and bumping the table again. Gravy splashes off his plate.

He looks up at her from under his curly fringe.

'Patrick, I—'

But Maureen is there with a cloth. 'It's no matter,' she says, wiping his front down like she would a child.

Chloe is conscious then of the empty chair at the table. The one with a short pile of magazines in front of it rather than a plate. Patrick looks up at her but doesn't say anything, then starts eating again while Maureen puts the butter back in the fridge.

'Chloe, while I'm here, I've cleared a shelf in here for you to put your things on,' she says, opening the door a little wider so Chloe can peer in.

'OK, thanks,' she says.

'I still feel uncomfortable about you making your own

meals,' she says, flipping the tea towel over her shoulder. 'Are you sure you won't eat with us?'

Patrick looks up, a piece of beef and dumpling suspended on his fork.

'No, no, of course not,' Chloe says. 'I can make myself something every evening.'

'Well, we've got cereal and toast for breakfast – all the essentials – so you don't need to bother getting any of that,' she adds, sitting down at the table. 'You can at least have your breakfast—'

'It's OK, honestly,' Chloe says.

Patrick sighs. 'Maureen, leave the girl alone. She's told you she'll sort herself out. Jesus Christ.'

'OK, Patrick, there's no need for language at the table . . . right.' Maureen picks up her fork. Her hands are smooth and her cutlery fits neatly into them.

The knife still sits heavy in Chloe's hand.

They eat in silence for a while, the tines of forks scratching against the willow on their plates. Patrick picks up the bread Maureen buttered for him and starts wiping at the blue and white pattern.

'You'll wipe that off,' Maureen says with a smile, and they all laugh politely.

Every so often Chloe looks up from her own plate, catching a glimpse of Maureen and Patrick eating beside her. Under the table, their knees are nearly touching. She hopes they can't tell that hers are shaking.

There are moments for Chloe when it feels completely natural. That if someone were passing this lonely lane, if they glimpsed into the kitchen and saw them all here, eating around this table, they'd look perfectly fine together. Just a regular family eating a regular dinner. Then there are other moments when Chloe's more aware of their cutlery scratching their plates, and then this tiny kitchen feels like a stage. The three of them actors who have forgotten their lines. It feels wrong in some ways, that she knows why she's here, that she has to keep her investigation at the forefront of her mind. She watches them as she eats, knowing all this will go in her pale blue notepad before she sleeps. She'd feel bad if she wasn't sure that one day they will thank her for it.

She points at the food with her fork. 'This is really nice,' she says. 'Thanks again, Maureen.'

She smiles and carries on eating. Chloe swallows, daring herself to go a little further, to throw some metaphorical bomb at the table. For something to happen. She doesn't just want to watch things happen, she needs to *feel* it.

'It reminds me of the food my nan used to make,' Chloe says.

Maureen stops chewing and looks at her across the table, tipping her head to one side, a smile more sympathetic this time.

'Was she a good age?' Maureen asks, as Chloe slips a forkful of food into her mouth. 'When she passed, I mean?'

Chloe nods as she chews, willing the food down so she can answer while she conjures up an age in her head.

'Ninety-six,' she says.

'Ninety-six! Goodness, she must have been quite old when she had your mum then? Or were your parents a lot older when they had you?'

There's a pause as Chloe stares back, trying frantically to do the maths in her head, wondering what she'd got so wrong. She feels Patrick stop eating and put down his fork. Under the table, she crosses her ankles, putting her left heel down hard on top of her right toes until they burn. The pain helps her to focus.

'Hmm-mmm,' she nods, looking back down at her plate. 'Yeah, quite old. I never knew my dad.'

That much is true.

Patrick looks up at her from the other side of the table. 'Where did you grow up, Chloe?' His tone isn't as friendly as Maureen's. Chloe feels the need to think before she speaks.

'In town,' she says, swallowing too quickly; the food hurts as it goes down. 'Peterborough. Various places. Nan lived in Dogsthorpe.'

'Oh, so did we,' Maureen says, nudging Patrick.

'Oh really?' Chloe says, thinking she manages to make it sound realistic.

'Yes, Chestnut Avenue. Do you know it?'

Chloe makes a point of looking up to the artex ceiling, furrowing her brow, and all the time inside she's congratulating herself at how she's making this appear, how she's pulled it back round. 'Er . . . I'm not sure . . .'

'Oh, you must do,' Maureen says. 'It's the big one, the one that crosses Central Avenue, with the shops.'

'Oh yes,' Chloe says, as if suddenly remembering. From the corner of her eye, she sees Patrick look back down at his plate. 'Of course I know it, Nan used to take me to church there when I was little.' She had *been* there, that wasn't a lie.

'Did she? Well I never . . . Patrick, did you hear that? Chloe only went to the same church.'

Patrick makes a sound from his chair.

'Did you know Father Cunningham? No, he's perhaps before your time, although . . . how old did you say you were, Chloe?'

'Twenty-nine.'

'That's it, of course,' Maureen says. She drifts back to her plate then, wiping a carrot round the willow pattern more times than is necessary. Chloe wonders if this is it. The moment they bring up Angie. Or is Chloe meant to ask? What is the etiquette? She thinks of the woman who had opened their front door to her in Chestnut Avenue just two weeks ago, her big gold hoop earrings. She pictures Maureen and Patrick handing over the keys to her and her snotty-nosed kids. How had she referred to Maureen? That was it, 'the old lady who used to live here.' Chloe looks across the table at her; she has a few frown lines on her face, no doubt carved from the worry of Angie's disappearance, but there aren't many crinkles around her eyes for a woman of her age. But then, what has she had to laugh about over these last twenty-five years?

Maureen continues eating, letting the opportunity to mention Angie slip by again. Chloe feels a desire then to pick at the scab. A detective would. Or at least they should.

'Nan was the only one there for me after Mum died,' she says.

There is silence at the table for a second. But then Maureen looks up, her brown eyes full of concern.

'You lost your mum as well?' She puts her fork down and covers her mouth. Patrick yawns from the other side of the table; he rubs his hands over his belly and pushes his chair back.

'I'm going to sit in front of the telly,' he says. He leaves his plate on the table. Maureen doesn't answer him; instead she puts a hand on Chloe's forearm. Her skin tingles in response.

'I was fifteen,' Chloe says, taking the last mouthful of her dinner.

Maureen's eyes are shining now, trained on nothing but Chloe. She's glad that Patrick has left the room, that she has Maureen all to herself. She feels as if she can relax a little.

Chloe points at her plate again, more confident now. 'That dinner really was lovely.'

'No mum, no dad, no other grandparents?' Maureen says slowly.

Chloe shakes her head.

'So you're all alone in the world, you poor love.'

Chloe feels her tap her arm and her blood pumps harder in response. She's reminded of visiting Nan when she had her fall – she blushes at the thought that that was only a week ago. She feels necessary.

'Oh, it's OK.' Chloe shrugs. The feeling is still there, right under her skin, but the problem is, it's addictive. 'I guess you get used to it. Loss, I mean.'

She holds her gaze this time and it's Maureen who looks away first. Chloe glances at Patrick's empty chair, feeling bolder somehow now he's left the room.

'Nan took me in after Mum died. I was fifteen then,

perhaps I was used to change. I was adopted, see. I've often thought about finding them but . . .'

She doesn't know why she says it. Perhaps to distance herself from the lie about Nan.

'You were adopted too?'

Chloe nods.

'How old were you then?'

'About four, something like that.'

'Do you remember anything of your birth parents?'

She shakes her head. 'I wish I did.'

She surprises herself then, how convincing she sounds. 'Sometimes there are moments – split seconds – when I think I remember something, when a memory comes back to me, but,' she sighs, 'it's all so foggy . . .'

Maureen has stopped eating. She sits at the table, her knife and fork suspended in the air.

'But can social services not tell you? Do they not have a record of your parents?'

It would make sense, and that makes Chloe panic. She feels rattled inside, though she stays calm. 'My social worker offered many times to get my file out of the archives, to show me all the paperwork but . . . well, there's no point in living in the past, is there? I'd rather focus on the present.'

She almost thinks she's gone too far now. She's strayed too much from the script, she knows that, but the temptation that fizzes inside makes her feel more alive than she has done in years. It always does.

Chloe dips her eyes back towards her plate. Maureen must understand from this tiny gesture that she doesn't want to talk anymore.

Maureen finishes off her food then puts down her cutlery and stands up. 'I'd better get this kitchen cleared up,' she says.

'I'll help—'

'No, don't you even think of it, Chloe. You go on into the living room with Patrick, make yourself comfy in front of the television. Knowing him, he'll have one of those CSI things on the telly, but we'll watch it together, the three of us. I only need a moment to clear up in here.'

TWENTY-THREE

Maureen is more than a moment, though. And Chloe sits stiffly on her hands on the sofa waiting for her. She's aware of clinking pots and pans in the kitchen even if Patrick is oblivious.

'Do you think I should go and help?' she asks.

'Hmm?' Patrick wafts away her suggestion. 'She's used to it, you sit yourself down.'

There's a detective series on the TV – just as Maureen had predicted. The fictional police chief is going over what they know so far about the case, what questions still need answering. Chloe imagines writing more of her own findings into her pale blue book later this evening: a description of the plates, the food, who sits where around the kitchen table, the way Patrick chews with his mouth open, the way Maureen fixes her hair – a nervous tic perhaps? How many detectives would want to be her right now? There have been moments, just odd split seconds, when she's felt that flicker of guilt, when Maureen filled her in on some detail about their life that she knew already. She had to remind herself there is a higher purpose to her being here, perhaps something that Maureen and Patrick might thank her for one day.

Across the other side of the living room, Patrick is absorbed in the TV drama, his feet up on the pouffe, his fingers tapping on the remote control every so often, utterly unaware of Chloe watching him. She remembers that cutting then, the one from when he was arrested. It's hard to imagine him now being bundled into a police car, kept in a dark, dank cell underneath the police station. She glances over her shoulder and wills Maureen to appear from the kitchen.

It's ten minutes before Maureen comes in, carrying a tray of three mugs of tea and a small plate of biscuits.

'Do you have to have the TV on that loud, Patrick?' Maureen says. 'I swear you need to get your hearing checked.'

'Huh?' he replies from his armchair.

Maureen looks at Chloe and rolls her eyes. She sits down beside her on the sofa. As she does, Chloe gets a whiff of her perfume, a sweet leafy scent.

'Are you sure you're full?' Maureen asks. 'You don't want anything more to eat?'

Patrick looks over quickly from the chair. 'You never bloody ask me that.'

'Nothing wrong with your hearing when I'm talking about food,' Maureen says, and the two women smile to each other.

It doesn't feel to Chloe like they're acting now. She imagines how they'd look to an outsider, dotted around the living room, lit by the lampshade hanging from the ceiling rose. Ordinary, that's how they must look. Chloe swallows down tea and feels a warm glow inside.

'That's a nice photograph,' she says, pointing over to the sideboard.

Maureen glances up slowly as she sips her tea and smiles. 'Angie,' she says.

Chloe's heart is thumping. 'Who's Angie?'

Immediately, she looks down into the milkiness of her tea, asking herself whether she made her question sound natural enough. But she's got to get them talking, isn't that why she's here?

'That's our little girl, isn't it, Pat?' Maureen says.

He looks up from the television at Maureen, and then at Angie. His face softens on cue.

'What's she up to now?' Chloe asks, this time going for a breezy tone. She hates herself for having to do it this way.

Maureen's eyes dip; she takes a moment to compose herself. When she looks up it's with an expression that appears mastered for moments like this.

'We don't know, love,' she says. 'She disappeared, when she was just a little girl.'

Maureen gets up and takes the framed photograph down from the sideboard, holding it in both hands. She smiles at it, wipes away an invisible layer of dust, then walks back and passes it to Chloe on the sofa.

'I'm so sorry,' Chloe says, taking the picture. That's not a lie. She holds the photograph in her hands and although she's looked at it – studied it – many, many times before, even on her old bedroom wall, this time it's different; the weight of the glass and frame in her hands, the specks of dust that cling to it, the volume turned up just that bit too loud on the TV, all of it adds to the picture, just like she knew it would.

'She's beautiful,' Chloe says. 'Do you have any more photographs?'

'Of Angie?'

Chloe swallows a little, then nods.

'Oh, hundreds.'

'Can I see them?' Chloe asks.

'You want to?'

'Of course.'

'Yes,' Maureen says. 'Yes, they're all here.'

Maureen keeps them in the same cupboard at the bottom of the sideboard where Nan keeps hers – like so many homes she's been in do. Maureen carries the albums over to the sofa, places them down one on top of the other on the seat cushion between them. Chloe picks up a brown leather-bound one first, starts flicking through the pages, cellophane and static sticking them together. Maureen points out Angie's baby photos as Chloe flicks slowly through: the ones of Angie lying naked on a sheepskin rug; sitting upright in the pram; holding up her cloth cat to the camera – the toy plumper then than the saggier version she'd come to know in the newspapers. Some of the photographs Chloe recognizes from the cuttings in the archive, not that she says anything. She can't, not yet. Not until she has something more solid. She's doing it for them really.

Chloe makes the mistake of saying, 'Look,' once or twice when she turns a page and finds a photograph she knows, but Maureen just smiles and says, 'Yes, Angie loved that little scooter,' or, 'Yes, that's Puss,' but of course Chloe already knew that.

Patrick looks across at them from the TV every now and then, although Chloe noticed a while ago – even if Maureen didn't – that he'd turned the volume up a couple of notches.

'Don't the police have any leads?' Chloe asks.

Maureen rolls her eyes, then shakes her head. 'Don't get me started on them.'

'Oh?' Chloe says. But she doesn't elaborate.

Maureen sits quietly for a moment, holding one particular photograph in her hand. It's a faded polaroid; in it, Angie stands next to a Christmas tree, her face covered in chocolate.

'What do they think happened to her?' Chloe asks.

Maureen puts the photo back in the album and fiddles with the cuffs of her jumper. 'They don't know, they . . . they say they'll never close the case completely, you know, without a . . . without . . .'

Chloe nods so she doesn't have to say it.

'But we don't know, do we, Pat?' Maureen says that last bit a little louder. 'I say, do we, Patrick?'

'Huh? What?' He springs round in his armchair, muting the television.

'Chloe was just asking what the police think might have happened to our Angie.'

He looks at Chloe, then back at the TV. 'If only we knew, eh, love . . .' he says quietly to Maureen.

He doesn't put the sound on again for a minute or two; instead he just stares at the screen, while Maureen picks up a couple of loose photographs and turns them over in her hand. Chloe decides not to ask too many questions tonight, reminding herself that there's plenty of time for that. She looks around the living room, still hardly believing this is her home now.

'Look, Pat, this one is from Hunstanton,' Maureen says. 'Our Angie loved it there, didn't she? Remember her on that carousel at the little fair they had at the end of the promenade?'

Patrick smiles to himself, then lifts the volume on the television again, the spirit of the room inflated once again by a happy memory. Chloe is always amazed how that happens.

Maureen hands the photograph to her. It's of Angie, aged around three, buried deep in the Hunstanton sand, only her head and her right hand poking out. She waves at the camera with her tiny fingers. Beside her sits Maureen, the pair of them giggling away. And behind them, on the sunbed, a shadow, a darker, more serious face, just out of focus.

'You're not cold are you, love?' Maureen says. 'You've got goosebumps.'

Chloe shakes her head quickly, while Maureen goes back to the picture.

'There's Patrick in his younger days,' Maureen says, her fingernail hovering over the face Chloe noticed behind them. She looks up at Patrick in his armchair – of course it's him. How strange that she hadn't recognized him, but the camera has a funny way of capturing people sometimes. Maureen holds her palm out and Chloe hands the photograph back to her, then she puts away the rest of the albums and goes into the kitchen for a packet of garibaldis she forgot she'd bought.

TWENTY-FOUR

Chloe opens her eyes, blinking in the blackness of the room. She can't sleep.

It's quiet, much quieter than Nan's. It's dark too. When she wakes in the middle of the night at Nan's, her bedroom is a dull orange colour, the light from the street lamp outside streaking through her curtains. But here, there are no street lights, she is surrounded by nothing but the whistle of the wind at her windows. On cue, the glass rattles slightly next to her bed. She pushes her covers back and dips her head behind the curtains, feeling the cold of the glass and a thin, freezing draught on her skin. Chloe searches the sky for the moon but tonight, there aren't even stars. Her breath soon fogs up the glass and she dips back under the curtains.

She checks the time on her watch. 1.21 a.m. It's only been two hours since she went to bed. Patrick had filled her and Maureen in on the show he was watching, so the three of them had sat in silence for the last hour of the evening to see the killer finally caught. Chloe had felt a small thrill when the mystery was solved, the idea of a resolution sitting far closer to the surface of her skin these days. Her attention had dipped in and out as she examined the room and the two people she sat beside. She'd filled two pages of her notebook before she fell asleep: Maureen has a habit of twiddling her feet at the ankles while she watches TV, and Patrick makes a groaning sound each time he gets up out of his chair. Every detail has to go into her book.

She'd come up to bed first, carrying her toothbrush, toothpaste and towel through to the bathroom like she was staying in a bed and breakfast rather than her new home. She still finds it hard to believe she's here. She can't say she feels she's deceiving the Kyles, not when her motivations are so genuine and her focus so fixed. How could she? She is here to help.

In the black of the night, she scans the room, only just making out the shapes of the furniture. Chloe knows it's going to take some getting used to; it usually does. It's not just the look of the place, it's the sounds too, or rather the lack of them. She'd got used to the noises Nan's house made after dark, the click and whoosh of the central heating, the slow tap of the radiator in her room that they never got round to bleeding. Here she has a whole other after-dark language to learn. And it's not just the noises, either. There are the smells in other people's homes, too. We forget each place has its individual notes. Ones we quickly become accustomed to; an infusion of dust and washing powder, perfume and aerosols, cleaning products, human skin. So far she's been struck by an old-fashioned potpourri smell about the Kyles' home, that and another bottom note, one she can't quite put a name to, some kind of earthy, damp scent. She casts her mind back and wonders how she would have once described Nan's house. Mothballs and old-lady perfume? There had been the cat then, too.

Suddenly light fills her room. Enough to define the shape of the wardrobe, the bed, a pile of her clothes on the floor. She scrambles up on the mattress, folding up her knees and wrapping her arms around them. A strip of light illuminates under the door. She sits on her pillow, holding her breath.

Outside on the landing, she hears the soft padding of footsteps. One or two floorboards creak underfoot. Perhaps Maureen or Patrick has got up to use the bathroom? But there's something different about the creak of the door that opens, as if the sound is contained in the wall beside her. And there's something else – it's not followed by the soft ping of the pulley light in the bathroom, the stir of the electric air vent. Just a dull click that could almost be coming from inside her own room.

She gets up, tiptoeing across the floorboards. She presses her ear up to the door. She tries desperately to still her breath or at least slow it down so she can listen, but instead the rush of her own blood pounds inside her ears. Her hand reaches for the brass doorknob; she turns it, feeling it click underneath her grasp. The latch breaks free of the frame, and Chloe opens the door slowly, peering out onto the landing. All is still, all is dark. The moon beams through the small window at the top of the stairs, falling on Christ on the wall inches from her own head. Each door is still closed. No light shines out from underneath the bathroom door.

Perhaps she had imagined it. Perhaps what she thought were footsteps was actually the soft tap-tapping of the radiators, of the copper expanding and contracting between the joists. There would be a simple explanation. Only she's about to return to the warmth of her sleepy duvet when she sees another slit of light. It is shining out from the room next to hers – the room Maureen told her is for storage. She stops still – something about the door is different. She realizes the shiny padlock has gone, and in the exact same second a shadow passes underneath the door. Someone is in there. Someone is in the padlocked room. And then, as quickly as that thought occurs, the light inside goes off. As if whoever it is knows she is watching.

Chloe stands once again in the darkness, the moon making her nightie shine whiter. She holds her breath, listens for another sound. But there is nothing. No one moving inside, no footsteps. All is absolutely still again.

Why would anyone be in there at this time of night?

She wraps her body around her own door frame as if it might offer something more solid. Now her mind really is racing. Her toes wriggle against the grain of the wood under her bare feet, a soft draught wraps itself around her ankles. She shivers.

She takes one step back into her room and closes the door, wincing as it clicks into place. Back in bed she peers out from under her duvet, once again unable to make out a thing in her room. She doesn't hear another sound, as if it had all been a dream.

TWENTY-FIVE

Chloe times her arrival at Park House for just after the staff have finished clearing away lunch.

'Hello, Chloe, we haven't seen you in a while,' says one of the care assistants as they buzz her in.

'Yeah, I know. Work.' She shrugs her shoulders and the woman nods like she understands.

'Sometimes it's hard to fit it all in, isn't it?' she says, throwing a tea towel casually over her arm. It's a generic line Chloe is sure she's used to rolling out here, but she nods as if it was meant especially for her.

'Is Nan around?' she asks.

'Yes, she's in her room, I think, but she usually has a nap after lunch.'

'Oh,' Chloe says.

'Pop along anyway, she wouldn't want to miss you.'

'Thanks, yeah,' Chloe replies. But she has no intention of waking Nan up.

Her door is closed when Chloe arrives at it. She doesn't knock. Instead she lingers for a while in the corridor, wasting a few moments looking at the watercolours of bland fields that line the walls, the same kind you'd see in any care home. What is so attractive about this one-size-fits-all approach? As if people find safety in keeping things the same. It's always been the opposite for her.

Chloe lets a few more minutes pass before she takes the circular corridor back round to the office.

'No luck?' the same carer says.

Chloe sighs. 'Never mind. Will you let her know I popped by?'

'Of course, no problem at all. Just sorry you had a wasted journey.'

Chloe heads out through the double doors. It's a sunny day. Spring is starting to coax daffodils to reveal their faces and birds flit here and there happily. Chloe takes the short path around the back of Park House into Ferry Meadows. She comforts herself with the fact that at least she has tried to see Nan today.

Nan had recovered quickly after her fall, and Miriam had assured Chloe on the phone that what she needed was more rest, not to be exhausted with visitors. At least that's how Chloe had interpreted it. Although, in truth, she only has one visitor, and that is her. But Chloe knows Nan finds it tiring to have someone sitting there, prodding at her with 2004 when she's far happier back in the fifties with Stella. She'll leave her there for another day – after all, she's not hurting anyone.

Chloe takes a familiar path. She knows both the curve and the camber by now. When she reaches the park she pushes through the short yellow metal gate and it whines a greeting back. She sits down on an empty bench, surprised to feel the cold through her coat. A mother watching her little boy on the slide looks over at her. From her bag Chloe pulls a Tupperware box; inside are two cheese sandwiches. She smiles as she remembers Maureen handing them to her this morning.

'Well, I was making them anyway for Patrick,' she'd said, excusing her fussing.

'I could get used to this,' Chloe said, and they'd laughed. She and Maureen had anyway. Patrick had taken his clingfilm-wrapped sandwiches from the worktop without saying a word. Maureen hadn't seemed to notice.

Chloe takes a bite of her sandwich – nothing tastes better than a sandwich made by someone else and Maureen has a particular way of spreading the mayonnaise on the top slice that makes it really perfect.

Chloe smiles to herself and the woman moves her child over to the swings.

The park is quieter than usual. Chloe has watched the toddlers playing in here while eating her lunch before. They race around with their wobbly gait, often falling onto their knees, their mums rushing to pick them up and wipe them down, sending them off again with a kiss in their ear. Chloe has pictured Maureen doing the same with Angie many times. She must miss having someone to make a fuss of. Perhaps that's why she's been making fewer and fewer excuses for fussing around Chloe. She's stopped pretending she'd made too much food by accident and now just serves up Chloe a plate of whatever they're having each night. Chloe and Maureen take their time at the small kitchen table, chatting about this and that. Patrick eats faster now, excusing himself to the television. Maureen notices less and less. Chloe helps her tidy up – she washes while Maureen dries – her small way of saying thanks. She likes to be extra particular about washing dishes, especially as it buys them more time together. Anyway, she knows Maureen enjoys the company, it must have been lonely for her with it just being the two of them all these years. She's often looked up from the soap suds and caught Maureen's eye in the glass that is made a mirror by the black night.

As she takes a bite of her sandwich, the child cries out from the swings, his fingers twisted in the cold metal.

Chloe finishes her sandwich and puts the Tupperware away. She pulls a packet of ready salted crisps from her lunch box – she'd only had to mention to Maureen once that she liked them – and opens the bag. She watches as the mother kisses her son's fat little fingers. Before Low Drove, Chloe would have felt lonely sitting here. She wonders if this mother knows what happened in this park all those years ago. People forget about Angie now. Perhaps they've never even heard of her. Or Maureen and Patrick. School teachers, neighbours, priests, public, people quoted in the newspaper articles Chloe's read – they cared once but then life moved on. Not for Maureen and Patrick. Not for Chloe. Not now.

She walks across the playground and puts the empty crisp packet in the bin. On the way back she sees the woman with the toddler watching her. Chloe checks her watch – it's almost three. She'll have a slow walk back to town and then it'll be time to get the bus home with all the other commuters.

Chloe arrives back to an empty house.

'Hello?' she calls. Then remembers Maureen telling her they always go supermarket shopping on a Thursday afternoon.

She's got used to their routines in the last week or so. Patrick has a part-time job at a local seed factory. He works on the production line there – just for pocket money, Maureen says. Some weeks he works days, others evenings. Chloe likes those shifts the best, the nights when she and Maureen get to eat alone at the little kitchen table and then chat in the living room until they hear his car pull up on the drive, his headlights illuminating the back garden. Then Maureen will get up and leave her sitting in the living room, and Chloe will listen as she dishes up Patrick's dinner and sits with him at the table while he eats. She goes up to her room then and from underneath her bed, buried way back behind a short pile of magazines and a pair of trainers, she'll pull out the shoe-box in which she keeps a selection of the original cuttings from her bedroom wall and, of course, her pale blue notebook. She'll write everything down in there. And when she looks at those cuttings, she barely recognizes the Maureen she sees in the pictures. She is sure some of those frown lines have been ironed out already, and she has wondered how much of that she could put that down to her own arrival.

She goes through the kitchen and out into the hall. The house feels still. She stands at the bottom of the stairs.

'Hello?' she calls again.

Nothing.

Maureen told Chloe that Patrick took early retirement from an engineering firm in the city before they moved out here, and coupled with the sale of their house and a decent pension, they have enough to live on. Renting this room gives them a little extra so they can afford treats, and when she'd told her Chloe had resisted the urge to look around their shabby kitchen and wonder what they might be. It's not a glamorous place, she knows it never will be. A little sign hangs on the wall beside the clock, in the kitchen. Another hope sign. This time it's an acronym: *H.O.P.E. Hold On Pain Ends.* She's seen Maureen straighten it once or twice as if each time she does might bring her closer to believing it.

Chloe goes upstairs to her room, familiar now with each floorboard that creaks on the landing. Out of the window at the top of the stairs, the flat Fens spread all the way back to the village and miles beyond the willow tree. She's learnt over the last week that wildlife is their neighbour out here. Just last night a barn owl flew right into the back garden and perched on the edge of the out-house roof. She and Maureen had got up and watched it from the patio doors. It sat there for at least ten minutes, blinking back at them with big black eyes.

'In the old house I used to find white feathers every now and then,' Maureen had said quietly, so as not to disturb the owl. 'Just out of nowhere, you know?'

Chloe had nodded.

'They say they're left by angels, but if that's so and it was Angie leaving them . . .'

Her sentence trailed off and Chloe had reached for her hand because that's what people do in films. She knew what Maureen was trying to say but Chloe found it hard to think that she really thought Angie might be dead. She'd never given that impression in the cuttings.

Maureen talks more about Angie now. It's as if Chloe being here has brought her daughter back to this new home. The dead flies are gone from this windowsill, and now there's a little photograph of Angie in a mother of pearl frame. As she reaches the top of the stairs, Chloe picks it up. It's one she never saw in the newspaper cuttings. She's aged around three or four. Her finger runs the length of her orange summer smock dress with mustard-yellow flowers, then across the child's smile. She puts it back and it falls face down. For a moment she thinks to leave it there, then walks back to return it to standing.

She looks out the window; from here she can see all the way up the lane to the willow tree. Maureen and Patrick will be back soon, their blue car will appear down this long straight road. The house feels different without them. Exposed, vulnerable even. Chloe looks towards the room next to her own, the one that is always kept locked, and that's when she notices – the padlock is missing again.

From the wall, the crucifix watches as she crosses the landing. Surely it would be a wasted opportunity if she didn't take a peep inside? It's not really snooping, not if you're investigating a disappearance. At least, if this were a police investigation, a chance like this would not be overlooked.

She glances over her shoulder, then tiptoes back to the top step to check down the road for Patrick's car. Nothing. She looks back at the door. Just a look, that's all she'll take, a peep inside then she'll close the door again. No one will know, and why would it matter anyway? It's just a room. A room that is usually locked. Locked from both doors.

She takes a step closer, then another. The floorboards creak underfoot. She stops, listens. Hears a sound downstairs, a click – she holds her breath – the back door?

No, it's just the fridge in the kitchen.

She takes another step, then another. The handle is

almost within reach. A second later her hand is on it. She takes it within her grasp, turns, feels the click of the lock releasing. She pushes the door, waits to feel it swing open.

Just a look, that's all.

But it doesn't budge. She pushes again, harder. Nothing. She turns the handle – perhaps it's stuck? It turns inside her palm, this way and that, but the door remains tightly shut. How can it be locked from the inside? She rattles it then, leans her shoulder into the wood, tries to push. The door resisting against the weight of her.

That's when she hears it, a sound from the road, the crack of pebbles under tyres.

Chloe lets go of the handle and rushes to the window in time to see Patrick's car pulling up on the driveway. She darts into her room and shuts the door behind her. Across the room her eyes fall on the connecting door through to the spare room – the identical padlock still in place. To lock the door to the landing from the inside, someone must have been in here. She scans her room – nothing looks out of place. But then a terrifying thought lands deep in the pit of her stomach. She is down on the floor in a second, searching underneath the bed among the dust and – there it is. Her archive. The panic stills inside her.

She sits back on her bed, hears the back door open, Maureen and Patrick's voices downstairs. She looks back at the wall that separates her from the room next door. She has to see inside.

It turns out Maureen and Patrick have brought fish and chips home tonight.

'We got you cod, I hope that's OK?' Maureen asks.

'Yes, thank you.'

'Didn't know if you liked mushy peas, though.'

Chloe guesses takeaways are the little treats they can now afford.

The three of them sit at the kitchen table, eating out of the chip paper. They eat in silence for a while. Maureen gets up every so often to butter bread for Patrick. He fills it with chips and folds it over in one hand.

Chloe can't stop thinking of the room upstairs. The room they've never mentioned. Who needs to padlock a door from the outside unless there's something in there you don't want someone else to see?

'You're a bit quiet tonight, Chloe,' Maureen says.

'I'm fine,' she says. 'Just a bit tired from work, you know?'

'What is it you do again?' Maureen says. 'I haven't asked you much about your job.'

She tries to think of something that sounds as boring as possible so as not to invite further questioning. For some reason Hollie's boyfriend, Phil, pops into her head.

'Insurance,' she says.

'Oh right,' Maureen replies. 'Pass the salt, will you, Pat?'

She's thought about asking them, of course she has. But they've already told her that the room is for storage. Why wouldn't she believe them? Would a detective believe them?

'Are you sure you're OK, Chloe?'

'Would you stop fussing, woman!' Patrick says between mouthfuls. 'She's said she's fine.'

SNerat ANNA WHARTON

'I'm only asking, Patrick.'

He sighs and gets up from the table, putting a plate underneath his wrapped fish and chips. He heads into the living room, then comes back for the ketchup. In the silence he squirts some onto his plate. He leaves again and a moment later, the last of the evening's news filters through into the kitchen.

'I was only asking,' Maureen says again, this time into her chip paper.

The two women eat for a while in silence. Chloe chews her food but there's a question she can't swallow. She looks to the open doorway, wanting to be sure Patrick isn't listening.

'There is something . . .' Chloe says.

'Yes?' Maureen looks up from her food.

Chloe hesitates. 'The room next to mine . . .'

Maureen's eyes flicker back to her plate.

'I just wondered why there is a padlock on it? I just wondered why it's always kept—'

'Patrick doesn't like me going in there,' she says in a whisper, looking quickly to the doorway. She is suddenly nervous in a way Chloe hasn't seen before.

'But why?' Chloe says. 'If it's just storage . . .'

Maureen picks up her plate from the table. 'It is storage, Chloe, but . . . it's best left, that's all.'

'But—'

Maureen scrapes the last of her food into the bin and puts her plate in the sink. She wipes her hands on a tea towel, then follows Patrick into the living room. Chloe hears her offering him a cup of tea, adopting a much lighter tone than a second before. Then nothing for a

198

while except for the sounds of the TV. There's been a big fire somewhere in Essex, two firefighters have been killed. Another is still missing.

Chloe makes an excuse to go to bed early that night. She yawns from the sofa to make it seem convincing, not that anyone protests.

After she's turned out the light in her room, she lies back in the darkness, the muffled sounds of the television creeping up through the house. She turns over on her pillow, once, twice, then sighs, switching on her bedside lamp. The duvet twists around her legs and she shakes it off. On the bedroom floor, she reaches for the box under her bed. It's pushed all the way to the back wall, and her hand fishes for it in the dust and darkness. Her fingertips find the cardboard sides of it and she pulls it out from under the bed. The box is black, or at least it once was. Now it is scuffed and scarred, having travelled with Chloe for years. Inside it is filled with envelopes, each one of them named. She pulls out the newest looking one. She sits back against the bed frame, the cool of the wooden floorboards under the back of her knees, her feet on the rug. She opens the envelope and empties it into her lap. She hasn't brought all the cuttings here, just a selection, in case she needs some reminders. The rest are back in her bedroom at Nan's. She knows she will need to go back for them, but when she thinks of Nan's house, she feels awkward and unsettled inside. She unfolds one photocopy after another, surprised how old photos that she had come to know so well now feel strange to her. She can't remember which cuttings she'd brought, and so each that she unfurls is a surprise, although none offer new clues, not even from this vantage point.

Raised voices filter through the floor. Chloe stops, the cutting in her hand. She can hear Patrick.

'Don't be ridiculous, woman . . .'

She shuffles closer to the floorboards, pressing her ear to a warm one where she had been sitting to get closer to their conversation. She holds her breath, the wood between them stealing much of what's being said in the living room, only tiny snippets floating up towards her.

Patrick continues: '. . . treating her like . . . turned up out of nowhere . . . know nothing about . . .'

And then Maureen interjects, her pitch higher, harder to decipher.

'Please, Patrick . . . know more than anybody . . .'

Patrick's voice cuts her off. Not that Chloe can hear what he says. Instead it's the way he says it, a coldness to his tone. She lies there, pinned to the floor. She waits for Maureen's response. But there is nothing, just fuzzy sound from the television. Her heart thuds against the floorboards. Should she go down? Has he hit her? Is that why she's suddenly silent? She listens closer for the sound of crying, but she can't pick up anything through the thickness of the oak between them. What had they been arguing about? She's read stories about this, women controlled by angry men, shocked into silence by the fear of them lashing out. Was this Maureen's life with Patrick? Is that how he appeared to her?

She finds a pen in her bag and writes down the date

along the side of the cutting she's holding: *Patrick angry. Maureen frightened into silence.*

A few minutes later she hears the click of the television going off in the living room, the soft pad of slippers mounting the stairs. She gathers the cuttings up quickly and pushes them back into their envelope. The one she'd written on is the last she puts away. She notices the headline then:

ANGIE'S FATHER IN SHOCK ARREST

She folds it up and gets back into bed. By the time she sees a pair of feet pause outside her door, she's already turned off the light.

TWENTY-SIX

There is a change in the atmosphere in the morning, she can tell before she's even reached the kitchen. Chloe lingers at the bottom of the stairs, listening out for Maureen and Patrick's voices, but there is only silence. From here her eyes settle on the front room, a room kept purely for storage at the moment and one she's never been in before. The door is still ajar, just as it was that first day Maureen showed her around. She can see through the gap in the door that it's filled with nothing more than boxes, each labelled with a different room in the house, but as she passes, she makes a note to take a look inside when she can.

She enters the kitchen, her flat heels clapping on the black and white lino.

'Morning, Chloe, love,' Maureen says, quieter than usual.

Patrick sits behind his newspaper at the kitchen table, his curly hair more unkempt this morning. He rakes his hand through it without looking up at Chloe. He is reading a story about the missing fireman Chloe had overheard on the news last night. He looks up and sees her watching him and turns the page of his paper.

Chloe goes about her usual routine, taking a bowl from the cupboard for her cereal, crossing the kitchen to take a spoon from the drawer. Its runners grate in the silence.

At the table, Chloe looks between Patrick's newspaper and Maureen, who stirs her tea slowly, looking down.

Outside, bare trees sway in front of a pale sky. Chloe spoons cereal into her mouth, watching Maureen when she gets up from her chair to cut Patrick's sandwiches slowly with a sharp knife. She wraps them in clingfilm and leaves them on the worktop. She steps back, returns to her chair. On cue – as if the pair of them have been choreographed – Patrick gets up and scoops his sandwiches from where she's left them. He hesitates then, as if, for a second, he forgets the steps. He goes to give Maureen a kiss as he usually would before he leaves for work, but she gets up and leaves the kitchen, his kiss hanging in the cool of the air she leaves behind. He glances at Chloe then and she quickly looks down into her bowl, then he leaves.

Maureen doesn't return to the kitchen until Chloe hears his car start.

What's gone on between them?

Chloe wonders whether she should ask about the argument she overheard last night. She eats her breakfast slowly while she considers how to put it. But Maureen is now setting up her sewing machine at the table, and Chloe feels the moment has passed. She watches Maureen as she gets ready, pulling a length of material from her sewing box that Chloe recognizes, although she can't say where from. Perhaps she's just seen Maureen working on it over the last few days.

She pretends to read the cereal packet, one eye on Maureen as she winds orange thread onto the bobbin. Chloe lifts her bowl to make more room for her. Maureen thanks her quietly.

Across the table, Maureen picks up the material and

breaks the silence between them by humming, winding the thread through the machine. Neither woman speaks, not even when Chloe gets up from the table and taps the contents of her bowl into the swing bin.

Chloe leaves the kitchen and goes upstairs to shower. She stands under the water, trying to piece together Maureen and Patrick's argument from the night before with the snippets she had heard. Whatever it was they had argued about had rolled into this new day.

She turns the water off and dries herself with a towel. Once she's put on her bathrobe, she opens the bathroom door to allow the steam to escape; it rushes out onto the landing, curling towards Maureen and Patrick's bedroom. Chloe watches it in the mirror on the bathroom cabinet. She stops still, listening carefully for any noise from downstairs, and hears the sound of the sewing machine going. She gently pulls the cabinet door open. Inside, the usual medical remedies are stowed away neatly: indigestion tablets and ibuprofen pain relief gel, spare tubes of toothpaste and extra toothbrushes, and four different bottles of prescription medicine, each with Maureen's name printed on them. One is out of date, the label faded, with only one or two tablets left inside the bottle, so Chloe puts that back on the shelf, but the other three were prescribed just ten days before Chloe arrived. She picks these up, one at a time. Diazepam she has heard of – isn't that some kind of sleeping pill? But the other two, sertraline and mirtazapine, she's not so sure about. Why would Maureen need all of these? Listening out again, the gentle hum of the machine gives her the cover she needs. She quickly returns to her room and grabs the pale blue notebook that she's not yet replaced in her black shoe-box. She hurries along the landing back to the bathroom and quickly scribbles down the name and dosage of each pill alongside her other notes. She's concentrating so hard on the spelling of each that she only realizes the sewing machine has stopped downstairs when she hears Maureen's footsteps on the tread of the stairs. Chloe quickly pushes the bottles back into the cupboard and shuts the door just in time to see the top of Maureen's head as she reaches the landing. She shoves her notebook inside her bathrobe, tucking it between her bare skin and her sleeved elbow, and desperately tries to rearrange her-self into someone who looks less guilty.

'You're having a slower morning today,' Maureen says as she appears on the landing. 'Ooh, those stairs, they don't get any easier, do they?'

'Oh, it's my boss, she's in a bit later this morning so I don't think anyone would mind if I . . . well, you know?' Now Chloe is aware of herself panting a little. As a dis-traction she grabs her pink hairbrush and starts pulling it through her hair, stumbling on a particularly stubborn knot. Maureen watches her from the landing and sees how she struggles. She steps forward.

'May I?' Maureen says. She holds out her hand, and Chloe hesitates for a second, knowing that just inches from her nose those bottles of pills may be standing in a haphazard fashion behind the small mirrored door – had she even remembered to put them back where she found them in her panic?

'Oh, yeah, sure,' Chloe says.

She hands the brush to Maureen, who steps into the

bathroom and takes her place between Chloe and the shower cubicle, still opaque with steam. Chloe pushes her hair back behind her shoulders as Maureen starts to tease the knot out of her hair silently.

She smiles as she brushes her hair slowly. 'I haven't done this in a long time,' Maureen says.

Chloe realizes she must be talking about Angie.

'No, I don't suppose you have,' she says.

Maureen holds Chloe's head so tenderly with her left hand while the right hand works on the knot. Chloe doesn't feel her head tug once.

'Wow, you've really got the touch, haven't you?' Chloe says as with each sweep of the brush more matted hair is released.

But Maureen doesn't stop once she's got the knot out; instead she starts to brush the rest of Chloe's hair, a look of deep concentration on her face. Chloe reaches for the sink to steady herself. In the clearing mirror, she watches Maureen's reflection. Does she really need all those tablets every day? Chloe isn't even sure what each one does, or what Maureen needs them to do.

Maureen stops brushing and sweeps her right hand down the length of Chloe's hair.

'Lovely,' Maureen says, 'almost black, just like . . .'

The two women meet each other's eyes in the mirror. Chloe sees the hint of a puzzle appear in Maureen's expression.

'Well, I'd better get to work,' Chloe says finally. She holds out her hand for the brush. It takes a second for Maureen to hand it to her.

'Yes, of course, there you go, love.'

Maureen leaves the bathroom and when Chloe hears her bedroom door close she crosses the landing to her own bedroom to dress.

Chloe catches the bus into town, sitting among her fellow commuters as she does every day. The only difference is that they're heading to jobs, whereas she's leaving hers until dusk. Because that's what her role is at the Kyles' house, it is a job of sorts. She has to keep reminding herself of that. As they drive towards the city, she envies these commuters their desks and when the bus slows for the roundabout beside the newspaper offices, Chloe looks up at the third floor and the safety of the archive. A place that had always seemed to yield answers, whereas now all she has is questions.

She can't face Park House today so decides to go to the library. It's warm and quiet there, the only other place in this city where she can sit peacefully among other people's stories.

She takes her phone from her pocket and sees that Claire Sanders has left another message for her. She doesn't need to listen to the voicemail to know what it is – talk of power of attorney and deeds and paperwork and a tangle of all the things Chloe tries hard to avoid. The bits of black and white that threaten to pin her down. In one previous message that Chloe made the mistake of listening to yesterday, Claire Sanders even mentioned how she'd called her office phone and someone had told her she'd left. Chloe's insides had twisted at the thought of the umbilical cord between her and the archive being cut so bluntly. Chloe curses herself again for ever giving

Claire her office number. But that was at the beginning when none of this could have been foreseen. Back then there hadn't been consequences, just the here and now, just what felt right on that particular day.

At the library, she heads straight for the research centre. It is housed inside a glass room in the middle of the main library floor and more often than not, it is empty. Just like the archive, Chloe knows, if people don't use it, they'll lose it. She's never understood why people enjoy novels more than real life. The research centre houses an archive of hundreds of digital newspapers, census records, old telephone directories. It seems a strange irony – even to Chloe – that she's more comfortable in fact than fiction.

She hangs her coat on the back of the chair and presses a key so the sleeping screen lights up. The research centre overlooks the children's reading corner, and while she waits for the program to load, she watches a mother with a little girl of about three or four. The girl toddles around, pulling books with colourful spines from the shelves and scattering them at her feet. Her red T-bar shoes march over their hard covers with little respect for the stories inside. Her mother has black hair – like Maureen – tied up in a messy bun and she tidies in her daughter's wake, trying her best to entice her over to some colourful cushions where they can read together.

Would Maureen have done this with Angie? Not that this particular library existed back then. Now the old red-brick library is a Chinese restaurant, although Chloe remembers it when it was fusty and full of books. She has a fuzzy memory of her own mother leaving her there once. A wall of books she can't see over is still enough to stoke that panic in her. A librarian had found her crying in fiction. She'd lifted her onto the counter and had let her stamp the return dates into the front of borrowed books. For those few hours of her childhood Chloe can honestly say she was truly happy. So happy that she cried sad tears when her mother returned, and, assuming they were tears of relief, the librarian tore strips off her mother. Strips that her mother then tore off her all the way home. Nothing was ever her fault, after all. It was always Chloe's. Her fault for being born.

Maureen wouldn't have been that kind of mother, she can tell from the way she fusses, the way she brings up a cup of tea for her in the morning while she's still in bed, how she's happy to mix Chloe's washing in with her own.

How different life might have been.

Back in the library, the mother has tempted her daughter onto her lap. They lie on two big red beanbags in the children's section, reading about a hungry caterpillar whose appetite was never sated despite how much he ate. Chloe knows that feeling, that hope that the next meal might be enough to turn her into a beautiful butterfly. The little girl kicks her red shoes off and her mother strokes her leg, as if the world was meant just for the two of them. Chloe had always had to share. Nan had Stella. Hollie had Phil. All the other people had someone, and when no one was left, then Chloe competed with memories of the ones that hung around to haunt them. She thinks of the cemetery, the flowers left week in, week out. She'd often wished she was loved with the same loyalty as a dead person.

She turns back to the screen and types in a particular date. She knows most of them by heart now, all the anniversaries that were revisited.

WE'RE STILL WAITING FOR ANGIE.

She reaches out and puts a hand up to the screen. She covers the last word in the headline and whispers her own name.

TWENTY-SEVEN

Chloe spends more than two hours reading over old cuttings in the library. All the ones she's read before, so they don't turn up anything new, but she likes to refamiliarize herself with the case. After all, she can't go over the facts too many times. Perhaps that's how some detectives get lazy. One of the more recent articles she found had a sidebar on police procedure in cases of potential child abduction and how the first forty-eight hours are the most crucial. It included some terrifying statistic that if an abductor intends to kill the child, most do it within the first five hours after capture. That thought alone makes a mockery of the reminders of hope Maureen has dotted around Elm House and Chloe's heart aches for her. She must redouble her efforts.

She opens an internet browser and types 'missing children investigation' into the search bar. A whole list of articles comes up and she devours each and every one in turn, writing notes in biro in her pale blue book as she goes. In one article from an American newspaper an expert from the National Center for Missing and Exploited Children talks about how important it is to interview people who live near to the site where the child disappeared. Not once, but over and over in the hope that extra – even tiny – details might resurface with every interview. She writes that down in her book. Then wonders who she might be able to talk to. Ferry Meadows is a park, there are no houses nearby. Even the ones that back onto it now wouldn't have been there twenty-five years ago. It's strange to think that Park House was probably the nearest building to the play park where Angie was last seen, but even that was just a building site then. She reads on carefully, scouring for interview techniques, the expert saying that it's not a case of asking witnesses if they noticed anything strange; even the seemingly normal, even a parked car, might be a significant detail. She writes that down too.

At lunchtime she walks to Central Park to eat her sandwiches. On a bench not too far from her own sits a homeless man watching the birds hop across the grass. Twenty-five years ago, Ferry Meadows might not have been surrounded by houses, but it could have been home to vagrants. She wonders if police interviewed any of them, or would they have gone as unnoticed then as they do now, slipping through the cracks of a society they don't choose or appear to fit into? She gets up and crosses the grass to him, offering the cheese and mayonnaise sandwich that Maureen had left out for her beside Patrick's. He takes it in both hands and thanks her. Chloe notices as he does the dirt that has accumulated under his fingernails, his messy beard and weather-beaten skin. She understands how he would prefer to drift from place to place. Not everyone needs to cast an anchor into one house, one home, one family.

She returns to the library and spends a couple more hours scanning through articles, but when she fails to fill her notebook with anything new, she knows it's time to go home. Only then she remembers the last thing she wanted to check. She flicks back a few pages in her book and types the name of the drugs she'd found in the bathroom cabinet into the search bar. She checks sertraline first and the results spring up. She clicks on the one at the top:

> . . . often used to treat depression, and sometimes panic attacks, obsessive compulsive disorder (OCD) and post-traumatic stress disorder (PTSD) . . .

She checks the next one. The same comes up:

> . . . depression, obsessive compulsive disorder, anxiety . . .

She double-checks diazepam and, as she suspected, among the answers is that it helps those with difficulty sleeping. Chloe can't imagine Maureen has slept easily these last twenty-five years.

She notes everything down, then packs her notebook away in her bag and heads back towards the bus station. She will arrive home early, but luckily she's already told Maureen her boss is away, so it won't raise too many eyebrows.

On the bus home she sends Hollie a message telling her she has an interview, knowing that it will please her to read that. Then she sinks back against the window and waits for the big sky of the Fens to open up as they leave the city.

*   *   *

Patrick beats her home from work; he and Maureen are working in the back garden when she walks down the drive.

'Hello, Chloe, love,' Maureen calls to her. 'Good day at work?'

Chloe gives her a generic response that seems to satisfy her, and Maureen turns back to supervising Patrick as he turns over earth and she bends to pick up the weeds he's churned up.

Chloe lets herself into the kitchen, pausing to get a glass of water to take up to her room. She plans to read through the notes she's taken today in the quiet of her room. Through the back door she watches Maureen and Patrick absorbed in their task. She walks into the hall, glancing into the front room and seeing the unopened boxes still stacked inside from their recent move. With so much to do inside the house, she's surprised they're working on the garden. Then, a thought occurs to her. She stops, looks back into the kitchen and down into the garden where Maureen and Patrick are still working. She puts her glass of water down by the high skirting on the parquet floor, and slowly pushes at the door to the front room.

The floorboards are exposed in here and dusty net curtains hang at the bay window. It is a dumping ground, just as Maureen had described, and along one of the walls, cardboard boxes balance on top of one another. Each is labelled with a different room, but the highest one, the lid of it sticking up, has a name on it: *Patrick*. Chloe pauses. From the garden she can hear Maureen giving Patrick instructions of where to dig and how deep.

She takes her bag off her shoulder and places it gently on the floor, then tiptoes over towards the box. Stacked on top of two other boxes, it's too high for her to look in without lifting it down. She reaches up and wraps her hands around the box; it's surprisingly light, so she lifts it down onto the floor. Carefully, she opens it, and peers in at what appears to be nothing more than paperwork and other odds and ends. But at the bottom there is a shoebox, not too dissimilar to the one underneath her bed. She pulls it out, and as she does so the paperwork collapses into the space it leaves. She sees an old CV, yellowing certificates and what look like school reports. Nothing that she thinks will be significant to this investigation. But this shoebox . . . Carefully, she lifts the lid and peers inside. There is white tissue paper, and nestled within it is a pair of child's T-bar school shoes. They are red, or once were, and scuffed at the toes. Chloe picks them up, and runs her hand along the soft leather, sliding her fingers inside and feeling indentations where each of Angie's tiny toes once sat. But why are they here, deep in a box marked *Patrick* and covered over with paperwork? Does Maureen even know he has them? She lifts them up, turns them around in the light. There's even still a little dried mud and a bit of sand on the sole. For some reason she thinks of the sandpit at the play park in Ferry Meadows.

Suddenly Chloe hears the back door open. Her heart starts thudding. She pushes the shoes back into the box as she hears Patrick cough in the kitchen, then footsteps, heading through the kitchen into the hall. She throws the shoebox back into the box, no time to cover it over with paperwork. She picks the whole thing up, quickly lifts it back into position on top of the other boxes. She's balancing it in place when Patrick appears at the front room door.

She turns to him, her hands still on the sides of the box. He stares at her, and then up to the box.

'Everything all right?' he says. He's holding the glass of water she left outside.

She follows his eyes then, up to the top of the box, the four sides of the lid still open.

She stares for a second into the blankness of the cardboard, her mind empty of excuses for why she's in the front room. Then she realizes that the black marker writing with his name on it isn't visible from this angle. She must have pushed it back on top the other way round. A small mercy.

'Oh, yeah,' she says. 'I . . . I just heard a noise and I think maybe this box . . .'

He glances from her to the box and back again.

'I think it might have tumbled onto the floor,' she says. 'Because when I looked inside . . . anyway, it's fine now.'

She taps the side of the box. Patrick's eyes narrow, just a little.

She picks up her bag from the floor, then goes to walk out, pausing beside him.

'Oh, thank you,' she says, taking the glass of water from his hand. And then, with a little bit more confidence, 'I don't know what would have made it fall down like that.'

'No,' Patrick says, quietly. 'Neither do I.'

He stands there after she takes the glass and walks out

of the room, but as she goes up the stairs – her heart still pounding – she sees him through the crack in the door, checking if anything has been disturbed inside.

When she comes downstairs later, the door is shut tight.

TWENTY-EIGHT

Chloe wakes on Saturday morning to sunshine burning through the curtains. Maureen had offered to line them with blackout material, but it had never felt necessary during the last dark mornings of winter. Now spring wakes her before her alarm.

She checks her watch and then picks up her phone. There is a text from Hollie: Hey, how are you? Sorry for late reply. We're off to Lanzarote this weekend so I've been packing. How did the interview go? Let me know you're ok xxx

She doesn't reply but instead lies back in the warmth of the sun that stretches across her pillow. She likes waking up in Low Drove, she loves to lie back in bed and hear the noises from downstairs drift up to her room: the clattering of crockery, the scraping of a chair leg. There's a safety in domestic sounds like these. The humdrum that other people take for granted.

She listens out for Patrick's voice, but instead it's the low buzz of the sewing machine that seeps up through the floorboards. She gets up, putting on the dressing gown and slippers she bought especially for Elm House.

Downstairs, Maureen is sitting at the kitchen table humming and sewing. She breaks her stitching to say good morning.

'Would you like me to get you some breakfast, love?' she asks, abandoning the floral material bunched in her hands.

'No, no, it's fine, thanks,' Chloe says. 'I'll get it.'

Though she likes Maureen to ask.

The gentle *whizz tap tap* of the machine resumes as she shakes cereal into her bowl. In the sink are two mugs and two plates still covered in toast crumbs. Next to them is an eggcup with *Angela* written on it, and a picture of a fairy. Chloe has never seen it before.

'Is Patrick working today?'

'Yes,' Maureen says, her eyes trained on the stitches. 'On the early shift this morning.'

Chloe nods as she pours milk on her cereal and sits down on a chair opposite Maureen, her eyes still trained on the egg-cup.

'I thought you might fancy eggs for a change?' Maureen says.

Had she noticed Chloe staring at it? She quickly looks down at her cereal.

Life had got back to normal in the last couple of days. Whatever Maureen and Patrick had rowed about had soon blown over and Patrick had never said anything about finding her in the front room, though the door had remained shut ever since.

Maureen looks up to see Chloe clutching her bowl to her chest. 'Set your bowl down, I can finish this after you've had your breakfast,' she says.

'It's no problem,' Chloe says. 'What are you making? It's nice material.'

Maureen smiles, pulling it out from the machine and biting off a loose thread. She flaps the fabric, the same orange pattern she's been working with on and off for the last week or so. She smooths out the cotton and Chloe can see that it's actually covered in mustard-yellow sunflowers.

'I'm glad you like it,' Maureen says, 'because it's for you.'

'For me?' Chloe drops her spoon into the bowl and puts it down on the table.

'Yes.' She holds it up then and Chloe sees that it's a sleeveless top with a white collar and three buttons in a V at the neck. The style you might describe as retro, but she is used to Maureen's taste, a little more old-fashioned. Maureen passes the top over to her.

'There are just the last few bits to do,' she says, 'but it won't take me a minute after you finish your breakfast.'

Chloe takes the top and holds it up against her chest, glancing down at it over her dressing gown. She runs her finger along the seam at the bottom; every last stitch is perfect.

'You really made this for me?' she says.

Maureen nods. 'Oh, it's just a little something. I had some material left over and . . . well, the pattern is a bit young for me now and, what with the warmer weather coming . . .'

Chloe remembers the notes she had made on the symptoms Maureen's drugs help to ease. She feels for her all over again.

'Nobody has ever made anything for me before,' Chloe says.

'Really?'

Chloe nods.

'Not even your nan?'

Chloe shakes her head.

'Well, there you go,' Maureen says, smiling.

'Thank you, I love it.'

She gets up from her seat and wraps Maureen in a hug. Maureen pats her arm gently. She steps back then, surprised by herself, by how naturally they had fitted together – she hadn't expected that. She looks down at the material in her hands.

'I'm so pleased you like it,' Maureen says as she gets up and finds some pots and pans to put away.

Chloe wants to show how much it means to her. 'Shall I try it on now?'

'Later,' Maureen says. 'Have your breakfast first. You can wear it tonight, let Patrick see you in it.' She takes it back gently. 'Anyway, I've got those last few bits to do.'

Chloe sits back down at the table. She picks up her bowl again and eats slowly while she watches Maureen's hands work fast, carefully, twisting the material this way and that under the needle. She lines up each sunflower until it is exactly so, taking great care over every stitch because she's making it for Chloe and she wants it to be just right.

'I can't believe you've done this for me,' Chloe says again.

Maureen smiles. 'The pleasure is all mine.'

After breakfast Chloe makes an excuse to walk up to the village shop on her own. Elm House sits in a black spot with patchy phone signal and she needs to make a call.

'I'm going to get a magazine,' she shouts up to Maureen who is in the bathroom. 'Do you need anything from the shop?'

She shouts a muffled 'no' from under the shower.

Chloe holds her phone inside her pocket as she walks, the willow at the top of the lane appearing in no time. She steps through the fronds as she has so many times now. Often it feels as if they mark a curtain between two worlds. She takes the phone out of her pocket and dials Park House. She's relieved when the answerphone picks up. She knows the routine well enough by now, when the overstretched and under-funded care staff are too busy to serve breakfast and answer the phone.

'Welcome to Park House,' the automated voice starts.

Chloe leaves a cheery yet brief message. She's missed a couple of calls from Park House recently but in every voicemail they'd said how they were sorry to call her during work, which had made Chloe feel better about not being able to get back to them straight away. They know she's busy. She looks back at the house, though of course it's not visible from here. In a way she is still working – because she still hasn't found Angie.

Back at the house, Maureen is washing up in the kitchen.

Chloe puts a celebrity magazine on the worktop between them.

'I thought you might like this,' she says.

Maureen glances back, her hands pushed deep in yellow gloves. 'Oh Angie, you . . .' Her voice trails off.

The two women look at each other quickly, realising the mistake. Soapsuds pop quietly in the sink between them.

'Chloe, I'm so sor—' Maureen starts.

'It's OK,' Chloe says quickly.

It is OK. Really it is.

Maureen looks down into the washing-up bowl and shakes her head as Chloe tries to busy herself rearranging the condiments on the table.

'It's not . . . I shouldn't . . . it's just sometimes these days I get confused,' Maureen says. 'It's just having you here, it reminds me . . . you understand, don't you?'

Chloe nods. She does understand.

'Patrick thinks I'm going mad, he says . . . he says . . .' She lifts a soapy glove from the bowl to waft away a thought. When she looks up at Chloe her eyes are teary.

Chloe swallows. 'It's actually quite warm outside, why don't we go for a walk? I haven't seen much of the area and, you know, with Patrick out all day, perhaps some fresh air would do you good?'

Maureen nods, pulling a tissue from her sleeve.

TWENTY-NINE

They walk along those straight Fen roads, the camber often pulling Chloe away from Maureen and into the verge. She picks up her pace to meet her back in the middle of road as Maureen points out the differences between the fields sown with sugar beet and those with barley. As they walk, Maureen paints a picture of the Fens in the summer, hares that box among the birds at dusk and dawn.

'You make it sound so beautiful out here,' Chloe says. 'When I arrived here it seemed so bleak.'

'Do you still think that now?'

'Not anymore.'

The two women's gaits fall in line and they walk on, silently.

'Now I think about it, maybe it was a bit bleak out here for me too before you arrived,' Maureen says, looking down at the tarmac. 'Patrick's noticed. I know it worries him.'

There's a beat before she answers. 'Why would it worry him?'

'After Angie, I was in a really bad way for a long time. I couldn't accept that she'd gone and Patrick, he was my rock. I don't know what I'd have done without him.'

Chloe knows she has prepared for moments like this, but she can't remember what to say for the thud of adrenalin in her veins. Instead she listens. This is the first time that Maureen has talked to her about Angie, about what happened – what *really* happened.

'Angie going, well, it took its toll on us, it was bound to.'

Chloe watches the tarmac, the dull grey of it allowing her to concentrate on every word that Maureen is saying. She's already filing it away for her notebook.

'I kept everything, kept her room, her toys, her books, her clothes, everything exactly how it was. Can you believe that?'

Chloe looks at her, but she's not waiting for an answer.

'But how long do you wait? How many years? I slept in her room, in her sheets until I realized that they didn't even smell of her anymore, they smelt of me, and I realized I'd have to wash them, but then I'd be washing her away, and that was all I had left . . .'

She stops on the road, and Chloe stops too. Maureen covers her face with her hands. There is no other life around them except for long fine grass that sways gently at the edge of the road. Maureen sniffs and walks on.

'Patrick was so worried about me. Sometimes he even said it: that I was clinging on to something – to someone – that wasn't there any longer. But she wasn't gone either, was she?'

Chloe shakes her head.

'That's the problem. We're stuck in this no-man's land, this place in between. We can't move on – you feel guilty for moving on – but then how could we carry on doing anything that we'd done before when everything was because of Angie? And the guilt . . . you feel guilty for laughing – smiling even. Imagine that, feeling guilty for putting a smile on your face.' Maureen shakes her head. 'It's no way to live. It's wicked. It's cruel, that's what it is. I wouldn't wish this not knowing on my worst enemy.'

Chloe wishes there was a script inside her coat. But instead it's Maureen who grabs her, tucking her arm inside her elbow. She pats the top of Chloe's hand and they walk on. Arm in arm. Like mother and daughter for all anyone else would see. But there is no one to bear witness, for the road is completely deserted.

'Listen to me,' Maureen says, 'going on like this to you. I'm sorry, Chloe, I shouldn't, I know I shouldn't, it's just . . .'

Chloe looks at her, she sees the way Maureen's eyes flicker across her face.

'What?' Chloe says. 'What is it?'

Maureen looks away, back down at the road. When she next speaks it's quieter, as if Maureen is daring herself to say the words.

'And then you turned up wanting that room. I remember when you said how old you were – twenty-nine, exactly the same age as Angie would have . . .'

Now it's Chloe's turn to look down at the tarmac. There's a lane turning right beside a disused signal box, where wild flowers run up to the road.

'Shall we go this way?' Chloe says, not because she wants to change the subject – far from it – but because she isn't sure how to respond. Or rather, she doesn't want her response to be too eager, too obvious. She almost feels exposed out here on these open fen roads.

Maureen nods.

The two women walk for a little while and as they do

Maureen points out snipe dipping their long beaks into the dykes that run alongside them, and lapwings pecking at fields sown with cereal. Chloe listens – half listens. She knows when she needs to nod, but she doesn't ask a single question about the flora and fauna because she so desperately wants Maureen to return to the same subject. She wants to hear her talk more about Angie.

'Do you have any other family?' Maureen says. 'I've probably asked you before.'

Chloe shakes her head. 'Just Nan,' she says.

'You have another grandmother still alive?'

Chloe looks back at her, then feels her cheeks sting with blood. She looks away. How had she slipped up like that?

'Oh, sorry. I forgot for a second, I . . .'

Maureen puts her hand on Chloe's.

'Don't worry,' she says. 'It's so easily done, isn't it? When you miss them so much, it feels like they're still here. I know for a long time after Angie . . . well, sometimes I even let myself pretend she was just at school. Anything to ease the pain, although I know some people thought I was mad.'

Chloe is grateful that her slip-up has brought them back to Angie. Now she just needs to keep her here.

'The day . . . the day Angie went . . . where were you?' Chloe asks.

'Me?' Maureen says.

Chloe nods.

'I was at home,' she says, 'in Chestnut Avenue, you know, our old house? Patrick had taken her out, to the park. He was with her when she . . . well, you know, when she disappeared.'

Chloe nods.

'He was a broken man, Chloe. Truly broken by it. The police could have done more too, Patrick knew it. But we were in their hands, we had to rely on them that they were doing all they could but . . . well, they called off the search that first night when it got dark, can you believe it?'

Maureen shakes her head as Chloe thinks back to those terrible hours when Nan was missing. Yes, she could believe it, especially back then.

'But Patrick, he had to be strong for me, see?' Maureen continues.

'Did you blame him? I mean, was it hard?'

'Never,' she says quickly.

Chloe looks at her sideways.

'What was the use? Especially when I saw how it had torn him in two. We had to stick together. That kind of thing happening, it tears most couples apart. We needed each other. I needed him.'

Chloe thinks of the cuttings she'd read about his arrest. She's surprised to hear Maureen criticising the police investigation – Patrick had praised them for look-ing at every line of inquiry so thoroughly. She hears his quotes again in her head.

'But if it broke Patrick too, why did he think you were hanging on to the past? Why didn't he want to hang on to things too?'

Maureen shrugs. 'People deal with grief in different ways,' she says. She looks up then, across the fields to the approaching crossroads. 'It's left back to the village, or right takes us all the way out on the Wisbech road,' she says.

Chloe indicates left with her eyes and intuitively Maureen follows her. The road is busier and they're forced to break off from one another to walk in single file as cars whizz by. Chloe watches Maureen from behind; the warmth of her still lingers, tucked in the curve of her elbow. Soon a grass verge curves up from the tarmac, a well-worn path within it. She thinks for a second of the carpet walkway to the archive at work and feels a longing for her old desk, the safety that office routine had offered. No wonder she still imitates it each day. She wonders how Alec is managing, whether the new computer systems have arrived, whether her beloved archive has lost its texture, whether it has turned yet from paper to metal to machine.

The two women walk in line on the single track. Chloe is grateful for a moment to think. She needs to keep Maureen talking while Patrick isn't around. It's obvious he doesn't understand Maureen like she does. She looks out at this flat landscape, the isolation, trees standing hundreds of yards from their neighbours. How lonely it must have felt for Maureen to have carried the weight of her grief alone all these years.

They walk for another half a mile or so back to the village. By the time they arrive at the house, cloud has stolen the sun and the air is cooler than it had been when they set off. They come in the back door, breaking the stillness of a kitchen they hadn't bothered to lock, and Maureen switches the heating on while they warm up beside the radiator.

'Chloe, love, stick the kettle on while I go upstairs to the loo,' she says.

Chloe does as she asks and listens to her footsteps disappear up the stairs. But five minutes go by, then ten, and she hears no footsteps returning back down. Their tea sits cooling, staining the rim of the mugs. Chloe walks to the bottom of the stairs in the hall. She listens out and hears a faint shuffling across the floorboards.

'Tea's ready,' she calls.

But there's no response. She puts her first foot on the step, waits. She takes another, then the next one, until she stands at the top of the stairs. She scans the landing. The padlock is missing from the spare room, the door slightly ajar. Inside, Chloe can just make out Maureen, moving around among cardboard boxes.

She steps onto the landing, walks slowly over to the door. How long has she waited to look inside? Maureen doesn't hear her enter. She is heaving and emptying boxes.

'Maureen?' Chloe asks quietly.

Maureen stands still in the middle of the room, her back to Chloe.

'Are you OK?' Chloe asks.

Maureen's head is bent forwards, her shoulders hunched. She's clutching something to her chest, and all around her toys from the seventies spill out of boxes: Sindy dolls, spinning tops, wooden bricks, Ladybird books and hard plastic baby dolls clothed in hand-knitted jackets. In the middle of the chaos, Maureen turns slowly on the spot, clutching what looks like a rag at first, squashed between her cheek and her neck. She buries her nose into it, taking a deep inhale. Chloe gasps as she realizes what it is, she recognizes it from the newspaper cuttings – Angie's cloth cat, Puss. Not that she says as much. But it's Maureen's response to her recognition that she notices, as if a tiny circuit board has been lit inside her. Chloe knows she could tell her why she recognizes these toys, that she *should* tell her. But she can't. Instead she watches as Maureen sobs into the soft cat, calling her missing daughter's name over and over again.

THIRTY

Maureen insists that everything in the room has to be put away before Patrick comes home. The tea sits abandoned downstairs, while the two women work together in the room that has been barred to Chloe these last three weeks of living here.

Maureen packs things hurriedly, but Chloe works more slowly, each toy sparking off a different memory, from newspaper cuttings or her own childhood – she and Angie were the same age, after all, and so, quite naturally, everything blurs into one. She picks up a Ladybird book – *Hansel and Gretel* – and flicks through its pages. She had the exact same one.

Beside her, Maureen searches for the box the cloth cat had been in. Chloe watches her push it back down among the other soft toys – a koala bear with real fur, a polar bear with black eyes and a sewn-on nose.

'Will you always keep these things?' Chloe asks.

Maureen pauses, bent over a box.

'I mean, if Patrick doesn't like you coming in here . . .' Chloe adds.

Maureen sinks down on a sealed box. She sighs and looks around at this museum of her missing daughter.

'In the old house we kept everything just the way it was,' Maureen says. 'We never changed a thing, even the sheets on her bed, like I told you. I had to keep everything the same, just in case.'

Chloe nods, remembering the gate at the old house and its peeling paint. She had probably brought the flakes of it in her coat pocket to Elm House. It was this same loyalty Chloe had come to admire in these two shattered parents.

'When we moved here, we had to take everything down,' Maureen continues. 'Patrick said it needed to be a new start in every sense. He knows I want to make her bedroom up again but he doesn't . . . well, he doesn't think it's good for me to live in the past. That's why he put that padlock on the door. I've got the key but he hopes it'll make me stop before I come in here, to think about him and his pain. That's why I sneak in at night while he's asleep. Sometimes just being among her things . . . it makes me feel closer to her, you know?'

Chloe nods, she knows a grave is not a marker for the one you love, not when they have already scored their name inside the skin and bones of you. How could Patrick deny his wife her grief? It's not like she's hurting anyone. It seems cruel, harsh, just because she grieves differently to him. But then, how does he grieve? Apart from the photographs in the newspapers, what grief has he ever shown Chloe inside Elm House?

'I've done these pieces in the newspaper every year,' Maureen says. 'Interviews, you know, because I wanted the world to keep talking about Angie. I don't want anyone to forget that she could be out there, that there's still a chance . . . so when would it be the right time to let go of all this? Surely if I did let go, I would be admitting that she's never coming back, and I'll never do that as long as I live. Never. That's what Patrick doesn't understand.'

Maureen's eyes fill with tears, the pain so obviously always sitting just beneath her skin.

'You know you can talk to me, Maureen – if you want to, I mean,' Chloe says. 'We can talk about Angie if Patrick won't.'

Maureen's face softens and Chloe feels sure that being granted permission to grieve so openly has ironed out some of the lines that the same pain created.

'Thank you, Chloe.'

Maureen reaches for a tendril of Chloe's hair, twisting it between finger and thumb. Chloe stands perfectly still.

'Angie's hair was so much like yours,' Maureen says. 'Almost jet black, just the same . . . I'm sure of it.' She whispers that last bit.

Chloe is silent, she dare not even exhale, as if this moment itself is made of fragile glass and even her breath might shatter it.

'I'm so afraid of forgetting the exact colour of her hair,' Maureen says. 'Forgetting anything would be a betrayal of my daughter. There have been times since you've arrived when I've just caught a glimpse of you, going out into the hall, or walking up the lane in the morning. Sometimes I've stood at the window at the top of these stairs and watched you. Does that sound ridiculous?'

Chloe shakes her head gently and her hair falls out of Maureen's grasp.

'But I've allowed myself to imagine, just for a moment, that you, with your dark hair, walking off up the lane towards the bus stop, are her . . . that you are Angie. I've let myself pretend that she's still here and she lives with us and it's her, not you, going to work every morning. You must think I'm mad.' Maureen closes her eyes and smiles. 'I know Patrick does. I made the mistake of telling him that once, I even said . . .' She pauses, and dips her gaze towards the floor. 'I even said . . .'

Chloe holds her breath. What?

A loud rapping on the front door shakes Maureen out of the moment. Her eyes dart around the room.

'Oh God, what if that's Patrick?' Maureen says.

'But why would he be knock—'

'Quick, get the last of this stuff away.'

Another rattle at the door.

'Quick.'

The two women hurry as they put the last of the toys back in the boxes. They throw them in, without the care they'd taken until now, pushing the cardboard sides down.

'Quickly,' Maureen says, panic staining her voice.

They step outside the room and Maureen shuts the door behind them, her hands shaking as she clicks the padlock back into place and slips the key inside her bra. She adjusts her hair and hurries down the stairs. Chloe is unsure whether to follow her. A mumbled voice meets Maureen in the kitchen, the sound of the back door closing shut as Chloe puts her first step on the top of the stairs. A woman's voice:

'. . . thought you might be in the garden . . . sunny out today . . . murder a cuppa . . .'

Chloe takes a few steps down the stairs and peers over the bannister. She can only see the back of a black coat on a chair, hear the scrape of the wooden legs on the kitchen lino as whoever has arrived sits down at the kitchen table. She sounds as if she's at home, whoever she is. Chloe listens but doesn't recognize the voice. But then, why should she? All the way out here she's never met any of Maureen and Patrick's friends and relatives. It probably would have been different if they'd still been in Chestnut Avenue, but out here, surrounded by all these fields, sometimes this house feels more like an island.

Downstairs the lightness has returned to Maureen's voice and Chloe hears her own name being mentioned.

'A lodger?' the stranger's voice asks. She sounds surprised, curious – shocked, even – which piques Chloe's own curiosity.

She decides then to recommence her descent down the stairs, trying as best she can to make her footsteps sound natural, not as if she's been eavesdropping.

'Here she is,' Maureen says.

The woman twists round from her seat with a smile that falls – just a little – when she sets eyes on Chloe.

'Chloe, this is my oldest friend, Josie,' Maureen says, introducing the pair. 'Josie, this is our new lodger.'

Chloe holds out her hand and Josie takes it tentatively. She's small and dumpy, with grey hair cut close to her head. Behind the years that she's grown into, Chloe can see that she was once a very beautiful woman. She wears a silk scarf around her neck and drops her gaze from Chloe to adjust it.

'How do you do?' Josie says.

'Nice to meet you,' Chloe replies.

Chloe crosses the kitchen to stand beside Maureen at the sink. This stranger's appearance at Elm House makes her feel more at home here herself, and she gleans some satisfaction from the way that Josie studies her and Maureen standing side by side. In the end it's Josie who looks away first.

As Maureen makes tea, she tells Josie how Chloe saw the advert in the newsagent's window. She fills the kettle and describes the first time she walked in the kitchen door. She drops a teabag into each mug and explains how easily she's settled in, as if she's always been here. As she adds the milk she raves about how nice it is to have someone to fuss over again, and Chloe smiles and blushes on cue, all the time knowing she is playing her part flawlessly.

But after a while, as the three women sip their tea, something about the way Josie watches her starts to unnerve Chloe. The way Josie's eyes flicker across her while Maureen continues chatting oblivious. In many ways Josie would be the perfect witness to interview. She wonders if Maureen and Josie would have been friends when Angie disappeared. If so, did detectives speak to her at the time? What might Josie have told them?

Maureen doesn't appear to have noticed that her friend has remained silent the whole time she has been talking.

'. . . and the most incredible thing is, how much does she remind you of our Angie?'

Josie had been about to sip from her mug, but it stops mid-air.

'I'm sorry?' Josie says.

'Chloe,' Maureen says, as she sits down beside her at the table. 'I was saying how much she reminds me of Angie, doesn't she you?'

Josie takes a slow sip of tea and over the top of the mug regards the two women in front of her. She shakes her head.

'No, Maureen,' she says, placing her cup back on the table. 'I can't say she does.'

Maureen looks up at her friend, and then at Chloe.

'Josie, but of course she does. Look at her hair, her pale skin, and she's even got this freckle on her neck – show her, Chloe. I saw it the very first night she moved in, not that I said anything but . . . Angie had one just like it. Josie, don't you see it?'

Chloe reaches up to her neck, her fingertip finding the freckle Maureen had never mentioned before.

Josie takes another sip of her tea without looking. 'I can't say I do, Mo.'

Maureen reaches up to fix her hair, and laughs a little.

'Oh Josie, you're making me feel like I'm going mad. Patrick's the same, he can't see it either.'

'Plenty of people have dark hair, Maur—'

'I know, I know, Josie, it's just . . .'

The two women look at Chloe and she dips her gaze down into her lap. Josie uses the silence as her opportunity.

'Angie was a little girl when she disappeared, Maureen,' she tells her friend. 'How can you say that Chloe reminds you of Angie when she's a grown woman?'

'Yes, but—'

'How old are you, Chloe? Thirty? Thirty-one?'

'Twenty-nine,' Chloe replies.

'The same age as Angie would have—' Maureen tries, but Josie talks over her.

'There you go, Mo, she said it herself – twenty-nine – how can she remind you of a little girl? She's a grown woman.'

'But if Angie hadn't—'

'Yes, but she did, Maureen.' Josie's voice is louder, as sharp as glass.

Silence. Maureen looks scolded.

'Now let's stop this talk and enjoy our tea,' Josie says. 'I'm sure Chloe has got things she needs to be getting on with rather than hanging around this kitchen with the likes of us.'

Josie looks at her, and Chloe looks at Maureen. Everything they'd shared that morning undone in front of her eyes. She doesn't know why but deep in her stomach, Chloe feels the ugliness start to stir. Maureen says nothing, just looks down at her hands wrapped round a warm mug of tea as if it were a lifebuoy in a particularly troubled stretch of water. Chloe looks between the two women. How many times have they sat across from one another over the years? How many years has this friendship endured? And has she always spoken to Maureen like this? Poor Maureen. She thinks of Patrick laying out the rules of her grief, and now Josie not allowing her a moment's fantasy. Perhaps it was Josie who had stirred sugar into sweet tea on the day that Angie disappeared. Couldn't she just allow her a little fancy now instead of shaming her for it? Why do people insist on being so tied to reality?

Maureen's chair scrapes the kitchen floor.

'How about a slice of cake?' Maureen says, trying to sound cheerful.

Is this how it's been for Maureen all these years? Both Patrick and Josie denying her an escape from real life, dragging her back to her heartbreak. She thinks of Park House, the residents there entitled to pick whatever year they want from their lives to revisit. They are living with a disease inside their brains, but is that really any different from the trauma Maureen lives with every single day? She thinks of that bathroom cabinet, and all the pills inside it that Maureen has to take just to get through the day. It's all right for Patrick, all right for Josie. How dare either of them judge how this mother grieves?

Chloe pushes her chair back abruptly, knocking the table a little as she does.

'Chloe?' Maureen says. 'Don't you want to stay for some cake?'

'No, I'll leave you two to it,' Chloe says, and she's sure she sees a smile curl at Josie's lips as she does. Maureen doesn't argue with her, and as Chloe leaves the kitchen and climbs the stairs, she hears the two women talking, returning once more to the safety zone of their usual chatter.

THIRTY-ONE

Chloe stays in her room for the rest of the afternoon while her signal comes and goes on her phone. She sends Hollie a text wishing her a good trip, and feels grateful to have a best friend like her and not Josie downstairs, one who doesn't ask too many questions. Through the gaps in the floorboards, their voices float up to Chloe's bedroom, not that she catches any of their discussion. She doesn't know why but something about Josie makes her feel nervous. She can't put her finger on it. Perhaps it was simply the way she looked at Chloe.

Josie's appearance at Elm House had momentarily made her forget all about the spare room. Does she feel any better for knowing what's in that room now? That it was Maureen moving around on the other side of the wall in the darkness? Her guilty secret to sit among her daughter's clothes and toys at night. No one could blame her for that. Except Patrick. Perhaps Josie thinks it's wrong, too. It makes perfect sense to Chloe, though. After all, she's blurred enough lines in her own life to stem disappointment, to ease the pain. Don't we all to some extent? Aren't we all just lying, even to ourselves, just to make life that bit more palatable? These are the little white lies that we tell every day to live with ourselves, and if we never tell anyone and they're not discovered, how can anyone say they're not true? If Maureen had kept her fantasy about watching Chloe to herself, then it would

241

have burrowed itself deeper under her skin, colluding with its keeper. But now she's told Patrick, she feels wrong – crazy even. But who's to say that he is right and Maureen is wrong? People, things, places, they're only as real as you make them.

At about four, she hears Patrick's car on the drive. She sits up and looks out of her window, watching him coming in through the back door. She listens out, holding her breath in her room, wondering what he thinks of Josie – perhaps he colludes with her to tell Maureen she's mad? Chloe reminds herself of her job here. She needs to see with her own eyes.

In the kitchen, Maureen and Josie are sitting at the table and Patrick is leaning against the worktop. No one says anything when Chloe walks in and starts making herself a drink, although she feels Patrick's eyes on her as she opens the cupboard above the kettle. Her hand reaches for the coffee before she decides she needs something that will keep her in the kitchen for longer – tea brews. She picks up a teabag and drops it into her cup. She fills the kettle up to the top because she knows then it will take longer to boil, gifting her more time watching the interaction between Maureen, Patrick and Josie.

She's surprised that Patrick doesn't sit down at the table with the two women. The seat next to Josie is free, but instead, he stands next to Chloe as she waits for the kettle to boil. From what she sees he is not particularly friendly towards Josie; if anything, he's quieter than usual. This piques her curiosity. Josie appears to be talking to both of them, telling them about someone they all know in Chestnut Avenue who has been ill. Maureen asks her questions but, Chloe notices, Patrick mostly keeps his eyes trained on his own shoes.

The kettle boils and clicks itself off.

'Would anyone else like anything? Patrick?' Chloe asks.

There's a split second before he answers, as if he's not really here in this room, as if he's somewhere else entirely.

'No, no thank you, Chloe.' Patrick has never been this polite; it's almost as if he's a different person now Josie is here, as if he's under scrutiny. But why?

Chloe watches Josie from under her fringe and she notices that since Patrick spoke Josie's eyes are now trained on him. Maureen carries on talking, oblivious. But Chloe sees it, the way Josie clutches her handbag a little tighter on her lap, the way she pulls her cardigan more tightly around herself, wrapping her arms across her body. Patrick's sudden appearance here has changed the atmosphere in the kitchen, thickening the air with tension.

Chloe pours the hot water over the teabag. As the tea brews, she turns her attention to Patrick. He's leaning against the worktop, his feet crossed at the ankles, and – Chloe now realizes – he has his own arms folded across his chest, mimicking Josie's body language at the table.

Maureen suddenly stands up, seemingly unaware of the change in the air.

'I shall have to start getting dinner ready soon,' Maureen says, crossing the kitchen.

And as Chloe goes to replace the milk in the fridge, she sees the way Josie watches Patrick. She looks away quickly and starts picking up her handbag.

'Yes, well, I should be getting on,' Josie says.

'Oh, really, Jo?' Maureen says, sounding disappointed. 'But Pat's only just got in, won't you stay for some tea?'

Josie's eyes again flicker to Patrick, but he's standing staring down at the floor. 'Oh, no thanks, Mo, not today. Why don't you come over to mine next week? We'll catch up with the girls?'

'OK,' Maureen says, 'that'll be nice. I've been so busy getting this place sorted I—'

'Don't worry, everyone understands. It takes a long time to get it how you want it, doesn't it? But it's all looking good. You'll get there.'

'Oh Josie, are you sure Pat can't run you back to town?'

Patrick looks at his wife quickly. Chloe notices how he doesn't offer the same.

'No, no, I'm perfectly fine on the bus,' Josie says. 'Well, goodbye, Mo. Goodbye, Chloe.'

The two women hug on the back door step, and it's only when Maureen follows her friend out and round to the drive that Patrick seems to grow inside his clothes somehow, standing taller. He takes his seat at the kitchen table, pushing Josie's cup into the middle of the tablecloth and unfolding his newspaper in the space it leaves.

Maureen comes back into the kitchen, fixing her hair.

'Right, what was I going to do tonight? That's right, I got some sausages out of the freezer.'

And with that, the kitchen at Elm House breathes easily again.

Back in her bedroom, her cup of tea beside her in bed, Chloe goes over Josie's visit. She can't remember ever seeing Josie's name mentioned in any of the cuttings. She curses herself again that she doesn't have her complete archive here in Low Drove. She could go to Nan's and collect it – the cuttings that are still in one piece – but then she pictures the place: the loneliness hanging behind curtains that she'd forgotten to draw in her haste to leave; the post piling up behind the front door, the curtain still hanging from the back of it, trailing on the carpet. Not so long ago that place had been a home, Chloe and Nan's home. Now it stands empty, neglected.

On the end of her bed is the top Maureen gave her this morning. Chloe pulls it towards her, tracing a finger along every stitch. The thought that Maureen made this for her warms her blood. She stands up and slips off her jumper, pulling the blouse on over her head. She stands in front of the mirror, twisting this way and that as the last of the evening's pink sky falls through the windows onto the mustard-yellow sunflowers.

She had a friend who had a blouse like this when she was little. Or was it her own? She has a vague memory of the colours – or is it the pattern? She can't place it. The day is muddling up everything in her head, but the blouse feels familiar and it fits perfectly. And it was made for her – just for her – and that is enough.

She sits back down on the bed in the blouse and fishes the pale blue notebook out from her small archive buried deep under the bed. Picking up a biro, she takes the lid off and opens the next blank page. She pauses, chewing the end of the pen, then flicks back a couple of dozen pages, filled with notes in various shades of blue and black ink. She knows she has so much to write in here today: there was the walk with Maureen, everything she

---

told her about the day Angie disappeared. There was the spare room and all its contents – a neat list of everything she saw in there should fill two pages alone. But instead, she returns to the blank page and writes, *Josie dislikes/ suspicious of Patrick. Why? Police tip-off? Look into this.* She circles that last bit, as if to highlight its importance.

Chloe closes the book. She doesn't really need to write everything down in her notes. For now, she sits back on her pillow, holding the material from her blouse between forefinger and thumb, and admiring every individual stitch. Every stitch that Maureen made, for no one else but her.

A few hours later, Chloe is sitting on her bed reading a magazine as she hears Patrick on the landing, then in the bathroom, the sound of the shower turning on and the boiler whirring into action. Afterwards, on his way downstairs, he gives her a knock when he passes by to let her know that dinner is ready. They have these routines now, the kind you find in normal homes. Or at least Chloe likes to think so.

Chloe waits until his footsteps have faded before she gets up from the bed and smooths the creases from her new blouse. She opens the bedroom door and the landing is cloudy with steam and mist from his body spray, a sweet musky scent lingering at the top of the stairwell. She stops there to admire her reflection once more in the glass window. She smooths out the white Peter Pan collar that Maureen so painstakingly sewed. Only that's when her eyes fall on the photograph on the windowsill and a frozen feeling crawls the length of her spine. It is the same picture she has passed by a thousand times, and yet how could she not have noticed this one thing? She picks it up. In it, Angie is standing in her back garden, long grass licking the back of her knees; she's laughing into the camera, her hair pulled into two bunches, and she's holding the same baby doll – Chloe now recognizes – from the spare room that very afternoon. But it's what Angie's wearing that takes the breath from her. Chloe looks down at the material on her own blouse – at every mustard sunflower – and then back at the picture. Exactly the same. She feels for her collar, to the starch white shape of it. She is wearing an exact replica. Even the buttons are identical.

She drops the photograph and it clatters against the windowsill.

'Chloe, love?' Maureen calls. 'Everything all right? Dinner's on the table.'

With shaking hands, Chloe stands the photograph upright again. She hears Maureen's footsteps heading down the hall.

'Chloe? Is everything OK?'

'Fine,' Chloe calls back, 'just coming.'

Maureen's footsteps disappear back into the kitchen.

In her room she looks down at her top. She moves in front of the mirror, and stares at her reflection. It is the same. The exact same. She takes her hands and makes two bunches from her almost black hair. She holds them at the side of her head and they hang loosely from her palms.

'Exactly the same,' she whispers. Under the blouse, her heart is racing.

Chloe drops her hair and it returns to her shoulders.

She pulls the top over her head and throws it onto her bed, exchanging it for the same jumper she has had on all day. Then, slowly, she descends the stairs for dinner.

It's quiet around the table. Patrick wipes bread around his plate and tells Maureen some story about his sick friend at the seed factory. Maureen asks more questions about the type of cancer he has and they count on their fingers how many friends they've known who've had the same.

Chloe eats slowly, like she always does, but this time the food on her fork gets tinier as she prepares every bite.

'You do like it, don't you, Chloe?' Maureen asks.

She nods, perhaps too enthusiastically, and Maureen's attention falls back to her own dinner.

She eats slowly, watching them. Had she imagined now that flicker of disappointment on Maureen's face when she came down for dinner wearing her jumper rather than her new blouse? Had she even remembered she'd asked Chloe to wear it tonight? She is waiting for Maureen to ask her about it, but the truth is, Chloe hasn't prepared an answer. Something like betrayal is beating in her blood, though she doesn't know why.

'And what did you do today, Chloe?' Patrick asks. 'Did you see any of your friends?'

Chloe looks to Maureen, who purses her lips as she chews, as if to remind her not to say anything about the spare room.

'I . . . er, no, just a quiet day, you know, tired from work.'

'And what is it you do again?' he says. He's finished his meal, his knife and fork in a neat line on his plate, but he makes no move to leave the table. In fact, he pushes his chair back towards the wall and crosses his legs, trailing his hands in his lap.

Chloe looks to Maureen again, but this time she seems more relaxed, her expression encouraging this sudden interest in her.

'Insurance,' Chloe says. Isn't that what she told them when she arrived? She's panicking now, she can feel it in every pore of her skin. Her hands are clammy. She pushes them under the table.

'Oh aye, which firm?'

Chloe tells him, quickly remembering the name of Phil's company.

'Oh, I have a mate who works there,' he says. 'Know him from school. John Bennett? Do you know him?'

Chloe shakes her head. Beneath the table, she presses her thumbnail into her palm. She's disappointed when she doesn't feel pain.

'No,' she says, looking up to the ceiling. 'I don't.'

Patrick waits a moment, then gets up from the table. He puts his plate in the sink. Chloe flinches a little when the knife and fork clatter to the bottom of it. What is it about his sudden interest in her that is making her so nervous?

'I'm surprised you haven't heard of him,' Patrick says, ''cos as far as I'm aware, he's still the managing director.'

Maureen looks up from her plate. Patrick stands behind her chair. Chloe twists her fingers together underneath the table, pinching the skin until it hurts. The kitchen burns with silence. There's a beat. Another.

'Oh, *that* John, yes, of course I know him . . . well, I

don't *know* him because I'm just, you know, in admin, but yes . . .' she nods.

Too fast?

She turns to look up to Patrick, nodding. 'Yes, I know John, of course, by reputation.' It's a thin line between making it seem convincing and overacting.

Patrick picks up his newspaper and walks out of the kitchen. Chloe turns back to Maureen and, as she does, she's sure she sees her shoulders relax.

THIRTY-TWO

Chloe sits beside Nan in the communal room at Park House. Between them are two cups of tea. Chloe's is empty and steam has long since finished curling out of Nan's. Chloe had reminded her several times that it was there, but it sits in the mug, the milk separating from the tea on the surface. An island breaks off and drifts away.

'Miserable day out,' Nan says.

She's said this at least a dozen times.

Chloe reaches over for her hand and squeezes it. She's all out of replies. She looks around the room, where each floral-patterned chair is filled with a grey-haired resident.

'All old folk here,' Nan mutters, cocking her head over at a group nearby.

A man and a woman sit on opposite sides of the room. Both of them staring outside at the trees and the park, the windows blurry with rainfall. Chloe hasn't seen them here before.

'Are they new here, Nan?'

'Hmm?'

'That man there and the lady sitting opposite him, I haven't seen them before.'

'Haven't seen them where?'

'Here, Nan.'

'Where are we?'

'Park House, Nan.'

'What about it?'

'That man and that lady?'

'Who?'

'Those two, there . . .'

'What about them?'

Chloe sighs. 'Doesn't matter.'

She stands up and picks up both mugs to put them back in the kitchen. One of the care assistants is washing up. Chloe throws the two mugs into the bowl.

It gets dark early that afternoon, the sun never having quite managed to cut through the thickest cloud that day. Chloe gets up from her chair just before three. Hollie is back from Lanzarote and they're meeting for coffee.

'I'll come again soon, Nan,' she says, kissing her good-bye.

She is about to leave Park House when Miriam calls her back.

'Chloe, did anyone give you the message from Claire Sanders?'

She tenses inside her coat.

'No?'

'She's been trying to reach you, apparently she's left lots of messages – she wondered if you'd changed your number, but it's the same one we have here, isn't it?' She peers her head into the office and runs her finger down a chart on the wall. Chloe had seen it once, a wall with every next of kin's emergency contact number. Her name fitting neatly among all the others.

'Ends in 248?'

'Yes, that's it, I haven't changed my number,' Chloe says, pulling her phone from her pocket, 'but there's not a great signal where I've been working, so maybe that's why her calls haven't been getting through?'

Miriam nods. 'How's it all going?'

Chloe shuffles her feet on the coarse matting in front of the door. She had been almost out of there when Miriam had called her back.

'Didn't you say that you had to go away for work?' Miriam says. 'I haven't seen you around as often.'

'Oh that, yes, it's going well.'

'Good,' Miriam says. 'I know your grandmother is really proud of you, well ... during her more lucid moments. How did she seem to you today?'

The automatic doors open and close as Chloe shifts on the carpet in front of them, stuck between Park House and the outside world.

'Yes, she seems good. I mean, forgetful but ...'

'Yes, well, you know that inside she knows you still. They say that even though people with dementia might not recognize you or remember your name, they still remember the love they feel for you and still feel the love you have for them.'

Chloe nods. The doors close behind her.

'Grace has been wandering again, she likes the bottom of the garden for some reason. I don't know what attracts her to the copse but the builders are moving into that area now so we're going to need to cordon it off somehow. Perhaps it's the lake she wants to get to. The staff walk out with them sometimes, but it's not the same as being able to go for a walk whenever you like, is it?'

Chloe shakes her head. She's going to be late for Hollie.

'You should take her sometime, she'd like that,' Miriam says. 'You don't have to always be stuck in here with all these old folk.'

'Oh yes, I will, I've just got to get off now.' She points to the doors which open on cue.

'Of course, I didn't mean now. Anyway, it'll be dark soon. I'll let you go, but see you soon, OK? Remember that your grandmother remembers you in here.' She pats her chest and Chloe feels the urge to roll her eyes because it's such a cliché, but of course she doesn't.

'And don't forget to give Claire a call. I think it's something to do with selling the house; she needs your signature on something.'

Chloe nods and walks out of Park House towards the bus stop. She takes her phone out of her pocket as she sits down on the bus, scrolling through dozens of missed calls, the voicemails stacking up. She deletes one after another and instantly feels better to see them disappear from her inbox.

The bus weaves its way through the streets back into the city. Chloe glances from the top deck down into living room windows illuminated one by one in varying shades of indoor afternoon glow. In some, children, still fresh from school, sit cross-legged on sofas and floors in their uniforms, the blue light of the television flickering across their faces. There would have been a time when Chloe resented them this, being the other side of the glass to her. But now she has Maureen's living room, and she knows that if someone peered into her back room – the brown swirl of the carpet, the teak sideboard, Chloe and

Maureen sitting beside each other on the sofa – it would look just as natural as these.

The bus slows to let passengers on. Chloe looks down the side of the window, at the tops of heads – the odd child trailing home late in their school blazer. Her phone buzzes inside her pocket. Hollie.

Where are you? We did say four, didn't we? xxx

Chloe taps out a reply, tells her she's on her way. She's concentrating, staring at her phone, so much so that she doesn't notice the woman who sits down in the seat opposite, though intuitively she moves her legs to make way for her shopping bags. It's only when the woman says her name that she looks up.

'Chloe?'

If Chloe's face looked blank for a second, she only wished she'd kept it that way. Because when she looks up, the recognition is immediately apparent. The mask slips. She feels it.

The old woman's hand flies to her mouth.

'I thought it was you.'

Chloe thinks fast, but it's far too late to strip the recognition from her face. It's much easier the other way round, to paint an expression on. Chloe knows that face opposite hers, of course she does. She would never forget the way her pink lipstick bleeds into the fine lines around her mouth, she can still remember all the gold rings adorning her fingers – the fascination she once faked in the stories behind every single one of them. The old woman's face crinkles with confusion. Chloe almost sees her brain scrambling to make sense of the situation.

'Chloe?' she asks again.

And this time she has more time to answer, even to put on an accent.

'Sorry?'

The wrinkles between the woman's eyes fold further into her face as her brow furrows, and then she says it, just as Chloe knew she would.

'Oh, I'm sorry, you just reminded me . . .'

But before she can finish her sentence, Chloe has rung the bell and the driver is slowing down. She runs down the stairs. Gets off the bus. She stands still at the bus stop. Her heart hammering against the inside of her coat.

It's only when the bus pulls away and she sees it indicate left at the end of the road that her breath escapes her.

She looks around, not recognising this residential street where she has been dropped off. She has no choice but to wait for the next bus, so she takes her phone from her pocket and, with shaking hands, texts Hollie to let her know she's going to be even later.

If truth be told, Hollie is the last person Chloe wants to see. And yet, she is the only person. As her best friend – as her only friend – Chloe knows she can see from her face something is wrong even as she approaches the table in the cafe. She is the one person who knows Chloe, *really* knows her, so well that she can't fake it.

Hollie pushes her chair back and stands up as Chloe approaches.

'What's happened?' Hollie asks.

It's not that Chloe isn't grateful for the concern written across her friend's face, but she knows what's coming next. What always comes next.

'Is it Nan?'

Chloe shakes her head.

'Well then, what? Chloe, you're shaking.'

'Just give me a second to sit down,' Chloe says.

The cafe is not long from closing, and around them staff wipe down the last plastic tablecloths and stack chairs on top of empty tables. Her friend has seen her like this before, of course she has – she's perhaps the only one – but Chloe needs to think, she needs to recompose herself. She can do this, she knows she can.

'Shall I order you a drink?' Hollie says, reaching for her arm across the table.

Chloe nods.

Hollie walks over to the counter and Chloe's head falls into her hands. She looks up a moment later, gazing outside of the cafe and its steamy windows, at people bustling by. She's looking again for that face in the crowd. She tells herself the woman has gone, that she's on a bus heading in the exact opposite direction from where they are now. She even knows where she is heading, which street, which house, she can even remember the colour of her curtains. But she needs to be absolutely sure, she can't relax. She's hot. She takes her coat off, then pulls it back up over her shoulders.

Hollie returns to the table with a milky tea. She can already smell the sugars her friend has put into it for her.

'Thought you might need something sweet,' Hollie says. 'They say it's good for shock.'

'Thanks.' Chloe picks up the cup and takes a sip. It's too hot, scalding her tongue, but she still drinks it.

Hollie doesn't say anything, not at first. Instead she

lets her friend recompose herself. But Chloe knows it's
coming, the interrogation.

'Who was it?' Hollie asks quietly and quickly.

Chloe's eyes flicker up to meet hers and quickly duck
away again.

'It was nothing,' she says, 'nobody.'

'Well, it obviously was—'

'Can you just leave it, Hollie?'

Hollie sighs.

She reaches out for Chloe's hand; they're still shaking
and she doesn't want her friend to realize. She flinches
away.

'You can't go on like this, Chloe, you know that, don't
you?'

Chloe says nothing.

'All these people . . . they're in the past now.'

'You don't understand,' Chloe says quickly but quietly.

'Chloe, you can't carry on living like this.'

'Look, it's fine. It was nothing today. It was just . . . it
was just . . . someone I thought I—'

Hollie lowers her voice: 'Was it anyone I knew?'

Chloe shakes her head quickly.

'Chloe, I know you don't mean to . . .'

Hollie is irritating her now, picking at a scab that is
already healing. She always does this. Why can't she leave
the past where it belongs? Her blood is burning now, hot
and red. She takes another sip of her tea and thinks of
Maureen. She would understand. But she can't even tell
Hollie that, and now she wants to cry because she feels
so alone, so misunderstood. She wants to be back at Elm
House, in the safety and sanctuary of Low Drove. She

knows now why the Kyles picked such an isolated spot. So no one can find them.

Hollie tries to take both of her hands across the table. Chloe shakes them free, pushing her chair back. She just wants to be back at the Kyles' house.

'I shouldn't have come,' Chloe says.

'Don't be like that.' Chloe sees that flicker of rejection on Hollie's face and feels better somehow, stronger. It reminds her of the same expression that woman had on the bus. Confusion, a hint of hurt sitting beneath it.

'Can we just talk about something else?' Chloe says.

'Of course,' Hollie replies, although she sounds less sure as she twists her thumbs inside her hands. 'It's just these people, they needn't be ghosts, they—'

That's it. Chloe gets up from the table. The cup clatters in its saucer, tipping over and spilling what was left onto the floor.

'Look at this mess you've made,' Chloe snaps at her friend.

Hollie is instantly wounded and a couple of people look round in the cafe. Why did it have to be like this? Why couldn't she have just left it like she asked?

'I just wanted to help,' Hollie says.

'Well, you're not helping, you never help, you just go on and on and on at me every time. But you don't under-stand what it's like. You think you do, but you don't know what you're talking about. I know what I'm doing. I know who I am.'

'Chloe.' She reaches for her friend, but Chloe is already pushing past the table. She knocks the one opposite as she goes; a chair that had been balancing on it clatters to the floor. She doesn't stop, not until she's out of the door, not until she reaches her bus stop, not until she's on the bus and she's leaving the orange lights of the city and she's heading out on the A47 into the blackness of the Fens, where she will be safe at last.

THIRTY-THREE

The moon shines brighter out here in this flat land. Chloe walks back towards Elm House under its glare. Tonight it feels like a lamp tilted directly at her, nature's own interrogation.

Maureen told her a Fenland folklore story about the moon a few nights ago, as they both stood out in the garden in their dressing gowns, hugging mugs of warm tea and staring up at the stars before bed.

'They say the moon couldn't believe how wicked humans are to each other,' Maureen had told her. 'So one night, she came down to earth in disguise to witness all the bad that humans can do to one another. She became stuck in the marshy bog and was caught by witches, who trapped her under a huge stone. When the moon disappeared from the sky, the Fens really were filled with ghouls and ghosts and, so the story goes, it was the locals who eventually found the moon and helped her return to the sky. That's why she shines brighter out here.'

Mostly the moon feels more like a guiding light leading Chloe home to Elm House. She feels bad about what happened with Hollie. But then why did she have to bring up all that old stuff? Why are people so determined to cling on to the past? And then she thinks of Maureen, who has no choice.

When Chloe sees the warm yellow glow of Elm House leaking out of the inky blackness, she puts the rest of the

ANNA WHARTON

day away somewhere. Nan is back in a box, along with the woman on the bus, even Hollie. They feel somehow like another lifetime. And in some way they are, once Chloe has walked back through that willow curtain.

Chloe steps through the back door and Maureen calls to her from the lounge. She pops her head around the door. Patrick sits in his chair, his feet up on the pouffe. He doesn't turn around.

'Good day at work, Chloe, love?' Maureen asks.

Chloe senses something in the air. She looks between Maureen and Patrick, his expression set, her smile that bit too wide. Somehow they appear further apart in here than usual, though they're sitting in the same seats they always do.

'Busy,' Chloe says, faking a yawn.

Maureen makes to get up, and Chloe notices Patrick looking over for a split second from his chair before he returns his gaze to the TV.

'Sit yourself down and I'll—' Maureen starts.

'No, it's OK,' Chloe says, putting her hand up before Maureen can offer to make tea. 'I think I'll go upstairs and have a shower.'

Patrick turns back to the TV and increases the volume.

'That's it,' Maureen says, 'scrub the day off.'

Upstairs, Chloe tiptoes across the landing, pausing to cock her head over the bannister. She can't hear voices, only the low hum of the evening news downstairs. The atmosphere feels the same as it did after Maureen and Patrick's fight. Every couple argues, she thinks, before looking again at the padlock on the spare room door. She knows so much more

262

now about how they live, though. How controlling Patrick is. At least, that's how she sees it.

In her room she strips off her clothes and wraps a bath sheet around her naked body. She closes her door and steps out onto the landing towards the bathroom, and finds herself pausing outside Maureen and Patrick's bedroom. Might more answers lie in there? She had always thought that it was the spare room that would hold the clues to Angie's disappearance. But wouldn't the real clues be found somewhere altogether more private? In any ordinary circumstance, she might feel bad for snooping around, but what if she found some clue that has been overlooked? What if her new eye on this story could actually help find Angie?

She looks behind her, backing up a few steps and leaning over the top of the stairs. She hears Maureen say something to Patrick about the programme they're watching, him grunt a reply, then Chloe looks back at their bedroom door. She tiptoes towards it, puts her palm on the handle, feels it turn and release before she can stop herself. Inside the bedroom, cool air hits her. One of the windows in the bay is open and deep salmon-pink curtains and nets billow at it, beckoning her inside. She obeys them and steps through the boundary, closing the door behind her. She stands there, her heart banging against the towel she holds in place with her hand. The room is painted white, but the pink of the curtains bleeds colour into the walls. Now she's in here, the curtains are still as if they'd never invited her in in the first place. She looks back at the door, wondering why she hadn't left it open. But then she'd only ever known this door closed, and it would raise suspicions if someone came upstairs and saw it ajar, she supposed. Anyway, she was in here now, it made sense to have a look.

Along one long wall facing the bed are fitted wardrobes, not too dissimilar to the ones in Nan's bedroom. The bed is made neatly with a frilly valance and a quilted eiderdown. There are two bedside tables that match the wardrobes, and on the side that she presumes is Maureen's there is a slim vase with a short fake white rose inside. Chloe thinks of the white rose etched into the front door at Chestnut Avenue – perhaps it had pained Maureen to leave it behind? Beside the rose is a box of tissues, and a pair of reading glasses, and beside that, a tiny charm. Chloe picks it up. It looks like a pendant, as if it should belong on a chain, but instead it rests here, next to Maureen's pillow. Etched into the metal is *St Anthony* and there is a picture of the saint cradling a child who Chloe presumes is Jesus. She turns the pendant over in her palm. On the back are three words: *Pray for us.* Chloe puts the pendant down exactly where she found it.

Patrick must sleep on the other side of the bed, nearest the window. Silently – and quickly – she crosses the room, around the bed, until she's standing in front of where he sleeps, feeling the cold of the wind at her bare shoulders. On his side of the bed there is a lamp, nothing else. She feels disappointed, as if this intrusion owed her a better insight. She opens the door to his bedside table: there's a nail file, a pair of reading glasses, an out-of-date slim green horse-racing diary. She closes the drawer quickly, flinching at the sound it makes. There must be more to him than this. She looks around, but there's nothing out of the ordinary that she can see. She goes to walk back around the bed and that's when she hears it, a footstep out on the landing, a sigh she knows as someone reaches the top step of the stairs – Patrick. She looks about her frantically. She's standing, clutching the towel around her, stuck between the bed and the window. If he comes in here now, that's where he'll find her. What would she say? She can't go out. Not now. She's trapped.

She throws herself down on the floor at his side of the bed just as the door starts to open. She rolls on her side, the towel coming undone, but more than half of her body disguised under the bed. She moves silently, shuffling an inch or so further under the bed. She lies on her back. Holding her breath, breathing with the very apex of each lung. There's less than an inch between the valance sheet and the floor. She sees his feet at the door. To her right, the towel trails out under the bed. If he walks around, he'll see it. But she can't risk moving a muscle. She holds her breath, her nose almost touching the underside of the mattress between the wooden slats. Patrick's feet start to move slowly round the bed. The valance sheet has caught on her bare shoulder, exposing it. She wriggles, only a little, and feels the sheet loosen, dropping towards the floor. She can't see his feet now, he must be at the very bottom of the bed. Then suddenly, she hears a faint sound from downstairs. Maureen calling him. Please say he hears it too.

'Yeah?' Patrick shouts downstairs to his wife.

Chloe's whole body tenses.

But there's no reply. He sighs, she hears a foot shuffle on the carpet, although she can't see it. Another sigh, this one longer. And then the creak of a floorboard as he walks out of the room, pulling the door shut behind him.

Chloe lets out a long breath. But she doesn't move, not until she hears him going down the stairs.

'What is it, Mo? I'd just gone to get my . . .'

What had she been thinking? Chloe knows she has to get out of the bedroom quickly. She shuffles back the way she came, only as she does, she sees what she disturbed when she launched herself underneath here. She can't tell how many there are, but there are dozens of them, more books than she's seen anywhere else in the house. But why would they keep them here under the bed?

She rolls out, dragging one with her. She rearranges the towel around herself and turns over the book so the cover is facing up. There's a black and white picture of some police tape on the front. It's a true crime book. Chloe picks up another, another, they're all the same: true crime, forensics, all real-life crime scene investigations – just like the programmes Patrick watches so obsessively.

Chloe stands up. She needs to get out of this room. She throws the two books in her hand back under the bed. The duvet cover is slightly askew where she has leant on the bed to get up and she quickly – frantically – tries to smooth it out, but she sees that her hands are shaking. She needs to get out of this room.

She opens the door to the landing. All is quiet. She takes three short steps and she's in the bathroom, she's closing the door, she's turning the shower on and she's leaning against the cubicle. Chloe steps under the water and its only then that her breathing returns to normal. She turns the dial hotter until her feet are pink and the air is thick with steam. She breathes deeply until she feels her pulse start to steady. She imagines the steam sterilising her from the inside, right down to the very core. She stands under the shower until the hot steam permeates her lungs, until she feels new again. She steps out and opens the window, and her day hurries away into the night.

She dries quickly with a rough towel, agitating her skin until it stings. She has been in the Kyles' home for almost five weeks now. The smells of the place have embedded themselves in her clothes; the scent of Maureen's washing powder is tucked in every cotton weave of her shirt and knitted into her jumpers. She sniffs at her hair. She has her own shampoo but recently she's preferred to use Maureen's. Two months ago she wouldn't even have known the toothpaste brand she uses, now they squeeze from the same tube. But who knows how long this will last? How much longer she can carry on paying rent here without a job? How much longer she can get a bus into town every day for a desk that doesn't exist? She pushes it to the back of her mind. She thinks instead of the true crime books she'd found under Patrick's bed. Her work in Elm House is far from done.

Who knows how long it is until she hears footsteps climbing the stairs. They stop outside her door and Chloe puts her magazine down. There's a knock and then the soft turn of her door handle. Maureen's head appears around the frame. Chloe sinks against her pillow.

'I baked today,' Maureen says. 'Banana loaf. I thought you might like some?'

'Oh thanks,' Chloe says. She shuffles up towards her pillow, still under her duvet.

'You're not cold, are you, Chloe?' Maureen crosses the room to check the radiator and as she does Chloe glances at the floor beside her bed, checking that her pale blue notebook hasn't been left open.

'No, no, I'm fine. Just wanted to relax, you know?'

Maureen nods, unconvinced. She hands Chloe the small plate she's brought up with a slice of cake on it. Chloe takes it, then hesitates for a second. Chloe hasn't seen this plate before. It has a pattern on it that she knows – tiny brown rabbits chase each other around the edge of the plate. She looks up to see Maureen watching her.

'I just had some bananas that were past their best and . . .' Maureen says, sitting at the bottom of Chloe's bed. She waits for her to take a bite.

Chloe picks up the slice of cake. As she does the image in the centre of the plate reveals itself: it's a river scene, bunnies in red and blue cardigans bathing in the water and lazing on the riverbank. Chloe knows it so well and yet can't quite remember . . . Maureen is still watching her. She takes a bite.

'It's lovely,' Chloe says. 'The cake, I mean.'

'Banana loaf was Angie's favourite,' Maureen says, smoothing out the cover of the duvet as she does.

Then it comes to her. Bunnykins. That's the design on the plate. She sees Maureen note her moment of recognition.

'Banana loaf is my favourite too,' Chloe says.

Maureen glows beside her dim bedside light. Chloe

takes another bite and this time the cake tastes even sweeter.

'Really? Is it really?'

Chloe nods. 'It's been years since I've had it,' she says between mouthfuls. 'In fact, I think the last time was when I was a little girl.'

'Really?' Maureen says. She goes to speak again, but seems unsure about how her words are going to sound. She rearranges her legs, crossing them over, and leaning one hand on the bed as she does. 'Chloe, I . . . well, I hope you don't mind me asking but . . . do you remember anything about your mum. Your real mum, I mean?'

Chloe stops chewing.

'My mum?'

'You said you were adopted and . . . I just wondered whether you have any memories of life before, you know, before . . . I mean you said you weren't curious about your background, but why?'

Chloe remembers and swallows a chunk of cake too quickly. She coughs and Maureen leans towards her. Chloe's eyes are watery again when she looks up. She has to think fast, distract her. She's not prepared for this.

'Like I said, they offered to tell me, but maybe I'm afraid, afraid of finding out that my real parents were bad people,' Chloe says.

'But why would they be? They might be good people, they might be . . .' Maureen stops and looks down at the sheet.

'I guess after Mum and Nan . . . it would have felt like a betrayal, as if they weren't good enough. It's hard to explain.'

Maureen nods her head, but Chloe can see that she doesn't understand. Why would she? This woman who hasn't stopped searching for her own lost family for decades. Maureen stands up from the bed then, straightening the legs of her trousers as she does and then her hair. She takes two steps towards the door, then pauses as if there's something she wants to say.

'I'll leave you in peace.'

Her footsteps down the stairs are filled with more purpose.

Chloe finishes the cake slowly and leans back on her pillow. She hears Maureen's voice floating up through the floorboards, not the words, just the tone – a persuasive, urgent quality to it. There's no reply from Patrick, just the sound of the TV turned up a notch or two.

THIRTY-FOUR

Chloe is in bed in Low Drove when her mobile rings, a rare moment when the signal is strong. It's one of the carers from Park House. Chloe lowers her voice to a whisper to speak to her and keeps an eye on her bedroom door. The carer is calling to see if Chloe has any special plans for Sunday. It takes Chloe a moment to register what she is talking about, then she sits up quickly and slaps her hand to her head. It's Nan's birthday tomorrow. What with everything that has been happening recently, Chloe has forgotten.

'No, I, er . . . just the usual really,' Chloe tells her, biting down hard on her lip.

The carer says they can bake a cake and Chloe promises she'll be there in the morning.

'We'll have your grandma ready,' she says.

As Chloe hangs up she thinks, ready for what? She doesn't like this panicky feeling. Her legs tangle in the duvet as she tries to get up. She starts making her bed. It almost feels as if the carer rang just to catch her out. Suddenly, she stops still. There it is again. Through the bedroom floor, the clatter of pans drifts up. And again. Then raised voices.

Chloe tiptoes quickly to the bedroom door. She opens it expertly, without a sound – something she has practised here – and she leans her head against the cool door frame. There's another clatter, more raised voices. Maureen and

Patrick. From the sounds she pictures them: Maureen cleaning up after breakfast, Patrick sitting at the table – a rattle of his newspaper confirms it. Then a fist goes down on the kitchen table.

'Oh Maureen, this is ridiculous, will you get a hold of yourself?'

'Why? Why is it so ridiculous? What if I'm right?'

'But you're not, you're . . . you're . . .'

'I'm what, Patrick? Say it?'

'OK then, you're crazy, that's what you are.' She hears the scrape of a chair on the lino. 'You're sick. Sick in the head. I mean, to even think . . .'

Chloe hears footsteps in the hall. She quickly pushes the door closed, the thickness of it muffling the rest of the argument. She gets down on her floor, pressing her ear to the boards, but it's no clearer. Then the thud of feet on the stairs starts reverberating under her head. She jumps up, stares at the door as if someone might just burst right through it. But it's Maureen and Patrick's bedroom door across the landing that slams shut. Then everything is still. Except Chloe's mind – that's whirring. What has she just overheard?

Chloe waits a moment or two and then opens her door again. Everything outside on the landing is still, but a residue of something hangs in the air. The photograph of Angie sits on the windowsill, offering no answers. Chloe looks across at the closed bedroom door opposite. Who is in there? Maureen or Patrick? Should she knock? She clutches the neck of her pyjamas and feels the bristle of carpet under her bare feet as she steps onto the landing. She takes the stairs, carefully, silently, egged on by nothing more than curiosity. She's almost at the bottom of the steps when she has a change in tact – she can't make it look like she's been eavesdropping. She coughs, landing with heavy footsteps. In the kitchen, it's Patrick she finds, not Maureen. His elbows are resting on his folded newspaper, his head is in his hands. He reminds her in that moment of the man she first knew in the newspaper cuttings – he looks fragile, close to breaking.

Patrick turns his head a little, looking up at her through his elbows. Chloe is motionless, waiting for him to speak, but he says nothing, just turns back, shaking his head a little as he does, and sighing loudly.

Should she ask what has gone on between them? No, of course not.

Patrick gets up then. He turns, as if to say something, then changes his mind. Instead he snatches his newspaper from the table and grabs a bunch of keys from the hook by the back door as he leaves. A moment later, Chloe hears his car engine on the driveway. She stands in the cold hall until the chug of his exhaust heads away from the house.

For a second all is still, then above her she hears the creak of Maureen's bedroom door.

'He's gone,' Chloe calls up to her. 'I just saw him go.'

Maureen creeps down the stairs.

'It's OK,' Chloe reassures her.

In the kitchen, Maureen stares at Patrick's chair. She fixes her hair, weaving a stray tendril back into her loose bun. But Chloe sees her hands are shaking, and she looks like she's been crying.

'Can I get you anything for breakfast, love?' Maureen says. Her voice unsure, wavering.

'What happened, Maureen?' Chloe asks.

'Don't mind Patrick, he'll be off to the bookie's.'

Chloe sits down at the table while Maureen puts bread in the toaster, obviously more out of habit than hunger. Maureen leans on the sink, bending at the elbows to look up at the sky.

'Looks like another grey day,' she says. 'It's beautiful out here in the summer but in winter you just want to stay home. You'll still be here in the summer, won't you, Chloe?'

That was the moment, just that short sentence, those ten words. Why would Maureen ask that? What makes her think she wouldn't be? Had that argument been something to do with her? Is that why Maureen is asking? But before she has time to question it, Maureen continues:

'I was hoping to get some gardening done today, but if it rains, I shan't be getting out there.'

Chloe doesn't say anything as Maureen passes by, in turn taking the butter from the fridge, putting jam on the table, side plates, two knives.

'Oops, forgetting myself,' Maureen laughs, scooping up one of the side plates she'd put down and replacing it with the same Bunnykins one. She pushes it towards Chloe.

The bread pops out of the toaster. Maureen puts it on a plate and carries it over to the table. She sits down opposite Chloe and offers her a slice of toast for her Bunnykins plate. Chloe takes one slowly. Maureen starts buttering her piece, then rolls her eyes, getting up again to go to the cutlery drawer. She rummages inside it, all the way to the back this time, then returns with a knife – a smaller knife – and places it in front of Chloe.

'Can't bear it with margarine,' Maureen says. 'It's got to be butter, don't you think?'

The knife she has handed Chloe has a plastic handle and a blunt curved blade. The handle is a pale cream and on it is a bunny that matches the ones leaping around on her plate.

'I don't even like these butter blends,' Maureen says, 'They call them things like I Can't Believe It's Not Butter. Well, it isn't, so I sure can believe it.'

She laughs to herself and Chloe manages a faint smile in return. This Bunnykins knife, with its faded pattern, feels too small in her hands. Chloe dips it in the butter and smooths it over the toast, on the bunny plate, with the bunny knife, while Maureen hums to herself as if desperate to fill the silence.

Chloe reaches out for Maureen's arm, touch seeming the best way to penetrate this facade.

'You know you can talk to me, don't you, Maureen? I mean, if anything's happened . . .'

Maureen's chewing slows, but she doesn't answer. Chloe continues:

'I heard . . . when I was upstairs in my . . .' Chloe says, swallowing a piece of toast. 'I heard you and Patrick arguing.'

Maureen doesn't answer her.

'I heard what he said to you,' Chloe continues, 'that you're crazy.'

Maureen stops chewing.

Chloe carries on talking: 'You know that's not right,

don't you? That no one should talk to you like that . . .'

Maureen struggles slightly to swallow her toast. Her voice is husky when she speaks.

'Maybe he's right,' Maureen says, dropping the slice in her hand to her plate. 'I have been having some strange thoughts lately.'

Chloe shakes her head quickly.

'You're not crazy, Maureen. If anything, Patrick is the one who won't face reality. He's the one who isn't at peace with the past.'

Maureen pulls at the cuff of her sleeve, twisting it round between forefinger and thumb. Chloe knows only too well that sometimes the truth can feel uncomfortable. But this is important, this is something Maureen *needs* to hear.

'Patrick says that it's too painful to look back,' Maureen says. 'But isn't it normal? It's grief, isn't it? But I can't even do that. I don't even know that she's . . . that she, you know . . .'

Chloe nods because she does know. She still remembers those hours when Nan was missing. Imagine decades spent in that no-man's land.

Maureen starts to cry, and on cue, Chloe gets up from her chair and wraps her arms around her shoulders. She feels Maureen relax into her arms, and she knows then that's she's got her. She can feel it. Between the soft sound of Maureen sobbing, Chloe listens out for Patrick's car on the drive. She hates him for doing this to Maureen, she doesn't want him to walk in and ruin this moment for them.

Maureen pulls a tissue from her sleeve, and reaches for Chloe's hand.

'Thank you, Chloe, I don't know what I would do if you weren't here. Things have been hard with Patrick over the years. He's a good man, but he's not always been easy to live with. But recently – well, since you arrived, or perhaps it's since we moved – he's been different, he's been . . .'

Chloe senses an opening. She sits back down opposite Maureen. Sometimes over the weeks, as she and Maureen have grown closer, it's been easy to forget why she is here. But that one sentence reminds her that she has a job to do.

'How has he been different?' Chloe asks.

'Oh, I don't know, maybe I'm wrong—'

'You're *not* wrong, Maureen, you've got to stop thinking like this, you've got to stop letting him tell you you're wrong or you're crazy or . . .'

Maureen looks up at Chloe and her face softens. She reaches for her cheek, tucking a loose coil of black hair behind her ear.

'Perhaps this does sound crazy,' she says, 'but I've often wondered what it would have been like if Angie . . . well, you know . . . and you being here, it's answered that for me. You're a good girl, Chloe. Your mum, she would have been proud of you.'

Chloe swallows down the mention of her mother. She doesn't want to talk about that. She needs to hear more from Maureen.

'Oh, don't listen to me, Chloe, love. I'm feeling emotional today. I don't like arguing with Pat, and you know what it's like, in an argument you both say silly things.' She gets up and tucks her chair in, but Chloe isn't ready to let this go.

'What did you say that was silly?' Chloe asks.

Maureen stops still on the kitchen lino. 'Well, I didn't, but I'm sure in the past—'

'But he said you were crazy, that was ten minutes ago. That's a terrible thing to say to someone, let alone his wife.' She leans back in her chair, feeling the front two legs lift from the floor.

Maureen goes to speak, but instead lets whatever it was drift away. She starts tidying the dishes, scraping her remaining toast into the bin. Chloe knows there's no need for her to say anything, that the seed she's planted will take root without her watering it with more words. Still, she is wholly unprepared for what Maureen says next.

'Maybe Patrick's right, maybe it's not such a good idea you being here.'

Chloe tips forward in her chair, landing against the kitchen table.

'What?'

Maureen bites the corner of her lip. She doesn't answer. Not right away. But Chloe feels something familiar stir deep inside her.

'You know he's jealous, don't you, Maureen?' Chloe says. She can't help it. 'That's the problem, he's jealous of how close we are.'

'But how could he—'

'It's not you and I that are the problem, it's him.' Chloe speaks quickly. She knows she should stop before she says too much. But the thought that Maureen thinks she should leave . . . 'Maybe . . . maybe he's the crazy one. I mean, why else would he think it's unhealthy for me to be here? What does he know that we don't?'

There, she's said it. The truth beats against the kitchen walls. Chloe stands up from the table and pushes her chair in.

'What do you mean, Chloe?' Maureen asks.

'I'll start looking for another place—'

'What do you mean?' A trace of panic in Maureen's voice.

'I'll be out of here as soon as I—'

'No, Chloe.' Maureen takes a step towards her. She grabs hold of her hand.

'But if Patrick thinks I shouldn't be here . . .' Chloe tries to shake her off. She hates doing this to Maureen, hates to see her broken like this, but sometimes, it's true, you do have to be cruel to be kind.

Maureen grips her harder, tries to weave her fingers through Chloe's, to make them one.

'No, he's wrong,' Maureen says. 'You mustn't go, Chloe. You can't—'

'I don't want to be a bother, you and Patrick were happy here before I—'

'No, not again. I won't lose you again, Angie.'

She lets go of Chloe, but the words hang there between them. Maureen wraps her arms across her waist.

'I . . . I didn't mean . . . I meant . . . well, it's not like you . . . and Angie . . .'

Chloe goes to speak, but there really isn't anything to say. It has already been said. Chloe is so much more than just the lodger.

The silence is broken by the sound of Patrick's car hitting the pebbles on the drive. Maureen lets go of her arm and spins around to fix her hair.

'I'll talk to him, Chloe,' Maureen says quickly as the car door slams and they hear his footsteps heading towards the house. 'The last thing I want is for you to feel uncomfortable here. I'll talk to him.'

Chloe turns to go up to her room, but as she climbs the stairs, she can still feel Maureen's grip on her arm. She reaches out to touch the pink marks that Maureen's grasp has left. She runs her fingers across them and remembers how insistent Maureen was, how determined she was not to let go.

THIRTY-FIVE

The carers at Park House have decorated Nan's bedroom door with two red balloons. The door is open when Chloe arrives and Nan sits on the leather chair next to her bed, two birthday cards on the bedside table beside her. Her eyes light up when she sees Chloe holding a bunch of daffodils.

'Happy birthday, Nan,' Chloe says, bending down to give her a kiss on the head. She no longer recognizes the shampoo she uses, or the scent of the washing powder her clothes are rinsed in here. Everyone knows the disease makes Chloe a stranger to Nan, but people forget that towards the end it works the other way around too.

'Are those for me?' Nan says, reaching for the flowers. 'My daughter Stella always buys me daffodils on Mother's Day. Is it Mother's Day today?'

Chloe picks up the birthday cards next to her bed, both illustrated on the front with flowers and fine copper-plate writing. One is signed by all the staff at Park House, and the other is from Claire Sanders. The one from Claire Sanders also has '85' on the front and Chloe hates her for remembering when she had not. She hasn't even bought a card this year. Last year had been so different when it had just been the two of them. She'd even baked a cake, Nan's favourite, lemon drizzle. She'd decorated it with candles and encouraged Nan to blow them out and watched as she made a wish – making her own wish that they would always be together. But it is true what they say, all good things must come to an end.

Chloe had stayed out of the way at Low Drove for the rest of the day yesterday. Patrick had put an old TV in her room during the week and so she sat upstairs watching classic black and white movies that barely held her interest. How could she follow any plot when what she really wanted to know was what was going on downstairs? She spent every few minutes turning the sound down on the remote control, but no voices had floated back up in response. She certainly hadn't heard any more arguing, which she was surprised to find disappointed her. No one had been there when she went down to breakfast this morning. She ate alone, each mouthful sticking in her throat, wondering if this was what awaited her now.

'Are you the florist?' Nan says.

'Sorry?'

'You're the lady who brought the flowers, aren't you?'

One of the carers bustles in.

'Of course she's not a florist, Grace, she's your grand-daughter.' This carer speaks in a loud, clear voice, articulating all her words. There's nothing wrong with Nan's hearing, Chloe thinks.

'Who?' Nan replies.

The carer sighs with a smile and rolls her eyes at Chloe. 'Right, shall we get your shoes on? We've got a little surprise for you in the communal room, a bit of a birthday party.'

'Is it your birthday?' Nan asks.

'No, Grace, it's yours.'

'Oh, is that why this young lady has brought some flowers?'

The carer sighs again, getting up from the floor as Nan wriggles her toes inside her shoes.

'Come on, Grace,' she says, helping her up off the chair.

The two women shuffle down the corridor and Chloe trails behind them. There was a time when she would have envied the ease with which this woman now chats to Nan. But as she passes the watercolours that line the corridor, she feels trapped inside her coat. She takes it off, but she doesn't feel any better as she follows Nan down the corridor, fitting her own feet into footsteps Nan leaves behind. Not that she says anything. She can't. She just allows herself to be swept along by it all. She plays her part.

'Here we are,' the carer says, guiding Nan towards two armchairs by the window, then she mouths to Chloe, 'I'll just go and get the cake.'

Nan sits in the chair and turns to Chloe.

'Oh, hello, dear, do you live here too? I'm just visiting.'

A few moments later, three carers come into the room holding a cake and singing 'Happy Birthday'. A few other residents start miming the words too – a familiar song embedded in their brain that dementia can't steal.

Chloe watches Nan blow out the candles. She longs to be released from this. She knows she's not alone; she's seen the other visitors here at Park House – they all have that same haunted look, ground down by the loyalty that has chained them here. But you can't just give up on someone, can you? Maureen and Patrick never have.

Chloe walks over to the window, and looks out over Ferry Meadows. Today the view is a little obscured by the scaffolding the builders have put up as part of the redevelopment.

'Nasty stuff,' a voice says at her side.

Chloe spins round. It's the matron.

'Already makes the room so much darker,' Miriam says. 'I hate the stuff – and its expensive – but we'd be hard pushed to get the extension done without it.'

Music is playing now – wartime tunes that ease residents back into a world they're more familiar with. Each resident sits alone, or chats to their neighbour, two trains of conversation running parallel. Chloe catches Nan's eye then and the old woman flashes her the brightest smile across the room, and for a second, there it is again, a whisper of the woman she once was. It happens still from time to time, as if she has risen to the surface, just for a moment as part of this long goodbye they are living.

Miriam nudges her. 'She wouldn't be without you, my love,' she says.

The lies we tell ourselves to live with ourselves, Chloe thinks. They even do it here, in this place, the last stop.

'She talks a lot about Stella,' Miriam says. 'Was that your mum or was your mum—'

'Mine,' Chloe says quickly. Too quickly.

'Oh, I see, I'm sorry,' Miriam says. 'And was it a long time ago, that she . . .'

'We don't really . . . I mean, it's not something I find easy to talk about.'

'No, no, of course not, Chloe. How silly of me to ask.'

Chloe feels hot inside her clothes suddenly. She crosses the room and kisses Nan goodbye. She needs to get back to Low Drove.

THIRTY-SIX

Chloe walks through the back door of Elm House and finds Patrick in the kitchen. She stops still, reticent now to shut the door behind her. He's sitting on a kitchen chair, leaning over some newspaper at his feet, a black leather shoe in one hand, a rag black with polish in the other. He looks up when she walks in, then quickly down again. He starts rubbing at the shoe while Chloe's insides twist. If she could go back outside, she would. But she's already in. She closes the door behind her. The rest of the house feels quiet, still somehow.

'Where's Maureen?' she says.

Patrick looks up, wipes his hair from his eyes. 'Gone to Josie's,' he says. 'The two of them are catching up with some old neighbour.'

'In Chestnut Avenue?'

Patrick looks up as if he hadn't expected Chloe to remember the name of the street where they lived.

Chloe continues: 'I mean, I didn't know that Josie had been a neighbour of yours.'

He goes back to working polish into the shoe.

'Yes, neighbours for nearly thirty years.'

'Is she still there? In Chestnut Avenue, I mean.'

It had never occurred to her that Josie – that anyone – could have been watching that day when Chloe had knocked on the door. What if she told Maureen that she'd seen her before? What if she's telling her right now?

Patrick shakes his head. 'Moved a year before we did,' he says, sighing as he gets up. He fills the kettle with water. 'You want one of these?' He holds up a cup.

Chloe looks down the hall, in the hope perhaps that Maureen might appear. It is still light despite the fact that it is nearly six o'clock, a reminder that the sunnier days are just around the corner. She wants to say no, but something – curiosity? – makes her nod her head instead.

'Yes, that'll be good, thanks.'

She pulls a chair out at the table while Patrick asks whether she prefers tea or coffee.

'Tea?' she says. She hadn't meant for it to sound like she was answering a question with a question. She puts the chair at an angle, further away from the table than she might ordinarily sit.

Chloe watches him as he moves about the kitchen, more confidently, she notices, without Maureen here. This is her domain, everything has her stamp on it, right down to the way that the tea towels are folded and left on the side of the sink. Chloe realizes she's never actually seen Patrick do so much as make a cup of tea here. When Maureen is around, he is passive, fussed over by her. It's strange to see him so out of context in his own home. He's not working today, and he's wearing jeans and a knitted burgundy jumper. He looks like he's had a trim, his curls less unruly, which make him look younger, less wild. She'd seen Maureen cutting his hair in the kitchen once not long after she arrived. He'd sat on a chair on the middle of the lino while Maureen snipped at his neck, pieces of hair falling onto the towel she had put there. She shifts in her chair, crossing and uncrossing her legs as the kettle reaches boiling point on the worktop. Should she start a conversation? She looks around the kitchen for inspiration, for something to say. Patrick interrupts her thoughts.

'Sugar?' he asks.

'Two, please.'

'Need sweetening up, eh?' he says, stirring in the milk. He smiles as he puts it down in front of her and Chloe swallows though she hasn't yet taken a sip. He pulls out a chair nearer to her than the one he had been using, and sits down. She coughs, shifting her chair back a little as she does.

Patrick takes a long sip of his tea, watching her over his cup. She looks down into her own drink.

'Too hot for you?' he asks.

'Yes, I add a bit of cold in the top usually.'

'Ah, so you do. Maureen would have known that,' he says.

Chloe nods.

'She likes to spoil you, eh?'

Chloe looks up at him, unsure how she is meant to answer, or if it's even a question.

'Yes, that's my Maureen, not happy unless she's fussing over someone.' He smiles as he says it. 'She's been the same since I've known her – thirty-six years this year.'

'Wow,' Chloe says.

'You'd get less for murder,' he says.

Chloe looks down at her tea.

'She was the last of her brothers and sisters living at home,' Patrick says, 'big Irish family like mine. You can just imagine it, can't you? She would have rather them come to live with us than leave, but then we had Angie and we got that little house just round the corner. Life goes on, doesn't it?'

Chloe tries her drink now, and nods.

'She's not very good with change, Maureen,' he says. 'Wasn't good leaving her mammy and daddy, and she found it hard at first, what with a new babby . . . Still, she was a good little mam – doted on our Angie she did. That kid wanted for nothing.'

Chloe listens, afraid to put her mug down, to break the spell. This is the most Patrick has ever spoken to her.

'Maureen was lost when she . . . when Angie . . . well, you know, when she went missing, like. I thought I'd lost her as well as Angie. I thought . . .' He trails off. 'Well, anyway, no point going over those times. Ent gonna bring her back, is it?'

He looks up at Chloe. She stares at him over the rim of her mug.

'I think what I'm trying to say is that she finds change, uncertainty . . . difficult. Moving here was a wrench for her, leaving that house. She had everything just' – he holds out his hands to demonstrate – 'just so. She even kept Angie's room, all her little toys, everything, just the way it was. The only way for her to get through it was to convince herself that Angie was coming home.'

Chloe nods.

'She was angry, see? Not just upset, but angry. The police, see, they . . . well, they didn't do everything right. They got things wrong and . . . well, Maureen coped the only way she knew how, I suppose. I'm different, stronger, I don't know. But Mo, she's fragile, always has been. God knows, I've tried to protect her, but . . .'

Chloe is still in her seat. The mug hasn't moved from her lips.

Patrick wipes his hand across his face. 'And then you turn up.'

Chloe swallows her tea quickly then, and it burns.

'It's funny how you arrived really,' he continues, 'how I found you, down that lane just looking at the house . . . just looking you were.'

Chloe feels her cheeks burn and blames it on the steam from her drink.

'We've had plenty of that over the years, people staring – not here, like, but at the old place. Maureen insisted on us doing these bloody newspaper write-ups every year. She wouldn't give up, wouldn't let go of our Angie. And it was the police she was angry at – well, I've already said that. Anyway, she wouldn't give up, not until, well . . . until a few months ago when you . . .'

He pauses and sighs, running his hands through his hair.

'I guess what I'm saying is that if you've noticed any-thing, out of the ordinary I mean, Maureen saying anything, acting . . . She's still a woman on the edge, Chloe. Losing your child like that . . . well, it does some-thing to a person. I've tried to distract her, tried to get her to move on over the years, we all have because, well, because you can't live in the past, can you? You just can't and you can't make everyone else live . . .'

His voice wavers and he gets up from his seat, begin-ning to pace the kitchen floor. Still silent, Chloe follows him with her eyes. He stops at the sink and looks out of the window.

'All I've ever wanted is for Maureen to be OK,' he says. 'She's not like the rest of us, she's . . . she's vulnerable, youngest of her family, doted on by her mammy and daddy. Christ knows, I haven't always got it right, but I've loved that woman, I've looked after her as best I could . . . I've tried, well, I've tried to make amends, as best I could.'

He turns round from the sink and looks at Chloe.

'You know what I'm saying, don't you?'

And even though she doesn't, even though her head is spinning trying to take it all in, she nods.

'She's had some funny ideas recently is all I'm saying, and I'm sure, I'm *sure* she'll see them for what they are because there ent no getting through to her when she's like this. It's like . . . it's like a one-track mind, but for now, I mean, I know this is a big ask, but for now, if you could just . . .'

He leaves that hanging, and Chloe nods, quickly, even though she's not entirely sure what he is saying. Is he asking her to play along with Maureen? Is that what he's saying? She can't think properly here, with him, she just wants to get to her room, to go over this whole conversation from the start.

Chloe goes to stand, picking up her cup from the table.

'I'm really tired,' she says, 'I've been at a friend's baby shower today and—'

'Oh Jesus, well, don't let me keep you.' Patrick moves forward, tidying up his own cup. 'Anyway, Maureen will be back soon. You're eating with us tonight, aren't you?'

'I'm actually a bit full, all that cake,' she says, tapping her belly.

'OK, right you are. Well, if you change your mind.'

Chloe leaves the kitchen, takes the stairs silently, her mind noisy with questions. If anything, she'd been expecting Patrick to ask her to leave, not this. Although, what exactly was he saying? Why did it feel like he was asking her to take part in some kind of collusion? And what did he mean when he said he'd tried to make amends? Amends for what?

She climbs to the top, past the photograph of Angie in the window, but one question follows her all the way up into her room. Of everything that Patrick has said, one thing stays with her. What exactly is he trying to protect Maureen from? But as she asks herself the question, she already feels she has the answer: the truth.

THIRTY-SEVEN

Chloe does end up eating with them that night. When she'd got home from Josie's, Maureen insisted. She'd tried to protest, but Maureen just put her hand to Chloe's forehead, whittling over whether she was coming down with something. At tea time she serves her the best bit of fish, chopping it up on the plate and searching for bones. Chloe sees Patrick glance at the plate that Maureen serves her food on – the bunnies, the mashed-up fish – but he says nothing, just looks at Chloe with some kind of conspiratorial look and a bit of a nod. Chloe eats her food slowly, watching him across the table, remembering times when he would snap at Maureen for doing something similar. But he makes no comment on her fussing. In fact, if anything, he shows concern too.

'Maybe you shouldn't go into work tomorrow, Chloe,' he says. 'It might be better to get a bit of rest instead.'

'I'll be fine,' she says.

'Well, at the very least Patrick will run you into town, won't you, Pat?' Maureen says.

'Honestly, I'm—' Chloe starts.

But Patrick nods between mouthfuls. 'Sure,' he says. 'I have some business in town anyway.'

'What's that then, Pat?' Maureen asks.

Patrick shovels another mouthful of mashed potato onto his fork. 'Just some banking, love,' he says, 'nothing interesting.'

Maureen shrugs at Chloe. 'I leave all that to him.'

Patrick doesn't seem to be in any hurry to leave the table. In fact, when he finishes, he puts his plate in the sink and sits back down with them.

'They say it's warming up next week,' Patrick tells them both. 'Sixteen and sunny Tuesday, Wednesday.'

'That'll be nice, could do with a bit of sunshine, couldn't we?' Maureen says.

'We could indeed, I'd like to get out in the garden if I can.'

Maureen sounds disappointed. 'Oh, I was hoping we might have a ride out to the coast on the first nice day.'

'Still be a bit nippy there, Mo.'

'You're probably right,' she says. 'Ooh, Chloe, I was meaning to ask, what was the name of your grandmother?'

Chloe is about to put a forkful of food in her mouth but it stops halfway. She doesn't answer, just looks at Patrick. He registers the surprise on her face and sits up a little in his seat.

'It's just,' Maureen continues, taking another mouthful of mashed potatoes, 'I was telling Josie that she lived in Dogsthorpe too and we were wondering if we might know her. Imagine that?'

Patrick shuffles closer to the table, not taking his eyes off her for a second.

Chloe puts the food in her mouth. She chews it, buying herself time before she can answer. Should she tell the truth? Make something up? What would be better? The two of them stare at her across the table. She coughs a little. And winces inwardly before she speaks. Her voice is small, unsure.

'Grace,' Chloe says, 'Grace Hudson.'

'Sorry? Hudson did you say?' Maureen asks.

She nods slowly and Maureen looks up to the kitchen ceiling. Patrick's eyes remain stuck fast on Chloe. Her appetite is gone but she looks down at her plate to shovel more food onto her fork.

'Hudson,' Maureen says. 'No, can't say I know a Hudson. What about you, Pat?'

He looks up like Maureen had a moment ago, then shakes his head.

'No, Mo, can't say I know anyone with that surname.'

His eyes return to Chloe.

Maureen shrugs into the space around the dining table. 'I'll tell Josie,' she says. 'She might know.' Then she carries on eating.

Chloe's appetite has gone. She lines her knife and fork up in the middle of the plate.

'Want me to take that for you?' Patrick says, extending his hand out for her plate. Chloe looks up at him but she doesn't want to meet his eye because she can feel her mask slipping and she's afraid he'll see it too. She hands him the plate.

'I've just realized,' Maureen says, turning to Chloe and breaking their gaze, 'we haven't seen you in your new blouse yet!'

Patrick puts Chloe's plate in the sink and returns to the table. 'What's that, love?'

'You know, the blouse I made for Chloe with that bit of material, the one you like with the yellow flowers.'

'Christ, you've had that for years, woman.'

'I know, but I thought . . .' She hesitates for a moment.

'Well, it suits Chloe's colouring, don't you think?'

Patrick looks across at Chloe; he leans back in his chair. 'Can't say I remember it all that well.'

'Oh, you do, Pat. Chloe, nip upstairs and put it on, let Pat have a look at you. Honestly, Patrick, it'll come straight back to you the minute you see it.'

Maureen looks at Chloe.

'That dinner was lovely, thank you,' Chloe says, pointing at the sink, trying desperately to change the subject.

'You're welcome, Chloe, love,' Maureen says. 'Now are you going to run upstairs and pop that top on so Pat can see you?'

She looks from Maureen to Patrick.

'Sorry?' Chloe says.

'The blouse I made you, Patrick would like to see it on.'

'Oh, it's just, well . . . I'm a bit—'

'Nonsense, my love, you're perfect. Go on, won't take you a minute.'

Chloe waits for Patrick to say something – anything – she doesn't know why, but instead he's looking at her expectantly.

'Well, go on then,' Maureen laughs, 'we haven't got all night.'

Chloe stands up slowly from the table, and with calls of encouragement from the kitchen, she heads out into the hallway and up the stairs. In her room, as instructed, she slips off her top and pulls the blouse over her shoulders. She stands in front of the mirror, as she had the last time she had worn it. She parts her hair in the middle, just like the photograph and picks up the same two bunches.

And it's there again; the resemblance is uncanny. Chloe shivers. She tells herself that Josie was right: that she is a grown woman, that Angie was a little girl. How could they be comparable? But as she shuffles out onto the landing, picking up the photograph in the frame, even she has to admit, the resemblance is striking, undeniable.

Downstairs, Maureen and Patrick are laughing. So different from the atmosphere of the last few days: the arguing, the shouting, the tears. What has changed?

Chloe puts her foot on the top step and takes a deep breath. She walks slowly down the stairs, clutching the newel post as she turns into the hallway, and the minute she does, she hears Maureen gasp from the kitchen.

'Patrick, will you look at that.'

Patrick spins around in his chair to face her, and there is a split second where he takes her in. But then all the colour drains from his face. In an instant, he is ashen white.

Maureen gets up from her seat, and leads Chloe into the kitchen. She stands beside her, encouraging her to twirl, while Patrick sits on the chair. Chloe spins slowly on the spot, her eyes never leaving Patrick's blank face.

'It's exactly the same, Pat. Can you believe I still kept the pattern and the material.'

'Maureen . . . I . . .' he says.

'And I told you she had just the right colouring for it, didn't I?' She stands behind Chloe, pulling her dark hair back from her face so it hangs down her back, limp. Chloe stands silent, still, like a doll Maureen has dressed up. Patrick's face is expressionless. Maureen chatters away, seemingly oblivious to anyone else's discomfort.

'Of course I didn't have the same buttons – you can't get the same now – so I borrowed some from the original—'

'Maureen, what?' Patrick says, looking up quickly. 'What did you say?'

Chloe's dinner turns over inside her stomach. Her skin under Maureen's touch is suddenly covered with goose-bumps. She looks down at the buttons.

'The buttons . . . oh Pat, you don't think you can still get the same ones, do you? I just borrowed them, that's all.'

'Maureen, this is too—'

'Oh Patrick, don't be so silly, it's just a few butt—'

'No it's not,' he shouts, his voice reverberating around the kitchen. In the silence that follows the glass lampshades on the ceiling lights ring faintly with the echo of his rage.

Patrick looks up at Chloe and then away again. 'Take it off,' he says, quietly at first. Then again, louder, pointing at the stairs: 'Take it off!'

'Patrick, I—'

'Maureen, this is too much. You've gone too far this time.'

Chloe rushes back upstairs. Behind her she hears the back door slam, and then a moment later, Maureen rushing into the garden after Patrick. In her room she closes the door, then behind the curtains searches for them out of the window that overlooks the back garden. She can't see anything, the blackness of the night swallowing them up, but she hears voices, a snatched conversation.

'. . . got to stop . . .'

'. . . the likeness . . . please.'

'coincidence, Maureen . . .'

'more than that . . . can't deny . . .'

Chloe pushes herself up close to the glass, her hair suddenly wet with condensation, her ear quickly frozen, but she can't hear anything else. All is quiet for a moment. She looks down at the blouse still hanging from her frame. She knows now what Maureen was trying to do. She had planned this. She wanted Patrick to see what she sees. She wanted him to see Angie.

Finally she senses something in the garden and looks down. Two figures move about in the shadows. She hears Maureen's voice, softer, coaxing. There's no sound from Patrick. She can't tell if he is being persuaded. But persuaded of what? It's not as if Chloe has made any claims. She's confident that she hasn't given Maureen the wrong idea. How could blame possibly be put at her door? All Maureen has done is put together the dots and drawn an entirely new picture.

THIRTY-EIGHT

Chloe is unsure how much time passes up in her room. She looks out on the garden occasionally but it is black, lit only by the moon that shines brightly tonight though casts no light on what might be going on beneath her. While she waits, Chloe changes out of the blouse, folding it carefully and putting it into the bottom of her wardrobe where it joins a space thick with bed linen and spare towels.

Eventually Chloe hears the back door open again, the *tap tap* of footsteps on the kitchen lino. The door closes, softly this time, and muffled voices float up the stairs. Chloe tries to establish the tone of them, but they're too muted to gauge. What was said? She can still close her eyes and picture Patrick's face as he stared at her in that blouse. How had Maureen managed to calm him so quickly?

'Chloe?'

She stands stock-still in her room. The voice floats up the stairs again, calling her name. It's Maureen.

'Chloe, love, would you come down? We want to talk to you.'

She opens the door a little and peers out. Maureen's face greets her at the bottom of the stairs. She's smiling, her features soft, not anxious.

'Come down,' she says, beckoning with her hand. 'Come on.'

Chloe leaves her room and takes the stairs. As she reaches the bottom, Maureen turns and she follows her into the living room. Patrick sits in his chair by the patio doors, but the TV is off; he sits upright, his feet on the floor, not the pouffe. He looks as if he has aged ten years.

'Sit down, Chloe,' he says, indicating the sofa. She sits by the door, in Maureen's usual spot, and Maureen sits beside Patrick on the pouffe. For once Chloe is grateful for another pair of eyes on them, for Angie bearing witness from the sideboard.

Maureen looks at Patrick, who clears his throat.

'What . . . what happened earlier, you'll have to forgive me,' he says.

Maureen pats his hand.

'It . . . it was just a shock to see . . . well, it's been a long time, I don't have to tell you,' he says.

Chloe nods. She cups her hands together in her lap. She is still, resenting even the requirement to breathe. She doesn't want anything to interrupt this moment.

Maureen interjects. 'Patrick's sorry for the way he reacted,' she says, 'he didn't mean to frighten you.'

Patrick coughs again. He looks at his wife, as if he's unsure of what he's going to say next, but she smiles at him, encouraging him on.

'I think, what I found so shocking was . . . was the resemblance between you and' – his eyes flicker up to Angie on the sideboard and he squeezes them shut – '. . . and to our Angie. Perhaps I haven't wanted to . . . acknowledge it before, but I guess that . . . well, seeing you there in that blouse . . .'

301

Maureen looks at him, nodding. He goes on.

'I know Maureen's felt like this for a long time, and to me, well, I guess I'd given up hope a long time ago. But maybe . . . well, tonight, I've had to admit that . . . maybe there is something in it, I mean, maybe there's a chance . . .'

Maureen rests her hand on his leg and he pauses.

Chloe's heart races inside her chest on the other side of the living room. She stays still, silent. She may still be wrong.

'What Patrick is trying to say is, we think . . . well, we know it sounds ridiculous' – Maureen laughs a little – 'but we think maybe there's a chance that you could be Angie. You could be our missing girl.'

Chloe takes a long, slow exhalation. She hadn't realized she'd been holding her breath the whole time Patrick had been talking. However many times she might have fantasized about this moment, it still manages to come as a surprise. She feels faint; her hands grip the cushion she sits on; the air in the room feels thin. Her head light.

Maureen and Patrick stare at her from across the room. Patrick wrings his hands in his lap.

'Could I . . . could I get a glass of water?' Chloe says.

'Yes,' Maureen says, springing up from her seat. 'Yes, of course.'

Maureen goes into the kitchen, and Patrick sits staring at the floor, giving Chloe a few precious seconds to think. Is it true, what they just said, that they think she is Angie? Maureen returns with the glass. She takes it.

'Oh, you're shaking,' Maureen says.

Chloe takes a sip. 'Yes, sorry, it's . . .'

'It's the shock, isn't it, love?'

Chloe nods, while Maureen goes to sit next to Patrick. She tells herself to focus on the glass, to let them do the talking, to convince her. That's what she needs them to do. She breathes into the glass.

'I mean, you said yourself that you were adopted, that you didn't really know your background,' Maureen says. 'I mean, didn't you say you were around four or five?'

Chloe nods, thinking back to that conversation, to the seed that she had planted all those weeks ago that had somehow grown into this.

'I mean, do you have any memories at all of before that? Anything?' Maureen asks.

Chloe looks up at the ceiling. She thinks of the boxes of toys in the spare room, how familiar some of them had been. She doesn't tell them that, though. She needs them to convince her. That's how this needs to go.

'I don't know, maybe, some things . . . maybe.'

'Listen, we're not saying this is definite,' Patrick says. 'Maybe we've got it wrong, maybe—'

'We don't think so, though, Chloe,' Maureen interrupts. 'There are too many coincidences: the way you look, your colouring, your background, the fact that your grandma was from the same area . . .'

Chloe reaches her hand up. It is shaking. Humans are pattern-seeking beings; they like symmetry; they like stars to align. She stares back at Maureen and Patrick across the room, sees how much this mother wants to be right. She'll ignore any facts that don't add up, taking only the ones that do. That's how horoscopes work – people only listen to what they want to hear. Every day we walk around with a fine filter that discards all evidence to the contrary of what we want to believe. She looks at these two parents, lost for nearly three decades – what we *need* to believe.

'I'm sorry,' Chloe says. 'It's all a bit of a shock, you know?'

'Of course it is,' Maureen says, and it's at this point that she crosses the room to sit next to Chloe on the sofa. She takes her hands in her own, examining the shape of them, as if searching for anything similar to her own.

'We're not expecting you to agree,' Maureen says, 'and we might be wrong, Chloe, but imagine if we're not, imagine if you are our daughter.'

Maureen takes her hands in her own and holds them against her chest. She looks into Chloe's eyes and finds the recognition she seeks there. Her eyes saying, *Imagine if it were true.*

Patrick interrupts. 'I mean, we'll know for sure, eventually, like.'

Maureen turns towards him. 'How do you mean?'

'Well, technology, it's moved on, hasn't it? Since our Angie was . . . well, they have all sorts now, DNA testing and—'

She drops Chloe's hands. 'Patrick, you still think I don't know, don't you?'

'What? No, Maureen, I wasn't saying—'

'After everything that's been said, after dragging this poor girl down from her room, you still think I'm crazy, don't you?'

'Maureen, I—'

'Patrick Kyle, after all these years, you still don't know me, do you?'

'Maureen, what?'

'Yes, I am your wife, but first and foremost, I am a mother. Do you think just because my child was taken from me that I stopped being a mother? Did you stop being a father that day?'

He shuffles in his seat.

'Actually, don't answer that. Because it's different for men, you don't carry them like we do, you don't wake up each morning and go to sleep at night cradling them inside your own body before they are even born. When they are, you claim you feel the same, but let me tell you this Patrick James Kyle, you're not even close.'

Maureen's face is set firm. She continues:

'The day Angie was born was the single best day of my life. It defined me. I was no longer just someone's daughter, someone's sister, someone's wife, I was someone's *mother*, and to me, that made me someone.' She prods herself in the chest. 'And then she went and I was nothing, I was no one, and I couldn't even grieve because I had nothing to grieve for. But in here' – she taps her chest again although her voice falters – 'I was still a mother. So don't tell me that I think some stranger is my child. Don't tell me that I can live with her as my lodger and forget that she's somebody else's daughter. I knew Angela. I *know* Angela.' She pauses then to look at Chloe. 'And I'm telling you, Patrick, with every fibre of my being, I know that this girl is my daughter.'

Maureen reaches for Chloe and tucks her arm underneath her own. Chloe sits beside her, passive, like a piece of driftwood caught by the current, swept away by the emotion in the room. And yet, isn't this what she had always wanted? To be chosen? To be loved more than a dead person?

Patrick puts his hands out, motioning for her to stop. 'Maureen, don't go upsetting yourself, all I'm saying is that there is a process—'

'What do you mean, process?'

'Well, of course there is. You can't just pull people off the street and say they're your . . .'

Chloe feels Maureen tense. Patrick continues:

'I'm just saying that there will be . . . formalities that we need to go through. The police will need to be—'

'Why? What's it got to do with them?'

Patrick sighs towards the carpet. He scrapes his hands through his hair; his grey curls are wild. He is drained, beaten. His voice fills the living room: 'Because they've been looking for her for twenty-five fecking years!'

Maureen jumps back, shocked by his tone. She lets go of Chloe, and lifts a hand to her face.

Chloe sees in Patrick's face that he instantly regrets shouting. He stands and crosses the room to Maureen, crouching down in front of her on the sofa. He reaches for her arms, holds them gently in his grasp.

'Mo, I'm sorry. I'm sorry that I can't just give you what you want . . . and my love, I know . . . I know more than anyone that this is what you want.' He looks at Chloe. She can see that he is trying, really trying to see what Maureen wants him to see.

'But, Maureen, we can't just decide for ourselves, for Christ's sake. We've been doing those pieces in the papers every year, people will want to know what's happened, there will be a big—'

'You're right,' Maureen says, standing up quickly. 'The newspaper, we'll have to let them know, they'll need to do a piece and . . .' She walks past him, over to the teak dresser. 'Patrick, where did we put that reporter's card? I'm sure . . .' She rummages through her address book.

Chloe glances quickly at Patrick, now kneeling on the floor, his face in his hands. She gets up and joins Maureen as she searches frantically for the number. She takes her by her shoulders, softens her voice, because if truth be told, something has just dawned on her, too. Patrick is right, they would need to do a piece in the newspaper, the same newspaper that she has been working at all these years, the same newspaper that fired her for taking the Angela Kyle file home almost three months ago. She can't risk outsiders getting involved – it would jeopardize her place in the house, it could undo all her hard work.

'Maureen, Patrick is right,' Chloe says, and she feels him look up from the floor. 'There is a process; well, I mean, there will be. We will need to let the police know, and he's right, there will need to be DNA tests. All that will have to be done before you tell the newspapers. It's the first thing they'll ask for.'

Maureen is half listening, but she can tell she's still distracted. Chloe looks over at Patrick and he gives her a nod, encouraging her to go on.

'To be honest,' Chloe says, 'I've had these thoughts, too.'

'You have?' Maureen says.

Chloe nods. 'Of course, like when we were in that

room, with all of Angie's things, I recognized so many of them, and not just because they would have been around when I was little, but because . . . I don't know, it's hard to put my finger on it. But there are other things, too. Just being with you and Patrick, it feels right somehow, like we've always been like this, like we were, I don't know . . .'

Maureen listens to every word. Chloe can see that her mind has let go of the newspaper story; that for now, it's just the three of them. Chloe continues:

'But tonight, it's been quite a shock, and I think . . . I think I need time to get used to the idea myself before we talk to anyone else. I want it to be just the three of us, for a bit longer, just so . . . well, then it's just like us against the world, isn't it?'

Maureen smiles. 'So you don't think we're crazy?' she asks.

Chloe shakes her head. 'No, not at all, but other people might.'

They laugh and Chloe continues:

'And so we have to be sure. We've *got* to be so sure.'

Patrick gets up and walks over to them. He puts his arms around Maureen and she leans back into his chest.

'Chloe's right,' he says. 'There's plenty of time for all that. Let's just allow it to sink in out here in Low Drove for now.'

Chloe looks out at the darkness that envelops them, the moon peering through the tops of the trees. Out here they could live any kind of life they liked. Maureen nods, reticently at first, but then more convincingly. And with that, Chloe notices, Patrick's shoulders relax.

'OK,' Maureen says, taking Chloe's hands in hers. 'OK, it's just between the three of us for now.'

And in all that had happened, everybody forgets about Angie watching from the shelf.

THIRTY-NINE

It is quiet in the car the following morning, the only noise the rumble of the tyres on the tarmac of the A47. Fields whizz past, tractors chugging across them, and the last of winter's frost clings to the leather seats inside Patrick's blue car.

A few times, Chloe has tried to think of something to say to break the silence, but nothing has come to her. She's tired – it had been hard to sleep last night. She'd spent hours going over and over the events of that evening, how perfectly it had all happened. She had to admit it felt strange going to sleep in Elm House knowing that across the landing, Maureen slept safe in the knowledge that after twenty-five years her baby was home.

Patrick looks as if he hasn't slept at all. His eyes are on the road, but Chloe can see from the passenger seat that they are bloodshot. His hands grip the steering wheel, his knuckles white.

Chloe has never been in his car before. She looks around; the cigarette lighter is missing, there are a couple of holes in the upholstery, new car mats that he's added in the footwell. In the back, something lies across the seat, covered by a sheet. She's grateful suddenly of an opening to break the silence.

'What's that?' she asks him.

He casts a glance into the back of the car via the rear-view mirror.

He turns to her. 'You really want to know?'

She nods.

'I can tell you,' he says, 'but you won't like it.'

Chloe pushes herself up a little in her seat.

'And you mustn't tell Maureen,' he says.

She turns around, and then she sees the long, slim shape of it.

'It's a gun,' Patrick says. 'Not that Maureen knows I've got it, and she must never know. She hates anything like that, she gets the wrong idea.'

'Why have you got it?' Chloe asks, twisting her fingers awkwardly in her lap.

'I'm taking it in to be serviced,' he says. 'Oh, don't worry, I've got a licence for the thing.'

She glances back at it, sleeping on the seat.

'But why do you need one? And why doesn't Maureen know you have it?'

'Rabbits,' he says.

The car slows to a halt. They're sitting in traffic now, waiting behind a lorry which is turning right across the single carriageway. He takes his hands off the steering wheel and mimes shooting a shotgun through the windscreen.

'It's a bit of fun really, but Maureen don't see it like that. There's a farmer I know, next place on from Low Drove, he lets me shoot on his land. Works for both of us, see? I get to shoot, he gets rid of the rabbits.'

Chloe eyes Patrick through her fringe. It sounds harmless to her – well, not to the rabbits. Why would Maureen care?

'She feels sorry for them,' Patrick says, as if reading

her thoughts. He rolls his eyes. 'But they're vermin, pests, ask any farmer out here.'

Chloe nods, and looks back over her shoulder.

'How long have you had it?' she asks.

'Now let me think,' Patrick says, sucking his teeth. 'Near on forty years. It was my eighteenth birthday present from my dad.'

'And it still works?'

'Oh, yes. Like I say, if you look after them . . .'

'And Maureen has no idea?'

'She thought I got rid of it when . . . well, when Angie was little, like.'

They both look away slightly at the mention of Angie. The sun shines straight into the car, bathing it with yellow light. Perhaps neither of them know what to say in the brightness of a new day.

'No, she didn't want it in the house with a little one around. I told her it was gone, like, put her mind at rest.'

'But you kept it?'

Patrick turns to Chloe with a smile and leans towards her. 'It's always best to have a few secrets in a marriage,' he says.

The traffic starts moving again, and they both stare straight ahead. Chloe wonders what other secrets he has kept from Maureen, and every so often, as they head into the city, she glances again to the back seat.

'It won't bite,' Patrick laughs.

Chloe attempts a smile. She's never been this close to a gun.

As they near the city, land makes way for round-abouts and concrete. Patrick takes each turn, over various roundabouts, as if he knows the way. As if he's been here a thousand times before. They leave the city centre behind them and Chloe looks over her shoulder as it disappears. He takes one dual carriageway after another, back out towards the sky, away from the newspaper offices. Chloe feels the back of her legs tense against the passenger seat. She has been so distracted by the thought of the gun that she's forgotten to give him directions.

'Where are we going?' she says.

Patrick turns from the wheel. 'Your office, ent we?'

'Yes, but . . .' She points over her shoulder, back towards the city, and it's then – only then – that she remembers it's the insurance company, not the newspaper, that he's taking her to.

'It's still over near the showground, isn't it? Unless it's moved since—'

'No, no,' Chloe says quickly. 'We're still there.'

'Oh good,' Patrick says, 'thought I was having a dementia moment then.'

He laughs, and she does too, expelling the breath she's trapped inside her lungs at last.

Patrick pulls up outside a glass-fronted insurance building, people in dark suits filtering in like ants to a nest.

'This is the place, right?' he says.

'Yes,' she says, undoing her seat belt.

He looks up under the sun visor to the building.

'I wonder if John's about . . . I could say hello.'

Panic sticks to Chloe's skin.

Patrick shakes his head. 'Probably have to get an appointment to see him these days.'

Chloe nods, grateful to be pushing on the car door, stepping out of the vehicle. In fact, she's so keen to get out, she doesn't notice who is standing there when her feet reach the pavement.

'Chloe?' a voice says.

Patrick indicates with his eyes and she turns around.

'I thought it was you,' Phil says. 'What on earth are you doing—'

'Phil,' Chloe says quickly, and strangely – for her – the first thing she can think to do to stop him talking is to wrap him in a hug. He seems surprised. He takes a step back awkwardly, then straightens his suit.

Patrick leans across from the passenger seat and looks up at the building. 'Impressive, ennit? Which floor do you work on, Chloe?'

Phil looks confused. He points to the building behind them. 'Oh, you're working—'

'Anyway, thanks, Patrick, thanks so much for the lift.' She slams the door before she hears his answer, and taps the top of the car. Patrick pulls away.

'Who's that then?' Phil asks, his forehead creased into a question.

'Oh, no one,' Chloe says. 'Just a neighbour who was heading the same way this morning . . . Anyway, I haven't seen you in ages. How are you?'

She doesn't care. Phil rattles on about a cough he's had that won't go away. He tells her they're getting quotes for a conservatory, about the holiday to Lanzarote. Chloe nods and smiles in all the right places, but she's also got one eye on the tail lights of Patrick's car; she sees him brake at the end of the car park, the orange indicator flickering left. Finally, he's gone.

'So you're working here now?' Phil asks.

'Well, not quite – an interview,' she says. It's all she can think of.

'Oh right, which department?'

'Oh, er . . .' She's rummaging through her bag then, pretending to search for a piece of paper. 'It's an agency that's sent me so . . .'

Phil starts shuffling on his feet, looking at the clock on the outside of the building that reads a few minutes past nine. He's carrying a briefcase that Chloe is sure will have nothing more in it than his sandwiches. When she notices him glance towards the doors, she starts searching deeper inside her bag.

'How's Hollie?' she starts.

But Phil's discomfort is obvious as he checks his watch.

'Listen, good luck with your interview – wherever it is. I'd better go. Duty calls and all that.' He smiles awkwardly, in that geeky, dull way of his.

'Yes, of course,' Chloe says. 'Send my love to Hollie, tell her I'll call.'

Phil nods, but he's already heading into the building through the revolving glass doors. Chloe pretends to be rifling through her bag for something – anything – until she sees him get into the lift in the lobby. Then she puts her bag back on her shoulder and walks towards the nearest bus stop.

FORTY

Chloe misses several calls on her phone that day. Two from Park House, and three from Hollie. Hollie sends a text too: Phil said you had an interview at his place today, how did it go? I miss you. Call me back. I'm sorry about before. xxx

She doesn't call back. Instead she sits on a swing in Angie's play park at Ferry Meadows and eats her packed lunch. Her feet scuff the woodchip floor intermittently. She can't face visiting Nan today, even though she is so close by. She is still reeling from the revelations of last night. She can't be Chloe for Nan today – not when she's Angie for the Kyles.

She closes her eyes, pushes herself back on the swing in her office shoes. It still doesn't feel real. She opens her eyes, hoping the world might be clearer, that one definite memory might make itself apparent if only she blinks and tries again. But today everything feels a blur, as if she's drowning, as if she's clamouring to stay afloat, as if nothing she tries to hold on to is real.

Her feet skid on the ground and she gets up from the swing, throwing away the last of her packed lunch. It's almost time to return to Low Drove.

On the bus home she gets out her phone – another missed call from Park House, one more from Claire Sanders. She reaches up to her breast pocket and pulls out the photograph of Nan and Stella. It's been weeks since she's looked at it. Those faces feel like another lifetime now. She's thought about replacing it with a photograph of Maureen, Patrick and Angie, that nice one of the three of them on Hunstanton beach perhaps, but then she remembers Patrick in the background, that looming shadow of him. No, she's sure she can find a better one. She replaces the photograph of Nan and Stella back in her pocket for now.

She rings the bell on the bus and gets off at her stop at Low Drove. Her stop. Even after all this time, she's never seen anyone else alight here. She makes her way through the willow and down the lane towards Elm House. Patrick's blue car is in the drive as usual. As she approaches it, she peers through the window to see if the gun is still lying across the back seat, but it has gone. Like much that happens at Elm House, she feels she might have imagined it.

Maureen greets her at the short garden gate beside the pebble drive. Chloe has the feeling she's been waiting for a long time. Her face lights up on spotting Chloe.

'I was beginning to get a bit worried about you, Chloe, love,' Maureen says. 'You're usually back by quarter to six.'

Chloe glances at her watch. It is eight minutes to six.

'Anyway, you're here now. Come inside, I've got your favourite for tea.'

Inside the kitchen, the windows are steamy, and on top of the counter are three plates colourful with food. Patrick sits at the kitchen table.

'Hello, love,' he says, as she walks through the door. She still isn't used to this change in Patrick's attitude, and she tries to keep the suspicion from her smile. Maureen helps her take her coat off and indicates for her to sit down. Patrick folds his newspaper and puts it on the table beside his knife and fork.

'Good day at work?' he asks.

'Oh, you know, same old.'

He nods.

'You didn't see my mate then?'

'Now, here we are,' Maureen says, interrupting and bringing two plates to the table. She puts Chloe's down first, the same plate that she has been giving her for the last couple of weeks. It's slightly smaller than the one Patrick has, and the fish fingers vie for space with the rabbits.

'Your favourite,' Maureen says, then stands back as if awaiting Chloe's reaction.

She looks down at the plate of fish fingers, mash and peas, and then back at Maureen.

'Of course, ketchup,' Maureen says, tipping the bottle this way and that and putting it on the table beside her.

Chloe stares at her dinner. 'This looks lovely,' she says. 'Thank you.'

Maureen smiles, bringing her own plate from the worktop. 'That's quite all right, Chloe, love. I thought we could try some of the old stuff, in case it brings anything back to you.'

'Oh,' Chloe says. 'Oh, right, yes, of course.'

Chloe picks up the cutlery – the blunt knife, a fork with three tines. She hesitates for a second, watching how easily Maureen and Patrick tuck in with cutlery that fits their hands more appropriately. Chloe glances down at the child's cutlery in her own hands, and then back at the

Kyles. They eat, oblivious, as if no one has noticed the absurdity of the situation.

'This takes me back,' Maureen says, putting another forkful into her mouth with a smile.

Chloe tentatively tries a small mouthful of food.

'That's it,' Maureen says. 'Eat up.'

After dinner, Chloe goes upstairs to change. She's grateful to be back in the sanctuary of her room. But as she lies down on the bed, she feels something uncomfortable under her neck. She fishes one arm behind her, onto the pillow, and pulls out Puss – Angie's cloth cat. She nearly drops it in surprise. She sits up quickly, looking this way and that.

'Who put thi . . . ?' she says to no one but Puss.

But she knows. Isn't it obvious?

She lies on her bed until the room turns black. She's grateful for the darkness that engulfs her. She holds Puss across her belly. Only then she hears Maureen calling to her from downstairs. She shuffles out onto the landing; the light is on and it makes her blink.

Maureen stands at the bottom of the stairs with a pile of photo albums.

'Come on,' she says, 'I thought this might help.'

Chloe obeys her command to join her downstairs, then on the sofa, side by side, she and Maureen sit down and look again through the same dusty photo albums she'd got out that very first night. This time, though, Maureen pauses over each photograph, searching Chloe's face for recognition, pointing out everyone, giving her every name. She seems disappointed when Chloe fails to feel what she does.

'It's all . . . it's all such a blur,' Chloe says finally, knowing Maureen just wants to hear something.

'Don't worry,' Maureen says, tapping her arm, 'it'll come back eventually. We can try again tomorrow.'

Across the room, Patrick watches the news on mute, ready to join in with their conversation whenever Maureen attempts to include him. She's talking to him when Chloe turns the last page and finds the photograph she was thinking of earlier. A day on the beach at Hunstanton. She opens the cellophane protector, and loosens it from its sticky page. It has been years, but eventually the photograph yields and it's there in her hands. There is something about this photograph that feels familiar. Maureen turns to see her holding it. She points to the place where they're sitting.

'Do you remember the steps down to that part of the beach, and the green that ran all the way up to it? Do you remember the carousel? The painted horses? Oh, you loved them. And we'd sit and eat fish and chips on that green, do you remember?'

Chloe nods, just a little, and as she does she's aware of Maureen turning round to Patrick and saying, 'Look, Pat, it is coming back to her, I knew it.'

But Chloe is distracted by Patrick's face in the picture, a different man to the one who sits with them now. She thinks of what he said earlier, about the secrets you keep in a marriage. She pictures again the gun on the back seat of the car, the newspaper article about his arrest. She brings the photograph towards her face. What else has he been hiding all these years?

'Can I keep this one?' Chloe says. 'Just up in my room.'

'Of course, love. It might even help.' Maureen gets up. 'I'm just going to get a tea. Would you like one?'

Chloe shakes her head, yawning. 'I think I'll just head to bed, busy day tomorrow,' she says, and pictures the same insurance building, as if that were really where she worked. It's amazing how quickly things can feel real.

'Poor love, it's getting that bus that does it to you. Pat, are you on a late tomorrow?'

'Yes,' he says. 'Late tomorrow and Wednesday, then nothing till next Monday.'

'Oh good. Well, you'll run Chloe into work, won't you?'

'Oh no—' Chloe tries to protest. She can't risk bumping into Phil two days running, and anyway, she was planning on visiting Nan tomorrow.

'Honestly, pet, it's no bother at all,' Maureen says. 'You don't mind, do you, Pat?'

'Not if you say so, Mo,' he replies, rearranging his legs on the pouffe.

'There, it's settled. Anyway, it would be good for you two to spend some time together.'

FORTY-ONE

Within days, it is a regular thing, Patrick giving her lifts to 'work'. Chloe managed to convince him after that first day that she missed stretching her legs on the walk from the bus stop, so he drops her there without question and as soon as she sees his car disappear, she crosses the road and waits for the bus back to town.

They've left a little earlier this morning. Chloe had hoped that she could steal out and catch the bus before he was up, only when Maureen realized, she had hurriedly shooed Patrick into action, standing over him while he quickly pressed his feet into his shoes.

The fields that they pass are bathed in a soft golden light that has yet to burn through the fog that still blankets the crops, and the radio fills the silence between them inside the car. At Elm House there is no time for awkward silences; Maureen fills them, mining memories as if searching for gold. Evenings in Low Drove for Chloe now are more often spent with faded polaroid pictures scattered across the sofa cushions as they pore over every photo album in turn.

Patrick obediently carries boxes from the storage room up and down the stairs, as Chloe is made to sit on the living room floor among Fuzzy-Felt and Playmobil sets while Maureen encourages her to open each battered box and handle its contents. It is now Maureen who ploughs Chloe for long-buried relics of the past – how the tables have turned. Even Patrick seems pleased to see his wife's new delight when one tiny gem is retrieved from the deep dark recesses of Chloe's memory – or something like that.

In the car, though, when it's just the two of them, Patrick seems less concerned with Chloe's fuzzy memory, as if part of him switches off the moment they pull out of the drive at Elm House. She can't explain this about-turn. Outside of Low Drove, he never mentions Angie. Although he never mentions DNA tests either, so Chloe has resisted picking at that particular scab. She wonders what their friend Josie would think of him going along with this idea that she really is Angie. Chloe would go so far as to say that Josie seemed suspicious of him. And even Chloe herself has been watching him more closely lately.

At night, when she has managed to escape to the sanctuary that is her bedroom, Chloe pulls out her own dusty archive where she now keeps the photograph that Maureen gave her. She has scanned it for clues and each time returns to the haunting face of Patrick, unable to pinpoint what about it unnerves her so much. At first she had thought this was a simple case of bringing Angie home, that however ridiculous it might have sounded, her fresh eye on the case could have brought some answers for these shattered parents. But more often these days her curiosity is replaced with a looming sense of dread about what really happened, and the closer she gets to Maureen, the more protective she feels towards her. But who exactly does she need to protect her from?

She glances at Patrick from the passenger seat.

'Another lovely day,' she says.

'Yeah.' Patrick stares straight ahead at the road.

Silence.

'I had the weirdest dream last night,' Chloe says. She leaves it hanging there, but Patrick doesn't bite. Maureen would. She goes on, curiosity gnawing at her insides.

'It felt so real, more like a memory,' she adds.

Still nothing. Chloe knows if this were Maureen beside her, meaning would already have been derived from every detail of this supposed dream. She swallows. The car hits a cat's eye and her stomach turns over.

'I was in a park . . . it felt so familiar.'

'Oh yeah?' he says, face straight ahead, too hard to read.

'Yeah, it was a play park, just a little one. It was surrounded by tall trees and long grass and nearby, there was a lake.'

Patrick's hands change position on the steering wheel.

'You were there,' she says, venturing further away from safety. 'It was actually just the two of us.'

He laughs a little. 'Dreams are strange things, ent they?'

'Yes, but this one, it felt . . . different,' she says. 'Like I said, more like a memory. I was on the swings and you were there, you were pushing me, or I was asking you to . . . it's all a bit fuzzy. It jumped around, the way dreams do.' She wishes that she could open the window, but she continues: 'The swings, they were yellow, and the ground wasn't covered in woodchip – not like you see at parks now – it was a concrete floor. There was a car park just nearby and I saw you. I watched you as you walked over to it, and then . . . and then suddenly, you were gone.'

Patrick's knuckles whiten. She's describing the park as it was that day, as she had seen it in the cuttings. He knows it, she knows it. She needs him to talk, open up, like he did that day in the kitchen.

'Yeah, well, don't pay too much attention to dreams,' Patrick says. 'I tell Maureen the same. Just your subconscious playing tricks on you, like.'

Chloe sinks down in her seat, her own eyes returning to the road. Why is he not asking more? Why is he not picking apart what she's telling him? She knows Maureen would.

'And I just thought, I mean, that's where . . . well, that's where Angie—'

'Like I said, I don't pay too much attention to dreams.'

He turns to her and smiles. But the smile stays too long, like a warning.

Chloe looks back at the road. They drive on in silence. Chloe twiddles her thumbs in her lap. She twists in her seat, rearranges her bag in the footwell. Then the news comes on the radio and Patrick quickly turns it off.

They drive across the city, Patrick indicating this way and that in silence. The atmosphere inside the car is thick with something, though Chloe doesn't know what.

One after another they cross roundabouts. The bus stop up ahead is her cue to relax. Patrick indicates and pulls over. Her hand is already on the seat belt catch.

'OK then?' he asks.

'Thanks,' Chloe says, and gets out of the car.

She is about to slam the door when Patrick leans across the passenger seat.

'And Chloe?' he says.

She stops still, her hand on the door frame. 'Yes?'

'We were never at the play park the day Angie went missing.'

FORTY-TWO

Chloe stands at the bus stop for a long time after Patrick drives away. She is still on the pavement exactly where he dropped her. She hears a plane cut through the clouds above, the rushing footsteps of office workers; she inhales the thick exhaust fumes of a bus that waits for passengers to alight, and still she stands there, trying to absorb exactly what Patrick had said. She knows this case inside out, she has spent hours reading through the cuttings, she can't have got something so vital wrong. How could Angie not have been at the play park that day when that was exactly the place she disappeared from? It doesn't make any sense. Chloe feels, standing there, as if suddenly everything she thought she knew about the Kyles' story is wrong. She wishes the cuttings were tucked inside her bag – she needs a reference point now to stop the world from spinning. But if what Patrick said is true, everything she knows about Angie's disappearance is mistaken. She blinks and shakes her head, ignoring the stares of people hurrying past her, though she knows her stillness uneases them.

But more worrying to Chloe is not what he said, but how he said it, and perhaps why? It seems a rather large bomb to have dropped so casually. Too casually.

It is a while before she pulls herself together, before she crosses the road to wait at the bus stop on the other side. Patrick's words swim around in her head.

How could he not have been at the park with Angie? And if they weren't there, where were they? And why would he tell her, of all people? It could only have been a test. Had she passed or failed? She hadn't even had time to react. Had it been her talking about the park which had prompted him to correct her? Does he want her to know that, whatever Maureen says, he *knows* she is not his missing daughter? But how can he be so sure?

Chloe looks down the road as she waits for the bus to appear, but as she does so another thought swirls around her mind. She tries to dismiss it, she's not ready for that. But as the bus pulls up alongside the pavement, as she buys her ticket, sits down, the thought takes its place beside her and follows her back towards town.

She gets off at the stop before the bus station and hurries through the underpass to the sound of her echoing footsteps. She takes the back streets, up and down kerbs, until finally she is there, standing outside a very familiar front door – one she hasn't visited for almost two months, but she has to see something for herself. She knows until she checks the cuttings she mustn't jump to any conclusions.

She takes a set of keys from her pocket, struggling to find the one that fits Nan's door. She pushes it into the lock and feels the click, that little resistance, and by the time she opens the door, it is all coming back to her.

Nan's house feels more like a museum these days. The air is stiff, the front door heavier than she had remembered. She looks down at the floor and understands why: envelopes and flyers, greetings cards and free newspapers have collected on the doormat.

She shuts the door behind her and starts collecting the junk mail from the floor. The curtain still hangs off the back of the door where she left it. She wanders through the house as if she has never been there before. She is scared to disturb it, afraid even for her feet to leave an impression on the carpet. Stopping in the hall and looking up into the mirror, in that split second she reminds herself that she has every right to be here. She quickly looks away from her reflection.

In the living room, everything is as she left it. Nan's mahogany sideboard has gathered more dust, but the freeze-framed faces smile as they always have. She picks up one photograph that she recognizes, the black and white photo of Nan and Stella on the beach. It had once been her favourite, and yet now, the faces in it are more like those of strangers.

Her eyes flit from one framed photograph to the next, but she feels nothing, like she is simply flicking through a magazine filled with models. Interesting how time makes strangers of us all, eventually.

She remembers then the reason she is here. She leaves the living room and takes the stairs, two at a time, hauling herself up by the handrail. She pauses on the landing, briefly glancing into Nan's bedroom, the light falling on her fitted wardrobes and the mirror inset within them reflecting an empty bed. She imagines Nan still here, shuffling round on her own, no one here to keep her company, to sit beside her watching television, to get up and make her a cup of tea. No one to take away that sting of loneliness. She imagines Nan dying on her own in the very same bedroom.

Things could have been so very different if it hadn't been for Chloe.

Inside her own room, the curtains are drawn, her bed is unmade. Blu-Tack still clings to the wall in places, and in others, the corners of A4 paper hang clumsily. Chloe drops to her knees and starts feeling underneath her bed, pulling out the cuttings that she had left there, that she had taken time to hide just in case. They come out, a bunch in each hand, and she turns and leans her back against the bed frame. She discards the first two – they are stories from later on in the enquiry. She even discards the update interviews that Maureen and Patrick did over the years. It's another story she's looking for, and as she sieves through them, Maureen and Patrick's faces fall on the bedroom carpet in a haphazard fashion. But then, finally, she finds it. The cutting is not on top of the pile in her hands, but the edge of it sticks out of the middle. She recognizes the photograph, even photocopied, even though so many pixels blur into one another; even with the blotches of newsprint, even with the age of the original, she recognizes it, because this photograph – this location – has been so vital to every single news story, every part of the investigation, that has followed since that day Angie disappeared. She is not mistaken.

She holds the cutting up. It's in two pieces so she grasps one page in each hand and fits them together into a jigsaw that at one time might have offered hope. Because right in the middle of both pieces of paper is the photograph she remembers. The one of Maureen and Patrick, her hand held tightly inside his, her head resting on his shoulder, the long grass around them almost obscuring their bodies. And in the background, just over their shoulder, the unmistakable landmark that was the park in Ferry Meadows that Angie had disappeared from. She reads the picture caption.

> *Devastated: Parents Patrick and Maureen Kyle join the search for Angie.*

Her eyes scan the cutting, and there it is, mentioned over and over again.

Play park where Angie disappeared from

Ferry Meadows Park

Only left her for a minute

Visit to the swings

The words start to move around on the page. She drops the two halves of the cutting and they flutter down either side of her legs. She tips her head back on the mattress, staring up at the artex ceiling. The thought she had on the bus resurfaces. She pushes it away. Blinks, restarts, but it's still there when she opens her eyes. What other explanation is there?

She sits up straight, grabbing the cuttings once again from the floor. And now when she looks at the photograph – when she *really* looks at the photograph – she sees something different. She doesn't see two broken parents, each holding up the other. She sees betrayal. She sees lies. She sees that same haunted expression in Patrick's eyes that she'd noticed in the photograph Maureen had showed her on her first night in the house. She sees Maureen's blind faith in him. She sees the gun he keeps secret from her. She sees the room he keeps locked. She sees why he wouldn't believe Maureen when she insisted Chloe is Angie. Because if he and Angie were never at the park that day, why had he allowed everyone to think that they were? Why had he allowed the police to comb it? Why had he been lying to everyone for nearly three decades? And the only answer Chloe can come up with is because Patrick knows what really happened to Angela Kyle.

FORTY-THREE

'Chloe . . . is that you? I can't . . . maybe it's a bad line. Chloe, are you there?'

The phone lies limply in Chloe's hand. Hollie sounds worried.

'Chloe, speak to me. Just let me know you're OK.'

She wants to talk to her, she really does. But where is she going to start? The beginning of it all feels decades ago now.

'Hollie,' Chloe says finally, her voice more of a croak. Hollie is the first person she has spoken to since Patrick dropped her off that morning. It is now nearly one o'clock. She has been sitting on her bedroom floor, combing through the discarded cuttings for hours, trying to find something – anything – that gives her an alternative explanation, one that doesn't involve Patrick's guilt.

'Oh Chloe, I was worried sick for a moment, you sound terrible. Are you OK?'

Chloe nods into the phone.

She hadn't known where to go after Patrick's revelation had sunk in. Back to Elm House? The thought now filled her with fear. She'd briefly pictured Maureen, wondered whether she might be in danger. Every time she thought of her, all she could see was her trusting face. But how could Chloe go back there now? How could she eat at their table? Hold that plastic cutlery while Patrick watched on? His confession hadn't just made a liar of him – perhaps that's what was breaking Chloe's heart.

She'd thought about going to see Park House, but what solace could Nan offer? If Chloe was really honest, what had she ever offered? Suddenly everything that Chloe thought she knew seemed different in this new light. Everything once solid now slipped through her fingers like sand.

And then there was Hollie. She'd dialled her number, not knowing what she was going to say. But she needed to reach out to the one real thing in her life. Her constant.

'Do you remember when we were kids?' Chloe says suddenly. 'Those games we used to play? The ones where our real parents would come and find us.'

Hollie laughs a little from the other end of the phone. 'I haven't thought about that for a long time.'

'We couldn't believe that they'd done that, that they'd left us,' Chloe says. 'And so we made them into new people. We shifted the shapes around until they made a different picture. One where we could like ourselves better. You remember, don't you?'

'My mum and dad were always doctors. Do you remember that?' Hollie says. 'I used to say they were too busy saving lives to come and get me. I invented all sorts of dramas that kept them at work.'

'We played that game for hours,' Chloe says.

'Months,' Hollie reminds her.

'Years.'

The two women fall silent down the handsets. In truth, their parents hadn't left them in the foster home where they had met as children, and they knew that

334

really. The reality was they were put there by people who knew that's where they would be safer. Two girls the same age, they had drifted towards each other, and then clung to one another in all the storms that followed. A bond was forged, they were one another's lifebuoys.

'They say that when we sleep, our brains make dreams that fit what we want to believe. Did you know that, Hollie?'

'It makes sense, I guess,' she says.

'But perhaps it's not just when we're asleep. When we were little, we had to write new stories in our heads, or make up games so that we could feel better, so that we didn't believe we weren't worth loving.'

'I guess that's why we did it,' Hollie says. 'I haven't really thought about it, but Chloe, all kids make up silly games.'

'But it wasn't just a game, was it? Not for me,' Chloe says.

There is silence on the other end of the phone. An understanding.

'What's happened, Chloe? You know you can tell me anything. You know that I'll understand.'

'You stopped making up stories. You had Dave and Rita. Then you met Phil. You got your house. You wrote yourself a new story and you left me.'

'I didn't, Chloe. I never left you, I promised you I wouldn't. I can't feel bad that it worked out for me . . . All that other stuff, it's in the past. And there's no point looking back, just forward.'

Chloe presses the phone to her ear and shakes her head. What does she have to look forward to? She feels that vulnerability then, the fear she dedicates her life to suppressing. Would she even know how to make the same life Hollie has, if she had the chance? Does she want to? She's not like everyone else, she knows this. She has always known this.

'It's funny how we get away with making things fit while we sleep,' Chloe says. 'But we do the same when we're awake, we sieve through everything, everyone, taking just the bits that fit what we want to believe – what we *need* to believe – and people think we're mad for doing so.'

She's not sure who she is talking about. She looks down at the photograph of Patrick and Maureen, and covers two fingers over Maureen's face.

'I don't think you're mad,' Hollie says. 'I've never thought that. Tell me what's happened, Chloe.'

She turns the cutting over, pressing Maureen and Patrick's faces against the carpet.

'I thought I could help,' Chloe says quietly into the phone. 'It sounds ridiculous now, doesn't it? But I really thought that I could bring her home, that I could fix everything. But maybe it wasn't Angie I was trying to bring home, maybe it was—'

'Wait, Chloe, you're not making any sen—'

'And then the lines got blurred, everything felt so confused and yet so familiar. I let them think . . . they told me . . . well, it doesn't matter, but then they made *me* think—'

'Who did? Chloe, who are you talking about? Who's Angie? Can you stop talking in riddles for a second?'

Chloe turns the picture back over. It was true that she had wanted to help. She always wanted to help. She looks up and around her room. She pictures the nights when she had lain here in bed, listening to Nan's soft breathing on the other side of the wall. It was enough for so long and she really thought this would be it. She always thinks that finally, she will be sated. In the early days, they'd chat through the wall, Nan always grateful to get a reply. For so long there had been nobody. Then her mind drifts back to the Kyles, wondering if it really had gone so wrong? Disappointment is nothing but reality failing to meet expectation. Hadn't she heard that somewhere? And what had she expected? All she'd wanted was to find out what had happened to Angie. That was it, wasn't it? She hadn't asked for more; it wasn't her fault if Maureen had convinced herself of something else. And then today, after all these weeks of searching for clues, Patrick had given her something bigger than anything he'd told the police. But why?

A horrible thought comes to mind, one so ugly she pushes it away before it has time to tie itself to her. Patrick had been the one to tell her that Angie was never at the park, but was he the only one who knew this? She pictures Maureen then, in her short pinny as she serves up dinner, her hands resting on her hips as she watches Chloe eat from the plate covered in bunnies.

No, Maureen doesn't know anything about this. It is inconceivable to think she is complicit in his lie. Chloe shakes her head. She won't have it. It is impossible to hold those two thoughts together. That woman, who has been so loyal in her grief all these years, who has trusted her husband implicitly. It would kill her to know he's been lying to her. It would kill her to know that he has known all this time just what had happened to their daughter.

Hollie is still speaking, but Chloe cuts her short.

'Hollie, I've got to . . . I've got to go.'

'What do you mean, go? Go where? Where are you?'

'I can't explain at the moment.'

'Chloe, you're worrying me . . .'

'Don't worry, I'll explain as soon as I can.'

And she hangs up. However hard the truth may be to hear, Maureen deserves to know what really happened to her daughter, and Chloe will be the one to tell her.

Chloe has decided to pretend she's come home from work sick. She can already picture how Maureen will whittle, how she'll reach a cold hand to her forehead to check her temperature, how she'll insist Chloe needs to go straight up to her room and she'll bring her a mug of hot steaming tea. Even this thought makes Chloe feel uneasy, of leaving Maureen down there with him, unknowing.

The bus rumbles along the potholed Fen roads and her stomach pitches up and down in time with the tyres. It reminds her of the first time she came out here – just for a look, she had promised herself. She had no idea then how things would turn out.

She stares out of the window, spotting the fields that are sown with sugar beet, the long straight lines of tiny lush green now competing with worms to push through the soil. Soon these fields will be thick with leaves, disguising the furrows that separate them by early summer. Chloe had thought she would still be here then, that she would watch this barren landscape turn technicolour with wild flowers, just as Maureen had described to her. But she knows that inside her coat she is carrying a bomb back to Low Drove. Information that will explode inside that house, maybe even further.

The bus pulls into a stop, and Chloe's racing head stills for the time it takes to let passengers off. The doors close and the bus moves on down the road and it's only then that she realizes. Her head has been so busy with thoughts of Patrick, for Maureen's safety, with exposing his lies, that she hasn't stopped for a moment to consider herself in all this. She pictures again Maureen's concerned face when she walks in the door. She is all that Maureen has now, and this information – this bomb that she can detonate – will destroy that too. A clammy coldness creeps across her skin.

Patrick hadn't told her as some kind of confession – why would he after all these years? No, he'd told her to make her as much of a liar as he is. He must feel confident she won't tell Maureen. He knows that would compromise her own place in their house. She thinks he's paid no attention to her all these weeks, but he knows her well enough to understand what she has come to mean to Maureen. What Maureen believes she could be to her. What she was convincing Chloe she may be. Now suddenly it makes perfect sense why Patrick had started to go along with it. Why he doesn't call Maureen crazy anymore. Why he had welcomed Chloe into his home.

She presses the bell on the bus. She stands up. Presses again. Again and again. The *Bus Stopping* sign flashes, but the driver continues. He looks up in the mirror as she makes her way to the front of the bus.

'Ent no stop now til West Fen,' he says into the rearview mirror.

Chloe clutches her stomach and heaves.

'Stop the bus,' she says.

'Ent no stop—'

'Stop the bus.'

Finally, it slows. She feels the other passengers' eyes on her as she makes for the front door. Her head is spinning. The doors open. Long grass disguises the step as the doors open. Chloe almost falls off the bus. She rights her balance as she lands in the soft mud. The doors close. The bus pulls away.

The thought rises along with the bile. There is a reason that Patrick is allowing Maureen to think that she is Angie. Because if she does, it'll mean keeping his own murderous secret.

She stumbles forward a few feet, and then, alone, at the side of the road, she vomits.

FORTY-FOUR

Low Drove looks like a film set as she approaches. An unsuspecting, end-of-the-road village. Its isolation haunting. The sky presses down today, dark heavy clouds thick with rain. At the other end of the village, the red Wall's ice cream sign flaps wildly in the wind.

Chloe had to wait almost another hour for a bus. She started walking but then pictured Patrick's blue car driving along the road and finding her. Instead, she sat on the banks of the dyke, among the long grass, her back to the road, listening out for the heavy hum of the bus as it approached.

Now in Low Drove, she walks across the road and passes through the fronds of the willow tree. She spins around as they close behind her, stopping for a moment as the leaf curtain flickers this way and that, obscuring her view back to the main road.

She turns and continues towards Elm House. She's relieved to see no car on the drive, and her gait quickens for a second as pictures flash into her mind: Maureen sitting at the kitchen table, a hurried explanation from Chloe, the two of them gathering their things. But she slows again as she remembers: to expose Patrick is to expose herself. She can only convince Maureen that he killed her daughter if she confesses that she can't possibly be the missing girl herself. She can't do that.

It's not as if Chloe hasn't tried to look for an innocent explanation. She wondered perhaps if the police had deliberately thrown the public off the scent. Perhaps Maureen and Patrick were somehow complicit in a cat and mouse game between the police and the abductor? But she knows enough about searches for missing children from her time at the newspaper to know that information made public is the only way of ensuring their return. That is, if they are searching in the right place to start with.

Chloe had also considered that it might have been an innocent mistake. Perhaps trauma had left Patrick with some kind of amnesia – you hear about these things, she figured. But whatever had impaired his thinking then had clearly worn off now. It didn't add up; how could he play the devoted, heartbroken father and not tell the police something so vital that might bring back his child? She thinks about their friend Josie – did she have a hunch that he had been lying all these years? Is that why she didn't seem to like him? Chloe wonders if she could speak to her, and then remembers how unfriendly she'd been to Chloe, too.

Whatever way she looked at it, she was always left with the most sinister supposition of all: Patrick had lied to conceal his daughter's murder. And he was allowing Chloe to pretend to be her in order to cover up the truth.

Elm House slowly comes closer. Chloe swallows. Once, twice. Her mouth feels dry. She has tried to run through the conversation she could have with Maureen, of course she has. But what's to say Maureen would even believe her? After Angie disappeared, Patrick was her rock. Why would she believe Chloe over a man she's been married to for nearly four decades? Chloe tells herself that if she truly believes she is her missing daughter, then she will. She has to. And then she ties herself up in knots all over again because of course she won't, not if Chloe tells her what she's really thinking.

Her hatred for Patrick swells inside each step. He's done this. If she keeps his secret, he will make her as guilty as he is. She hates him for that. Hates him and fears him because if these thoughts – these suspicions – are correct, Patrick is guilty of infanticide. He is his own daughter's killer.

Chloe reaches the house, but it feels different now. Every one of her senses is alert to a new sound, a new smell. She arrives at the back door. Through the glass panel, she can see Maureen sitting at the table, head bowed, lost in a book. If only she could keep her that way, locked in innocence. Chloe doesn't want to blow her world apart – has this woman not suffered enough? – but she needs to know. She deserves to know. Chloe pushes her hand down on the handle. She thought she'd come here to find out the truth – just not this truth.

'What are you doing home at this time, Chloe, love?' Maureen says, looking up, double-checking the clock as she does.

Chloe had forgotten for a moment that she was going to feign illness. If Patrick had been there, she would have needed an excuse for coming home early. For a split second she is unsure whether to reach for her head or her stomach. She goes for her head.

'Oh lovey,' Maureen says, getting up from her chair

and rushing to her side. She puts her hand out to her forehead just as Chloe knew she would. She holds it there, and Chloe presses her head forward, as if Maureen's palm could take away not just this fictional pain, but all of it. All of it always. Why is it that nothing can stay the same forever? Chloe feels like she might cry.

'Well, you haven't got a temperature, so that's a good thing,' Maureen says.

She guides her by her elbow to a chair at the table, pulling it out and encouraging Chloe into it. On the draining board, upside down, there are six pink plastic beakers, the kind you might find in a school or a nursery. Maureen sees her staring at them.

'Let me get you a glass of water,' she says. 'These are new – for you.'

Maureen pours her water into one of the beakers and Chloe takes it in two hands. She takes a sip as Maureen sits down opposite her.

'Patrick not here?' Chloe asks.

'Hmm? No,' Maureen says, 'though he shouldn't be too long. Why? You're not thinking you need running to the doctor's, are you? I mean, I'm sure he would – of course he would – but you don't feel that poorly, do you, love?'

Chloe shakes her head. 'I'll be fine, I just need some rest. There's been something going round at work, it's probably that.'

Maureen sighs. 'Probably . . . I remember when you . . .' She stops.

'When I what?' Chloe asks.

'It's nothing,' Maureen says, looking down at the

tablecloth and running the seam of it round her index finger. 'Well, I was going to say, I remember when you . . . well . . . I remember when Angie started school, there wasn't a day when she didn't come home with something – when *you* didn't come home with something.' She says the last bit as if it's a new dress that she's still trying on for size.

Chloe looks down into her lap. All she can see, all she can hear, is him. She looks up again quickly, into Maureen's trusting face, just inches from hers. She wants to tell herself that there is enough between them, that even if Maureen knew for sure that she wasn't Angie, that she would still keep her, that they'd still have each other.

'What is it, love?' Maureen says suddenly. 'You really don't seem yourself.'

Chloe reaches for Maureen's hand. The two parts of her heart pulling away from each other. Had she come here to deceive? That wasn't what she had thought she was doing. And yet, she can't tell the truth.

'It's just . . . it's just . . .'

Maureen takes her hand and holds it.

'What is it, Chloe, love? Has something come back to you, is this what it is? Have you remembered? Is that why your head is hurting?'

Chloe clutches her temples, because now it really is hurting. She flashes back for a moment, to the car, to the conversation with Patrick. Snapshots race through her mind. She has to tell her. She *has* to tell her. But Chloe's uncertainty – or perhaps hope – that she's still got some-thing wrong nags at her. Worse is a fear that Maureen hasn't been honest either, that she knows Patrick wasn't at the park that day. But hadn't she run through that thought earlier? Hadn't she discarded it as impossible?

'It's just I was telling Patrick this morning, about a dream I had.'

Maureen shuffles closer; she's on the edge of her chair.

'It was different – to others, I mean.'

Maureen nods. She feels her squeeze her hand, as if to help her go on.

'It felt . . . it felt like I'd been there before, and, well . . .'

'Been where, love?'

'A park.'

Maureen blanches. Chloe tries to read what she can from the look on her face, but it's blank. Why? Because she knows nothing, or she wants to make it look like she does? Chloe reaches for her head again.

'I was in a park, and it was only me and Patrick, and the grass, it was long . . .'

Maureen sits straighter. 'What length?' she says.

'What?'

'The grass. I mean, here?' She points to ankle height. 'Here?' She moves up to over her knees.

Chloe thinks of the picture, the one she had studied that morning back at Nan's. Thank God.

Her hand hovers just around her own knee.

'Well, it would be here now, but then . . .'

'When?' Maureen says, quickly. 'Try and remember, Chloe.'

Chloe hears a car on the road outside; her eyes flicker to the window – not that she'd be able to see – but

Maureen remains bolt upright in her chair, pleading with her eyes for more. Chloe starts speaking faster, in case it is Patrick arriving home.

'I was little. The grass, then, it was . . . it was almost to here.' She shows Maureen by making a line right across the middle of her neck. 'And there were swings, yellow ones.'

Maureen lets go of Chloe's hands just in time for the pair of them to hear for sure Patrick's tyres crunching on the pebble drive. A little gasp escapes Maureen's mouth.

The car door slams.

'Well, Patrick . . . he was there one minute and then the next . . .'

'Gone?' Maureen asks.

'Well, yeah, gone . . . I, I don't know . . .'

Maureen gets up from her chair and almost floats across the kitchen just in time to see Patrick heading from the car past the window by the sink.

'I don't know what it means,' Chloe says.

'What it means?' asks Maureen, her face a wide and brilliant smile that takes two decades off the woman standing before Chloe. 'What it means is that your memory is coming back. Don't you see? The park is where Angie disappeared from. I can still see it that day: long grass – just like you said – yellow swings. That's where you were with Dad when . . . when . . . oh Chloe! Oh Angie!'

'So I did disappear from the park?' Chloe asks.

'Yes! Yes,' Maureen says. Half laughs, half cries. She's wiping those same tears away when Patrick comes through the back door. He stops when he sees Chloe there. He hesitates, one foot suspended above the step. He puts it down slowly, then steps into the kitchen, looking between Chloe and his wife.

'Oh Patrick,' Maureen says, going over and wrapping her arms around him. He pats his wife's back, looking straight at Chloe as he does. She looks away.

'Oh Patrick, you're not going to believe this . . . come in, come in, sit down . . .'

She directs him to his chair; he sits down opposite Chloe. He looks again, between them.

'What's going on, Mo?' he says.

'It's Angie, Pat – Chloe . . . oh, whatever.' She tosses her hands up, offering them to the air. 'She's remembering, it's working, it's . . . it's all coming back to her.'

Chloe glances up at Patrick in time, she's sure, to see his eyes narrow a bit.

'Don't you see? She's remembering, Pat, it's all coming back. She had a dream, she said she was at the park, with you. She described it, she . . . she described it just as it was that day. Oh Pat, our Angie.' She squeezes his hand inside hers. 'We're getting our girl back.'

Patrick smiles at his wife. Chloe sees how he squeezes her hand in his fist. He reaches down, kisses it. He strokes the top of her head and gets up.

'You always knew it, didn't you, love?' he says, and she swells under his touch.

Half of Chloe expects he might put Maureen right then, if there had been a genuine mistake. Wasn't this the time to finally say it? But instead he stands next to the sink and shakes his head, smiling.

'Well, if she remembers the park,' he says.

Maureen nods enthusiastically, and then playfully stands up and taps him. 'And you thought we needed DNA tests,' she laughs. 'You watch too many of those CSI programmes, that's your problem.'

He laughs. The two of them laugh. And Chloe sits at the kitchen table alone.

Inside she is screaming.

FORTY-FIVE

Chloe watches Patrick. This is her life now. She watches the way he holds the knife if Maureen asks him to help her peel spuds for dinner. She notices how comfortable the blade looks in his hand, how natural his grip is on the handle. Is this how he did it?

When he puffs up the cushions on his chair before sitting down to watch one of his CSI programmes, Chloe looks up from the sofa. She notices the way he grips the cushions, with two hands. Her eyes flicker to his face, searching for a moment of recognition, but it is so hard to tell. People like him are experts in deceit.

When Maureen and Patrick are out of the house, she has searched – and searched – for where he keeps his gun. But she has found nothing, which doesn't make any sense at all. Yet again, wouldn't he need to be a master of deceit to have kept it hidden all these years?

She can't say she feels uncomfortable in the Kyles' house now, not all the time. In the daylight, when the kitchen is filled with the sound of the radio, when Maureen is humming as she wipes down the worktops, when the sound of the horse racing on the TV floats up the stairs, Chloe can almost pretend that nothing has changed. And yet, everything is different.

She lies on her bed in the evening light. Maureen has left Puss on her pillow again. The clocks went forward last weekend and hope lingers at the end of each day now.

Not for Chloe anymore. She could leave, she knows she could. She could just pack up her things and go. But – she looks out of the window, across the tops of the trees that disguise the garden in these desolated fields – something keeps her here. Maureen? Her unwavering belief that Chloe is her missing daughter? Or is it what had pulled her to Elm House in the first place: a search for truth? Everything is so blurred now, it's impossible to tell.

She leans over the side of the bed and fishes underneath for her archive. Her hand sweeps dusty floorboards, a pair of old trainers, nothing else. She leans further off the bed, waiting to feel her fingertips touch the box, but instead there is a space where it should be. She slides off the bed, looks underneath, all the way back to the wall. Her heart is gripped with panic. She is on her belly now, frantically pushing aside the trainers, a few discarded magazines. There is no box. She pulls herself out. Scans her room. Did she leave it out? Might it have been found? But the shoebox is nowhere to be seen. She stands, circling the floor. Her head is pounding now. She strides back to her bed, strips off the duvet. Has it become tangled inside it? She strips the bed all the way back to the mattress, but it isn't there. She throws the pillow onto the floor. She opens the cupboard of the bedside table, nothing. She pulls out the bed. She looks down the gap between the bed and the window. The box is gone. Her archive is gone.

Her archive is gone.

Her heart is pounding as she reaches for the door handle. The sweat on her hands makes it turn inside her palm. She's trapped, she thinks, just for an instant. But then the door releases and the air on the landing is cooler, and downstairs the same old sounds float back up to her.

'Is everything all right, Chloe?' Maureen says, appearing at the bottom of the stairs. 'I heard some banging up there . . . ooh, you do look pale.'

Chloe wipes her hands on her clothes. 'No . . . no, everything is . . . I'm OK. I mean, it's OK. There's nothing.'

She goes back into her room and closes the door. Inside the room is turned over. But she starts her search again, this time in places that she would never keep her archive. She checks the bottom of the wardrobe, among the spare blankets and the blouse Maureen made her. She even walks over to the door that connects her room to the spare one and tries it. But the padlock is still there, keeping it locked tight. She climbs on top of her bed and peers onto the top of the wardrobe. She checks behind the curtain. Then finally flops down onto the bare mattress. Her archive has gone. And there's only one person she can think of who might have it.

She stays up in her room that night. She doesn't go down to dinner. Maureen brings her a plate of mince and potatoes up on a tray but she doesn't touch a thing. She lets the room fall dark. She doesn't switch on her own television. Instead she lies in the darkness, listening to the sounds that drift up through her floorboards: the chimes of the *Nine O'Clock News*, Maureen and Patrick chatting easily. There are no arguments to be overheard between the pair of them now. It's as if everything has been settled. Chloe is Angie. Patrick has got away with murder.

A few hours later, she hears Maureen come up to bed. She makes out the sound of the bathroom cabinet opening, of Maureen running the cold water tap and swallowing down the tablets that regulate her days, that keep everything normal. Chloe wants to laugh – what is normal anymore?

She gets up and makes her bed in the darkness, then slips under the duvet. But she doesn't sleep. Instead, she stares at her door, at the slit of light from the landing that casts a dull shine on the first few feet of floorboards inside her room. She can't rest. Not when he's downstairs. She imagines his hands all over her cuttings. Her cuttings . . . She wants to cry. So now they both keep a secret. And his only silences Chloe further.

Half an hour later, Chloe hears Patrick's footsteps on the stairs. A dull thud that comes closer. He stops at the top of the landing. Chloe grips the duvet underneath her chin as a pair of feet come to a standstill outside her door. The light dims. She hears his breath on the other side of the door frame. She stares at the door handle, praying not to see it turn but she's sure it moves momentarily. Someone's grip on the handle the other side. She freezes in bed. But a second later the footsteps move away, towards the bathroom. She listens to the sound of the toilet flushing, to the taps in the sink, the water whooshing past her down the creaking drainpipes. Every sense is alert in the darkness. And long after he closes their bedroom door, Chloe lies awake staring at her black ceiling.

They say that at night, when the frontal lobes are least active, we are left with the more primeval parts of our personality. Intuition takes over from logic. So it makes sense that it is in the middle of the night, the early hours, when Chloe's suspicions are strongest, when she rehearses in her head what she will say to Maureen come the morning, what she will reveal about the husband she adores. She practises over and over so she will get it right as the sun bleaches the black night blue behind her curtains. But by the morning, when she goes downstairs for breakfast, when the kitchen table is filled with bright packets of kids' cereals, a plastic bowl and spoon for her, the world somehow looks more normal again. Normal, and at once strange.

Chloe rubs her eyes. She has hardly slept.

'Let me get the milk for you, Chloe, love,' Maureen says, as she tucks her chair under the table.

Patrick sits across from her. She doesn't look up. Instead she feels his eyes on her. She thinks of her archive. She has no appetite.

Maureen fusses around her as usual, trailing a hand down the back of her hair as she moves between the table and the sink. Chloe shivers a little.

'Any more dreams?' Maureen says.

She has asked her this the last three mornings.

Chloe shakes her head. Maureen looks disappointed, as she has every other day.

'We'll have to be feeding you cheese before bed,' she laughs.

Patrick laughs too.

'Pat's got some business in town later, so he's offered to pick you up from work.'

Chloe looks up quickly.

'Oh, I—'

'It's no bother, Chloe, love. Is it, Pat?' Maureen says.

'No, no bother at all,' he smiles at her, and underneath the table, Chloe presses crescent shapes into her palm with her nails.

'It'll save you getting the bus, and they say there might be rain later,' Maureen says.

Maureen shakes some Frosties into Chloe's bowl, as she looks out of the window. Bright sunlight fills the kitchen.

Chloe nods as Maureen hands her Angie's spoon.

Chloe eats slowly, the cereal sticking in her throat. She's thinking of Patrick's gun. Is that what business he has in town today? Is that why he hasn't told Maureen? She's picturing it lying in the back of the car later as they drive along isolated roads in the dark, back towards Low Drove. Not a soul around.

Chloe swallows her cereal too quickly. She coughs.

'I was going to meet a friend later,' she says, trying to clear her throat.

Both Maureen and Patrick look up.

'A friend?' Maureen says. She looks at Patrick quickly. 'What friend, Chloe, love? We didn't know Chloe had a friend, did we, Pat?'

Patrick shakes his head and leans forward on the table.

'Hollie,' Chloe says.

'Hollie?'

'Yes, Hollie.'

Maureen sits down slowly in the chair. She picks up a tea towel on the table and starts winding it around her hand.

'You haven't mentioned Hollie before, has she, Pat?'

Patrick shakes his head. Chloe looks between them, wondering why Maureen had found it necessary to check with him.

'I've known Hollie my whole life,' Chloe says.

Maureen lets out a little laugh. 'Well, you can't have known her your *whole* life . . .' she says. 'We've never heard of a Hollie, have we, Pat?'

Again, he shakes his head.

'Can't say we have,' he says.

'Oh . . . no, well, maybe not my whole life,' Chloe says, suddenly backtracking. 'But since, well, we were in foster care together.'

Maureen's shoulders sink.

'Oh,' she says. Then again, 'Oh. She doesn't have parents either then?'

Chloe sees how she glances at Patrick. She quickly looks down into her cereal bowl.

'Well, she does but . . . well, they couldn't look after her, or at least they did but not how social services thought they should so . . . yeah. But she got a new family, Dave and Rita. They're nice. And then yeah, we stayed friends afterwards. We've always looked out for each other, I guess. We tell each other everything.'

She looks at Patrick when she says that last bit.

'Hmm,' Maureen says, and looks down at the tea towel in her lap. 'You should bring her here.'

'What?'

'Hollie. Is that what you said her name was? Shouldn't she, Pat? Wouldn't it be nice to meet Chloe's friend?'

Patrick pauses.

'Well, Mo, I . . .'

'Whyever not, Patrick?'

'Well, it's not that I . . .' he starts.

Chloe sees how he squirms in his seat.

Patrick stands up, goes to the sink. He taps the side of the worktop with his signet ring as he searches the big Fen sky for something.

Maureen turns to Chloe.

'So you'll bring her tonight?'

'Sorry?' Chloe says.

'Hollie. You'll bring her home, here?'

'Tonight?' Chloe says, one eye still watching Patrick at the sink. His head is bowed now. Even the back of him looks guilty. She thinks of her archive and her stomach twists inside. 'Oh, I think she's busy tonight.'

'But you said—' Maureen starts.

'Actually, I've just remembered' – Chloe mimes slapping her forehead – 'she text last night to say she's going out for dinner with her boyfriend.'

'She's got a boyfriend, has she?'

'Yes, Phil.'

'That might be you some day, bringing a boyfriend home to meet Mum and Dad.' She nudges Chloe's elbow. 'Still, we wouldn't want you to leave us here, would we, Pat?'

'Hmm?' He turns round from the sink.

Maureen rolls her eyes. 'Oh, men, no point talking to them about this stuff. Anyway, that settles it, Pat'll bring you home tonight. It's five you finish, isn't it, love?'

Chloe nods as Maureen stands up and clasps her hands together.

'Why don't you two bring fish and chips home with you? We haven't had them in ages.'

*   *   *

Chloe makes her excuses after a while, and mounts the stairs, saying she needs to get ready for work. Only when she gets to the top of the landing, something feels different. The door to her room is slightly ajar – she hadn't left it like that, she never leaves it like that. Slowly, she pushes it open, the door creaking a little as she does. Inside, everything looks the same. For some reason, her eyes fall under the bed. She closes the door and gets down on her hands and knees. She slides one arm underneath, into the darkness, and feels her fingertips hit something familiar – her archive.

She squeezes herself under the bed, pulling it out with both hands. Tentatively she takes off the lid. It's all there, just as she had kept it. She feels relief and fear, because she knows it wasn't here last night. Someone had removed it. The box has been returned, but perhaps everything has changed now – maybe whoever has looked inside now suspects her. She leans back against the bed, her fingers feeling for each cutting in turn, each small brown envelope. She holds the archive to her chest as her heart beats against it.

FORTY-SIX

Chloe arrives at the glass building that houses the insurance company an hour before Patrick is due to collect her that afternoon. The last thing she wants is for him to catch her getting off the bus and hurrying across the road towards the office. When she walked by the other day, she noticed that there was a small cafe in the atrium on the ground floor, complete with a couple of chairs and tables spilling out of it. She arrives early and goes inside. She had worried, of course, about bumping into Phil again, but she figured the chances were slim and, anyway, she could always say she had a second interview.

At reception, a woman dressed like an air hostess with a silk scarf round her neck asks if she can help. Chloe points towards the cafe, and she nods, smiles and waves her forward.

Chloe buys a KitKat and a can of Diet Coke then sits there, in her winter coat, in the atrium, her bag at her side. A copy of the local newspaper peers out the top of her bag, but she resists reading it and instead sits staring out at the road, waiting for the first flash of Patrick's blue car.

Chloe doesn't want to get in that car. She hasn't wanted to get into it all day. Not tonight, not on her own. Not without Maureen. Chloe has a thought that maybe Maureen has changed her mind and come along with him for the ride. How relieved she would be if they pulled up and Maureen was sitting alongside him in the front, ready to collect her. And then she stops and ponders on that image, how happy it would have made her not so long ago to have a mum and dad driving to pick her up from work. She always promised herself she wouldn't take a proper family for granted.

Her phone vibrates in her pocket, making her stomach turn inside the padding of her coat. She pulls the phone out in case it's Patrick and is filled with relief when she sees it's Park House. But she can't answer, not now. And so that same relief turns to guilt. She turns her phone off, as if that might dilute the unease. She has missed a few calls from Park House in the last few days. She's deleted the voicemails without listening. Claire Sanders has called, too. Twice. Chloe knows what about. The house, the paperwork, the fees, but Chloe is not in that head-space now. Not when she's living with a killer. She's shocked even at her mind's ability to use that word. A child killer. A man capable of murdering his own daughter, then lying to the police – to his wife – for decades. This is not the time to be filling out paperwork for social services. She shakes her head and takes another sip of her drink, then pulls her coat around her. She doesn't want to get in that car.

She'd forgotten her watch that morning, so now her phone is off she can't check the time. She looks around, towards the glass lift and the open staircase which criss-crosses the atrium. A wall of plants rises the entire way up to a few square metres of blue sky above them. Chloe can't help thinking they must attract flies in the summer. When she pictures Phil coming here every day, she thinks of her own desk back at the newspaper. She still catches herself sometimes, walking through the archive in her mind, mapping the aisles made up of metal filing cabinets; she can even feel the old blue carpet tiles underneath her feet. She pauses to pull open drawers. She can still conjure up the scratch and squeak of their runners, see the spines of envelopes that lie inside. That had been home, among those files, those people. She had been happy there. Perhaps she'd even imagined a file being opened up for her if she'd solved this case. She'd even thought for a while that by bringing Angie back she could save the archive, that it would be a huge news story that she had reinvestigated the files – bigger even than the local news – and then perhaps it wouldn't just be her archive that would be saved, but so many others at newspapers up and down the country, that people would see just how vital that human touch is to a story, just how seriously archivists take their jobs, that they're not just caretakers of stories, but vital gatekeepers of them. But that's all fantasy now.

She's startled by a voice at the top of the staircase. A navy suit begins its descent down the steps. Chloe is sure she recognizes the same dark hair. She can't risk bumping into Phil again. She grabs the newspaper from her bag, opens the page at random and buries her head in the stories. She takes a deep breath, inhaling the scent of the newsprint which instantly calms her. She has missed this.

A few moments later, she peers over the top of the newspaper. It is another man, not Phil. She replaces the paper in her bag, and looks up in time to see Patrick's blue car rounding through the car park. She gathers up her bag and leaves the KitKat wrapper and can of Coke on the table. She's aware of the receptionist watching her as she walks across the atrium and out through the revolving doors.

Patrick leans across the empty passenger seat to open the door for her.

'Good day?' he asks when she gets in. She puts her bag between her feet and turns around to check the back seat. She's relieved to see there is no gun.

'Yes, thanks,' she says, pulling on her seat belt and plugging it in at her side. 'Busy.'

She checks the seat again, and then her eyes flicker further back – could it be in the boot?

'All set?' Patrick asks. 'Better not forget those fish and chips on the way, Maureen would murder us.'

They don't speak as they leave the city; instead the radio fills the space between them in the car. The DJ makes cheesy jokes and Patrick laughs quietly, adjusting his hands on the steering wheel. When Chloe feels him look at her, she smiles back, though in reality she has no idea what the DJ just said. When Patrick watches the road, she watches him, his big hands on the wheel.

Traffic queues to get out of the city at rush hour. She taps her feet, aware of the extra time she'll have to spend trapped in the car with him. She reassures herself that the A47 becomes a dual carriageway at the next roundabout, but still she sinks a little into her seat. In her lap, she picks the skin around her fingernails, not watching the road, willing this journey over.

Patrick drums his hands on the steering wheel and

turns up the sound on the radio. But at the next round-about, Chloe feels them take a left. She looks up – they're heading away from the traffic that's starting to move up ahead. This isn't the usual route home. She looks at Patrick quickly, but he doesn't return her gaze. Instead he pushes his foot on the accelerator, and as she feels herself pressing into the passenger seat, she grips the sides of the leather upholstery with both hands. Patrick's eyes flicker down to the handbrake. Chloe moves her hand back into her lap.

'Bloody traffic,' he sighs.

She looks straight ahead. The windows have started to steam. Chloe looks to her left, but the fields beyond them are hazy. She skips ahead on their route – one mile, two – then remembers they are picking up fish and chips.

'Is this the way to the fish and chip shop?' she asks.

The sports results are on the radio and Patrick turns up the volume before answering.

'I need petrol,' he says after a moment. 'There's a place just up here.'

'Oh right.' Chloe tries to allow her body to sink into the leather of the upholstery.

Ahead, at the next roundabout, is a large village, and just before it, the petrol station Patrick had mentioned. He pulls onto the forecourt, and gets out of the car. Chloe sits, frozen, the sweet smell of benzene floating into the car when he opens the door to get his wallet. She watches him cross the forecourt. Just an ordinary man to every-body else. There is a long queue to pay inside, and Chloe makes the most of a few moments alone in the car. Her eyes flicker around, and she checks the back again, behind

Patrick's seat, just in case the gun is propped up there. But she finds the footwell empty. Her imagination is getting carried away. She looks up at Patrick again behind four or five other people. Just an ordinary man.

She sighs inside the car. The windows are still steamy. She watches him, though she knows he'd struggle to see her. And that's when she notices the glove compartment in front of her. It has a tiny lock on it, one that fits a tiny key. She looks up at Patrick, still stuck in the queue, tapping the side of his leg with his keys. Chloe leans forward, restricted a little by her seat belt, but enough to try the tiny door – it opens. Inside, there is the usual paraphernalia you find in cars. She takes each item out in turn: screen wipes, a log book, a small first aid kit. And then, pressed tight against the bottom, something that seems unusual. Her fingers feel for it, fishing it out, and then there it is, exposed in her hand – a newspaper cutting she recognizes from her own collection at Low Drove:

ANGIE'S FATHER IN SHOCK ARREST

Her heart stops still in her chest. Her hands start to shake as she reads the words she knows so well, the ones she's already committed to memory, the quotes from Patrick that had once put her mind at rest. She looks from the cutting to Patrick in the queue. He took this from her archive. She knows this because she recognizes the same biro writing down the side of it: *Patrick angry. Maureen frightened into silence.* And the date, just a few weeks before.

The cutting flutters in her hands. She looks up. Patrick is paying at the till. He turns around, heading out of the petrol station, back across the forecourt. She takes the cutting, pushing it into her coat pocket, feeling it tear as she does so. Quickly, she shoves everything else back into the glove compartment, closing the door tight just as Patrick gets back in the car beside her. He stops for a moment and looks at her, as if sensing a shift in atmosphere. He looks down at her hands in her lap. She places one over the other, so he doesn't see how they're shaking.

'Bloody queues,' he says, heaving the car door shut behind him. Then he pulls on his seat belt and puts his key in the ignition. And as he does, Chloe closes her eyes and longs for the safety of home. Nan's home.

They continue on the road towards the Fens. Inside, the car is filled with the white noise of tyres on the dual carriageway. Chloe's head is spinning beside Patrick. He taps the steering wheel, humming along to the radio. She watches his hands as he changes gear; the rest of the time, she focuses on the dull grey of the road in front of them, pictures swimming in front of her eyes. She is still in her seat, but her heart thumps behind her ribs and hot blood spins in her ears.

Then Patrick turns off the dual carriageway onto a single track they haven't taken before. Chloe grips the sides of her seat as he pushes his foot down on the accelerator. In the wing mirror she sees dust kicked up by the tyres. Her feet press into the footwell.

It is early evening out in the Fens and the big sky is turning pink, dyeing silhouettes of the trees an inky blue. She would usually see beauty here, but not tonight. She doesn't recognize this road. She has never been here before. She pictures the boot of the car. Patrick's gun. Maureen at home waiting for fish and chips.

'Would you look at that?' Patrick says.

Suddenly he lunges towards her. She flinches, squeezing her eyes shut. But when she opens them, out of the window, at exactly the same level and even speed, a barn owl flies alongside them. Its beautiful white plumage streaks across the dark green of the fields, its black eyes fixed straight ahead. It moves as if it flies in slow motion.

'Ent that a sight, eh?' Patrick says.

For a moment the pair of them are mesmerized by the sight: the bird's round moon face, its dangling feathered legs, within them a mouse, or perhaps a vole.

A bump underneath the wheels jolts them out of the moment. For a second, black tyres tear across the road. Patrick clutches hold of the wheel, which spins under his grip, and he slams on the brakes. Chloe grips the upholstery harder as she jolts in her seat. A moment later and the car is still, the only thing moving a cloud of dust chewed up from the road behind them.

Patrick checks the rear-view mirror. 'Oh Jesus,' he says, quickly undoing his seat belt. Then again: 'Oh Jesus Christ.'

He's out of the car before Chloe has time to turn around. He leaves the driver's door open. Chloe thinks of the cutting crumpled in her pocket and looks quickly at the keys hanging in the ignition. She glances through the back windscreen, and sees Patrick striding swiftly back the way they came. She turns further in her seat to see why. Not too far in front of him, there is something unidentifiable writhing in the road.

Chloe unfastens her seat belt and opens her own car door. Out on the open road, Patrick marches closer to the figure on the tarmac. Chloe follows him. He looks up.

'Stay back,' he says, holding his hand up to stop her.

She jumps slightly, but obeys him.

He turns back to the creature, and she hears him say again, 'Oh Jesus.'

A hare lies on the road, its deep brown eyes bulging in pain. Even from this distance, Chloe can see the whites of its eyes. The terror in them as Patrick approaches. She can feel it. The hare makes a pathetic attempt to run, but its hind leg is stuck fast to the road, a mass of pink and red seeping into the tarmac.

Patrick kneels down beside the hare. The animal jerks away, a bloody part of its leg tearing from the tarmac, but not enough. Flesh and fur enmeshed on the road.

Patrick reaches for its long angular head with both hands. The animal struggles, but his strength is too much. She sees the hare's black-tipped ears poke out of the top of Patrick's palms. There is no time for Chloe to look away. The wind carries the sound towards her: the snap of the hare's neck breaking in two. It is the swiftest of movements that does it, and in the same second the animal stops struggling. Patrick returns its limp body to the road. Its wide eyes reflecting the last of the amber sun.

Chloe stands as still as the hare on the tarmac. In this barren landscape, the only witness to this death.

Patrick makes to stand, then bends back down. He pulls what's left of the hare from the road and tosses it onto the grassy verge. A pinky stain remains where it lay. He turns back towards the car and that's when he looks up and sees Chloe's face. He stops still. The pair of them twenty paces apart. His own face drained of blood.

'Chloe, it was the . . .'

She stares at the blood on his hands. Those big hands.

'There was nothing more . . .' He takes a step towards her.

Chloe instantly jumps back. She feels the boot of the car against her back. She whips round, searches the land-scape for another car, another witness. There is nothing, nobody.

Patrick holds his hands out as if surrendering. But he knows she's seen it, the ease with which he stubbed out that animal's life. There is no going back and she cannot hide the horror on her face. He knew how to break that hare's neck. He did it as though he had done it a thousand times before. But there is only one occasion now that runs like a reel through Chloe's head. He sees it too. He must do.

'Don't come near me,' she says, her hands feeling behind her for the side of the car.

'Chloe, what—'

'Don't move another step.'

'Ah, come on, Chloe, you saw the poor fecking crea-ture, it was the kindest—'

What will she do out here on this lonely road? She reaches into her pocket for her phone, then remembers it is off. And who would she call, anyway? What would she say? What is there to tell? That's when she hears herself say it.

'You did it, didn't you?'

'Did what?' Patrick asks.

'You killed Angie.'

FORTY-SEVEN

There is silence between the pair, just the whistle of the wind as it finds the only two things around which to coil.

She stares at Patrick. His face is blank. Her own hot blood pounds in her ears.

Patrick staggers backwards and forwards in the road, his hands reaching for his temples. For a long while, he can't speak. When he does, all he says is, 'What?'

His tone is incredulous, frayed at the edges.

Patrick takes one step towards Chloe. She inches back. Two fields away, she hears the hum of traffic from the dual carriageway. Too far to run. Closer, she hears the rustle of the sugar beet leaves in the fields that surround them, and then her voice as she calls across the asphalt to him: 'I've known for a long time that you did it. I just didn't know how I knew for sure . . . but seeing that just then, how easily you—'

'Chloe, it's a fucking hare.'

Chloe is silent. It's not just the hare.

On the road, Patrick clasps his hands together. He shakes his head as if he cannot believe what she is saying. Then he rests his forehead in his hands.

He tries again, stepping forward, but Chloe moves back.

'It's a fucking animal, Chloe. There's a big fucking difference between an animal and . . . and . . .'

'It's not just that, though, is it?' she says. 'It's everything.

You told me yourself you weren't at the swings the day Angie disappeared. So why would you have people looking there? The whole investigation was based on that play park . . .' As she says this she spreads her arms wide, as if the police had been combing this very field.

Patrick stops, as if the thought has suddenly hit him. He looks up to the sky and then puts his head into his hands.

'Chloe, I . . . look.' He pauses, staggering around. 'Would you get a hold of yourself.'

But she won't give up. She's come this far.

'All these years you've let Maureen think that Angie was taken from that park. All these years. And yet you were hiding the biggest secret of all, from everyone.'

'Chloe, it's not what you thi—'

'Why else would you let Maureen think that I was Angie unless you didn't want her to know what had happened to her? What *you* had done to her?'

He takes another step forward. 'I think you've got your wires cr—'

'Don't move,' she shouts. He stops suddenly, and he must see it then, the terror in her eyes. Her absolute fear of him.

'Don't take another step closer,' Chloe says. 'You killed your daughter and now what? You're going to kill me?'

With that thought, she looks around, across the fields that surround them. She hasn't thought this through. Just what is she going to do now? There is a house, across two fields, where smoke files from its short chimney stack, a warm glow from one downstairs window. Could she make it there? Could she get there before him? She turns back to Patrick. He's standing, wide-legged, wide-eyed on the tarmac. She weighs up whether she could run, but she has no chance. She knows that. If he has that gun in the boot of the car, her chances of making it even fifty yards are slim. She hadn't expected it to happen like this. It wasn't meant to. But there was the car journey, the hare, his hands. *His hands.*

Patrick is cradling his head in them now. Pacing up and down, talking to himself – not that Chloe can hear what he's saying.

He goes to speak, but he can't find the words. Instead he sinks down onto his haunches in the middle of the road. He wipes his hands across his face, and sighs, defeated. Chloe is surprised to feel her back relaxing into the boot of the car. By instinct she knows she's got him, that a confession will follow. He is so obviously undone by her accusation that this is surely over. She's won. And now what? What does she do with him out here? In that moment she isn't sure. All she does know is that the mystery is over. It has ended. She pictures Maureen at home, waiting innocently for fish and chips, naive to the fact that what will return home to her will blow her world apart. But what choice has Chloe had? She is not Angie. She never was, and once she knew Patrick only allowed Maureen to believe she was to hide his own crimes, how could she keep up the facade? There was no more fantasy, only the truth.

She stares at Patrick, almost as broken on the road as the hare he discarded. She has done this – Chloe has done this. It had taken her appearance in their home to show

Patrick Kyle for who he was. Hadn't she always vowed to find out the truth about Angie? Perhaps now, she was one step closer to that.

It seems to be a long time before either of them move. When Chloe looks up again, the sky has darkened and the pair of them are little more than shadows. Finally, Patrick gets up from the road. He holds up his arms as if in surrender.

'I'm going to walk back to the car, Chloe,' he says slowly, a resigned tone to his voice that she's never heard before. 'I don't want you to be frightened. I've got my hands up, I'm not going to come anywhere near you. I'm just going to walk back towards the car, OK?'

Chloe nods, then realizes he can't see her in the darkness. 'Yes,' she says. 'OK.'

He's moving already, walking towards her. She sees the way he moves, his head bent, his shoulders slumped. Something in his stance tells her he's not a danger now, he can't hurt anyone ever again. Somehow, instinctively, she is no longer afraid.

Slowly, Patrick walks back to the driver's door. They face each other, the car between them.

'Get in,' he says. Then more gently, 'Get in and I'll explain everything.'

She hesitates. Does she want to get into a car with a murderer? But she looks around her, at the deserted road, the two of them in utter blackness, too early for the moon to shine its torch. If he was going to kill her, wouldn't he have done it by now? She looks across the fields for the house she saw, but it's now lost in the blindness of dusk; there is no light to run towards.

Patrick indicates again for her to get in. Then, without waiting for her, he slips into the driver's seat, leaving his door wide open. Slowly she moves back towards her side of the car. She glances in; he is staring at the steering wheel. She takes her place alongside him, but like him, keeps her door open. They sit like that for a while, both doors open, the air whistling through the open car. Finally, Patrick speaks.

'I am guilty,' he says, his voice shaken and small. 'I am. But not in the way that you think I am.'

Chloe swallows beside him. She knows she needs to let him speak.

'I couldn't have killed Angie, she was the most' – his voice breaks – 'she was the most precious . . . she was . . .' He clutches the steering wheel with both hands and leans his head in the middle of them.

Chloe looks over at him, the light in the car highlighting his hair.

'She was everything.' He starts to cry.

Chloe sits still beside him. She has never seen a man cry like this, she's mesmerized – mesmerized and horrified. She watches him without making a sound. It's a while before he recomposes himself. He wipes his face on the sleeve of his jumper and rubs his eyes. It's a few more minutes before he can speak.

'It is true that we weren't at the swings the day that she disappeared and you . . . you were the first person I ever told in all those years. Can you believe that?'

Chloe shakes her head under the glow of the car's interior light.

'I don't know why, why I chose to confess that to you,

a perfect stranger, when I had carried that secret all that time.'

He stops talking to shake his head in disbelief.

'Perhaps I felt so out of control,' he says. 'Maureen, she's so convinced you . . . well, you know. And I've tried, all these years I've tried to make her . . .'

He drops his head down again and sobs.

Chloe waits. Her mind is ablaze with questions. But she has to let him tell her himself. She has, after all, waited this long.

'OK . . . all right.' He turns to her in his seat. 'The truth is, I was having an affair. Can you believe it? I was the man who had everything. I had Maureen, I had my little girl, but like a lot of young men, it just wasn't enough.'

Chloe tips her head back against the headrest. An affair? She hadn't seen this coming. What? What is he saying?

He runs his hands through his hair, and bangs the steering wheel with both hands. Chloe jumps in her seat, and Patrick turns to her quickly, his hands out to calm her.

'But it doesn't make me a killer, Chloe. A fecking eejit, yes, but not a killer.' He shakes his head. 'Not a killer.'

Chloe moves a little towards the door, still nervous of being so close to him. Her mind was racing to join the dots, to understand what he was trying to tell her. What exactly had Patrick Kyle done if he had not murdered his daughter?

'But I knew, though, I knew I was risking everything,' he says. 'That's why I took Angie with me on that day. I took her with me to break it off, to end it. She was the best reminder of all I had to lose – I knew if I took Angie I would go through with it. We met not far from the park, but not in the park itself – a copse nearby. I couldn't risk . . . I couldn't risk anyone seeing . . . ah, it was a stupid thing, a stupid secret, and it cost me my daughter. It cost me everything.'

Chloe's brain scrambles. An affair. With who? What is he saying, that he *lost* Angie? But why not just confess? And why would he have taken Angie? Wouldn't she have told Maureen when they got back? So much isn't making sense.

Patrick continues: 'Angie, she played just beside us . . . unaware of anything her stupid eejit father was doing. And perhaps I thought if Angie said anything, I could just tell her we bumped into someone at the park, that kind of thing. Jesus, I don't know.' He turns to Chloe quickly. 'I swear I only took my eyes off her for a minute but . . . that was all it took. It's all it ever takes.'

Chloe is silent. She thinks of losing Nan in the cemetery. But that was not the same. Nan didn't die. But maybe neither did Angie. Why didn't he say anything? Why didn't he just tell Maureen he wasn't at the park?

'I'd told Maureen that I was taking her to the park and, you've got to believe me, I wanted to tell her, I did, but . . . how could I break that woman's heart twice over? She'd already lost her daughter . . . I'd already lost *my* daughter, I couldn't lose my wife too.'

He breaks down again, great big wracking sobs as Chloe sits beside him.

'So I told them I was in the park with her. It was near

enough, a stone's throw away, and I was sure – I was *so* sure – they'd search a bit further, a bit wider. But Maureen's probably told you about how the police cocked everything up? How they stopped searching when night started to fall. Ridiculous, right? But they were worried about trampling over evidence. So they searched for a few hours and then they gave up. You've got to remember this is more than twenty-five years ago. If it had happened today . . .' He holds his head in his hands. 'If it had happened today . . . I remember, there was a building site nearby, a waste area; I even pointed it out to them, I showed them myself, and they said they'd searched but . . . ah, how do you know? How do you know unless you get down on your hands and knees and . . . but I had Maureen, Chloe. And she could hardly function. She'd lost her daughter and I was the only thing she had to cling to and if I'd . . . if I'd told her . . .' He turns to Chloe, pleading. 'It would have destroyed her, Chloe. You've got to believe me.'

'But . . . but how could you have let them look . . . ?' She's still trying to piece it all together in her head.

'I know . . .' He rakes his hands through his hair, then bangs his fist on the steering wheel again. 'I know, and don't you think I've lived with it all of these years? Eh?'

Chloe isn't sure whether to answer.

'At first I was so sure, *so sure* she would come back. You picture it, your girl found, you wrapping her in your arms, kissing her, snuggling into her neck and promising yourself you will never let her out of your sight for even a split second, ever again. Because you hear about people

– you see it even – they lose their kids in the supermarket and you can hear the desperation in their voice and the absolute relief when . . . well, the relief when they get them back and they squeeze them . . .' He makes as if he is squeezing a daughter that never returned. 'I never thought she wouldn't come back. Never. All these years, living like this. I never . . .' His voice trails off. He stops and shakes his head, putting forefinger and thumb to the bridge of his nose.

'In the end, it got so that I wanted them to find her dead. Can you believe that? I can't stand to say it but I did. A dad who wanted the police to knock on his door and tell him that his daughter was found in a ditch some-where. I wanted the nightmare to end for Maureen because she wasn't good . . . she was hardly . . . I kept her alive, Chloe, in those early days. I was the only thing that Maureen had and I promised her that Angie would come back, day after day, then week after week, month after month, and then it was years and decades . . . and then you . . .' His voice trails off. 'It was a split-second mistake, one look away and she was gone. And I lied, I lied to the police, I lied to my wife, and I've lived with that little white lie ever since. It has killed me, Chloe, you've got to believe me.'

But Chloe is only thinking of Angie. She doesn't care what happened to Patrick. Does she believe him? She's not sure. But this story, it's too elaborate to be made up. And she thinks of Maureen, how broken she's been by the whole thing, how she herself protected her. Is it possible he's telling the truth?

'In the end I realized that my punishment for what I'd

done was this nothingness, this limbo, this bit trapped between living and dead, without answers. That was my punishment for my little white lie, and the only thing I could do to make anything right again was to devote myself absolutely to Maureen. To love her and keep on loving her, and try somehow to make up for what I had done.'

He sighs. 'So I went along with it all, I went along with the appeals in the newspaper, the certainty that our little girl would one day come home. Hell, I even went along with it when she was so convinced that you were her, but in here' – he pats his chest – 'I knew you weren't her, and I had this anger, this utter resentment that not only had I suffered so much but now I was being goaded for it, and when you started saying you'd had a dream and I just realized how utterly stupid the whole thing . . . perhaps I did want to confess to you, I wanted you to know that I thought the whole fecking thing was crazy, because I'd tried telling Maureen and . . .'

He drops his head into his hands.

'Does it sound strange to you? Does it? That perhaps I wanted you to put an end to it once and for all . . . I don't know.' He sweeps his hands over his face and sighs. 'I don't know.'

Chloe sits alongside him. The road and the fields are completely black now. Not a single car has passed in all this time. It is cold and so she shuts her passenger door. Patrick does the same, then switches the interior light back on. He turns to her.

Chloe swallows in the darkness, then tries to speak: 'But I don't understand . . . I mean, an affair? That was it? You could have told Maureen, people forgive people who—'

'You don't understand, Chloe.'

'So tell me,' she says. 'Because whatever you'd done, whatever you said you—'

'Because it was Josie, all right? Because the woman I was having an affair with was Maureen's best friend. We were the two people who had to pick up the pieces after Angie disappeared. How was I meant to tell her what we'd done? The two people who she needed more than anyone.'

'Josie?' Chloe gasps. She'd convinced herself Josie hated Patrick, that perhaps she even suspected him like she did.

'Did she know? Did she search for Angie with you?'

Patrick shakes his head. 'She'd left by the time I turned around and realized Angie was gone . . . I searched for her myself, and when I told everyone she'd disappeared from the park, well, Josie knew that's where we were going afterwards . . . I lied to everyone, Chloe, just to keep my family together when it had already fallen apart.'

He sinks back against his seat and stares at the roof of the car. Chloe has noticed that the windows have steamed up now. Nobody could see in, or out.

'But Josie?' Chloe says finally. 'How could you?'

Patrick turns to her quickly. 'We all have secrets, Chloe,' he says. 'What about you and all those newspaper clippings?'

Chloe looks at him quickly at the mention of her archive. So he had seen it.

'Yes, I saw them,' Patrick says. 'You're not so innocent yourself, are you, Chloe? None of us are, not if we're really honest. Not one of us can get through this life without telling some lies, we just better hope the consequences aren't too painful. But we've all got something to hide, Chloe.'

'So why didn't you tell Maureen? About the cuttings, I mean.'

'And extinguish the only flicker of hope she's had in twenty-five years? I'm a coward, Chloe, don't you know that by now? Perhaps that's another reason I told you we weren't at the park. Maybe I knew by then that somehow we were bound in this together.'

They sit there like that for a long time. Patrick broken by his confession, Chloe trying to take it all in – even her own culpability. Finally, he speaks.

'So what now?'

'What do you mean?' she says.

'Well, are you going to tell Maureen? Are you going to be braver than I ever was? Are *you* going to be the one who breaks her heart? To tell her that her husband and her best friend . . .'

Chloe looks out of the window. Patrick continues:

'I mean, she's sitting there at home, waiting for fish and chips, all this time thinking that you could be our Angie come back. So what are we going to do? What the hell are we going to do?'

She hates the way he says 'we'. But he is right. She is complicit.

'I . . . I don't know,' Chloe says. Where to start?

Patrick sighs. 'I thought she'd have given up this silly fantasy by now. I thought she would have woken up to the truth, but she's talking about doing a piece in the paper, about informing the police, and what do we do then? I mean, it's ridiculous, it's all out of control, and all because I couldn't break my wife's heart nearly three decades ago. I'm a fucking coward.'

He leans his elbows on the steering wheel and covers his face with his hands. In the dimness of the interior light, Chloe sees his hands are still stained in places with the blood of the hare. She knows that will wash off, but some things cannot be undone. If this is really what happened, then she had got Patrick wrong. Perhaps he was right, perhaps it would have been crueller still to break Maureen's heart all those years ago. The chances that it could have brought back Angie were still slim. He had weighed them up and decided to risk it, and he had lived with that decision every day since. In some ways, yes, he was responsible for his daughter's death, but not in the way that Chloe had imagined. Patrick wasn't a killer.

'Let's go home,' Chloe says. She can't think straight and they can't spend all night on this road.

'Yeah?' Patrick says.

She nods and slowly he sits forward and turns his keys inside the ignition.

They don't speak for the few miles that it takes to drive back to Low Drove. There is a solemnness inside the car, a silent undertaking that they will each keep the secret that has been revealed out on that lonely flat road. Just like Patrick all those years ago, Chloe doesn't know if it is the right thing to do. For some reason she thinks of Nan, of all the times that she has pretended that Stella was coming home soon, or was just out shopping. Was it so different to let Maureen live with that little bit of hope if it made it easier for her to get through each day? Why should we keep forcing those who have lost to accept it and move on? Maybe there is no moving on when you have lost a child. Who knows if the decision she and Patrick have made will be the right one? We can only live the best way we know how, and that's what Patrick has done all of these years. But he has suffered for it. Maybe even no one more than him.

They arrive into Low Drove through the back way, down the lane that Chloe and Maureen had walked the day that she had broken down talking about her missing daughter. She remembers that day, how it had been so painful to watch, and as they drive closer to Elm House, Chloe feels sure she can't bear witness to any more of Maureen's pain.

The road they take, unusually for the Fens, has a slight curve in it that hides Elm House from view from this direction, so they don't see the police car on the drive until they are almost there and the car's headlights reflect back the blue and yellow chequered pattern.

'What the . . .' Patrick says as he pulls up outside on the road, already tugging at his seatbelt.

They are out of the car quickly, forgetting in an instant everything that has occurred in the last hour. As they hurry down the drive, Maureen must hear their footsteps on the pebbles because she comes flying out of the back door and straight into Patrick's arms, followed quickly by two stony-faced uniformed police officers.

'Maureen, thank God . . .' Patrick says, wrapping her up inside his arms. 'What on earth's going on?'

He holds her face in the same hands that had ended the life of that hare. Though it is not with tears of distress that she looks back at him, but relief.

'It's Angie, Pat,' she says. 'They've found our Angie.'

FORTY-EIGHT

It had taken a while for the driveway to empty. Maureen's legs had gone from underneath her just moments after she had given Patrick the news, which had meant that everyone's attention had been directed towards getting Maureen back inside and onto the sofa. She sits there now alongside her husband, whispering something over and over into a scrunched-up tissue in her hand. Chloe can't quite make out what.

The living room is more cramped than Chloe has ever known it. There are two detectives here – one who sits in Patrick's chair, the other standing – and two uniformed officers. They are here only to keep the press away, and when they'd said this, Chloe's stomach had turned underneath her clothes. But no journalists have turned up yet at Elm House.

The uniformed officers turn down the volume on their radios, and Chloe sees one of the detectives nod at them. They leave the living room and go into the kitchen, offering to make tea.

When they've left, the standing detective pulls up a pouffe in front of the sofa and sits down with Maureen and Patrick. She's young, not much older than Chloe, she reckons. Her knees are almost touching Maureen's as she sits on the pouffe. Her voice is gentle when she speaks.

'Mr Kyle, I know this must be a huge shock—'

'Wait, let me just stop you there,' Patrick says. Since

Maureen collapsed in his arms on the drive, he hasn't taken a hand off her, he hasn't said a word. Now he holds her, as if propping her up under his right arm, his left hand holding hers in his. Maureen leans into his chest – just like she did in those photographs in 1979 – the two of them immediately resuming the poses they'd assumed for the cameras back when Angie disappeared, some instinct to get through this the only way they know how, a muscle memory instantly flexed. Patrick drops Maureen's hand for a second, though he keeps his other arm tight around her waist. He wipes his face and then, taking a deep breath, says to the detective, 'What do you mean, Angela's been found?'

The detective moves an inch closer. When she speaks, her voice is almost a whisper.

'We're sorry to inform you that a body believed to be that of a four-year-old girl was discovered in some undergrowth this morning.'

A body? Chloe leans against the sideboard to steady herself. She feels Angie looking down from the shelf, witnessing this whole scene unfold, but she can't turn around and face her. She can't bear to meet her eyes. A body means Angie is dead.

Inside Patrick's arms, Maureen makes a wounded crying sound, almost animal-like, and her husband dips his head to meet hers. They sit like that for a while, the other people in the living room fading away. They are back where they started, just the two of them. When Patrick looks up, Chloe sees that his eyes are filled with tears. He looks at the detective.

'Are you sure? I mean, is it definitely her?'

'Obviously, due to the length of time and . . . well, and decay' – the detective speaks slowly – 'there will need to be a formal identification, but from initial records it does seem that . . . that yes, it is the body of your daughter, Angela Kyle. I'm so sorry, Mr Kyle.'

The detective reaches out and touches a hand to his shoulder, just for a second. Patrick glances at it, unsure how to respond. Instead his attention falls again to his wife under his arm. He wraps her up tighter as she sobs quietly into his chest. Her right hand clutches the wool of his jumper. It's only then that Chloe makes out what Maureen has been whispering on repeat.

'It's over, Patrick,' Maureen cries softly. 'Angie's come home.'

Chloe stands in the kitchen now, stirring milk into seven cups of sweet tea. She'd gone out there to help the uniformed officers find their way around the kitchen. Somehow it had felt wrong to hear them raking through the contents of Maureen's kitchen cupboards; she didn't want them judging Maureen for the plastic pink beakers she keeps just for Chloe, or the Bunnykins cutlery they would find in the drawer. They wouldn't understand. They couldn't comprehend a mother's pain, why she has desperately clung on to these things of Angie's all these years.

To be honest, Chloe is glad for the breathing space. The air is thin in the living room and after a while her head had started to spin. Whatever she has been doing here in the Kyles' house these last fourteen weeks, something about the rawness of emotion she had just seen had made her feel uncomfortable – guilty even – about bearing witness to Maureen and Patrick's pain. After twenty-five years this was a moment that belonged to no one but them. Chloe needs to give them time to take it all in.

She stirs the tea and listens out. There is no sound coming from the living room now. In the kitchen, the uniformed officers' radios crackle quietly as they sit at the small pine table.

'Have you been renting a room here long?' one of the officers asks her.

She stops stirring the tea. Her back to both officers. They make it sound so impersonal. Chloe takes a split second to remind herself that she has done nothing wrong, that these police officers are not here to interrogate her. They've come to tell Maureen and Patrick that Angie has been found. She still can't quite believe it.

'A few months,' Chloe says, turning round and pressing two hot mugs into their hands as if she hopes it might distract them from too much questioning. It seems to work.

The officers nod and thank her for the tea. She suddenly would rather be in the living room with Angie watching from the sideboard, the solemn faces of the two detectives and all of Maureen and Patrick's pain.

Chloe turns and faces her reflection in the black kitchen window, realising that in all the commotion she is yet to remove her coat. It's over for her here now – with this news, Maureen's fantasy must come to an end. She's known that since that moment on the drive; her mind had leapt two steps forward in an instant to know what this news meant for her. She doesn't know yet how it will all play out, when they might ask her to leave, but she's surprised to find that she doesn't care. Tonight is about Maureen and Patrick. Hadn't she always planned to bring Angie home? And now that was done, her reason for being here was gone.

She puts five mugs onto a round tray and carries them carefully through to the living room. The detective now sits on the sofa beside Patrick and Maureen, who have recomposed themselves a little and seem ready to hear more about how their missing daughter was found.

Chloe hands a mug from the tray to the officer in Patrick's chair. He thanks her with a tight smile, everyone unsure of how they are supposed to behave after this bombshell has swept through the room. The detectives do a good job of seeming awkward, but surely they are used to this? Surely they do this all the time? She thinks about the reporters at the newspaper who were often sent out on death knocks just hours after someone had put an announcement in the newspaper. The receptionists would ring up and tell the news desk if it was a sudden death, or a young age, and a reporter would be dispatched to their home. They'd return to the office the same as they'd left, with a breezy demeanour, their priority only to empty their shorthand pads onto their screens in time for the next day's paper. Perhaps they had sat in living rooms like this, an intruder into someone else's most personal moments. Chloe's job was only ever to file away what they had written. She'd never thought of the reporters' lives outside of the office, of how close they were to both life and death.

Patrick sniffs and shakes his head when Chloe offers him tea. She puts a mug down in front of Maureen, who thanks her with a small voice, and the detective places her cup beside her feet.

Chloe takes her place at the very edge of the room in the hope of not being noticed. She'd always been good at fading into the background, of disappearing into the wallpaper. Over the years she likes to think she's perfected the art of camouflage.

Patrick sits forward, balancing his elbows on his knees. He holds his head in his hands and then looks up.

'Sorry,' he says, 'it's just, well, it's a shock, you know? After all these years.'

The detective nods, and glancing at Maureen again, Patrick reaches for his wife's hand. Chloe notices how she squeezes it in return. He's right, how could he have let go of her hand twenty-five years ago?

'I don't . . . well, I don't quite know what to ask first, like,' Patrick says. 'I mean how . . . how was she found?'

The detective takes a sip of her tea and then holds the mug between two hands.

'Another person was reported missing and it was actually during the search for her that Angela's remains were found.'

Patrick nods. 'I see . . . and where? I mean, where was she found?'

'Not far from the park where she went missing.'

Maureen looks up quickly and a tiny sob escapes from her mouth.

'You mean, she's been there all this time, out in the cold?' Maureen asks, her voice small, child-like.

Patricks wraps her up in his arms again, rocking her as she cries. But Chloe sees something that no one else in the room would notice, a relief in him that is almost palpable. She had been found not far from where he'd left her. They had been looking in the right place all along.

'You may remember there was a building site nearby the park at the time of Angela's disappearance . . .' the detective explains. Patrick and Chloe quickly exchange glances. 'That building site is now a care home for the elderly.' She stops to check her notebook. 'Park House.'

Chloe looks up quickly at the mention of Park House.

'Park House was under construction at the time of Angie's disappearance, and recently they've been having some building work done. The ground was disturbed during those excavations at a copse at the back of the care home and so during our search for the other missing person, Angela's body was found in a shallow grave.'

'She was that close by all the time?' Patrick says.

Chloe looks to the detective, as eager as these two parents for an explanation that will make sense right now.

'There have been diggers and all sorts of building equipment raking over that earth recently while they were excavating footings for the new extension at Park House,' the detective explains. 'We deepened and extended the search area for the other missing person, and that's when Angela's remains were discovered.'

'So no one . . . ?' Maureen can't finish her sentence. But everyone in the room senses a mother's need to write off the unthinkable after all these years.

The detective shakes her head. 'No, it seems from what can be understood by forensics that her death was a very tragic accident. There'll need to be a full post-mortem, of course, but we don't suspect any foul play and at this stage, we're not launching a murder investigation. I'm just so very sorry.'

'But it doesn't make sense . . . I mean, surely that building site was searched at the time . . .' Maureen says.

'We have no way of knowing how thoroughly it was searched all those years ago, perhaps resources were allocated elsewhere – it appears that mistakes could have been made and we can of course review the case if you—'

Maureen shakes her head and looks at Patrick. 'I just want this over now, Pat. I just want Angie properly laid to rest.'

He nods and pulls her in closer.

The room falls silent, and Chloe – still holding the empty tea tray – shuffles from one foot to the other. She feels twitchy somehow at the mention of Park House. She needs air. She needs to breathe.

'I'm just . . . I'm just going to find some biscuits in the kitchen,' Chloe tells the room, but it's only the detective that looks up and nods. Maureen and Patrick still cling on to one another as if they are each lifebuoys and they are trying desperately not to drown in this ocean of grief.

In the kitchen, the two uniformed officers look up when she walks past them to open the back door. The windows are filled with steam which quickly starts to shrink as the cool air rushes in. At the back door she inhales lungfuls of the cold Fen night. She thinks of the recreation room at Park House, of the residents who spend hours looking out onto the garden, all the way down to the copse at the end of the sloping lawn. She has looked out onto that copse herself. Could it really be true, that the whole time Nan has been in Park House, Chloe has been unknowingly watching over Angie's grave?

From the kitchen, as she opens a cupboard to find the biscuit tin, she hears Maureen asking more questions and the detective answering her carefully.

'And what about the other missing person?'

'I'm sorry?' the detective says.

'You said that they found Angie when they were searching for someone else. Did they find them? God knows, I wouldn't want someone else to suffer like we have all these years.'

Chloe finds the biscuit tin and takes out a small plate from the cupboard. On it she arranges bourbons, custard creams, digestives, fanning them out in a semi-circle. She can hear the detective consulting with her colleague about the other missing person.

'I don't think we have much information, except that she was found and taken to hospital. Is that right, Pete?'

When he speaks his voice is louder and clearer than his colleague's, weaving its way across the living room, round the door frame and through to the kitchen where Chloe stands arranging the biscuits.

'Yes, it was an elderly lady who went missing from Park House.'

Chloe stops as she returns the packets to the tin. She can hear him flicking through his notebook in the living room.

'Yes, that's right, IC1 female, eighty-five years old, taken to hospital suffering from hypothermia ... I'm afraid we don't have any update on her condition.'

Chloe's heart beats hard in her chest, the packets of biscuits fall from her hand. She's already out of the kitchen into the hall, running up the stairs. She hears Maureen and Patrick, the detectives in the living room, but she runs into her room, slamming the door shut behind her. She pulls her phone from her coat pocket. Switches it on. Waits for it to light up.

'Come on, come on,' she says as she clutches it in both hands.

Finally it is on. She waits for the signal – it's there, but patchy. She curses this black spot as the signal wavers. Her phone blinks with voicemail messages. Three more missed calls from Park House, one from a blocked caller – please not the police. Her heart is beating so wildly, tremors reach her hands. She grips the phone, a split second when she is afraid of the news that it might bring. She stands beside the window, and tentatively presses the voicemail button. Perhaps everything will be fine, she tells herself, Nan can't be the only eighty-five-year-old woman in Park House. She pleads inwardly for her phone to offer a connection that lasts – just this once. Yet, at the same time, she wants to delay her own heartbreak just that bit longer. But life chooses its own moments to send a meteor down to destroy your world. And so it is that, alone in this room, far out in the Fens, Chloe hears enough through the patchy phone signal to realize that everything she has come to know as family has ended:

ANNA WHARTON

'*Been trying to call . . . police search . . . sorry to have to tell you . . . your grandmother passed away in hospital this afternoon.*'

FORTY-NINE

It had taken a few weeks to release the body for the funeral. With it being a sudden death there were the inevitable tests that needed to be carried out. It was only once the authorities were satisfied that the death certificate was released. The coroner had recorded a verdict of death by misadventure.

So much time had passed that it was almost summer when a small crowd gathered in the city's cemetery for the burial. The sun was shining so brightly that the usual black garb worn at funerals conducted the heat and everybody hoped – for more reasons than one – that the Rite of Committal would soon be over. No one likes to see a child go before an adult, except in this case, so many adults had gone before they had found her. The priest mentioned each of them by name during the church service, relatives of the Kyles who hadn't lived to see little Angela returned to her parents, and even as he did, everybody thought again inwardly what a shame it was that she had been returned to them in death instead of in life. Some people, as ridiculous as it might have seemed, had never given up hope. Sometimes, in the face of so much despair, it really is all we've got.

At first Chloe had thought it was best to hang back, but it was Maureen and Patrick themselves who had picked her out of the crowd as they filed into St Gregory's. Maureen's hand had found Chloe's and it has not left hers

395

since. Nobody asked who Chloe was as they filed out of the church to make their way to the cemetery, but Chloe had overheard Patrick telling one group of friends that she was their lodger, and then Maureen had interrupted – her hand still wrapped firmly around Chloe's – to tell them that she was 'practically family now'. This had made Chloe glow inside, even on such a sorrowful day. She understands now that Patrick wants only what will make the pain easier to bear for Maureen, and for now, that is Chloe.

As they'd waited for the priest to arrive to commence the committal Maureen had made sure to introduce Chloe to even the most distant of relatives, and if they noticed – by coincidence – the resemblance between Chloe and Angie, nobody commented. Perhaps it wouldn't have felt right on this particular day.

Chloe stands at the front now, right beside the grave as the tiny coffin hovers over it. On her right, Hollie's hand fits neatly into hers and she feels her best friend – her only friend – squeeze it every now and then as if to remind her that she is here, that she is always here for her. As they recite the Lord's Prayer, Chloe looks behind her, and Phil gives her a tight, embarrassed smile.

On Chloe's left is Maureen, and beside her, Patrick. Maureen's fingers are wrapped so tightly around Chloe's that her bones ache, but she doesn't let go of this mother's grasp, not for one second. She can see now why Patrick didn't. And behind Maureen, a hand on her left shoulder, stands Josie. Perhaps she had proved her friendship a hundred times over in all the years that followed. Who knows how much she has also suffered for her own deceit? We rarely have a way of telling.

The priest concludes his prayers:

'Loving God, from whom all life proceeds
And by whose hand the dead are raised again,
Though we are sinners, you wish always to hear us.
Accept the prayers we offer in sadness for your servant, Angela Rose Kyle:
Deliver her soul from death,
Number her among your saints
And clothe her with the robe of salvation
To enjoy forever the delights of your kingdom.
We ask this through Christ our Lord.'

The congregation, Maureen, Patrick and Chloe, all whisper, 'Amen.'

Maureen and Patrick stand beside the grave until the crowds disperse and people finish telling them that the service had been 'lovely' and 'fitting' and 'beautiful' and all the other adjectives that people hope will make grief that much easier to bear. In truth, what it takes most of all is time, and haven't Maureen and Patrick had enough of that already? But their grief starts again at day zero, now they have finally laid their daughter to rest.

Most people are heading for the wake, but Maureen and Patrick understandably want to have the last few moments alone with their daughter.

'Are you sure you'll be OK?' Chloe asks Maureen.

She nods. 'I've got Patrick,' she says, squeezing his arm underneath hers. 'I just feel that I need to be near her, you know? After all that time that she had to lie there alone, I just need to make sure she's truly rested now.'

'Of course,' Chloe says, planting a kiss on Maureen's cheek. 'Take as long as you need. I'll see you at the wake.'

She slips her hand from Maureen's, the first time that morning.

'Thank you, Chloe,' Maureen says. 'Not just for today but all these days. You've been my rock. I don't know what I'd have done without you.'

Patrick smiles from behind her shoulder, and reaches out a hand to Chloe's arm.

Chloe leaves them with Angie, assuring them she will get a lift to the wake with one of the other mourners.

'I'm sorry we can't come with you, Chloe,' Hollie says. 'But we've both got to get back to work.'

'It's OK,' Chloe says. 'Thank you for coming, both of you.'

Hollie wraps her in a hug. 'Remember, you're never alone,' she says. 'You're as good as family to me and Phil. You've always got us.'

Chloe breaks away and nods. 'Thank you,' she says.

'Are you going to walk out with us?' Hollie asks. 'We could drop you off at the wake?'

'It's OK,' Chloe says. 'I want to take a little time here . . .'

Hollie nods. It's not necessary for Chloe to explain herself to her friend. She has been there from the start, after all. She knows all her secrets. She just hopes that one day there will be fewer of them to keep. Chloe has felt the same, of course, each time she has hoped that this would be the one, that she would finally be content. She is as disappointed as anyone that her life has worked out this way.

Chloe waits until the very last of the mourners have

filed out of the cemetery and then heads towards what would appear to be the wrong way out. She has one other thing she needs to do first.

She wasn't there for the service, so it takes some searching, but finally she finds it among all the others. The earth has not yet sunk back to level on this particular grave, and a stone has only finally been put in place in the last week. Chloe bends down beside it. She lays her coat on the ground and sits on top of it so as not to ruin the new black dress that Maureen had run up on her machine.

'Hello, Nan,' Chloe says, gently smoothing the blades of grass with the palm of her hand as if they were fine strands of Nan's own soft white hair.

She reads out loud the inscription on the grave:

Here lies Grace Hudson
1919–2004

Wife to Hugh

Mother to Stella, taken from
this earth still an angel

Rest in Peace

It was simple enough, and even if Chloe had been able to have any input, she knew Nan well enough to know there wasn't much more she would have wanted except to be mentioned alongside her husband and the daughter she lost at just six years old. If anyone knew the pain of losing a child, it was Nan. Her little girl had died of polio, the cruellest of childhood illnesses. Grace had been able to lay her daughter to rest, unlike Maureen, who had endured all those years of not knowing.

Chloe had considered coming to the funeral, even just to watch from afar, but in the end she had decided that it was too risky. Better to blend into the background. She had always been so good at that. She knew that she would celebrate Nan's life in her own way, or all fifteen months that she had known of it.

Chloe had needed to change her mobile number, of course, but she was used to that. The only person who needed her new one was Hollie. She knew Hollie always understood, each time Chloe convinced her that this time would be the last. But what are best friends if they're not someone who believes in you utterly? Hollie might not have liked it, but she at least understood Chloe's search to feel whole, for that perfect place where she would finally belong. Perhaps it had just become one of those annoying habits you come to accept in those you love. We all have them, Chloe thinks.

She sits up and looks around the cemetery. She has other friends here, people she has said goodbye to, other services that she has attended – most that she hasn't. She's experienced enough loss in her life to know that you celebrate people inside – that's where you carry them with you, the people who have made a difference. And she hopes that she has at least done that – made a difference.

Chloe still has her own archive back at Maureen and Patrick's. In fact, now she has left Nan's, she has more of it there. In it, this morning, she had found among all the others one envelope marked Grace Hudson, and she had pulled from it a single cutting. The one where their story together had started. It only felt right to read it here today.

WOMAN THANKS BLUE WATCH FOR SAVING CAT

DINKY the tabby got more than she bargained for when she decided to steal up the drainpipe of a local block of flats.

Quick-thinking residents called 999 when they heard miaows coming from piping thirty feet off the ground.

Firefighters attended the block in the city's Garton End Road with the turntable ladder, and under the watchful eye of residents, returned the cat to its owner, Grace Hudson.

Mrs Hudson, eighty-three, praised Blue Watch for rescuing her beloved cat. 'I lost my daughter Stella when she was just six years old and my husband has passed, too. Dinky is all I have left in the world,' she told this newspaper. 'I have recently been diagnosed with dementia and so a local charity is helping me look after Dinky because I keep forgetting to feed her. She's nineteen years old so, like me, she hasn't got long left. We only have each other for company . . .'

Chloe pauses. She can still remember that day in the office, how her scalpel had hovered over this story before she cut it out to file it in the archive. Who wouldn't have felt sorry for a poor old lady who had nothing in her life

left except for her cat? She'd taken round some choco-
lates – and some cat treats for Dinky – and it turned out
Chloe had lasted months longer than Dinky. At least she
and Nan had each other, not that other people would
have seen it like that. That's why Chloe had to disappear.
People never understand.

She will replace this cutting when she's back home in
Low Drove with all the others she has kept over the years.
One day she will have a sideboard in a home of her own,
and that's where all the people who have made up her
family will be kept. Family doesn't have to be the same
blood that runs around in your veins; its more what you
curate over the years, the people you collect. Or that's
what Chloe likes to think. People say you can't choose
your family, but that's where they are wrong.

Chloe sits for a while with Nan, until she remembers
the wake. She knows Maureen will be looking out for her.
It is true that she has been there more than most these last
few months. She just hopes this one lasts. She always
hopes they will, that this time it will be enough.

Chloe stands and folds her coat over her arm. She
kisses the top of the gravestone so tenderly, it could
almost have been Nan's very own head.

'Sleep tight, Nan,' she says. 'You were one of the very
best.'

She knows her way out of the cemetery from here.
There are, after all, several of Chloe's nans, grandmas and
grannies dotted around. Grace was the first with dementia, though, and that had made things a lot less
complicated. Who would question the sudden appearance
of a granddaughter who had arrived to take care of her

confused grandma? It might even sound sinister if she'd had anything to gain except the company. A family to call her own, for a while. An invented history more palatable than the one she had lived, waiting for parents who never came, a life spent in foster homes, never properly putting down roots.

She leaves the cemetery and walks back to town to the bus station. Maureen won't mind her being a little later than the others; she knows she can rely on her, after all. Or as much as you can rely on anyone living.

She waits outside the bus station, and there beside it is a newsagent's. She arrives in time to see a new bound batch of the local weekly newspaper arrive. Advertising is down so much they've dropped it from its evening circulation. She's heard that half the reporters have been made redundant, so it wasn't just the archive that had to go. She hands over seventy pence to the cashier in return for a thinning copy of her once beloved newspaper. She flicks through as she waits for the bus; it's more adverts than news now. Although there is one story that catches her eye:

WIDOW'S PLEA: DON'T TAKE MY ALLOTMENT

The old woman looks sweet in the photograph. A curly-haired grandmother with kind eyes and a pearl necklace. She hasn't a soul left in the world. The only pleasure she gets is growing her tomatoes, she tells the reporter. Chloe feels that familiar tug at her heart.

She folds the newspaper just in time for her bus to pull up, and soon blends in among all the other passengers. As the city passes at the window, she sees that old lady in her mind's eye. She has always fancied an allotment of her own – and a grandma just like that.

ACKNOWLEDGEMENTS

This novel would not have been possible without a whole bunch of people behind both it and me. My name may appear on the cover, but publishing a novel is in fact a huge team effort.

First thanks go to Sue Armstrong, my extremely kind agent who waited five patient years for this book to be delivered, offering positive affirmations and encouragement throughout – especially when I wanted to give up. I am so pleased I didn't.

Thank you to my editor, Sam Humphreys – I feel very lucky to have had you championing this book. Thank you to Josie Humber, Rosie Wilson, Elle Gibbons, Kate Tolley, Samantha Fletcher, Holly Sheldrake and Siân Chilvers – you have all done magnificent work in helping this book into the world. Thanks also to those in the UK Sales, International Sales, Finance, Operations, Contracts and Digital teams at Mantle who have all worked hard to do the very best for this book, as well as all those behind the scenes at C&W Agency.

When it comes to personal thanks, I will be forever indebted to many friends for their enthusiasm, endless patience, advice and often hours sacrificed to reading various drafts. In particular, I would like to thank: Veronica Clark, Joanne Kurt-Elli, Lee Knight, Greg Buchanan, Jon Elek, Jane Gould, Dyfed Edwards, Sarah Salway, Jo Schneider and Wendy Mitchell. Thanks also to my fellow students in my workshop groups at UEA who helped me untangle this story, and to ever-encouraging tutors Giles Foden, Henry Sutton and Philip Langeskov.

Mum, thank you for spending hours on the end of the phone listening to me witter that I couldn't or wouldn't ever finish this book. And special thanks must go to Gracie, my daughter, who is eight years old as I write this, but was two when the idea of this novel was conceived, and to whom this book is dedicated. All those hours watching cartoons so Mummy could work did not go unappreciated. Thank you.